CONQUER
THE
KINGDOM

By Jennifer Estep

CONQUER THE KINGDOM

A GARGOYLE QUEEN NOVEL

JENNIFER ESTEP

HARPER Voyager

An Imprint of HarperCollinsPublishers

CONQUER THE KINGDOM. Copyright © 2023 by Jennifer Estep. All rights reserved. Printed in the United States of America. No part of this book may be used or reproduced in any manner whatsoever without written permission except in the case of brief quotations embodied in critical articles and reviews. For information, address HarperCollins Publishers, 195 Broadway, New York, NY 10007.

HarperCollins books may be purchased for educational, business, or sales promotional use. For information, please email the Special Markets Department at SPsales@harpercollins.com.

Harper Voyager and design are trademarks of HarperCollins Publishers LLC.

FIRST EDITION

Designed by Angela Boutin
Maps designed by Virginia Norey
Title page and chapter opener art by Angela Boutin

Library of Congress Cataloging-in-Publication Data has been applied for.

ISBN 978-0-06-302346-8

23 24 25 26 27 LBC 5 4 3 2 1

To my mom—for your love, your patience, and everything
else that you've given to me over the years.

To all the readers who wanted more stories set in my
Crown of Shards world—this one is for you.

And to my teenage self, who devoured every single
epic fantasy book that she could get her hands on—
for writing your very own epic fantasy books.

To conquer a kingdom, you must first crush its heart.
—MAXIMUS MORRICONE, FORMER KING OF MORTA

Andvari shall never fall, so long as one gargoyle lives.
—ARMINA RIPLEY, FIRST QUEEN OF ANDVARI

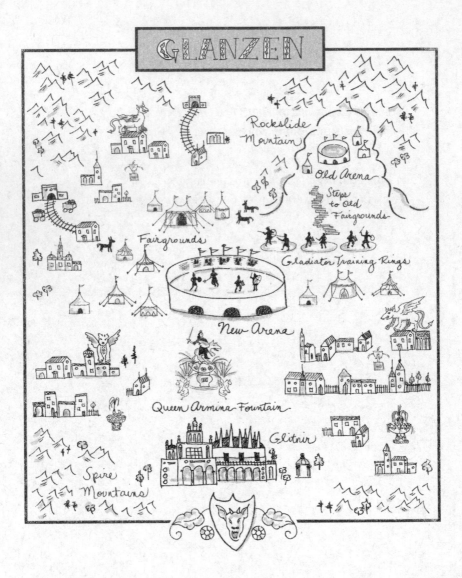

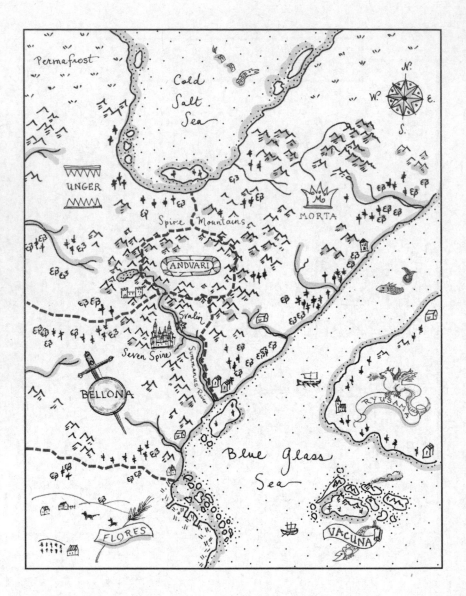

CONQUER THE KINGDOM

PART ONE

THE
BOUNTY
HUNTER

CHapter one

'vе played a lot of parts in my life.

My most frequent and famous role is that of Gemma Armina Merilde Ripley, crown princess of Andvari, also snidely known as Glitzma. I suppose Princess Gemma is who I *am*, for better or worse.

But it's not *all* that I am.

Princess Gemma is just one part of my persona, a carefully crafted role that enables me to travel throughout Andvari and into the kingdoms beyond, spying on those who would harm my people, gathering intelligence on their schemes, and thwarting their plots both great and small.

Being a spy is much more useful and far more satisfying than being a princess. In recent weeks, I had masqueraded as everything from a miner to a jewelry maker to a gladiator. Right now I was playing a new part, one that just might be my most important role yet.

Bounty hunter.

I crouched down, eased forward, and peered around the side of a large wooden crate. Similar crates were stacked all along the riverfront, while thick ropes were curled up like coral vipers on the grimy flagstones. Small rowboats rested on the muddy shore in the distance, and the watery stench of fish filled the November air. Everything looked perfectly normal, and my gaze moved over to a ship tied to a dock that stretched out into the Summanus River.

The vessel was the biggest one along the riverfront, with masts that towered high in the air. The ship's hull might have been a bright cobalt at one time, although the elements had weathered and dulled the wood to the same murky blue gray as the river. The only real bits of color were the bloodred letters on the side that spelled out the vessel's name—*The Drowned Man*. I hoped the name was an omen of things to come, although drowning would be a much quicker and far more merciful death than what my prey deserved.

"Do you really think Milo is on that ship?" a voice murmured.

I glanced over at the woman crouching beside me. She was wearing a dark green cloak over a matching tunic, along with black leggings and boots, and a sword dangled from her black leather belt. Her long black hair was pulled back into a fishtail braid, and her emerald-green eyes and golden skin gleamed in the growing dawn, as did the dragon face with emerald-green scales and black eyes that adorned her right hand. All morphs had some sort of tattoo-like mark on their bodies that indicated what larger, stronger creature was lurking inside them.

Despite the burgeoning light, Lady Reiko Yamato, my friend and fellow spy, remained almost invisible in the departing shadows. Even though I was dressed the same way, in a dark blue cloak and tunic, I felt as exposed as a gladiator standing in the middle of an arena floor. But even if the noontime sun had been shining brightly, Reiko still would have found a way to blend in to her surroundings. She was simply that skilled a spy—the best, in my opinion.

Reiko and I had been watching *The Drowned Man* for more

than half an hour. No one had approached the vessel, and no one had appeared on the deck. The riverfront was eerily quiet, except for the steady *slap-slap-slap* of water up against the ship's hull and the whistling breeze that ruffled its dingy sails.

"Do you really think Milo is on that ship?" Reiko repeated.

"Let me see if I can find out."

I drew in a deep breath, then exhaled, reached out with my magic, and scanned the ship. As a mind magier, I could sense when other people were nearby, especially if I'd had dealings with them before. Unfortunately, I knew Crown Prince Milo Maximus Moreland Morricone of Morta far better than I wanted to.

A few months ago, dozens of merchants, miners, and guards had been killed along the Andvari-Morta border. Some had died in a bandit attack. Others in a mine collapse. And several people had been swept away by a violent, sudden storm. King Heinrich and Crown Prince Dominic Ripley, my grandfather and father, had assumed the incidents were senseless tragedies, but the deaths of so many people so close together had struck me as extremely suspicious. As Princess Gemma, I had visited each site to offer my condolences to the victims' families, and I'd discovered something deeply concerning—large amounts of tearstone had been stolen at every spot.

My investigation had eventually led me to Blauberg, a city near the Andvari-Morta border. As Miner Gemma, I'd gone undercover and realized that Conley, the mine foreman, was stealing and selling tearstone to Mortan guards. Conley had shoved me into a chasm and left me for dead, but I'd been rescued and taken to Myrkvior, the royal palace in Majesta, the capital city of Morta.

Despite the danger, being at Myrkvior had been a golden opportunity to figure out which Mortan was ultimately stockpiling the tearstone and why, so I had played yet another part—Armina, a noble lady and jewelry maker. But my disguise wasn't as good as I'd thought, and Queen Maeven Morricone had revealed my true identity as Princess Gemma Ripley at her own birthday ball.

And then she had let Milo torture me.

The riverfront flickered and vanished, along with *The Drowned Man*. Suddenly, I was back in Milo's workshop, staring down at my own unconscious body chained to a table. Whipped back, punctured hands, burned skin. Blood dripped out of my wounds and hit the stone, every soft *drop-drop-drop* blaring as loud as a bell in my mind. Even though the torture had happened a couple of months ago, my heart still picked up speed, my breath puffed out in ragged gasps, and sweat prickled the back of my neck.

Desperate to stave off more unwanted memories, I grabbed the silver pendant hanging off the chain around my neck and focused on the bits of black jet that glittered in the shape of a snarling gargoyle face—the Ripley royal crest. Tiny midnight-blue shards of tearstone formed the gargoyle's horns, eyes, nose, and teeth, turning the crest into the face of Grimley, my own beloved gargoyle. The same jeweled crest was embedded in the light gray tearstone dagger hanging off my belt. Alvis, the Glitnir royal jeweler, had made the pendant and the dagger for me years ago, when I was first learning how to control my mind magier magic—something I still struggled with to this day.

I squeezed the pendant tight, making a dull ache ripple through my fingers. That uncomfortable sensation, combined with the sharp prick of the jewels against my skin, helped me force the memories away. Milo's workshop vanished, and the riverfront snapped back into focus, although the abrupt change in scenery made my head spin.

"Gemma?" Reiko asked. "Are you okay?"

"Fine," I lied.

I released the necklace. The soft, familiar *thump* of the pendant against my heart further steadied me, and my head slowly stopped spinning.

Reiko arched an eyebrow, clearly not believing my lie, but I ignored her concerned look. Compared to all the times when my magic threw me back into the distant past and completely immersed and overwhelmed me with memories, this brief glimpse of my own tortured self was a relatively minor annoyance.

"If you're so fine, then why are you rubbing your hands?" she asked.

I had been massaging first one palm, then the other, trying to rub the dull aches out of my hands and snuff out the hot sparks of phantom pain twinging my fingertips. I froze mid-rub and lowered my arms to my sides.

Reiko's face remained blank, but her inner dragon grimaced, and its black gaze skittered away from mine. Milo's barbed arrows and lightning magic had scarred my hands, both front and back, as though someone had painted vivid red starbursts onto my skin.

My fingers clenched into fists, reigniting those dull aches and hot sparks, but I didn't mind the pain now. It further fueled my determination to find out if Milo was truly on *The Drowned Man*—and if so, to finally kill him for everything he'd done to me.

So I exhaled and reached out with my magic again. This time, the riverfront remained still and solid, and I examined the ship.

In addition to telling when other people were nearby, I could also hear their thoughts and sense their emotions. Ironically enough, given our current location, I had always pictured that aspect of my mind magier magic as though I were leaning over the deck of my own tiny internal ship and dipping my fingers into the sea of other people's musings and feelings, which constantly churned around me.

Right now, that sea was utterly calm, and I didn't hear any

whispered thoughts or sense so much as a flicker of emotion. No sizzling anger, no icy malevolence, nothing that would indicate Milo or anyone else was nearby. The ship could be completely empty or full of sleeping sailors.

I let out a frustrated breath, released my power, and shook my head. "I don't think he's on the ship, but I can't be certain. Not without us actually going on board and searching the vessel."

Reiko's hand dropped to her sword. "Well, we might as well get on with it."

This time, I arched an eyebrow at her. "Isn't this the point where you tell me it might be a trap? That Milo might have a dozen men hiding belowdecks just waiting to rush out and kill us?"

She snorted. "If I have to tell you that, then you haven't been paying attention to everything that's happened, especially a few weeks ago during the Summit."

I grimaced. The Summit was supposed to be a peaceful meeting of nobles, merchants, guilders, and leaders of the various kingdoms to discuss trade agreements—but this year, it had devolved into a bloodbath.

Milo had attended the Summit as part of the Mortan contingent, and he had been working with Corvina Dumond, his fiancée and a powerful weather magier. Milo had wanted Corvina to kill me, along with his younger half brother, Leonidas, but the noble lady had been determined to kill *all* the Morricones, especially Queen Maeven, and capture the Mortan crown for herself.

During the Summit, Corvina had ordered the Dumond fighters to attack all the other royals in attendance, including my father. I'd managed to kill Corvina, but Milo had escaped, along with Captain Wexel, his loyal guard and Corvina's secret lover.

Afterward, Crown Prince Dominic Ripley had joined forces with some of the other royals to put an enormous bounty on Milo— one hundred thousand gold crowns. According to my sources, every bounty hunter and mercenary on the Buchovian continent was searching for Milo so they could collect the reward.

And I had joined their ranks.

In public, Princess Gemma was performing her usual duties as a traveling ambassador, going from city to city in Andvari and meeting with nobles, merchants, and the like. But in private, Reiko and I had spent the last few weeks tracking Milo from one hiding spot to the next. A deserted farm just outside of Caldwell. An inn near Haverton. A tavern on the outskirts of Blauberg. The crown prince had been running like a deer, trying to escape the bounty hunters' greed, as well as the wildfire of my wrath.

I reached out to every source I had in every city we visited, asking for news and gossip, and I had read dozens of letters from people all across Buchovia, scanning them for the smallest scrap of information about Milo and Wexel. A couple of times, Reiko and I had gotten oh so close to the Mortans, missing them by mere hours, which only added to my anger and frustration.

I might have embraced this new bounty-hunter persona, but I didn't care about collecting any reward. I just wanted to find and kill Milo before he hurt anyone else.

Especially my gargoyles.

Despite the bloodshed at the Summit, I had finally figured out one of Milo's main goals—to slaughter Andvarian gargoyles. With their stone skin, gargoyles were largely indestructible, although they were vulnerable to the crown prince's tearstone arrows, which were coated with dried fool's bane flowers.

I still wasn't sure how killing gargoyles would help Milo conquer my kingdom, but I was certain it was only part of some larger, deadlier scheme, which is why I wanted to find and eliminate him as soon as possible.

"Gemma?" Reiko asked. "Are you ready to search the ship?"

I shoved my dark thoughts away. "You're not usually so eager to walk into a potential trap. Most of the time, you're trying to talk me out of doing something reckless."

"True. But I also know exactly what you'll say." She waggled her eyebrows. "Come on. Say it with me. That boarding the ship is . . ."

I rolled my eyes, but I joined in with her words. "Worth the risk."

Reiko grinned. "Exactly! So we might as well sneak on board, spring whatever trap Milo and Wexel might have left behind, and get on with our day. If we hurry, we can return to Glitnir before the cook masters run out of those delicious apple-cinnamon scones."

"Your love of sweet cakes is going to get you in trouble some-day," I teased.

Reiko's grin widened. "Maybe. Either way, I want some of those scones, so let's go. Traps and sweet cakes await!"

She stood up, drew her sword, and moved forward. I rolled my eyes again, but a smile spread across my face as I plucked my dagger off my belt and followed my friend.

Reiko slid from one shadow to the next, as silent as smoke snaking through the air. I crept along behind her, but my boots scraped across the flagstones, making far too much noise. If Milo and Wexel were hiding on *The Drowned Man*, then they were certain to hear me coming.

As we neared the ship, I reached out with my magic again. For the first time, I sensed several presences on board, like dim candles flickering in a dark room, but I didn't feel the bright, hot sting of Milo's lightning or the raw, brute force of Wexel's strength magic. Perhaps the ship's thick hull and the churning water were blocking my power.

We stepped onto the dock, and a wooden board *creaked* ominously under my weight.

Reiko shot me an annoyed look. "Do you have to be so bloody *loud*, Gemma? You're tromping around like a gargoyle in a glass shop."

"Sorry, your royal spyness," I sniped back. "But some of us aren't as light on our feet as dragons are."

She huffed, as did the dragon on her hand, and moved forward. I sighed and followed her, once again trying to be as quiet as possible.

We quickly reached the gangplank that led up to the ship's main deck. Reiko raised her eyebrows in a silent question, and I shrugged back. I still didn't sense Milo anywhere nearby.

Yesterday, we'd come across an innkeeper in a nearby village who claimed he'd recently hosted a Mortan noble eager to book passage on a ship headed south from the docks here in Allentown. We'd arrived at the docks several hours ago, closer to midnight than morning. Everyone had already been in bed, which had made it easy for Reiko and me to break into and search the dockmaster's office.

According to the records, *The Drowned Man* had sailed into Allentown early yesterday morning, unloaded its passengers and cargo, and taken the rest of the day to resupply. It was supposed to sail back down the Summanus River later today, on a return journey to Fortuna Island, and it was the only vessel here that was large enough to accommodate passengers. If the innkeeper's information was correct, and Milo was planning to escape on *The Drowned Man*, then he was either already on board or he'd have to come here sometime soon.

Either way, this was the closest we'd been to him in weeks, and I was determined to finally catch him.

Reiko eased up the gangplank and stepped onto the ship. I followed her, for once managing to be almost as quiet as she was.

Weapons in hand, we both glanced around the wide, rectangular deck.

Several barrels filled with arrows were spaced along the railing, with longbows propped up against the sides of the containers. Other barrels featured swords, while spears, many topped with wicked-looking barbs, were nestled in a net that was dangling from the main mast in the center of the deck. Still more spears gleamed a dull silver in another net that was close to the wheel on the starboard side of the ship.

The plethora of weapons wasn't surprising. Plenty of pirates sailed up and down the Summanus River, boarding ships, murdering sailors, and stealing cargo.

"Could Milo be belowdecks?" Reiko whispered, her breath frosting faintly in the chilly air.

Clomp-clomp-clomp-clomp.

As if in answer to her question, footsteps sounded in the distance, and a sixty-something man climbed a set of steps and ambled out onto the deck. Wavy iron-gray hair brushed the tops of his broad shoulders, and his dark brown skin was covered with even darker freckles from years spent in the sun. His eyes were a light golden-brown, like the glossy varnish that coated the deck, and a jagged scar curved through one of his bushy gray eyebrows, as though he'd been hooked like a fish at some point in his sailing days.

Despite the early hour, the man's hair was neatly brushed, and the smell of his spicy cologne overpowered the stench of fish in the air. He was wearing a short sandy-brown jacket, along with a matching tunic, leggings, and boots, and the crest of a man's face with bulging eyes and an open mouth glimmered in gold thread over his heart. That same crest was carved into the main mast and marked him as the ship's captain. A cutlass with a gold hilt dangled from his brown leather belt, along with a spyglass and several long, thin knives. I could easily imagine the captain shedding his jacket, rolling up his tunic sleeves, and gutting the catch of the day with those knives, right along with any sailors who disobeyed him.

The captain yawned and stretched his arms over his head. He glowered up at the sky as if the pretty pink dawn displeased him, then dropped his arms and his gaze back down to the deck.

Reiko jerked her head to the side, silently asking if I wanted to hide behind the barrels, but I shook my head. I was tired of creeping around, especially since the captain might have the answers—and passengers—we were so desperately seeking.

The captain blinked a couple of times, as if surprised to see us standing on his ship, but a grin spread across his face. "I wasn't expecting visitors this early in the morning. I'm Captain Davies. And who are you two lovely ladies?"

"Armina," I replied, using my middle name the way I always did whenever I was on a spy mission. "And this is Resplenda."

Reiko arched an eyebrow, apparently not liking the hastily chosen moniker, but I ignored her chiding glance.

Captain Davies looked us both up and down, his gaze lingering on our breasts and hips. His grin widened, and lust rolled off him in clear, palpable waves, making my stomach churn.

"Have you two ladies come to warm my bed before we set sail? If so, I'll have to give my crew a bonus for their exceptionally good taste." He leered at us both, revealing a mouthful of straight gold-capped teeth.

Reiko growled, and smoke boiled out of the mouth of her inner dragon and skated across her skin. Davies's grin faltered, then vanished altogether. Anyone with even a lick of common sense was wary of morphs, especially dragons. Plus, Reiko looked like she was one more lascivious comment away from charging across the deck and plunging her sword into his chest.

Davies puckered his lips and let out a loud, earsplitting whistle that sounded like a strix's shrill shriek.

I tensed, as did Reiko. For a few seconds, nothing happened, but then more footsteps *clomp-clomp-clomp-clomped*, and more than a dozen men climbed the steps and streamed out onto the deck. The men were all wearing dark brown tunics, along with matching leggings and boots, and each one of them was carrying a cutlass. The men spread out across the deck and started leering at us the same way the captain had.

Davies drew his own cutlass and stabbed it at Reiko and me. "What do you want?" he demanded. "If you've come to take my ship, then you're in for a nasty surprise, because the crew of *The Drowned Man* never gives up without a fight."

The sailors murmured their agreement and hefted their weapons a little higher.

Reiko growled again, ready to fight, but I slid my dagger back into its scabbard, then held my hands up in a placating gesture.

"We're not here to cause trouble. We just want some information." I reached down and jiggled the blue velvet bag tied to my belt. "And we're prepared to pay for it."

Davies's eyes brightened at the distinctive sound of coins *clink-clink-clinking* together. "What kind of information?"

"I want to know if any Mortans have booked passage on your ship—especially any Mortan nobles."

The captain scratched his chin. "Nope, no nobles have approached me. I only sail down to Fortuna Island and back up here again." He glanced around. "Has anyone approached you lot?"

The sailors shook their heads, and frustration washed over me. Milo wasn't here. He had probably *never* been here, and I had wasted yet more time chasing down another rumor that had led me nowhere. I'd thought Milo was heading south, away from both Andvari *and* Morta, but it looked like I had been wrong about that, just like I'd been wrong about so many other things lately.

Davies swept his hand out wide, gesturing at the ship. "No

Mortans have booked passage, but you lovely ladies are more than welcome to sail with us. I'm certain we could find a good use for the two of you."

The sailors leered at us again, and waves of lust rolled off them and slammed into my chest. I resisted the urge to snarl at the men.

"Forget it," Reiko snapped. "We're leaving."

Davies grinned again, but cold calculation filled every deep crease and wrinkle on his weathered face. "I can get an excellent price for a pretty little dragon like you at the Fortuna Mint." His gaze flicked to me. "I won't get nearly as much for you, but I'm sure someone would add you to their collection."

My stomach roiled, even as anger scorched through me. Davies and his men weren't simply sailors hauling cargo up and down the river. No, they were pirates—kidnappers—who waylaid innocent people and sold them to the DiLucris, the wealthy, powerful family who ran the Fortuna Mint. The DiLucris traded in all sorts of unlawful things, but they were especially known for their auctions, which included men, women, and children who were sold to the highest bidders. Supposedly, those folks were indentured servants who could earn back their freedom, but really, they were slaves—and used for much, much worse things than just forced labor. Grandfather Heinrich, along with Queen Everleigh Blair of Bellona, had been trying to shut down the DiLucris' auctions for years, although they had never been successful.

Despite the anger still scorching through my body, I glanced at each man in turn, but I didn't see any familiar faces. All of these bastards were the sailors they appeared to be. Still, the fact that Reiko and I had just *happened* to run into pirates was more than a little suspicious.

"Where's Wexel?" I demanded. "Tell that weasel to show himself."

Captain Davies frowned, and his eyebrows drew together, forming a solid gray line across his forehead. "Who's Wexel?"

I opened my mouth to tell him, but he waved his hand.

"Ah, it doesn't matter who sent you here." Another cold, calculating grin creased his face. "Because we're going to have a lot of fun with you and your friend before we deliver you both to the DiLucris."

Davies puckered his lips and let out another loud, earsplitting whistle. The pirates lifted their weapons and moved forward.

For once, this didn't appear to be one of Wexel and Milo's traps, but Reiko and I were in grave danger just the same.

CHAPTER TWO

The way I see it, we only have two options—run or fight," I murmured.

Reiko snorted, although she never took her gaze off the approaching pirates. "Aren't those always our only two options?"

"They haven't thought to block the gangplank yet. You're the one who wanted sconces. If we run now, you can get them a lot faster."

"And let these bastards find some other women to abduct and sell into slavery?" Reiko growled. "No bloody way."

I grinned. "I was hoping you'd say that."

Reiko grinned back at me. Magic flared in her eyes, making them burn like green torches, and long black talons sprouted on her fingertips as she partially shifted into her larger, stronger morph form.

I plucked my gargoyle dagger off my belt and twirled it around in my hand, getting it into just the right position. Then, together, we both charged forward.

Reiko ducked the first pirate's swing, then lashed out and raked her razor-sharp talons across his throat. He screamed and clutched his bloody neck. Reiko shoved him away, then charged forward again, swinging her sword at first one pirate, then another, then another.

I dove into my own pack of pirates. First, I sliced my dagger across one man's stomach, then turned and buried the blade in another man's throat. I ripped my weapon free and spun around, searching for a new enemy to kill. A gleam of gold glimmered off to my left. On instinct, I jerked to the side.

Clash!

I brought my dagger up just in time to block Davies's cutlass, although the brutal blow knocked me off balance. I lurched backward, my boots skidding on the slick deck, but Davies followed me, swinging his cutlass back and forth in a series of quick, confident strikes. Not only was he an excellent fighter, but Davies was also a mutt, a somewhat derogatory term for someone with a relatively simple, straightforward power, like enhanced strength or speed.

Unfortunately for me, the captain had both.

He swung his cutlass at me over and over again, and it was all I could do to block his hard, fast blows and keep him from knocking the dagger out of my hand. Using both his strength and speed, Davies quickly drove me across the deck. I lunged to the side, and he slammed his cutlass into the railing hard enough to make chips fly up out of the scarred wood. He growled, whirled around, and came at me again.

Davies drove me back in the opposite direction. Two other pirates joined in, and they all took turns lashing out at me time and time again. I dodged yet another blow and whirled around, putting my back to the main mast so they couldn't attack me from multiple sides at once.

Across the deck, pirates surrounded Reiko, and the dragon morph used her sword, along with her talons, to attack the men, who shrieked and screamed every time one of her vicious swipes connected with their throats, chests, or guts.

Davies stopped and brandished his cutlass at me, as did the other two pirates.

"You shouldn't have come here, girlie," the captain crowed, his spicy cologne rapidly turning sour with sweat. "I was going to save you and your friend for myself, but now I'm going to let every man on my crew have a turn with the two of you."

White-hot rage roared through me at his vile threat, and a storm of magic erupted deep inside me, just begging to be unleashed. For a moment, I considered giving in to that rage, that storm, and showing the captain and his men just how dangerous I truly was. But that wouldn't get me any answers about Milo and Wexel, so instead I stared at each one of my enemies in turn.

"You're not going to hurt me or my friend or anyone else ever again."

The other two pirates shifted on their feet at the icy fury in my voice. Davies hesitated, but he quickly found his bravado again.

"And why is that?" he asked, a sneer on his face.

"Because you're not the only one who brought reinforcements."

I puckered my lips and let out a loud, earsplitting whistle, just as Davies had done earlier. The captain grimaced, as did the two pirates. They all tensed and glanced over their shoulders, but when no one came running up the gangplank, they pivoted back to me.

Davies sneered at me again. "Seems like your reinforcements didn't get the message—"

A shadow zipped over the deck, and what looked like a large boulder dropped down from the sky, smashing into the pirate on Davies's right. The man grunted once, too wounded to even scream as his bones *snap-snap-snapped* one after another. His arms and legs spasmed for a few seconds, but the pirate swiftly went silent and still as death claimed him.

Everyone on the deck froze, including the pirates who were still battling Reiko. The boulder let out a loud, jaw-cracking yawn and sat upright, morphing into the familiar, blocky shape of a gargoyle.

The gargoyle was about the size of a horse, although his stocky, powerful body was set much lower to the ground. Two curved horns jutted up from his forehead, while black talons protruded from his large, wolfish paws, and a sharp arrow tipped the end of his long tail. His flexible stone skin was a dark gray, with pinprick bits of blue that shimmered in the early morning sunlight. His eyes were also blue, the color rich and deep, like that of the finest sapphires.

Grimley yawned again. *Pirates?* His low voice rumbled through my mind, sounding like pieces of gravel crunching together underfoot. *You woke me up just to battle a bunch of mangy, scurvy pirates?*

So sorry my being in mortal danger interferes with your nap schedule. I sent the snide thought back to him.

Putting yourself in mortal danger is becoming a nasty habit, Gemma. Grimley yawned for a third time. *Well, since I'm already up, I suppose I should help you. Which pirate do you want me to kill next—*

Another shadow dropped down from the sky and landed on the pirate to Davies's left, crushing him just like Grimley had crushed the other pirate. The shadow perched prettily on the pirate it had just killed, lifting its head and morphing into the sleek shape of a strix.

Like Grimley, the strix was also about the size of a horse, although with a much stronger and more streamlined body, making it resemble an oversize hawk. The creature's eyes were a dark vibrant amethyst, as were its feathers, which were tipped with razor-sharp pieces of onyx that looked like arrows. Its equally sharp beak and talons were the same shiny, glossy black. Another beautiful, if deadly, creature.

Thank you, Lyra. I sent the thought to the strix.

You're welcome! Her high singsong voice sounded in my mind. Lyra winked at me, then hopped across the deck and plunged into the group of dumbstruck pirates.

Grimley watched the strix stab her beak into the throat of another enemy. *That stupid bird ruins all my fun,* his voice grumbled through my mind again.

But he loped over and started battling the pirates side by side with Lyra. The two creatures quickly worked their way over to Reiko, who was once again fighting her own enemies.

I focused on Davies again. "Now, where were we?"

The captain brandished his cutlass. I braced myself for another attack . . . but he whirled around, ran across the deck, and sprinted down the gangplank.

My mouth gaped in surprise, but I hurried over to the railing and glanced down below. Davies was using his mutt speed to its full advantage, and he was rapidly leaving *The Drowned Man* behind—

A man strode out from behind one of the wooden crates stacked up along the riverfront. He stepped right into Davies's path, causing the captain to pull up short to keep from crashing into him.

This man was a year or two older than me, thirty or so, with tan skin; sharp, angular cheekbones; and a straight nose. His longish wavy hair gleamed like polished onyx, while his eyes were a deep, dark amethyst that was the same color as Lyra's feathers. He was wearing a long black riding coat over a black tunic, leggings, and boots, and the layers of fabric perfectly outlined his tall, muscular body. Black gloves covered his hands, and the cool, steady breeze pushed his black cloak back and forth like a hungry greywolf snapping around his legs. A light gray tearstone sword and a dagger dangled from his black leather belt, but he didn't reach for the blades. Even without a weapon in his hand, this man was still extremely dangerous.

"Who the fuck are you?" Davies asked.

Instead of answering the question, Prince Leonidas Luther Andor Morricone looked up at me.

Dead or alive? he asked, his low, husky voice curling through my mind and sending a shiver down my spine.

Alive, please. The captain might know more than he thinks.

A grin stretched across Leonidas's face, softening his angular features. *As my lady wishes.*

"Get out of my way," Davies snarled. "Or I'll gut you like a fish."

Leonidas's warm, teasing grin vanished. His face settled back into its usual cold, blank mask, and he gave the captain a bored look, as though Davies's threat was no more worrisome than the winter wind tangling his hair.

"Fine," Davies snarled again. "Have it your way."

The captain raised his cutlass and rushed forward. Leonidas waited until the last possible second before calmly, smoothly spinning out of the way. Davies couldn't stop his reckless charge, and he crashed into one of the wooden crates and bounced off like an oversize ball. The captain growled, whirled back around, and charged again.

Leonidas watched him come with the same bored expression as before. Once again, at the last second, right before Davies would have skewered him, Leonidas lifted his hand and curled his fingers into a tight fist.

Davies stopped in his tracks.

The captain growled again and tried to move. His biceps bulged, and the muscles in his neck stood out like taut ropes, but Leonidas flexed his fingers, then curled them into an even tighter fist. Despite all his growling and straining, Davies remained frozen in place, like a statue that had been perched along the riverfront.

Leonidas was a mind magier just like I was, and he could do many of the same things I could with his power, including moving objects with his mind—or holding them in place, in the captain's case.

Every person, creature, and object had its own energy, an invisible layer of power that surrounded it just as surely as Leonidas's black cloak covered his body. As mind magiers, we could both tap into that energy and bend it to our will.

I'd always thought of my power as invisible strings radiating out from my fingertips and connecting to everyone and everything around me, as though I were a puppeteer moving dolls and scenery around a stage. All I had to do was push and pull, and grasp and release those strings, and I could do almost anything I wanted, from making a flagstone fly up out of the ground, to tearing the top off one of the wooden crates, to holding Davies in place, like Leonidas was doing right now.

Even up here on the ship, I could feel the prince's power and how smoothly and effortlessly he was manipulating the strings of energy surrounding Davies. In some ways, Leonidas was much stronger in his mind magier magic than I was in mine. He could always completely control his power, whereas I still struggled to wrangle mine. Sometimes, that mercurial storm of magic deep inside me did exactly what I wanted it to. Other times, the power squirted out of my grasp and either drowned me in memories or overwhelmed me with other people's thoughts and feelings, leaving me paralyzed and useless.

Are you sure you want him alive? Leonidas's voice sounded in my mind again. *I'm happy to toss him into the river and drown him like the rat he is.*

That's a bit extreme, don't you think?

His eyes glittered like dark amethysts. *Not when it comes to you, Gemma. I would tear that whole ship apart and drown every man on board if that's what it took to keep you safe.*

Another shiver swept down my spine. *Well, for now, let's keep the captain alive. He can't answer questions if he's dead.*

Leonidas tipped his head. *As my lady wishes.*

He flicked his fingers, and Davies sailed through the air and smashed into a nearby crate hard enough to splinter the thick wood. The captain dropped to the ground, unconscious.

A couple of low moans caught my ear, and I glanced over my shoulder. Reiko, Grimley, and Lyra had killed most of the pirates, and the ones who were still alive were too injured to threaten us anymore.

"Well, that was fun." Reiko stepped over a whimpering pirate with a nasty gash across his chest and walked over to me. "Just the thing to work up an appetite for those apple-cinnamon scones waiting for me back at Glitnir."

"Don't worry," I replied. "You'll get your scones, but we still have work to do here."

Reiko saluted me with her bloody sword.

I turned to Grimley and Lyra. "Stand guard, and make sure none of the pirates try to escape."

Grimley and Lyra both nodded. The gargoyle hopped up onto the railing, perched there like an oversize cat, and started licking the blood off his talons, while Lyra flapped her wings, shot up, and landed on top of the main mast.

"Let's search the ship," I said. "Davies might have been lying when he said Milo hadn't approached him about booking passage down the river."

Reiko grinned and swept her sword out wide. "After you, princess."

I rolled my eyes, but I couldn't stop an answering grin from spreading across my face. "Come along then, spy."

Reiko and I went down the steps into the lower part of the ship. Sunlight streamed in through the round windows, illuminating a long hallway that ran the length of the vessel, with several rooms and corridors branching off it. In the largest room, dozens of hammocks were strung up like gray spiderwebs swooping from one wooden post to the next, while shelves had been built into the walls, stretching from the floor up to the low ceiling. Metal buckets were also lashed to the bottom of the posts, and the sour stench of urine filled the air, despite the lids that topped each container.

"Not the most luxurious accommodations for the pirates and their passengers," Reiko said. "No matter how desperate they might be to flee from Andvari and Morta, I can't imagine Milo or Wexel willingly enduring these conditions for days on end."

"Me neither, but let's see what we can find."

Reiko searched through the shelves on the right side of the room, while I took the ones on the left. Small, framed painted portraits of loved ones. Wooden carvings of krakens, mermaids, and other sea creatures. Books, playing cards, and other odds and ends that were either sentimental, entertaining, or useful in some way. All the objects were perfectly ordinary, and nothing looked like it might have belonged to either Milo or Wexel.

"Find anything?" I asked when I reached the end of my shelves.

"Just an alarming amount of licorice. Blech." Reiko's face crinkled with disgust, as did the one of her inner dragon.

I laughed. "Let's keep looking."

Together, we moved through the rest of the lower deck, searching all the rooms. A small galley, a dining hall with scarred wooden tables and chairs, several storage areas for sails, ropes, tools, and weapons. Nothing unusual, so we plodded down another set of steps into the cargo hold in the very bottom of the ship.

No windows were set into this level, so Reiko and I grabbed a couple of black iron lanterns hanging on a peg by the door. The round fluorestones inside flared to life, casting out gloomy gray light. Instead of wooden crates full of goods, dozens and dozens of hammocks were also strung up down here—along with shackles.

Coldiron shackles attached to short chains were embedded in every single post, while several more sets lined the walls. I crouched down and shined my lantern on the closest set of shackles. Dried blood covered the cuffs, along with the attached chain, and even more blood stained the floor, along with urine, shit, and vomit.

Anger, revulsion, and sorrow surged through me at the thought of all the people—women—who had been trapped in here and all the horrors they had suffered at the hands of Davies and his crew. Given the number of shackles, Davies probably made most of his money kidnapping and selling people to the DiLucris, rather than hauling cargo and paying passengers up and down the river. Greedy, heartless bastard. I should have let Leonidas drown him after all.

"Hey, Gemma. Look at this."

Reiko plucked something off the floor and tossed it over to me. I caught the object and held it up to the lantern light.

It was a coin.

I squinted at the gold, which was stamped with a familiar crest—a woman's face that featured two tiny coins for her eyes and a third coin for her mouth. "This is a DiLucri gold crown. What's it doing here?"

"Maybe it belonged to one of the pirates' victims," Reiko suggested. "It would be easy to lose a coin from your pocket in the dark, especially if you were struggling not to get shackled."

"True," I agreed, then swung the lantern around and looked out over the cargo hold again. "But that doesn't explain all these hammocks. More than a hundred of them are squeezed in here."

Reiko shrugged. "Maybe Davies brought a bunch of people up the river for some reason."

"Maybe," I replied. "Or maybe the Mortans were here after all. Back in Blauberg, when Wexel was buying the stolen tearstone, he paid Conley with DiLucri gold."

Reiko shrugged again. "A single coin doesn't mean Wexel or Milo were here. Anyone could have dropped that DiLucri crown at any time."

She was right, but frustration filled me all the same. Despite our searching, we still had no idea if the Mortans had been here or not.

We didn't find anything else noteworthy in the cargo hold, so I shoved the gold coin into my pocket and we went back upstairs to the captain's quarters. Unlike the rest of the ship, which was devoid of finery, Davies's room was crammed full of expensive furniture, with a bed shoved up against one wall and a writing desk perched in the corner. Shelves lined the walls, but they were filled with spyglasses, maps of the Summanus River, and other navigational tools, rather than the books, bags of candy, and knickknacks that had populated the crew's quarters.

I sat down in the desk chair and riffled through the drawers. More spyglasses, a couple of daggers, some feather pens and pots of stoppered blue ink. Nothing interesting—except for a thick black ledger.

Curious, I cracked open the ledger and scanned the notations inside.

GIRL, THIRTEEN, RED HAIR, BLUE EYES—100 GOLD
CROWNS.

WOMAN, MID-TWENTIES, OGRE MORPH, BROWN HAIR
AND EYES—500 GOLD CROWNS.

MAN, MID-THIRTIES, MUTT WITH STRENGTH MAGIC,
BLACK HAIR AND EYES—50 GOLD CROWNS.

More anger, revulsion, and sorrow surged through me. Davies kept detailed records of all the people he sold to the DiLucris—and how much money he got for them.

Disgusted, I slammed the ledger shut hard enough to make a couple of compasses perched on the desk *rattle-rattle* together. "There's nothing here. Not the smallest hint that Milo and Wexel ever set foot on this ship."

"Maybe the rumor we heard was wrong," Reiko said, leaning one shoulder against the doorjamb. "Or maybe this is simply the wrong ship. Maybe Milo has already left on *another* ship. We both know it's his best option at this point."

So far, everything indicated that the crown prince was fleeing south and trying to get as far away from Andvari and Morta as fast as possible, since he was now a pariah with a hefty price on his head in both kingdoms. And given the deals my father had struck with the other royals, Milo wouldn't find safety in Unger, Ryusama, Bellona, Flores, or Vacuna either. No, his smartest, safest course of action was to run south to Fortuna Island and somehow convince—or bribe—the DiLucris to shelter him.

From there, Milo could board a ship and sail far, far away across the Blue Glass Sea to another kingdom, where he might find favor in some other royal's court. But even that was a faint, tenuous hope, since most leaders would not look kindly on a crown prince who had tried to depose and murder his own queen mother, along with several other royals. Plus, it would be a long, hard, dangerous journey—one that Milo might not survive, even with all his lightning magic, cleverness, and cruelty.

I rocked back in Davies's chair, which *creaked* in protest. "Well, according to all the rumors we've heard, Milo and Wexel have definitely been heading south."

"But?" Reiko asked.

"But you saw Milo during the Summit. Even though his plan to have Corvina murder me and Leonidas failed, he didn't give up—not for an *instant*. Instead, he barreled straight ahead with his plot and tried to assassinate *all* the other royals."

"So?"

I shook my head. "So I don't think he's running. At least, I don't think he's running away from us—more like *toward* something that will further his plans."

Reiko chewed on her lower lip, while her inner dragon's face scrunched up in thought. Worry radiated off them both, joining what was already churning in my stomach. We all knew the same unsettling truth—that we needed to figure out what Milo was plotting before he struck again and finally found some way to conquer my kingdom.

CHAPTER THREE

I grabbed the ledger, and Reiko and I returned to the top deck.

Grimley and Lyra were now both perched on the ship's railing and keeping a watch on the injured pirates, many of whom were still moaning with pain. A few feet away, Captain Davies was sitting on his ass in the middle of the deck, with Leonidas looming over him like an angry storm cloud threatening to wreak havoc on the landscape below.

I tossed the ledger down on the deck next to Davies, who flinched at the loud, accusing *thump*.

"I'm going to ask you some questions. Answer them honestly, and I'll let you and what's left of your crew live."

The captain gave me a wary look. "And if I don't?"

I jerked my thumb over my shoulder at Grimley. "Then I'll let the gargoyle gnaw on your bones."

Grimley growled and raked his talons across the railing, playing his part to perfection. Davies's eyes widened, but he didn't start blubbering up information, so I looked over at Leonidas.

"Or perhaps I'll let the strix have a turn with the good captain. Does Lyra like to eat humans?"

A sly grin spread across Leonidas's face. "Oh, Lyra *loves* to feast on humans. She snaps their fingers off one by one with her beak, like they're little worms she's snatching up out of the dirt. She also likes to pluck people's eyes out of their heads and gobble them down like grapes."

Lyra let out a loud, fierce *caw!* and stretched her wings out wide, also playing her part to perfection.

Davies's face paled even more. He glanced back and forth between Grimley and Lyra, eyes wide, clearly terrified of each creature and the gruesome ways they could kill him. After a few seconds, the captain ducked his head, as though wishing he were a ghost who could melt right down through the deck.

"What—what do you want to know?" he stammered, his voice far less arrogant and hostile than before.

I reached into my cloak pocket and pulled out a flyer that featured Milo's likeness, along with his name and the reward being offered for his capture or death. "Have you seen this man?"

Davies peered at the paper, then shook his head. "No, I haven't seen him. I swear. Like I told you before, no . . . Mortan noble has approached me about anything."

Suspicion filled me, and Reiko and Leonidas both tilted their heads to the side. They too had noticed the captain's hesitation.

"But someone *has* approached you about something," I said.

Davies wet his lips, his gaze flicking between Grimley and Lyra again. "Yes. A man boarded *The Drowned Man* yesterday morning, right after we docked. He claimed to have heard some gossip about a couple of folks who planned to stow away on my ship to get a free ride to Fortuna Island."

"And what did you tell him?"

Davies shrugged. "That I would treat those folks the same way I do all stowaways—either kill them or sell them to the Di-Lucris. He laughed and said either one was fine with him."

Reiko, Leonidas, and I all exchanged glances. Then I reached into my cloak pocket and pulled out another flyer, this one featuring Captain Wexel's likeness.

"Was it this man?"

Davies took one look at the flyer and started nodding. "Yes! Yes! That's him!"

"Did you see where he went? Did he get on another ship?"

"No idea," Davies replied. "He was only on board for a few minutes. Besides, I had too many passengers to unload to worry about some stranger."

Frustration shot through me, and I started pacing back and forth. Wexel had been here—*right bloody here*—on this very deck less than twenty-four hours ago, but once again, he had slipped away before we had even arrived.

I stopped pacing and had started to ask Davies another question when the image of all those hammocks in the cargo hold filled my mind, along with the gold coin Reiko had found. "What kind of passengers? From where?"

The captain shrugged. "Gladiators, from the looks of them. From Fortuna Island. This is the fifth load of them I've hauled up the river in the last few weeks. Going to the Sword and Shield Tournament in Glitnir like everyone else." He wet his lips again and jerked his head at the flyers in my hand. "Who are those people?"

"Dead men walking," I growled.

Davies ducked his head again, as if he suddenly feared me as much as he did Grimley and Lyra. Smart man.

I reached out with my magic and skimmed his thoughts, but they whipped back and forth like sails in a hurricane, and all I could really sense was his worry that I was going to kill him after all—or, worse, let Grimley and Lyra do it. Images of the gargoyle gnawing on Davies's bones and the strix pecking out his eyes filled my mind. The captain's fear was most definitely genuine, which meant his words most likely were too.

"What are you going to do with him?" Reiko asked.

Davies sucked in a breath, and I finally got a clear thought off him. *Please don't kill me, please don't kill me, please, please, please . . .*

I wondered how many innocent men, women, and children had huddled on this deck, thinking the exact same thing when they realized what Davies and his crew had planned for them. Rage crackled like lightning inside my chest, and my fingers itched with the urge to toss Davies into the main mast and snap his bloody spine, and then do the same thing to the remaining pirates. But that would be far too merciful a death for these bastards.

"The royal guards can deal with the captain and his crew," I replied. "It's only fair that Davies and his men wind up in shackles—before they're hanged."

The captain started to protest, but I stared him down, and he wisely shut his mouth.

Reiko nodded. "I'll summon the dockmaster."

She walked down the gangplank. Grimley and Lyra flapped their wings and took off to do some hunting, while Leonidas kept an eye on Davies, as well as the injured pirates.

I stalked over to the railing. Down below, the river churned and churned, and the *slap-slap-slap* of the waves up against the hull matched the anger and frustration pounding in my heart.

Milo Morricone had escaped yet again. Even worse, I had no idea where he had gone—or what horrible thing he might do next.

❖

A few minutes later, Reiko returned with the dockmaster. I explained who I was and what Davies and his men had tried to do to Reiko and me. The dockmaster's eyes bulged with surprise, but she summoned some royal guards, and Davies and the surviving pirates were clapped in chains and dragged off to the city prison.

Reiko, Leonidas, and I left *The Drowned Man* and walked along the riverfront. By this point, the sun was up, and people were starting their daily work and chores. We showed the flyers of Milo and Wexel to sailors, fishermen, and other folks, but no one remembered seeing the two men.

When it became apparent the Mortans were gone and we were wasting our time, the three of us left the riverfront and ducked into a nearby alley.

Lyra . . .

Grimley . . .

Leonidas and I called out to the creatures. A few minutes later, Lyra landed in the alley, followed by Grimley, along with another gargoyle.

This gargoyle was a bit smaller than Grimley, since she wasn't quite fully grown like he was, and her stone skin was a lighter gray and ribboned with tiny veins of jade green. Her eyes were the same bright green, and her mouth split into a smile at the sight of us.

Fern bounded over to Reiko and nuzzled up against her legs. "Lady Reiko! Did you have a good time battling pirates? Are you ready to fly home?"

Reiko grimaced at the word *fly*, but she scratched Fern's head in between her two horns, as many gargoyles liked. Fern's tail *thump-thump-thumped* against the flagstones in a quick, happy rhythm, making chips of stone zip through the air.

Reiko looked at me. "Are you sure we can't take the train back to Glanzen?"

Leonidas frowned in confusion. "Why would you take a train when you can fly?"

I slung my arm around the dragon morph's shoulders. "Oh, Reiko is not *nearly* as fond of flying as we are. Although she will do it for scones, right?"

Reiko shot me a sour look and elbowed me in the side. I

hissed and rubbed my ribs. Leonidas chuckled at us, then strode over to Lyra and stroked his hand along her feathers.

"It's no wonder you and Prince Leo are perfect for each other. You both have your heads in the clouds—literally," Reiko said.

Longing filled her face, and her inner dragon silently sighed, causing a cloud of smoke to skate across her skin.

I had a good idea what—or rather, whom—she was thinking about. "Have you heard from Kai?"

Reiko crossed her arms over her chest. "No, and I don't expect to. We said our goodbyes at the Summit."

Kai Nakamura had attended the Summit as one of the personal guards to Queen Ruri Yamato of Ryusama, although he was much better known for being a ferocious gladiator and the winner of last year's Tournament of Champions during the Regalia Games. Reiko used to be a gladiator too, and the two of them had been in the same troupe, the Crimson Dragons. Not only had Kai and Reiko competed against each other in the gladiatorial ring, but they had also butted heads at every turn—until they'd had a passionate encounter during the Regalia Games.

The last time I'd seen the two dragon morphs at the Summit, Kai had been trying to convince Reiko to give their relationship a real chance, although I didn't know if he'd succeeded. Reiko Yamato excelled at ferreting out other people's secrets, but she was stubbornly reluctant about sharing her own, no matter how many times I told her that I was happy to listen, if she ever wanted to talk.

Reiko dropped her arms to her sides. "You're right about one thing, though."

"What?"

"The sooner we get back to the capital, the sooner I can have those scones." She grinned, but sadness washed off her and pinched my own heart tight. Despite her light tone and cheerful words, Reiko was missing Kai far more than she would ever admit.

Reiko climbed onto Fern's back, while I did the same thing to Grimley, and Leonidas mounted Lyra. Then, with a whisper of wings, we all took off.

I tilted my face into the chilly November breeze. In, out, in, out. The more slow, controlled, steady breaths I took, the smaller my problems became, just like the boats, crates, and people along the riverfront shrank the higher into the air Grimley climbed. Oh, I was still deeply concerned about where Milo and Wexel were and especially what they were plotting, but flying always made my worries a little lighter and easier to bear, at least while I was soaring through the sky.

Grimley moved away from Allentown and flew north, following the Summanus River, which snaked through the forested landscape like a dull blue-gray thread embedded in a speckled brown and green carpet. Fern and Reiko were off to my right, while Leonidas and Lyra were off to my left.

Reiko didn't like flying—the dragon morph always claimed she was a mere gust of wind away from losing her seat on Fern's back and plummeting to her death—but Leonidas loved it as much as I did.

He grinned, and his voice filled my mind. *Race you?*

I returned his grin with an even wider one. *Only if you and Lyra want to lose again.*

I heard that. This time, the strix's voice sounded in my mind. *And I did not lose. Your rocks-for-brains gargoyle cheated.*

Grimley snorted. *It's not cheating just because I know the Glitnir rooftops better than you do. And it's certainly not my fault that you clipped a tower with one of your wings and lost precious seconds righting yourself.*

Lyra answered him with a loud, annoyed shriek and dove closer to the river. Grimley growled and followed her. The strix pumped her wings, and the gargoyle matched her swift pace.

Soon, the two of them were racing across the surface of the water. Cool spray misted over my face, and the wind tangled my hair, making me laugh with delight.

Idiots. Reiko's thought floated through my mind. *All four of them are idiots who are going to get themselves killed.*

For once, she was wrong, and we didn't hurt ourselves, although there was no clear winner in the race, since Lyra and Grimley both had to swerve to the side to avoid a steamboat that was slowly chugging up the river.

We flew for about an hour, although it seemed much shorter than that, given how much I enjoyed the journey. The forested landscape gave way to thinner woods, then farms surrounded by rolling hills. Faint trails turned into dirt paths and then into cobblestone streets. Clusters of homes popped up here and there, along with plazas lined with shops. Eventually, the streets, homes, shops, and plazas all ran together, stretching out as far as I could see and forming an enormous city nestled in the Spire Mountains—Glanzen, the capital of Andvari.

Grimley tucked his wings into his sides and dropped down, skimming over the rooftops the same way he had above the river earlier. Lyra and Fern followed his lead.

At our approach, several guards manning one of the city walls snapped to attention and raised their crossbows, although they relaxed when they recognized Grimley and me. I waved to the guards, who returned the gesture.

Over the last few weeks, Grandfather Heinrich had greatly increased the number of guards stationed along the city's borders, and everyone in Glanzen had been told to keep a wary eye on the sky and watch out for large groups of strixes. Everyone knew about Milo Morricone's attempt to assassinate Crown Prince Dominic Ripley and the other royals during the Summit, although we'd managed to keep the threat of his tearstone arrows under wraps—for now. But it was only a matter of time before Milo tried to implement his ultimate plan, whatever it was, and we wanted everyone to be prepared for trouble.

We left the outskirts of the city behind and headed for Glitnir, the royal palace that was the gleaming heart of Glanzen. Pinpricks of blue, purple, green, red, and white sparked in the distance, growing larger and brighter as we neared the palace, like flowers opening in the morning sunlight. Eventually, the sparks and colors solidified into faceted sapphires, amethysts, emeralds, rubies, and diamonds, which were arranged in mosaic patterns that complemented the opalescent sheen of the pale grayish marble walls. Hammered ribbons of gold, silver, and bronze also snaked up the steps, outlined the windows, and curved over the archways, making the palace look like an opulent wedding cake strung with precious gems and metals instead of spun sugar and fluffy icing.

Since it was midmorning, most of the gargoyles had flown out into the surrounding countryside to hunt, but a few were lounging on the palace rooftops, soaking up the sun. As we flew by, the gargoyles lifted their heads and called out welcoming cries. Lucky, Boodle, Pansy, Iris . . . All the creatures had names, either ones I had given them or ones they had chosen for themselves.

Grimley answered their gravelly grumbles with ones of his own, as did Fern. Lyra also let out a few caws, although the other gargoyles didn't respond. They still weren't used to having a strix in their midst, and most of them gave the other creature a wide berth.

Grimley sailed down and landed on a terrace. I slid off his back, while Reiko dismounted Fern, and Leonidas did the same thing with Lyra.

"You're getting better at flying," I teased Reiko. "Your face isn't *nearly* as green as it was when we landed in Allentown."

She scowled and made a rude hand gesture. I laughed, as did Leonidas.

Grimley, Fern, and Lyra flapped their wings and took off to do some hunting, while Reiko, Leonidas, and I headed inside the palace to get cleaned up and prepare for our next mission of the day. Bounty Hunter Gemma might have failed miserably this morning, but perhaps Princess Gemma would have better luck.

Thirty minutes later, we met in the hallway outside my chambers. Reiko had donned a fresh tunic, while Leonidas was sporting a clean riding coat. I was now clad in a gray gown covered with dark blue thread that had been stitched to resemble frost pansies blooming all over me.

"You look lovely," Leonidas said.

I huffed. "I look like I rolled around in a flowerbed."

He grinned. "That too."

Leonidas offered me his arm, and we strolled through the palace, with Reiko striding along beside us.

Plenty of precious metals and gems adorned the exterior palace walls, but the interior corridors resembled a life-size jewelry box, and something glittered and gleamed around every corner. Fluorestone chandeliers studded with white, gray, and black diamonds blazed with light, while opals, topazes, and other gemstones were set into many of the furnishings, glimmering like stars embedded in the dark wooden chairs, tables, and bookcases.

Servants and palace stewards dressed in dark gray tunics hurried to do chores and check on things, while guards stood in the corners, their hands on their swords. Everyone nodded as we walked by, and I returned the gestures, once again playing the part of Princess Gemma.

We stepped through some open glass doors and entered the Edelstein Gardens, which lay in the center of Glitnir. The Edelstein Gardens were famous for their mix of real, live trees, flowers, and other plants, along with those made of gold, silver, and sparkling jewels. The gardens were one of my favorite places in the entire palace, although right now, the shimmering branches, colorful blossoms, and soft floral perfumes did little to improve my mood. Once again, I had left home to hunt down Milo, and once again, I had failed to return with his head.

Leonidas, Reiko, and I left the trees and flowers behind and stepped into the hedge maze that was the gardens' main feature. The maze was always shaped like a snarling gargoyle face—the Ripley royal crest—although the plant masters came up with new twists and turns every year.

I led my friends to the gargoyle's nose, which served as the center of the maze. The hedges fell away, revealing an enormous open space that featured a wide, grassy lawn, a pond filled with water lilies, and a lovely gazebo. It was a beautiful place to enjoy a late fall morning—or a garden party, in this case.

Dozens of nobles, merchants, and guilders milled around, sipping warm apple cider and gossiping in their usual cliques. Even though today's garden party wasn't a formal occasion, most folks were still decked out in colorful gowns and jackets that made them look like oversize hummingbirds flitting around the lawn.

As per tradition, Grandfather Heinrich always hosted a gathering for the Glitnir court the day before any major gladiator competition was held in Glanzen. This year, it was our city's turn to host the Sword and Shield Tournament, the final event of the season, which would decide the best individual gladiator in Buchovia, as well as the top overall troupe. A larger, more formal breakfast would be held tomorrow to welcome all the tournament competitors to Glanzen.

Several tables boasting platters of fresh fruits, cheeses, and sweet cakes had been spaced around the lawn, along with smaller tables and cushioned chairs where guests could sit, relax, and enjoy the refreshments. Ice sculptures shaped like swords, shields, and gargoyles glimmered like cold diamonds on stone pedestals that had been positioned all around the gazebo.

Gray ribbons twined through the ebony railing and wound up the white marble columns that supported the gazebo, giving the structure a fun, festive air. Even the silver gargoyle faces embedded in the columns seemed to grin, while their jeweled eyes continuously winked their approval.

But the longer I stared at the sculptures, the more color bloomed in the ice, turning the clear, frosty figures a dark, bloody red. The gazebo flickered, and the sculptures and ribbons vanished, along with the bright sunlight.

Suddenly, I was seeing the structure as it had been some sixteen years ago, the night Dahlia Sullivan, my grandfather's mistress, and other members of the Bastard Brigade, a group of bastard-born Morricones, had tried to murder Queen Everleigh Blair.

The nobles, merchants, and guilders disappeared, replaced by cloaked assassins clutching swords who were creeping closer and closer to the gazebo. My heart galloped up into my throat, and a sharp tang of fear filled my mouth. The assassins were going to kill Evie before I could reach her—

"Gemma?" Leonidas's voice broke into my memories. "Are you okay?"

I blinked. The assassins disappeared, the sunlight returned, and the blood dribbled out of the ice sculptures. My heart was still stuck in my throat, but I swallowed it down. "I'm fine."

"Mmm." Leonidas's noncommittal reply indicated he didn't believe my lie.

"Well, I see a platter of apple-cinnamon scones that are demanding to be eaten," Reiko announced. "You two have fun making nice with the nobles."

I shot her a sour look, but Reiko laughed and moved away.

A sigh escaped my lips. "As much as I hate to admit it, she's right. We should make the rounds."

"Well, then, let me escort Princess Gemma through her throngs of admirers," Leonidas murmured, and offered me his arm again.

Together, we ambled across the lawn. Audible whispers surged through the crowd at my walking arm in arm with Leonidas, and even more silent thoughts buzzed in my ears.

Prince Leonidas is handsome—for a Mortan . . .

Look at the two of them strolling along as though they aren't both traitors to their kingdoms . . .

I still can't believe that Gemma Ripley is fucking a Morricone. What a bloody disgrace to Andvari . . .

Rage erupted in my heart, burning even hotter than a Vacunan volcano. I whirled around. As soon as I figured out the source of that horrid thought, I was going to give that person a piece of my mind—

"Forget it, Gemma," Leonidas murmured. "They're not worthy of your time or attention, much less your anger."

I grimaced, knowing he had also heard the snide thoughts and wishing he hadn't. "I'm not angry for myself. I'm enraged for *you*. Because you are smart and thoughtful and kind and generous, if only they would bother to look past their petty prejudices and see you—the real *you*."

Leonidas smiled, but it was a sad, resigned expression. "Some people will *never* see me as anything other than a Morricone, than Maeven's son, especially here in Andvari." He shrugged. "I don't blame your people for their mistrust. My mother hasn't exactly endeared herself to Andvarians or anyone else during her reign."

No, no, she had not. Maeven Morricone was one of the most notorious queens, well, *ever*. She was most famous—some would argue infamous—for murdering her brother Maximus during the Regalia Games sixteen years ago so that she could seize the

Mortan throne. But that was hardly her first or only crime. Maeven had also tried to start a war between Andvari and Bellona by orchestrating the Seven Spire massacre, and she had hatched myriad other schemes, some successful, some not, against all the kingdoms on the Buchovian continent.

"Come," Leonidas said. "We should greet your family."

We strolled over to an open section of the lawn, close to the cattails that lined one side of the rippling pond. Through the throngs of people, I spotted a seventy-something man with blue eyes, tan skin, and wavy hair that was more silver than dark brown. King Heinrich Aldric Magnus Ripley had finally gotten over a cough that had been bothering him for the past several weeks, and he looked as fit and hearty as ever. Grandfather Heinrich was holding up a jar of honey, showing off the sweet rewards of his beekeeping hobby.

A few feet away, Crown Prince Dominic Heinrich Ferdinand Ripley was sipping cider and nodding at something a merchant was saying. My father had the same tan skin and blue eyes as Grandfather Heinrich, although his hair was still more dark brown than silver, since he was in his fifties.

Rhea Hans, my forty-something stepmother, stood nearby, talking to a noble lady. Her ebony skin gleamed in the sunlight, as did her topaz eyes and the gray crystal pins that held her black hair back from her face. Rhea's hand rested on the hilt of the sword belted to her waist, and her gaze continually scanned the lawn. Rhea was the captain of the royal guard, and she had been on high alert ever since we had first learned of Milo's plot against Andvari.

Leonidas and I stopped, not wanting to interrupt their conversations, and I studied all the nobles, merchants, and guilders gathered on the lawn. I might have swallowed my earlier rage, but I still wanted my people to give Leonidas a chance. If they were too stubborn to realize how wonderful he was on their own, then I would have to arrange some other, more pointed form of enlightenment.

My gaze snagged on a sixty-something lord standing by himself and staring down at the ground beside the front entrance to the gazebo. He was short and slender, with silver-rimmed glasses, dark brown eyes and skin, and iron-gray hair and a matching mustache. A gold oak tree dripping with gold acorns was stitched on his green tunic right over his heart. Instead of a sword or dagger, a small pair of pruning shears dangled from his belt, along with a large pouch.

A smile lifted my lips. Oh, yes. He would do quite nicely.

"Come," I told Leonidas. "There's someone I want you to meet."

Lord Eichen turned at the sound of our feet scuffing through the grass. "Your Highness. Prince Leonidas." He greeted me warmly, although his voice turned noticeably cooler when he said Leonidas's name.

I tipped my head to him. "Lord Eichen. I'm so glad you could attend the garden party. It's such a lovely fall day. The good weather is supposed to last through the entire Sword and Shield Tournament."

Eichen smiled at me, although his gaze kept skittering over to Leonidas. The prince's face was calm and blank, but his arm was as stiff as a board under my fingers, and tension radiated off his body.

I hadn't expected things to be *easy* for Leonidas at Glitnir, but I had severely underestimated just how difficult they would be. The nobles, merchants, and guilders either openly shunned him or made snide comments behind his back, as did the palace stewards, servants, and guards. That obvious hostility was bad enough, but with his mind magier magic, Leonidas could hear their vicious thoughts just as clearly and easily as I could.

He never reacted to any of the audible insults or silent mockery, although at times like these, I could tell just how much they bothered him. My heart ached for him, even as my rage boiled up again. People were wrong, petty, and cruel to judge the Morricone prince based solely on his family name and who his mother and brother were. But Andvarians and Mortans were much like gargoyles and strixes: constantly fighting. And the two peoples preferred to embrace old prejudices rather than try to get along.

Determination flared inside me. Well, I was going to do my best to change that.

I gestured at Leonidas. "Lord Eichen, let me formally introduce Prince Leonidas Morricone. He is visiting Glitnir as part of an effort to improve relations with Morta."

That was the official story for Leonidas being at the palace, although everyone knew we were involved. In recent days, I'd heard more than one hushed whisper and silent speculation about whether I would be bold enough to actually marry Leonidas—and what Grandfather Heinrich, Father, and Rhea would think of such a union.

Those comments were as kind as kittens compared to the callous quips about us fucking.

People probably thought they were being daring, bold, or shocking by discussing my personal relationships, but sadly, I'd grown used to it over the years. All I had to do was dance with a man at a ball, and people assumed we were fucking. Or if I had a private tea with a noble lady. Or if I asked a servant to bring something to my chambers. Despite the hundreds, thousands of innocent ways I could interact with someone, the conclusion was *always* the same: I was fucking that person.

The gossip, comments, and speculation had never particularly bothered me before, but now they cut me like razors scraping across my skin. Because what I felt for Leonidas went so far beyond anything I had ever imagined possible. I loved him with all my heart, mind, and magic, and I would do anything for him, including making his stay at Glitnir a bit more pleasant—or at least getting one noble to see him as more than a Mortan, a Morricone, an enemy.

"Of course," Eichen murmured, matching my politeness. "Everyone at Glitnir has been buzzing about Prince Leonidas and his . . . unprecedented visit."

Sadly, *unprecedented* was among the nicer things people had said and thought about the Morricone prince.

"Lord Eichen," Leonidas replied, his voice also polite and smooth. "It's so nice to be formally introduced. Have your grandchildren arrived yet? Gemma has told me about their impressive fighting skills. I'm looking forward to seeing them compete in the Sword and Shield Tournament."

Eichen's eyes brightened, his lips lifted, and his shoulders straightened, as though the plant magier had used his magic to make his own body bloom with happiness. The lord was known for his rabid love of gladiator bouts and tournaments, and he'd already been at Glitnir for more than two weeks, overseeing preparations for his grandchildren and their respective gladiator troupes to compete in the tournament.

Eichen opened his mouth to answer Leonidas's question, but then he remembered whom he was talking to, and the warmth vanished from his features.

The lord cleared his throat. "Thank you for your kind words, Prince Leonidas. I always look forward to seeing my grandchildren compete, especially against the Mortan troupes."

As far as insults went, his words were rather mild, but they still made me grind my teeth. Eichen was one of the wealthiest and most powerful nobles in Andvari. If I could convince him to accept Leonidas, or at least be civil, then much of the hostility toward the Morricone prince would die down.

And then maybe—just maybe—I could let myself dream of

a future with Leonidas beyond the next few days, or weeks, or however long it took us to find Milo.

When it became apparent Eichen wasn't going to further the conversation, Leonidas turned to me. "I'm rather thirsty. Something to drink, Gemma?"

I recognized his words as the escape they were. "Yes, please. Thank you."

"Lord Eichen?" Leonidas asked.

Eichen waved his hand, declining a drink, and Leonidas headed over to one of the refreshment tables. The lord watched him go with a curious expression.

"I can see why you are so . . . enamored of Prince Leonidas," Eichen said. "He is quite handsome. And from what I saw at the Summit, he is an excellent fighter. Killing an arena full of enemies by yourself is no small feat. He could have easily been a gladiator himself, if not for his familial duties."

I grimaced, even though the lord's voice was more thoughtful than snide. During the Summit, Maeven had invoked the Gauntlet, an arcane Ungerian tradition that consisted of three challenges, in order to force Leonidas and me to become engaged—and eventually marry. Eichen was referring to the second Gauntlet challenge, where Leonidas had been required to battle a dozen enemies to the death in the gladiator arena at Caldwell Castle.

"Prince Leonidas's triumph was quite thrilling. One of the best bouts I have ever seen." Eichen eyed me, but when I didn't respond, he cleared his throat again. "But enough about that. You saw the fight for yourself. Let us move on to other matters."

He drew in a breath, then let it out, along with a rush of words. "Did I ever tell you that I once received a letter from Queen Maeven Morricone herself?"

I had braced myself for more benign talk of gladiators, and

I blinked at the unexpected change in topic. "*Maeven* contacted you? When? And why?"

Eichen's face darkened, and anger surged off him, the emotion strong enough to make my own cheeks burn. "I received the letter about a month after my wife was murdered."

Sympathy filled me. From all accounts, Lady Odella, Eichen's wife, had been a lovely woman. She too had been a plant magier. Several years ago, she had been out hunting rare mushrooms when she'd had the bad luck to run into Mortan bandits. The men had killed Odella and left her body to rot in the woods.

Eichen had dearly loved his wife, although he rarely talked about her death, which made me even more curious why he had brought it up now.

"What did Maeven say in her letter?"

He clasped his hands together behind his back. "She apologized for the bandits' actions."

"That's . . . unusual."

A small, bitter laugh tumbled out of Eichen's lips. "Oh, yes. Believe me, I was as stunned as you are, but the letter was quite cordial. Queen Maeven said she deeply regretted the pain that had been inflicted on my family, and she assured me the bandits had been dealt with to the fullest extent of Mortan law. She even sent along some proof."

"What proof?"

He stared at me, his expression ice-cold. "Their heads."

Surprise shot through me. Not that Maeven wouldn't do such a thing. Ordering heads to be chopped off and then sending them to people was perfectly in keeping with the queen's ruthless nature. But why would she care about getting justice for a murdered Andvarian noble?

"I planted the heads around Odella's grave," Eichen continued. "They made excellent compost material. Her favorite roses continue to thrive to this day."

I nodded. "As they should."

Eichen fell silent, but he didn't seem angry about Maeven's gesture, and his mood appeared to be more contemplative than vengeful. Still, I kept thinking about his story—and wondering why he had shared it with me.

"Prince Leonidas hasn't made the impression at court you hoped he would," Eichen said.

We both looked over at Leonidas, who was standing alone, sipping a glass of cider. Nobles, merchants, and guilders moved all around the prince, but they pointedly ignored him, as though he was as irrelevant as one of the ice sculptures. Leonidas stared off into the distance, as though he was admiring the gardens' beauty, but a muscle ticced in his jaw, and his fingers curled around his crystal goblet like he wanted to hurl it at someone.

Once again, my heart ached for him, even as more determination flared inside me. It was time to stop dancing around in this courtly game and ask for what I wanted.

I turned so that I was facing Eichen. "I would consider it a great personal favor if you would extend your friendship to Leonidas."

His bushy eyebrows shot up on his face. "A personal favor? That is no small thing to offer."

"There is nothing small about how I feel about Leonidas," I replied in a soft voice.

"Oh, yes. I can see how much you care about him, and his concern for you is as plain as that Morricone crest on his tunic."

I ignored the not-so-subtle dig about Leonidas's family. "So will you help me?"

Eichen shrugged a shoulder, neither agreeing nor disagreeing. "Mine is not the help you need."

"Modesty does not become you, my lord. We both know how powerful and influential you are. The other nobles follow your lead in a great many matters. Why, gladiators wouldn't be *nearly* as popular as they are in Andvari without your long-standing enthusiasm and patronage."

Eichen shrugged again, although a sly smile crept across his face. "True. But not even I can overcome centuries of hostility, bloodshed, and prejudice simply by offering my friendship."

"We must start somewhere," I replied in a sharp voice. "Lest we all be destroyed by those prejudices."

Eichen shrugged for a third time. "Perhaps. Or perhaps those prejudices exist for a reason."

Equal parts frustration and disappointment filled me. He wasn't going to help, and even worse, he was right. No matter whether they were nobles, servants, or guards, certain Andvarians would *never* accept Leonidas, no matter what he or I did or how much we cared about each other.

"Although there is one thing I have always liked about Morta," Eichen said.

"What?" I asked in a wary voice.

He gestured at the ground beside the gazebo. "Liladorn."

For the first time, I realized what the plant magier had been looking at when Leonidas and I had first approached him—a tangle of black vines with sharp curved thorns that were longer than my fingers.

"Liladorn is such a fascinating plant," Eichen continued. "Most people, including the Mortans, think it's nothing more than a noxious weed, but it has a surprising number of uses. Why, I've heard some people even make salve and other healing ointments with liladorn."

My fingers flexed, and the familiar dull aches rippled through my hands. Delmira Morricone, Leonidas's sister, was one of those people, and the liladorn salve she'd slathered on my whipped back and burned, punctured hands had helped heal the gruesome wounds Milo had inflicted on me at Myrkvior.

"Liladorn is thought to be native to Morta and Morta alone,"

Eichen continued. "So I was quite surprised to find it in the Edelstein Gardens. I've strolled past this gazebo at least a hundred
times over the years, but I don't recall ever seeing it here before."

I had never seen it here before either. At least, not around the
gazebo, although a few weeks ago, before the Summit, I'd found
it in another section of the gardens, curled around a bench with
a memorial plaque that honored my mother, Merilde Ripley. Perhaps some of the vines had slithered over here.

We liked Merilde. She planted us everywhere she went. That's
what the liladorn at Caldwell Castle had told me, although I still
didn't know why she had been so interested in the vines.

"My mother must have planted the liladorn," I said. "She
was always bringing flowers, vines, and shrubs back from our
travels and adding them to the gardens here. I used to sit in the
shade and read books while she would plant them. Those are
some of my fondest memories."

I couldn't quite keep the longing out of my voice, and sadness
splattered all over my heart like a cold rain.

We miss your mother too, a voice whispered in my mind.

I glanced down at the liladorn again. The vines vibrated ever
so slightly, then snaked in my direction. I tensed. The liladorn
had helped me before, but it had also scratched me more times
than I cared to remember. The sentient plant was just as likely to
harm as to heal, just like everything else that came out of Morta.

Eichen didn't notice the liladorn headbutting the toe of my
shoe like a cat demanding to have its back scratched. I thought
about scooting my foot away from the vines, but that would probably just annoy them and make them lash out at me, so I remained
still.

But watching the plant slither around gave me an idea, another way I might convince Eichen to help me. "Would you like
some liladorn to take back to your estate? It would make a very
lovely and unique addition to Oakton Manor."

His face brightened again. No plant magier could resist the allure of having something special in their gardens. "Why, yes, it would. I would be honored to accept your offer."

"I'll make the arrangements and have a cutting delivered to your chambers."

Happiness rippled off him, although his wide, genuine smile quickly turned sharp and calculating. "Excellent! Now, please excuse me, Your Highness. Prince Leonidas had the right idea. I suddenly find myself exceptionally thirsty."

Eichen tipped his head to me, then went over to the refreshment table where Leonidas was still standing and pretending to admire the gardens. The lord got his own cider and engaged Leonidas in conversation. At first, the Morricone prince looked surprised, then wary, although his unease slowly melted away.

"Gladiators . . . My grandchildren . . . Great hopes for the tournament this year . . ." Snippets of Eichen's words drifted over to me.

The other nobles had taken note of their conversation, and more than a few people wandered over to blatantly eavesdrop. Within minutes, a crowd had gathered around the two men, and Eichen was clapping Leonidas on the shoulder and laughing at something the prince had said.

Eichen was right. One conversation at one party on one day wasn't nearly enough to change people's minds and hearts about Leonidas, or the Morricones, or Mortans in general.

But it was a start, no matter how small.

I glanced down at the liladorn still curling around my shoe. I'd seen the power just one strand of the sentient plant could have, and I hoped Eichen reaching out to Leonidas would have the same effect and help us all build a lasting peace between Andvari and Morta—one strand, conversation, and party at a time.

CHAPTER FOUR

An hour later, the garden party finally ended. After exchanging goodbyes with all the guests, I retreated to Grandfather Heinrich's study, along with Father, Rhea, and Leonidas. Reiko also appeared from wherever she had been skulking about and joined us behind closed doors.

"I abhor those bloody parties," Grandfather Heinrich muttered, sitting down behind his desk in the back of the room. "They get longer and more tedious with each and every tournament of the season."

"Well, this is the last major tournament of the year," Father replied, taking a seat at his own desk, which was off to the right. "Once it's finished, and the individual champion is decided, along with the overall winning troupe, then the nobles will jump into the yuletide season, and we can finally have a few weeks to ourselves."

"If Milo doesn't murder us all in the meantime," I muttered.

I told Grandfather Heinrich, Father, and Rhea everything that had happened in Allentown, including the fact that Milo and Wexel had slipped through our fingers yet again.

"Perhaps the Mortans left on another ship," Rhea suggested,

gesturing at a map on her own desk. "That is the most logical conclusion."

"I'll use my Cardea mirror to speak to the dockmasters in other towns along the Summanus River, both in Andvari and Bellona," Father said. "Perhaps one of them will remember seeing Milo or Wexel."

I nodded, trying to hide the frustration still bubbling inside me.

Rhea cleared her throat and looked at me, then Leonidas. "What about the other matter we discussed yesterday?"

Everyone stared at Leonidas, who was leaning up against a bookcase a few feet away from the rest of us. "Everything has been arranged, as per your requests. It should be *quite* the grand, momentous occasion."

I arched an eyebrow at his sarcastic tone, and he shrugged back at me.

Grandfather Heinrich grumbled something under his breath, while Father rocked back in his chair and Rhea tapped her index finger on the hilt of her sword. Anger, tension, hostility, and suspicion radiated off all three, matching the emotions that were simmering in my own heart. But this was the course of action I had suggested, and one we had all agreed on, and we had no choice now but to see it through to the end.

Like Queen Everleigh Blair before me, I had set a Bellonan long game into motion. I just hoped my plan wouldn't doom us all.

"Do you really think Milo is fleeing south?" Grandfather Heinrich asked. "And that he can somehow convince the Di-Lucris to shelter him?"

Once again, all eyes fell on Leonidas, whose forehead creased in thought. "Milo is smart enough to see the advantages of running south, of getting as far away from both Andvari and Morta as possible. He probably has enough money squirreled away to pay the DiLucris to take him in, at least long enough for him to book passage to another continent."

"But?" Father challenged.

Leonidas shrugged. "But Milo is also stubborn, petty, and vindictive enough to try to attack us again, regardless of the risk to his own personal safety. Milo is perfectly cold, calm, and logical—until he's not. And when he is not cold, calm, and logical, then *anything* can happen. Milo's unpredictability makes him extremely volatile and dangerous. He's far more of a threat to Andvari than King Maximus ever was, because there's no way to tell what he might do next."

No one spoke, but worry blasted off Grandfather Heinrich, Father, and Rhea and twisted my stomach further into knots.

Images of all the notes and journals in Milo's workshops in Myrkvior and on Antheia Island flashed through my mind. The crown prince had spent years experimenting with tearstone, dried fool's bane flowers, and other items, and now he had finally created arrows that could kill both people *and* gargoyles. Milo Morricone had devoted his life to three things: learning how to murder his enemies, becoming king of Morta, and ruling the Buchovian continent. Milo might run for a while, but he would *never* give up on those goals—not until he was dead.

"Regardless of Milo's whereabouts, we need to focus on the tournament," Grandfather Heinrich said. "Let's review the security protocols again. I don't want a repeat of what happened at the Summit . . ."

He started riffling through some papers on his desk, and Father and Rhea chimed in with their own reports. I also added my own thoughts when called upon, as did Reiko and Leonidas, but I was only listening with half an ear.

Instead, I kept thinking about Milo, wondering when and where he might strike again—and if he would finally succeed in his relentless, ruthless quest to conquer my kingdom.

We reviewed the tournament security protocols for another hour. After that, Grandfather Heinrich, Father, and Rhea kept working in the study, while Leonidas returned to his chambers to double-check the arrangements for my plan, which would kick off tomorrow morning. Reiko announced that she was going in search of more apple-cinnamon scones, although I knew she was just using the sweets as an excuse to skulk around the palace and spy on the nobles, servants, and guards.

I climbed to the top of one of the palace towers and knocked on a door made of blue, black, and silver pieces of stained glass that formed a lovely frosted forest scene. A muffled voice told me to enter, so I turned the knob, opened the door, and stepped inside.

Glass cabinets ringed the round room, each one filled with sheets of precious metals, along with sparkling jewels in every color imaginable, from the clearest, pinkest diamonds to the darkest, blackest pieces of jet. Large windows were set into the walls, while fluorestones embedded in the ceiling flooded the area with even more light.

Some *tink-tink-tinks* rang out, drawing my attention. An eighty-something man was perched on a stool at a long table in the center of the room. A fluorestone lamp sitting by his right elbow burnished his ebony skin in a soft glow and highlighted the many strands of silver in his wavy black hair. The man leaned forward, his hazel eyes narrowing in concentration as he peered down through a magnifying glass that was clamped onto the edge of the table.

Alvis, the royal jeweler and a metalstone master, didn't look up as I walked over to him, although the two creatures in the room perked up at my approach.

The first creature was a gargoyle that was even bigger than

Grimley, with a thick, wide body, enormous wings, and a long tail. Bits of white glimmered like strings of opals embedded in the gargoyle's dark gray stone skin, while his light gray eyes gleamed like moonstones. His right horn was sharp, curved, and intact, but his left horn was broken off into a jagged stump—thanks to Milo Morricone.

When he was young, Otto had been captured by Milo on Antheia Island in Caldwell Lake, and the crown prince had tortured and eventually shattered the gargoyle's horn. Otto was as haunted by Milo's cruelty as I was, and we both had a burning desire to see him pay for all the awful things he'd done to us.

Otto was stretched out on the floor in front of the table, although his head lifted at my footsteps. He might have appeared to be relaxing, but he was ready for trouble. Good. Alvis could take care of himself, but it never hurt to have a gargoyle watching your back.

The second creature was much, much smaller—a baby strix with light lilac feathers and big, bright matching eyes. Her beak and talons were a dusky gray, as were the tips of her feathers, although they would all blacken and harden as she grew older. Violet was perched on the table by Alvis's elbow, trying to peer through the magnifying glass right along with him.

I had asked Alvis to watch over Violet while I was off chasing Milo, and the baby strix seemed fascinated by the tweezers, polishing cloths, and other jeweler's tools strewn across the table. Leonidas had given Violet to me as part of one of the Gauntlet challenges during the Summit, and I fell a little more in love with the strix every time I saw her.

Violet caught sight of me and let out a loud, happy *cheep!* She hopped forward and waggled her wings in a furious rhythm. At first, I thought she was just greeting me, but then her body lifted off the tabletop an inch, then two, then three—

Suddenly, Violet's wings sputtered to a stop, as though she'd run out of the skill and energy to keep pumping them so hard and fast. She plummeted down and landed with a loud *thump*. The baby strix let out a dismayed cry and raked her tiny talons across the wood, clearly upset.

Otto yawned, stretched, and got to his feet. "She's been practicing all day," he rumbled. "She can almost fly, but not quite."

Violet dropped her head and let out a sad little chirp of agreement. I reached out and stroked my fingers along her silky feathers.

"It's okay, little one," I said. "You'll be flying soon enough, and then no one will be able to keep up with you."

Violet's head lifted, her eyes brightened, and she let out a happier, far more hopeful chirp.

I stroked her feathers again, then looked over the other objects on the table—different bunches of dried flowers and herbs, along with several mortars and pestles. My nose twitched, and I resisted the urge to sneeze at the rose, lavender, dill, and other floral and earthy scents swirling through the air.

I sidled up beside Alvis and peered over his shoulder and down through the magnifying glass. One of Milo's tearstone arrows lay on a white velvet work tray. The shorter-than-normal projectile was only a little longer than my hand, but its wicked design still made me shudder, especially the razor-sharp tip and the oversize arrowhead lined with hooked barbs whose sole purpose was to tear through as much of a person's flesh as possible. This arrow was currently a light starry gray, although I knew from past, personal experience that it would turn and remain a deep midnight blue once it was covered with blood.

"Any progress?" I asked.

Alvis sighed and leaned back on his stool. "None—absolutely none. So far, I haven't found any flowers, herbs, or other plants that will nullify the dried fool's bane Milo is putting on his tearstone arrows. The dried fool's bane itself isn't poisonous, but it does greatly amplify any magic that touches it."

He waved his hand. Magic gusted off him and sank into the arrow, making it glimmer a bright gray as the tearstone absorbed his power.

"Watch carefully," Alvis said.

He picked up a dried flower that featured three light purple cloverlike petals perched atop a green stem covered with prickly, sticky fuzz. He laid the fool's bane on top of the arrow and snatched his hand back. As soon as the flower touched the tearstone, the purple petals began glowing like electrified amethysts, and even more magic surged through the air, far more magic than what Alvis had first directed at the arrow—

Whoosh!

The entire flower—petals, stem, and all—erupted like a volcano. Purple sparks and smoke spewed up into the air, along with a watery, fishy stench, and the tearstone arrow glowed even more brightly than before. In addition to the visible display of power, I could *feel* the arrow's magic increasing, growing hotter and hotter the longer the flower burned.

Violet squeaked in surprise and alarm and scuttled back, pressing herself up against my arm, and a shiver swept through my own body at the odd, horrific sight.

Alvis grabbed a cup of water and doused the burning fool's bane, reducing it to wet ash, but the arrow kept right on glowing with magic. Another shiver swept through my body.

"I still don't know how or why the dried fool's bane reacts that way to the tearstone and my power," Alvis said. "But Milo can do even more damage with his arrows than we previously thought."

"How much damage?"

Alvis crossed his arms over his chest, his gaze locked on the still-glowing arrow. "Each arrow could probably absorb enough magic to shoot right through two or three gargoyles, as though their skin were made of paper instead of stone. If Milo could somehow link enough arrows together, and hit them all with his lightning magic, then he could potentially kill dozens of gargoyles all at once."

My stomach churned with nausea, but I forced myself to keep asking questions. "What else could he do with the arrows?"

Alvis shrugged. "The beauty of using arrows is that you can target anything you want to with them. Gargoyles, people, even buildings."

I frowned. "Buildings?"

He nodded. "Oh, yes. If Milo strung enough arrows together, and then blasted them with his lightning, then he could potentially set off a chain reaction of magic strong enough to take down an entire building."

"Or an arena full of people," I murmured, thinking of the upcoming tournament.

Alvis shrugged again. "That too."

My gaze dropped to the wet, ashy remains of the fool's bane flower. "And there's no way to stop the magic once it starts building?"

He shook his head. "Not that I've found so far. In many ways, magic is like a campfire. Once it's created, then it burns and burns until it either runs out of wood or is extinguished by some greater outside force, like a bucket of water. But the combination of the tearstone *and* the dried fool's bane on Milo's arrows keeps that magic, that fire, from being so easily extinguished. Add his lightning power to the mix, and the consequences are potentially catastrophic for whatever creatures, people, or objects Milo targets with his weapons."

Every word he said tied another tight knot of worry around my heart, as though they were anchors on a ship plunging me

down, down, down into icy waters filled with despair, desperation, and hopelessness.

"I'm sorry, Gemma," Alvis said in a soft voice. "I wish I had
better news."

"Me too," I murmured.

"But let's try to look on the bright side of things," he continued.

I arched an eyebrow. "You *never* look on the bright side of
things. Only the annoyed, aggravated, grumpy side."

Alvis harrumphed. "Well, at least Milo won't be able to get
his hands on any *more* tearstone. The last of it was delivered to
the royal treasury this morning."

After the Summit, Grandfather Heinrich had sent royal
guards to secure every tearstone mine in Andvari, as well as escort shipments of the raw ore back to Glitnir. So far, all the shipments had arrived without incident, and the loads of tearstone
were being stored in the treasury, which was one of the most secure parts of the palace.

Grandfather Heinrich had also ordered the mines to be
closed for the next several days, so that the miners and other
workers could have a holiday and attend the Sword and Shield
Tournament, if they so wished.

"You're right," I said. "It is good news that the last of the tearstone arrived safely."

"But?" Alvis asked.

I gestured at the tearstone arrow, which was still glowing
brightly through the wet ash of the fool's bane flower. "But I'm
still worried about how much damage Milo can do with what he
already has."

CHAPTER FIVE

I stayed in Alvis's workshop another hour, helping with his experiments, but we didn't find anything that would dampen the power of Milo's arrows once the tearstone and the dried fool's bane were triggered with magic. Alvis decided to retire to his chambers for the evening, so I headed to my own suite of rooms, with Otto following along behind me, and Violet riding on his back.

I opened the double doors with a wave of my hand and stepped into a sitting room filled with cushioned chairs and settees, which were arranged around a fireplace that was shaped like the Ripley gargoyle crest. An iron grate stretched across the creature's wide, open mouth, which formed the actual firebox, while its horns were carved into the stone chimney and stretched all the way to the ceiling. The crackling flames behind the grate made it seem like the gargoyle was perpetually snarling fire and baring its red-hot teeth.

Grimley was stretched out on the rug in front of the fireplace. Violet cheeped with excitement, hopped down off Otto's back, and raced over to the other gargoyle. Then she stopped and rubbed her head all over his front paws. Violet liked all the gargoyles, including Otto and Fern, but Grimley was her favorite.

"Hello, runt," Grimley said in an affectionate tone, raising his head to peer at the much smaller creature. "Did you miss me while I was gone?"

"Yes, yes, yes!" Violet replied in her high singsong voice. "Missed you lots!"

The baby strix fluffed out her feathers and settled herself in between Grimley's front paws. Within seconds, she was fast asleep, with small snores squeaking out of her throat.

Otto rolled his eyes. "That bird has you wrapped around her little talons."

Grimley snorted. "Please. As if *you* weren't letting her ride around on your back like you were her own personal pony while we were gone."

Otto's gray eyes narrowed to slits. "That's different. She can't fly yet, so she can't keep up with me any other way."

Grimley snorted again. "Right. Whatever you say."

Otto huffed, and his long tail lashed from side to side, as though he wanted to smack Grimley with the arrow on the end. "I will go patrol, princess."

"Thank you, Otto," I replied.

The gargoyle huffed again, then trotted over to the balcony doors. I opened one of them, and he leaped up onto the railing, flapped his wings, and shot up into the evening sky.

"Why doesn't he sleep in here? Or somewhere else inside the palace?" Grimley grumbled. "There is plenty of room, even for a big, annoying brute like him."

I stared up at Otto, who veered around a tower and vanished from view. "I think it reminds him too much of being trapped in the manor house on Antheia Island, where Milo tortured him."

A shudder rippled through Grimley's body. "If that had happened to me, then I wouldn't want to stay inside much either."

Grimley laid his head down and went to sleep, with Violet still cradled in between his paws. Soon the two creatures were snoring in unison, with the gargoyle's deep rumbles punctuated by the strix's higher trills.

I walked through an open door into an adjoining room that served as my study. An ebony desk squatted near the back of the chamber, while a picture window with a gray cushioned seat offered a sweeping view of the Edelstein Gardens below. A bookcase filled with my favorite storybooks and other childhood mementos stood in a corner, while maps of Andvari, Morta, Bellona, and the other kingdoms hung on the walls.

I wandered over to the bookcase and picked up a silver-framed portrait of my mother that had been painted a few weeks before her death. Dark blond hair, rosy skin, pretty features. Merilde Ripley looked the same as always, although her blue eyes were much dimmer than I remembered, and her smile seemed more weary than genuinely happy. Or perhaps my own worry and exhaustion were coloring my senses tonight.

A tired sigh escaped my lips, and I glanced longingly at the window seat. Right now, I wanted nothing more than to curl up on the cushion and lose myself in a story I knew would have a happy ending. But that wouldn't help me find Milo, so I placed my mother's portrait back on the shelf and sat down at my desk.

More than three dozen letters—a relatively light load—were stacked up on a silver tray. During my ambassador travels, I made friends with as many people as possible, then encouraged those folks to write letters to keep me abreast of the goings-on in their parts of Andvari and beyond.

Given how many of my sources had journeyed to Glanzen for the Sword and Shield Tournament, I had expected twice as many missives, along with invitations to teas, luncheons, and the like. Everyone always wanted to meet face-to-face with Princess Gemma whenever they were in the capital. Another tired sigh escaped my lips, but the correspondence wasn't going to read itself, so I grabbed the first envelope.

Lady Ingrid, a noble from Blauberg, had written three pages detailing everything from the new porcelain teapot and cups she'd received from Ryusama, to the high silk prices at her local marketplace, to her neighbor's cow, which kept escaping its field and trampling her vegetable garden. Nothing important, and absolutely nothing that would help me track down Milo and Wexel.

I sighed again, set Ingrid's letter aside, and opened the next one. They were all more of the same. Missives about the weather, the price of goods, and the like, peppered with complaints about neighbors, family members, and other nobles, merchants, and guilders. A few included small gifts, like pretty ribbons, striped seashells, or polished rocks, which warmed my heart, even if they didn't help further my goals.

An hour later, I was reaching for the last letter when I accidentally knocked the tray off the table, sending it clattering down onto the floor. Frustrated, I rocked back in my chair, tipped my head up, and stared at the ceiling, which featured a carving of Armina Ripley, the first queen of Andvari.

This carving was part of a series that adorned my chamber ceilings. This one showed Armina standing next to her loyal gargoyle Arton, the two of them preparing to fight the Mortans who wanted to enslave Andvari and its gargoyles. The second carving out in the sitting room featured the two of them streaking through the sky, while the third and final carving above my bed showed Armina and Arton engaged in a fierce battle against their enemies.

I had always loved the carvings and the story they told of my ancestor's and kingdom's history, but tonight, thinking about Armina and Arton's triumph was just another reminder of my own failure to find Milo—and my growing worry that I wouldn't be able to stop him from hurting more gargoyles and people, just like he had hurt Otto and me.

After a few minutes, I roused myself from my brooding, dropped my gaze from the carving, and grabbed the tray from the floor. Then I opened the final letter and read through the contents.

This letter was from Adora, one of Lord Eichen's grand-daughters, who worked as a ringmaster for the Gray Falcons, an extremely successful and popular all-female gladiator troupe. The Gray Falcons had arrived in Glanzen last week, although Adora's letter had been written earlier today, according to the date at the top.

I'd met Adora a few weeks ago when I'd been visiting Oak-ton Manor, Eichen's estate near the Mortan border. Some of the Gray Falcon gladiators had performed during a luncheon, and I'd struck up a conversation with Adora afterward. Her sly wit and strong leadership had impressed me, and we had been exchang-ing letters ever since.

The ringmaster wrote about how excited she was to present her troupe at the palace, as well as compete in the Sword and Shield Tournament. Everything was perfectly ordinary, although a paragraph near the bottom of the letter caught my eye.

> Several new troupes have arrived in Glanzen to par-ticipate in the tournament. Some of the troupes are just the same old gladiators with new names, crests, and colors, but there is one troupe I've never heard of—the Storm Clouds. They are supposed to feature several good fighters, and I'm eager to learn more about them . . .

I leaned forward and read the passage again. And then a third time. Now this—*this* might be something.

Back on *The Drowned Man*, I'd told Reiko my suspicion that Milo was running toward something, rather than simply away from us and the other bounty hunters on his trail. If Milo was determined to attack Andvari, then there was no better opportunity than the Sword and Shield Tournament, especially given the throngs of people who had flocked to Glanzen for the event. Of course, Rhea had voiced this same thought to Father and Grandfather Heinrich, and she'd greatly increased security around the fairgrounds where the tournament was being held, along with here at the palace.

Still, joining a gladiator troupe would be an excellent way for Milo and Wexel to sneak into the city. After all, Everleigh Blair had used the same ruse to get close enough to challenge her cousin Vasilia for the throne all those years ago. Milo might despise the Bellonan queen, but he was smart enough to remember that piece of Buchovian history—and so was I.

If Milo and Wexel were here in Glanzen, either with the Storm Clouds or another gladiator troupe, then the trick would be getting them to show themselves—something I hoped to accomplish with my long game. Because I had invited someone to the tournament that Milo despised just as much as he did me, someone I hoped he wouldn't be able to resist trying to murder again—

A knock sounded on the hallway door. A familiar presence filled my mind, and I smiled and waved my hand. The lock turned, the door opened, and Leonidas entered.

"What are you doing?" he asked, staring down at the papers on my desk.

I set Adora's letter aside with all the others. "Wasting my time. None of my sources has heard anything about Milo or Wexel."

I sighed, leaned back in my chair, and gestured at the pile of letters. "After we came up empty in Allentown, I was hoping a bit of good news might be waiting here, but this is all just more of the same *nothingness*."

Leonidas scooted some of the papers off to the side and

perched on the corner of the desk. "We'll find Milo sooner or later. If he's smart, he really has set sail down the Summanus River and is heading to Fortuna Island."

"But what if he's more vindictive than smart?" I countered. "What if he is sneaking into Glanzen at this very moment? Slipping in with the gladiators and spectators streaming into the city for the tournament?"

Ice filled Leonidas's eyes. "Then we'll find him and kill him."

The cold promise in his voice matched the ruthlessness beating in my own heart, and it comforted me to know he was just as determined to stop Milo as I was. I reached out and squeezed his hand, and Leonidas threaded his fingers through mine. Some of my worry eased, but it was quickly replaced by more tension.

"I'm sorry about how everyone acted during the garden party. You've been here for a few weeks now, and I was hoping things would at least get . . ."

"Tolerable?" he suggested, arching a black eyebrow. "Don't worry, Gemma. I didn't expect to be greeted with open arms. No Morricone ever expects that, no matter what kingdom they're in. Why, there are even some shops in Majesta where I can't show my face for fear that a tailor will come after me with a pair of scissors, or a butcher will do the same with a carving knife."

His voice was light, and he was trying to make a joke about not being welcome in his own capital city, but his body was stiff with tension, and hurt rippled off him and pinched my own heart tight.

"Tell me, though," Leonidas continued. "What did you promise Eichen to get him to speak to me? Because after the two of you had your private chat by the gazebo, he practically talked my ear off about the tournament for the rest of the garden party."

I grimaced. "Was I that obvious?"

He shrugged. "Only to me. My mother has played similar

games with the Myrkvior nobles over the years, especially recently, with those who have sons she thinks might make a suitable match for Delmira."

"First, your mother tries to force us to get engaged by invoking the Gauntlet tradition during the Summit, and now she's set her sights on Delmira?" I shook my head. "I don't envy your sister's position."

Leonidas shrugged again. "Out of the three of us, Delmira has always rebelled against Maeven the most, even more so than Milo, in some ways. My sister is much more like our mother than she cares to admit, and neither one of them will bend to the other. I've always admired Delmira for standing up to Maeven. For me, it was easier to just go along with whatever Mother wanted. It caused me far less trouble and heartache than what Delmira has endured."

His words made me think of various conversations I'd overheard and had myself with both his mother and sister indicating that something was amiss between them.

"Did Maeven ever . . . do something to Delmira?" I asked. "Something . . . bad?"

His face turned thoughtful. "I'm not sure. All I remember is that something happened when Delmira was very young. Mother took her on a trip, supposedly to see our father, and Delmira was different when they returned. Some of her . . . joy was gone, as strange as that might sound. I don't think Mother physically hurt her, though."

"Not like Maximus did you," I said in a soft voice.

A muscle ticced in Leonidas's jaw, and even more tension radiated off his body. My gaze dropped to his many layers of clothing, which he wore like a suit of armor. Beneath the fine fabrics, scars covered Leonidas's back from where King Maximus, his uncle, had whipped, burned, and otherwise tortured him as a boy.

"You didn't answer my question," Leonidas said, changing the subject. "What did you promise Eichen?"

"Just a cutting of liladorn to take home and plant in his own gardens."

I got up and walked over to the bookcase. Beside my mother's portrait, a strand of liladorn was sitting in some water inside a crystal bowl, with its thorns stretched out on either side of the rim like arms, as if it were a person lounging in a hot, soothing bath.

Liladorn was incredibly tough, and I doubted even boiling water would so much as scorch its rock-hard yet strangely flexible skin. This particular strand had been wrapped around a bouquet of ice violets that Leonidas had given me during the first Gauntlet challenge during the Summit, and it had saved my life when Corvina Dumond had shot me with a poisoned arrow.

I gestured at the vine. "Perhaps I'll just give Eichen this bit of liladorn. That would save me the trouble of trying to figure out how to actually cut a piece of it out of the stands in the gardens."

We decide where we go, Not-Our-Princess, that familiar voice whispered in my mind again. *Not you. And we don't want some silly plant magier poking and prodding us with his pesky shears.*

I leaned forward and stared at the vine. *Why not? He can't hurt you with them. Why, it might be fun for you to frustrate him the same way you have me.*

True, the voice mused. *Perhaps you are right for a change, Not-Our-Princess. Very well. You may remove a piece of us from the Edelstein Gardens to give to your plant magier. But only a small piece.*

How kind of you.

The vine sniffed at my sarcasm, then settled itself a little deeper in the water.

Leonidas came over to stand beside me. "Is it talking to you again?"

For some reason, the vine often spoke to me, although it had never communicated with him, despite the fact that liladorn covered Myrkvior, the Morricone palace, from top to bottom.

"Unfortunately," I muttered. "The liladorn enjoys mocking me. It reminds me of your mother that way."

Leonidas laughed, and the low, husky sound warmed my heart. I adored hearing him laugh, something he didn't do nearly often enough. Then again, he hadn't had much to laugh about in his life, something I was hoping to change.

I looped my arms around his neck. "How was your afternoon ride with Fern? I saw the two of you zooming around the palace rooftops through the windows in Alvis's workshop."

His eyes brightened, and his hands gripped my waist. "Wonderful. Although I think Grimley was jealous that I didn't pick him to ride today."

Leonidas loved flying just as much as I did, so I had asked Fern, Grimley, and the other palace gargoyles to let the prince ride them to his heart's content. Gargoyles had far fewer prejudices than people did, and they had quickly warmed up to Leonidas, especially since he brought them citrines and other gemstones to eat. Now the gargoyles practically fought for the chance to fly Leonidas around the palace.

Of course Lyra got a little jealous, crowing that she could fly much faster and smoother than any of the gargoyles. I had ridden Lyra a few times, and she was right. The strix was far more graceful through the air than the gargoyles were, although I would never hurt the other creatures' feelings by admitting that.

"Perhaps we can go riding together tomorrow afternoon, after the tournament festivities are finished," I suggested.

His eyes brightened a little more. "I would love that."

Leonidas's hands tightened on my waist, and his gaze dropped to my lips. In an instant, the mood between us shifted from light and playful to hot and intense.

Sometimes, I thought I would *never* get tired of looking at him, of seeing the many subtle shades of purple glinting like individual facets in his eyes or admiring how the ends of his longish black hair always curled slightly up, like the onyx tips on Lyra's feathers. Of studying how the light brought out his sharp cheekbones and straight nose or how his black clothes hinted at the coiled strength of his body. And especially of sensing his thoughts, his desire, and especially his love for me mixing, mingling, and merging with what was beating in my own mind, body, and heart.

"I would love to kiss you right now," Leonidas murmured.

"So why don't you?"

He jerked his head to the side. "Because we have an audience."

I glanced over at the bookcase. The liladorn had moved to the front of the crystal bowl and propped its thorns up on the rim like hands supporting its head, clearly watching us with avid interest, despite its lack of an actual face.

One of the thorns waved like a dismissive hand. *Please. We have no interest in watching you. We are enjoying our bath.*

Liar, I teased.

That voice snorted in my mind, but the vine slithered back to the opposite side of the bowl to give us a bit more privacy.

"Perhaps we should retire to a less-crowded chamber." I tilted my head toward the door at the other end of the room. "Like one with a comfortable bed waiting inside."

Leonidas flashed me a wicked grin, then lifted me up off the floor. I locked my legs around his waist, feeling his hard cock settle in between my thighs. I rocked forward, and he groaned.

"I don't care what kind of audience we have," I whispered. "But just in case you need further encouragement . . ."

I rocked forward again, and Leonidas groaned for a second time. I tangled my fingers in his silky hair and breathed in deeply, letting the soft, masculine scent of his honeysuckle soap fill my nose even as the rest of him flooded my senses. His strong, sure hands gripping my hips, his muscled chest pressing up against mine, the warmth of his body mixing with my own. I rocked forward again, not to tease him, but just to get closer, to feel *more* of him.

Leonidas strode forward, still carrying me. He left the study, stepped into my bedroom, and kicked the door shut behind us. Then he stopped in the middle of the room and eased me down so that I was standing before him again.

I took all the proper herbs and precautions, as did he, and I was eager to explore every inch of his body. I reached for him, but Leonidas stepped back. He flicked his fingers, and the silver gargoyle pin that hooked my cloak around my throat loosened. He flicked his fingers again, and the pin floated over and landed on a nightstand, even as the cloak slid off my shoulders and pooled at my feet.

I arched an eyebrow. "What game are you playing?"

His smile widened. "Let me show you."

He curled his fingers, and the laces on the back of my dress slowly opened, as if pushed apart by a set of invisible hands—*his* hands, thanks to his mind magier magic. Leonidas curled his fingers again, and the dress opened wider and wider, until it was completely undone. Another curl of his fingers sent the fabric sliding off my arms and down onto the floor. A few more flicks, dips, and curls of his fingers did the same thing to my shoes and undergarments. In seconds, I was standing naked before him, with clothing strewn on the floor all around me.

Desire flared in his eyes, making them burn with amethyst fire. I shivered, even as my stomach clenched in anticipation.

"No matter how many times we're together, I'm always awed by how strong and beautiful you are," he said in a hoarse voice.

I reached for him, but Leonidas held up his hand, asking

me to stop. I stood there, waiting and shivering. He hadn't even touched me yet, and heat was already pooling between my thighs.

Leonidas flicked his fingers yet again, and my dark brown hair slid back over my shoulders. His magic twined around me like a ribbon, velvet soft but with a hint of strength behind it. His power flowed across my neck and collarbones, then trailed down the center of my chest in a gentle caress. Then, all at once, his magic morphed into two invisible hands that were cupping my breasts.

I gasped and arched back, my nipples hardening. Those two hands slid lower and lower, those invisible fingers dipping down to stroke the most intimate part of me. I stood there, shivering and trembling, as Leonidas teased me with his magic, touching me over and over again.

"Such smooth skin, such lovely curves, such power and strength and passion."

His voice flowed over me, but I barely registered the compliments, too caught up in the heat building inside my body.

Leonidas stroking, caressing, and teasing me with his magic was one of the most thrilling things I had ever experienced, but it wasn't enough. I wanted *all* of him—his skin, his body, his lips and tongue and actual hands on me—so I stepped forward and flicked my fingers the same way he had.

The silver strix pin at his throat loosened and floated over to join my gargoyle pin on the vanity table, even as his cloak dropped to the floor. A small black journal slid out of one of his cloak pockets, rousing my curiosity, although Leonidas quickly scooted the book aside with his boot, shoving it back under the fabric.

"Copycat," he teased.

I gave him the same wicked grin he had given me. "Oh, I'm just getting started."

I waved my hand. One by one, the amethyst buttons on his black riding coat popped open, and I peeled the fabric off his body with my magic just as he had removed my dress. I made quick work of the rest of his clothes, and soon he was standing naked before me.

The smile vanished from his face, and his hands clenched into fists by his sides. In that moment, he reminded me of a fierce, beautiful strix just waiting to strike out and latch onto its prey. Well, I wasn't ready to be caught just yet.

I slowly circled around Leonidas, admiring everything about him, from the way his black hair gleamed underneath the fluorestones to the solid planes of his muscled chest to his firm ass. I walked around behind him and stopped, studying the scars that covered his back—from the long, thin white lines left behind by a whip to the smaller, round, puckered burn marks to the eerie zigzag patches that always reminded me of jagged, uneven seams of thread.

"Your scars are beautiful," I murmured.

Leonidas shuddered out a breath, his fists loosened, and some of the tension in his shoulders eased.

I moved around so that I was standing in front of him again. Then I reached out with my magic, slowly trailing the invisible fingers of my power down his chest and stomach. When I grasped his cock, a hiss escaped his lips.

I stopped. "Is this okay?"

Leonidas nodded, the desire in his eyes flaring even brighter and hotter than before. "I love it when you touch me, Gemma."

I grinned and stroked him with my magic, watching every bunch, flex, and twitch of his body. In seconds, he was trembling.

"You know what would be even better?" he asked. "This."

Another wicked grin curved his lips, and Leonidas used his own power again, stroking me the same way that I was him. By this point, we were both trembling and gasping, but we both kept going, using our magic to bring as much pleasure to each other as possible.

The more power we used, the closer our bodies drew together, those invisible strings of energy pulling us toward each other. Soon, we were inches apart, staring into each other's eyes. My magic flowed, caressed, and teased his skin, just as his magic was still curling around my own body, as though we were standing in a silent storm of passion.

I didn't know which one of us made the first move to physically touch the other. Or perhaps it was both of us, at the same time. His hands settled on my waist again, while my arms looped around his neck. Leonidas dipped his head, even as I lifted mine toward his.

That first soft brush of our lips was like throwing a lit match into a mine full of gas—everything went up in flames.

In an instant, our tongues were stroking together, and our hands were roaming over each other's bodies. Leonidas cupped my breasts, and I dug my fingers into his shoulders and arched back. He tore his mouth away from mine and trailed kisses down the side of my neck. His tongue darted out and scraped against my right nipple; then he closed his teeth around it and sucked hard. I gasped, and desire twisted through my whole body. Leonidas did the same thing to my other breast, and I tangled my fingers in his hair, urging him on, even as my other hand snaked down in between us.

I wrapped my hand around his cock and stroked him, sliding my fingers back and forth in a quick rhythm.

"Gemma," he rasped against my chest. "Gemma."

His magic curled around us again, and my feet floated up, even as my body tilted backward. Somehow, I ended up on the floor, on top of all the clothes we'd shed earlier.

Leonidas hovered right above me, passion making his eyes

blaze like purple stars. I looped my arms around his neck and drew him down on top of me, finally feeling every delicious inch of his hard, muscled body pressing against my own. I trailed my hands up and down his back, my fingers gently tracing over his scars, trying to show him how strong I thought he was, how brave, and especially how much I loved him.

I know. His low, husky voice filled my mind. *I love you too, Gemma.*

Then show me.

He smiled, his eyes soft and warm, then dipped his head and kissed me again.

I lost myself in Leonidas. In the firm press of his lips against mine. In the teasing strokes of his tongue. In the slide and glide of his fingers across my skin. In his rich honeysuckle scent and light, feathery magic that filled me with a burning need that could only be quenched by one thing—him.

Leonidas raised his head and looked at me again. I gripped his shoulders and opened my legs. Still staring at me, he moved forward and thrust deep inside me. We both groaned, and I locked my legs around his hips, even as he rocked forward again.

And then again, and again, and again.

That silent storm of passion shattered, and we both started moaning each other's name. Those waves of pleasure arched higher and higher, merging into sharp, aching need, and we both kept going, moving together. That delicious pressure built deep inside me, then erupted all at once, like shooting stars streaking through the night sky.

The orgasm ripped through me, and I felt it move through Leonidas too. In that moment, our bodies, minds, and magics were one and the same, and I happily drowned in that tidal wave of passion, power, and pleasure.

CHAPTER SIX

We fell asleep on the floor, right in the middle of our discarded clothes. Sometime later, I woke up to find myself nestled in Leonidas's arms, and his cloak wrapped around the both of us. His face was soft, warm, and relaxed in sleep, unlike the icy mask he so often wore during the day to keep everyone from realizing just how much their cruel words hurt him.

I pressed a kiss to his temple, but Leonidas didn't stir, so I slipped out of his arms and used my magic to gently float him up off the floor and onto the bed. I covered him with a blanket. He rolled over onto his side and murmured something incoherent, although his body quickly relaxed again.

"Sleep well, my love," I whispered.

I grabbed my clothes, got dressed, and then tiptoed into the study. The liladorn was still sitting in its bowl, although the vine was now curled up into a tight ball, much like a cat, as though it too was sleeping. Next, I slipped out into the sitting room, where Grimley and Violet were still asleep and snuggled up together by the fireplace. Just like with Leo, the sights warmed my heart—and filled it with cold dread.

If I didn't find Milo before he implemented his master plan,

then these happy scenes and serene safety would be gone forever, drowned in blood, bones, and bodies. So I threw on a cloak,
raised the hood to hide my features, and left my chambers.

I moved from one section of Glitnir to the next, steering clear
of the many guards. Captain Rhea had spread her men throughout the palace, and they were all alert and doing their jobs, but
none of them spotted me. Lady Xenia Rubin, the famed spymaster, had trained me to slyly creep around, although I would never
be as naturally stealthy as Reiko was. Plus, Father used to sneak
around the palace with my uncles Frederich and Lucas when they
were all boys, and he had taught that game to me as well.

Most nights when I couldn't sleep, I climbed out onto one of
the tower roofs to sit with the gargoyles and stare up at the sky.
But tonight, I was on a mission, so I trudged down, down, down
several sets of steps into the very bowels of Glitnir. As I moved
from one level to another, the precious metal and jewel adorn-
ments vanished, and the walls became much plainer, thicker,
and sturdier. No guards were posted down here, and few people
even knew the palace contained so many underground levels.

Eventually, I reached two stone doors that stretched from the
floor all the way up to the ceiling more than a hundred feet above.
The Ripley royal crest was carved into many doors throughout
the palace, but the image here was truly stunning. Enormous
pieces of black jet fitted together to form the snarling gargoyle's
face, while rows of gray diamonds curved up and out in the shape
of its horns. Two sapphires larger than my fists glittered as the
gargoyle's eyes, while bright, glowing, jagged red shards formed
its teeth, making the creature look like it had just taken a big,
bloody bite out of an enemy.

Most people would have mistaken the red shards for rubies,
but they were actually common glass. The lack of facets on the
shards was an old Ripley signal and warning. Each one of the

gargoyle's teeth was filled with coral-viper venom, and the poison would break through and spew out of the glass if someone tried to force the doors open.

No footsteps echoed behind me, and no shadows snaked along the floor. I also reached out with my magic, although the walls were so thick down here that I couldn't sense anything but the surrounding hallway. When I was certain I was alone, I turned back to the doors. No locks or keyholes adorned them, and nothing was visible except the gargoyle's face.

I blew out a breath, then carefully pressed in on various parts of the face.

First, its left horn. Then the right eye. The tooth in the center of its mouth. Right horn. Left eye. And finally, the gargoyle's nose.

Only a few people knew the correct sequence of jewels and glass and exactly how long and hard to press in on them. I counted off seven seconds, then released the gargoyle's nose and stepped back. The bright glow dimmed, then snuffed out of the red glass teeth, indicating that the poison trap had been disarmed. Several soft *click-click-clicks* rang out, and the two doors slowly swung outward.

I blew out another breath, squared my shoulders, and strode forward.

White fluorestones shaped like flying gargoyles were embedded in the ceiling, and the lights clicked on at my approach and then clicked off as I moved past them. A shiver snaked down my spine. I'd always found the flare and dousing of such lights a little unnerving, but even more so down here, as though the fluorestones were silent guards watching my every move.

A plethora of precious metals and jewels adorned the common areas of the palace, but they were small, cheap trinkets compared to the overwhelming wealth and sheer opulence stored in the Ripley royal treasury.

Crowns, tiaras, necklaces, rings, and bracelets that had been worn by the kings and queens of old were resting on velvet pillows covered with glass boxes, which were sitting atop marble pedestals. Small white cards trimmed with gold and silver leaf were also tucked inside the glass, each one describing the item, its place in Andvarian history, and its estimated worth, although everything down here was priceless in its own right. The royal-blue sapphires, violet-purple amethysts, forest-green emeralds, bloodred rubies, and star-bright diamonds glinted under the lights, and their facets winked at me like sleepy eyes as I walked past, as if they were wondering why I was disturbing their midnight slumber.

The treasury featured several different sections, each one containing similar items, from the royal jewels, to gowns, jackets, and other garments, to statues, carvings, and paintings that chronicled important figures and moments in Andvarian history. I rounded a bookcase filled with thick tomes, along with rolled-up maps and scrolls, and moved into my favorite part of the treasury—the armory.

Dozens of swords, shields, and daggers were housed under glass cases, along with cards that described who had used the items, and when, and why. Those swords, shields, and daggers were all polished to a high gloss, and many were crusted with even more precious jewels than the crowns and tiaras, but I had always preferred to wander through the freestanding racks of weapons, most of which were nicked, scratched, and dented. To me, the signs of battle that scarred the blades were far more fascinating than the gold filigree and diamond chips that covered the ceremonial weapons that had never drawn so much as a drop of blood.

I stopped in front of my favorite object in the entire treasury—a suit of armor worn by Armina Ripley, the first queen of Andvari. Armina's armor was mounted on a wooden mannequin and consisted of a simple silver breastplate, along with two matching gauntlets. The Ripley snarling gargoyle crest had been etched into each piece, although the dips and curves made the symbols look hollow and empty, as though someone had pried out all the jewels that were supposed to complete the intricate designs.

Most people probably would have thought the armor dull, dim, and disappointingly plain. And truthfully, it was all those things, as well as horribly scratched from Armina's many battles. But I loved the simplicity of it, along with the bits of blue that shimmered like tiny sapphires in the silver breastplate and gauntlets. I could easily picture Armina wearing the armor into battle, her chest and arms blazing as though she had the power of the stars burning inside her.

A silver framed painting of Queen Armina and Arton, her beloved gargoyle, was hanging on the wall behind the armor. The image showed them streaking through the sky, with Armina holding her arms out wide, Arton flexing his wings, and a legion of gargoyles hovering in the air behind them. It was one of my favorite paintings, even though it always made me feel like a fraud. Armina had been a mind magier, just like me, but she had been able to communicate with hundreds of gargoyles at once, whereas I could only manage two or three at a time.

I focused on the armor again, and those pinprick bits of blue brightened, as though they were burning with some inner flame. The more the color intensified, the more magic that rose inside me in commensurate measure, as though the two were somehow connected, even though I knew they weren't. I tried to shove my magic down, but it squirted out of my grasp and kept rising and rising, like a high tide slapping up against a ship it was determined to drag out to sea.

I stepped back, but those bits of blue continued to burn in my eyes, no matter how hard and fast I tried to blink them away. Despite my best efforts to contain it, my power crashed over me, even stronger than before, and swept me back into the past . . .

The royal treasury vanished, replaced by the dull grays, browns, and greens of a forest. I frowned and took another step back, trying to figure out when and where I was—

My left boot sliced through empty air, and I jerked to the side, staring down at the canyon below. Even though this wasn't really happening—at least not happening right now—I still scuttled away from the edge. I had never been injured in one of my memories, and I didn't want to find out the hard way if getting hurt in the past would affect me in the present.

A frustrated, resigned sigh escaped from my lips. In addition to my mind magier magic, I had also inherited some of my mother Merilde's time magier power. My mother had often gotten visions of the future, but most of the time, my magic tossed me back into the past, forcing me to relive all my awful memories of the Seven Spire massacre, along with everything else that had happened after that horrible day. Ghosting, it was called.

Despite all the strides I'd made over the past few months learning how to better control my power, my ghosting ability was something I hadn't quite mastered yet. I snorted. That was a bloody lie. I hadn't mastered it at all, not in the slightest way. My magic rose up whenever and wherever it wanted to, and anything could trigger it, from a certain color to a sharp sound to a pungent scent.

All I could do now was wait for my magic to release me, so I studied the landscape. The sun was rising, gilding the tops of the evergreen trees with a soft golden sheen, and a thin layer of snow crusted the ground, turning it a brittle white.

Three people wrapped in cloaks were huddled around a fire pit in the open space between the canyon behind me and the forest in the distance. The first was a sixty-something woman with coppery red hair, bronze skin, and golden amber eyes. An ogre face with the same red hair and amber eyes that the woman herself had was visible on her neck. Lady Xenia Rubin, the famed spymaster.

Sitting beside her was Alvis, with his hazel eyes, ebony skin, and wavy black hair studded with silver. The metalstone master hadn't changed much in all the years I'd known him.

The third and final person was a twelve-year-old girl with the same dark brown hair, blue eyes, and pale skin that I had. Gems, as I always thought of this younger version of myself.

I chewed on my lower lip, trying to place this particular moment in time. Ah, yes. This had been about six weeks after we'd fled from Svalin following the Seven Spire massacre, and we had been so close to the Andvarian border that I could practically smell the scent of home in the air.

"I'm bloody sick and tired of your cheese-and-jam sandwiches," Xenia grumbled, staring down at the pieces of bread in her hand. "Can't you make something else for breakfast?"

"I would have made roasted rabbit, if your snare had managed to catch one last night," Alvis said in a chiding tone.

Xenia shot him an annoyed glare.

"If you would rather be hungry, suit yourself." Alvis took a bite of his own sandwich. "I, on the other hand, prefer to be sensible about such things. And if I have to eat toasted cheese-and-jam sandwiches every day until we reach Andvari, then so be it."

Xenia glowered at him, but she too wolfed down her sandwich. Gems hid a smile at their bickering and ate her own sandwich, which featured tangy apricot jam, melted gruyère cheese, and toasted sourdough bread. My mouth watered, and my stomach rumbled with longing.

The three of them finished their breakfast, and Xenia and Alvis got to their feet.

"We're only about a mile from Andvari." Xenia stared off into the trees. "All we have to do is make it across the border, and we'll finally be safe. This is the last chance the turncoat guards have to catch us, and I want to make sure they haven't set up any ambushes nearby."

Alvis nodded. "I'll go with you."

They both looked at Gems, who sighed in resignation. "I'll stay here and pack up our things."

"Be quiet and careful," Xenia warned. "We'll be back soon."

Magic rippled in the air around her, and long black talons sprouted on her fingertips as she partially shifted into her larger, stronger ogre form. Alvis drew the sword on his belt, and together, the two of them vanished into the trees.

Gems sighed again, then packed up the remaining scraps of food. She had just put the last half-eaten wedge of cheese away when a sharp scrape rang out, along with a low, angry growl.

Gems scooped up the cast-iron skillet Alvis had used to toast their sandwiches and hoisted it up over her shoulder like a staff. Her gaze snapped back and forth as she tried to figure out where the noise had come from—

Scrape. Scrape-scrape-scrape. Scrape.

Instead of floating out of the forest, the noise was drifting up from the canyon below. Still clutching the skillet, Gems tiptoed in that direction. I eased up beside her, and we both peered over the edge.

Something shifted on a ledge about thirty feet down, causing even more rocks to scrape together and tumble into the canyon. Gems gasped, and my own breath caught in my throat.

It was a gargoyle.

The creature was little more than a baby, still too young to fly. The gargoyle stood up on its hind legs and dug its black talons into the cliff face. It managed to sink its talons into the rocks and hoist itself up a few inches, but then its talons slipped free, and it slid right back down. Another angry, frustrated growl rippled out of the gargoyle's throat, but it surged to its feet to try again.

The gargoyle finally spotted Gems, and it quirked its head to the side, its bright, sapphire-blue gaze locking with hers. Even now, all these years later, a jolt of awareness zinged through my body, making my fingertips tingle. All the creature's anger and frustration punched into Gems's—my—heart, along with its growing fear that it would never be able to escape the ledge.

Gems's jaw clenched, and memories surged off her and flickered through my own mind. The gruesome slaughter and screams of the Seven Spire massacre. The turncoat guards surrounding Xenia and Alvis in a clearing. Bandits advancing on Gems and a young Leo by a rushing river. All the horrible things that had happened over the past several weeks, and all the times she had felt the same anger, pain, frustration, and fear as the baby gargoyle.

Determination flared in Gems's heart, drowning out the screams and scorching through her memories. "Don't worry, little one," she called out in a soft voice. "I'll help you."

The gargoyle quirked its head to the side again, as if it didn't quite understand her words.

Gems hurried away from the edge of the canyon, went over, and dug through Xenia's knapsack until she found a long length of rope. She tied one end of the rope around her waist, then looped the other end around a boulder close to the canyon's edge.

"This is a really stupid idea," she whispered to herself.

"No kidding," I whispered back, even though she couldn't hear me and this had all happened long ago.

Gems drew in a deep breath to steady her racing heart, then stepped off the side of the canyon and started lowering herself down to the ledge where the gargoyle was trapped . . .

A fluorestone in the ceiling clicked on, blasting light right into my eyes. The canyon vanished, and I was once again standing in the royal treasury, staring at the bits of blue glimmering in Armina's armor.

I blinked, shaking off the last dregs of my magic. That vision had been relatively quick and painless, but I still shivered and wrapped my arms around myself, silently cursing my magic for tossing me back into the past yet again. Then I hurried away from the armor before another random glimmer of color could trigger my power.

I left the armory behind and stepped into the final, largest section of the treasury. Instead of crowns, books, and weapons, something completely different filled this space.

Tearstone.

Shelves filled with jagged chunks of tearstone marched down both sides of this area, while even larger pieces were either piled up in freestanding metal carts or stacked together on wooden pallets. Most of the ore was the more common light starry gray, but dozens and dozens of pieces boasted the rarer midnight-blue hue. As I walked along, every single piece of tearstone shifted color, flickering from light gray to dark blue and back again. In addition to changing color, tearstone also had another dual nature—it could both absorb and deflect magic.

Grandfather Heinrich had long stored tearstone in the treasury, since it was such a valuable resource, but ever since the

Summit, he had ordered that every available shard of tearstone in Andvari be brought here for safekeeping. After all, if Milo Morricone couldn't get any more ore, then he couldn't fashion it into more arrows to use against our people and gargoyles.

Still, having this much tearstone in one place made me uneasy, which is why I came down here every night to make sure it was still safe and secure. In some ways, it felt like we were setting out a giant pot of honey and *not* expecting a grizzly to try to get inside it. Because if Milo ever got his hands on this much tearstone, then he could make as many weapons as he wanted, and we wouldn't be able to stop him.

I did a slow circuit of the area, but all the tearstone was exactly where it should be, so I left the treasury and stepped outside into the hallway beyond. I pressed in on the gargoyle's nose, much longer than I had before, and the double doors slowly swung shut. I pressed in on the nose again, and another series of *click-click-clicks* rang out. The glass shards that made up the gargoyle's teeth started glowing red again, indicating that the coral-viper-venom trap had been rearmed.

I stared at the Ripley crest, but the bloody, steady gleam of the poison didn't comfort me. The Andvarian royal treasury might be one of the most secure places on the Buchovian continent, but Milo Morricone had proven he was exceedingly clever. A hard truth filled my heart, weighing me down like a boulder crushing my chest.

No matter how secure the treasury was, and how many precautions my friends and family took, the tearstone and my kingdom would always be at risk—until Milo was dead.

I thought about returning to my chambers and climbing into bed beside Leonidas, but I was still worried and restless, so I went back up to the ground level of the palace, slipped outside, and plunged into the Edelstein Gardens. I had one more mission to complete tonight.

I followed the twists and turns of the hedge maze to the gargoyle's right eye. The Ripley family mausoleum dominated much of the grassy area, and the granite building gleamed a dark gray in the moon- and starlight. The mausoleum doors were shut and locked, but my magic still let me sense all the hollow spaces inside that were filled with the bones of my ancestors. Andvari tradition dictated that all the Ripley royals be entombed here, that we give our bodies back to the earth as payment for all the precious metals and gems that our people had dug out of the Spire Mountains.

Sometimes, when I came here late at night, I thought I could hear the ghosts of all the Ripley kings and queens whispering to me, although I had never been able to figure out exactly what they were saying. The raspy murmurs and odd howls of air used to frighten me as a child, but right now I would have been happy to endure the scare of my life if it meant receiving any advice from my ancestors about how to find Milo Morricone. But alas, the ghosts were quiet tonight.

I walked over to a bench made of delicate tendrils of silver that was sitting beneath a pear tree. The tree had already lost its scarlet leaves, making it look like a dull brown skeleton hulking over the landscape, although a silver plaque in the bench's backrest glimmered brightly in the moonlight.

Merilde Edelle Irma Ripley, Beloved Mother, Daughter, and Wife

Bittersweet longing flooded my heart. My mother and I had spent hours in this spot, reading storybooks, soaking up the sunshine, and hiding from all the cares and concerns inside the palace. After her death, my father had erected this bench in my mother's honor, and I often came here whenever I needed a quiet moment alone.

But tonight, I had a bargain to keep, so I went over and dropped to one knee in front of the bench. Several strands of liladorn were curled around my mother's plaque, as though they were an ebony frame holding a pretty portrait. The vines stirred at my approach, and I cautiously held out my hand to them.

May I please have a strand of you to give to Lord Eichen?

The liladorn quivered, as though it was considering my request. I held my breath, wondering if the thorns would lash out and scratch me, as they had done in the past. The liladorn had its own set of rules, and I could never quite tell if it would help or hinder me.

Very well. That familiar voice sounded in my mind. *Since you asked so nicely, Not-Our-Princess.*

One of the vines moved forward, even as another vine rose up beside it. A long, sharp thorn whipped forward and sliced through the first vine, which fluttered down onto the bench like a falling leaf. Purple sap oozed out of the cut section, and the sweet scent of lilacs filled the air.

Touching the clipped vine without permission would probably earn me another painful scratch, so I waited. Although I did find it strangely fascinating that the liladorn could use its own thorns to cut itself. I would have to mention that to Eichen, lest it completely take over his gardens.

You may pick us up now, the liladorn whispered in my mind.

I held out my hand, and the cut strand snaked up and wrapped around my wrist, almost like it was a bracelet. The motion reminded me of how the vine in my study had wrapped around my arm at Caldwell Castle, and then had dug its thorns into my skin to release its sap to throttle the fool's bane that Corvina Dumond had poisoned me with during the Summit. I held back a shudder.

Even though the liladorn had saved me, I would never forget the foul, watery poison slithering through my veins and filling up my lungs, and my painful struggle to breathe, as though I were drowning on dry land.

I shuddered again, lowered my hand to my side, and climbed to my feet. I started to leave when a flicker of movement caught my eye.

I'd been wrong before. There *was* a ghost in the gardens tonight—my mother.

Merilde Ripley was standing in front of the mausoleum, staring pensively at the closed, locked doors as though something about them greatly troubled her. Curious, I walked over to her.

My mother didn't move or speak to me, and I had no idea how this was even happening—if my ghosting ability had thrown me back into the past yet again, or if some other aspect of my time or mind magier magic was out of control.

I studied the mausoleum doors, trying to figure out what she was looking at, and especially why. But the doors were the same as always—solid slabs of dark gray granite bearing the Ripley royal crest—and I didn't see anything special about them. Similar doors could be found throughout the palace.

Since I couldn't figure out what my mother was staring at, I studied her instead, my gaze tracing over the soft waves in her dark blond hair, her kind blue eyes, her mysterious smile. My heart ached again, the pain even stronger than before. Seeing her like this was different, and far more intense, than staring at her portrait on the bookshelf in my study, and it made me miss her even more fiercely, even though she had been dead for almost twenty years.

As if hearing my thoughts, Merilde turned and smiled at me—really, truly, fully smiled at me, as though she were actually *seeing* me in this moment the same way I was seeing her.

"Mother?" I whispered. "Are you here?"

Her smile widened for a moment, but then her form flickered, and she vanished altogether.

"Mother?" I asked. "Mother!"

I whirled around and around, but she was gone. Still, I could have sworn there was a . . . *presence* in the air that hadn't been here before, a faint fluttering, as though she were stroking my hair. Or perhaps that was just my imagination again, fueled by the breeze gusting through the gardens. Either way, I froze, hoping my mother would return.

But nothing happened, and the minutes ticked by in cold, quiet silence.

A disappointed sigh escaped my lips and steamed in the chilly night air. First, my magic had thrown me back into the past in the royal treasury, and now it had shown me . . . whatever sort of mirage this had been. Perhaps it was a good thing we hadn't found Milo on the ship earlier today. Because I needed to get a much better grip on my power if I had any chance of killing the crown prince when I saw him again.

I glanced around, but my mother was gone, and it didn't seem as though she was coming back. Another disappointed sigh escaped my lips.

With the strand of liladorn still curled around my wrist, I left the gardens and the memory of my mother behind, still wondering what she had been trying to show me, if anything—and especially why she had seemed so very, very worried.

PART TWO

THE
PRINCE
OF LIGHTNING

CHAPTER SEVEN

Early the next morning, I stood in the Glitnir throne room and waited for my enemy to arrive.

"Are you sure it's not too late to cancel?" Grandfather Heinrich grumbled in a low voice that only Father, Rhea, and I could hear.

Grandfather was sitting on the throne atop the royal dais. Father was standing to his right, while Rhea was standing to his left. I was lurking at the bottom of the dais steps, eyeing the nobles, merchants, and guilders who had gathered for the breakfast refreshments and competitor introductions that marked the unofficial start of the Sword and Shield Tournament.

"Considering that we are only halfway through greeting the gladiator troupes?" Father scoffed. "You know the answer to that as well as I do."

Grandfather sighed, but he waved his hand, signaling for the next troupe to enter the throne room and mingle with all the others already inside.

A shadow crept up on the floor beside me, and, suddenly, Reiko was standing next to my right elbow, holding a napkin filled with sweet cakes.

I bit back a surprised shriek. "How many times have I told

you not to sneak up on me?" I hissed. "I don't know how you can even *do* that, considering we are in a room full of people in broad daylight."

Reiko gave me a smug smirk, as did her inner dragon. "Because I'm a much better spy than you are, princess." She popped a chocolate-orange sweet cake into her mouth, and her inner dragon smacked its lips in appreciation.

I huffed and looked toward the open doors in the distance.

"Where's Leo?" Reiko asked.

"On his way here," I replied in a tense voice. "Along with the rest of them."

Reiko gave me a sympathetic look. "When you first proposed this scheme, I thought it was utter madness, and that no one on either side would agree to it. But yet, here we are. Although I still can't believe they're actually going to stay *here*, in the palace."

"I know," I muttered in a dark tone. "But at least if they stay here, then I can keep an eye on them. That's slightly better than not knowing exactly where they are and especially what they're doing."

Reiko shrugged, neither agreeing nor disagreeing. She popped another sweet cake into her mouth and gestured out at the throne room. "This is a bit grander and more formal than I expected it to be."

"How do you greet gladiators when championship tournaments are held in Ryusama?"

She shrugged again. "It's done in the arena. All the troupes march around so that everyone can see them, Queen Ruri makes a brief welcome speech, and then the tournament begins. It's not *nearly* as ostentatious as this soiree. You Andvarians certainly do love showing off your wealth."

As much as I hated to admit it, she had a point. During normal court proceedings, the throne room was an impressive, if cavernous, space, but the servants had spruced it up for the gladiator introductions. A wide black carpet patterned with the Ripley royal crest stretched from the open doors all the way across the floor before stopping in front of the dais. The silver threads glimmered underneath the fluorestones, making the snarling gargoyles look like they were about to erupt from the fabric and take a bite out of the gladiators strolling across them. Matching black banners boasting the same silver-thread crest adorned the walls, while several more banners dangled from the second-floor balcony railing.

The servants had also polished all the columns, making the gargoyles carved there look like they were a breath away from breaking free of their stone shells. Long tables laden with scones, sweet cakes, and other treats marched down one wall, while several musicians huddled in a corner, trilling out each troupe's arrival with a flare of flutes, violins, and trumpets.

Nobles, merchants, and guilders lined both sides of the carpet, all clad in fine clothes, dripping with jewels, and doused with floral perfumes and spicy colognes. Up on the dais, Grandfather Heinrich and Father both sported short, formal dark gray jackets. A silver crown studded with pieces of jet, along with white and gray diamonds, perched atop my grandfather's head, while a matching signet ring winked on one of my father's fingers. Rhea was also clad in a dark gray jacket, with her ruby-studded sword hanging off her belt like usual.

Reiko nibbled her sweet cakes while I watched the gladiators arrive. Each troupe entered through the main doors, marched down the carpet, and stopped in front of the dais. The leader of each troupe stepped forward and introduced themselves, and Grandfather Heinrich wished them good luck in the upcoming tournament.

"And now, introducing the Golden Stallions!" the announcer called out.

Lord Eichen straightened up with pride and moved forward

so that he was standing at the edge of the carpet. He beamed as his grandchildren presented themselves to Grandfather Heinrich.

"How many grandchildren does Eichen have?" Reiko asked. "Because that's several more than I remember seeing when they performed for us at Oakton Manor."

"He has thirteen grandchildren at current count, some with this troupe, and some with other troupes."

"How fitting that a plant magier like Eichen would produce such a *fruitful* family." Reiko snickered at her own bad joke.

Eichen's grandchildren stepped off to the side, mingling with the crowd.

"And now, presenting the Gray Falcons!" the announcer bellowed.

That name caught my attention, and I looked over at the dais.

Lady Adora walked forward, stopped, and bowed to my grandfather. She was in her late twenties, with short, curly black hair and dark brown eyes and skin. A silver sword dangled from her black belt, and her hands bore the tiny nicks and scars of someone who spent their time fighting for a crowd's applause.

Adora wore a ringmaster uniform of a white ruffled shirt under a short, tight, light gray tailcoat with gleaming silver buttons shaped like flying falcons, as befitting her troupe's name. Black leggings and boots completed her ensemble.

I caught Adora's eye and smiled. The ringmaster winked back at me.

Adora and her people moved aside, and the next group moved forward.

"And now, introducing the Crimson Dragons!" the announcer called out. "Led by the winner of last year's Tournament of Champions, Kai Nakamura!"

Reiko's final sweet cake squirted out of her fingers and hit the floor, along with the napkin she'd been holding. She froze for a moment, then darted forward, slipping between people and sidling up to the edge of the carpet so that she had the best view possible. I hid a grin and followed her.

Kai Nakamura swaggered down the carpet. Like many of the gladiators, he was tall and muscled, but the determined glint in his golden eyes hinted that he was far more dangerous than most of the other warriors. Kai's black hair and golden skin gleamed under the rainbow prisms of light cast out by the jeweled chandeliers, and a dragon's face with red scales and black eyes adorned the side of his neck.

He was wearing an ordinary black tunic, leggings, and boots, but his long crimson coat was magnificent. Dragons made of glittering black thread covered the garment from top to bottom, their wings spread out wide as though they were flying through the fabric, and the matching jet buttons gleamed as though they had been freshly shined. A light gray tearstone sword and dagger dangled from his black leather belt, completing his fierce, fashionable ensemble.

Kai stopped in front of the dais. He kept his eyes trained on my grandfather, although the dragon on his neck swiveled around to look at Reiko, who was staring back at him with a guarded expression. My friend had never told me exactly what had happened between the two of them during the Summit, but she wasn't happy to see him right now.

"King Heinrich, Crown Prince Dominic, Captain Rhea," Kai said, his voice deep and smooth. "It is a great honor to be invited to your court."

My family murmured the appropriate responses, and Kai dropped into a perfect Ryusaman bow, although his inner dragon never took its eyes off Reiko.

The gladiator exchanged a few more pleasantries with my

family, then stepped aside as the next troupe was announced. He murmured something to another member of the Crimson Dragons, then headed in our direction.

Kai stopped and dropped into another formal bow. "Your Highness," he murmured, his words dripping out of his mouth like the sweetest honey.

I smiled. For all his arrogance and swagger, Kai had a natural charm that made him exceedingly likeable. "Lord Nakamura. So lovely to see you again. Given everything that happened at the Summit, I think we can dispense with the formalities. Please, call me Gemma."

He tipped his head. "Gemma. And please, call me Kai."

He grinned at me, then focused on Reiko. The smile faded from his face, replaced by a blank expression, although his inner dragon kept staring at Reiko.

"What are you doing here?" she asked in a low, wary voice. "I thought you were still serving as one of Ruri's personal guards."

"After the Summit, I decided to rejoin the Crimson Dragons." Kai reached into one of his coat pockets, drew out a small white envelope sealed with gold wax, and held it out to her. "Also, Tatsuo wanted me to deliver a message."

Reiko's black eyebrows climbed up her forehead, and even more surprise and wariness surged off her than before. Reiko and her father, Tatsuo Yamato, had a . . . well, perhaps *complicated* was the best word to describe their relationship. The two of them had never seen eye to eye, and Tatsuo had been upset Reiko had wanted to be a spy, rather than following in his gladiator footsteps. But their relationship had shifted a bit, for the better, after Reiko had helped Kai protect Tatsuo, as well as Queen Ruri, during the Summit.

Reiko plucked the envelope out of Kai's hand. His fingers flexed, as though he was thinking about reaching out and touching her, but he dropped his arm.

She slid the letter into her pocket, then crossed her arms over her chest and speared the gladiator with a hard look. "You didn't come all this way just to deliver a letter."

"Of course not. I plan on winning the Sword and Shield Tournament. It's the only major event that has eluded me so far." He paused, and when he spoke again, his voice was much lower and huskier than before. "Rather like you."

Reiko snorted. "Oh, please. Save the simpering seduction for someone it might actually work on."

A smile curved one corner of Kai's lips, which only made him that much more ridiculously handsome. "From what I remember, my simpering seduction has worked on you a time or two."

A hot blush streaked across Reiko's cheekbones, but she lifted her chin. "I'll admit you are not without certain . . . charms."

"Perhaps I can remind you just how very *charming* I can be later this evening," Kai said, his voice dropping even lower. "After the day's battles are won."

Reiko snorted again, but her lips twitched up into an answering smile. Kai bent down and whispered something in her ear—

Without warning, an intense tingling erupted in my fingertips, and my hands instinctively clenched into fists, causing that dull ache to ripple through them again. I hissed out a breath and forced myself to relax my hands. That lessened the ache, but my fingertips kept violently tingling, as though I was somehow clutching a lightning bolt.

This time, I was the one who sidled up to the edge of the carpet and peered down the length of it. The double doors had been closed after the last of the gladiator troupes had arrived, but now they slowly, silently swung open again, revealing a woman standing in the hallway beyond.

She was sixty, and her golden hair was sleeked back and up into a high bun, although thick seams of silver glimmered along her temples. Her skin was pale, but her eyes were such a dark amethyst that they looked black from this distance. Her gown was that same deep color, more black than purple, as was the berry balm that stained her lips.

A silver choker studded with amethysts ringed her neck, while matching silver cuffs adorned her wrists. Rings flashed on her fingers, and the amethysts nestled in the silver settings flickered like purple lightning dancing across her knuckles. I shivered, the winking gems reminding me of the actual lightning this cursed woman could so easily wield.

Everyone turned toward the open doors to see who the late arrival was. A hush dropped over the crowd, and even the boisterous, loquacious nobles fell silent, stunned by the sight before them. Even though I knew it was coming, even though I was the one who had arranged for it to happen, the sight still stunned me as well.

The announcer cleared his throat, finding his voice again. "Presenting Her Royal Majesty, Queen Maeven Aella Toril Morricone!"

With her head held high, and a smug smirk on her lips, my enemy strode forward—right into the heart of Glitnir.

Maeven swept inside as though this were her throne room, instead of my grandfather's, and her black heels seemed to stab directly into every silver-thread gargoyle on the black carpet. She ignored everyone's shocked, curious looks and kept her gaze fixed on the dais at the far end of the room. Then again, Maeven always had her eyes on one throne or another.

She was halfway down the carpet when another woman stepped into the room behind her. This woman was younger, in her mid-twenties, with pale skin and black hair, but she too had the ubiquitous amethyst eyes that marked her as a Morricone. Her dress was a light, dreamy lilac, and a soft, fuzzy cape fluttered around her shoulders. Her only jewelry was a silver ring with black jet vines and thorns studded with tiny amethyst spikes that formed three liladorn strands snaking up her finger. A long, thin dagger made of actual liladorn dangled from the black velvet belt cinched around her waist.

Delmira Myrina Cahira Morricone also moved along the carpet, although hers was a much more graceful and far less annoying stride than Maeven's spiky swagger. Or perhaps that was just my ire toward the Morricone queen bubbling up to the surface, the way it always did in her presence.

Leonidas was walking alongside Delmira, and he looked as handsome as ever in his long black riding coat, with his black cloak nipping at his heels.

The Morricones might present a pretty, regal picture, but the mood toward them was decidedly hostile. Anger, bitterness, and resentment swelled up and off the Andvarian nobles, merchants, servants, and guards like a tidal wave arcing high into the sky. Even some of the gladiators from the other kingdoms shot the Morricones venomous looks. For once, everyone's feelings perfectly meshed with my own, and I had to grind my teeth to keep from snarling at the intense, hateful emotions cascading over me.

But there was far too much at stake for me to indulge in my feelings, as Grandfather Heinrich was so fond of saying. Even though I had saved Maeven's life not once but twice during the Summit, part of me still couldn't believe this was actually *happening*, that the Mortan queen was actually *here*. Armina Ripley had raised an army of gargoyles and forcibly ripped our kingdom out of the Morricones' clutches, which is where and how the Ripley family name and crest had originated. I didn't know of any Mortan king or queen who had set foot inside Glitnir since then.

Something that made Maeven's presence even more remarkable—and fraught with peril on all sides.

Maeven stopped at the bottom of the dais steps. Delmira stepped up to her mother's right side, while Leonidas moved to her left.

Grandfather Heinrich and Father glared down their noses at Maeven, while Rhea dropped her hand to her sword. The captain's fingers curled around the three rubies embedded in the hilt, which would augment her own natural strength magic, if need be.

No one moved or spoke, and the silence was so profound I could hear the feathers fluttering on Delmira's cape, still stirred up by her walk along the carpet.

"Queen Maeven," Grandfather Heinrich called out. "Welcome to Glitnir."

Maeven tipped her head to my grandfather, as protocol dictated. "Thank you, King Heinrich. Crown Prince Dominic. Captain Rhea." Her head turned in my direction, and she speared me with a cold, hard gaze. "Gemma."

Mine was the only title she didn't use, but I didn't mind the insult. Even though the two of us had agreed to a tenuous truce after the Summit, we were well beyond any sort of niceties. Maeven would still be utterly delighted by my death, despite her wanting Leonidas to stay here at Glitnir, where he might be safe from Milo's plots. I would also be utterly delighted by Maeven's death, should someone finally manage to murder her.

Sometimes, I still fantasized about doing the deed myself, about picking Maeven up with my mind magier magic, slamming her into the closest wall, and snapping her spine. Not only had she arranged for me to be murdered along with my fellow Andvarians during the Seven Spire massacre all those years ago, but she'd also sent assassins to kill Father, and she'd helped Dahlia Sullivan poison Grandfather Heinrich. More recently, she had added to those past sins by exposing my real identity during her birthday ball at Myrkvior to hang on to her crown, and then of course by letting Milo torture me in his horrid workshop.

Oh, yes. I still wanted her to die, and I burned to do the deed myself.

My fingertips tingled again, not because of Maeven's lightning magic, but with the urge to grab my dagger off my belt and bury the blade in her black heart. I clasped my hands together behind my back until the sensation faded away, although that icy, murderous rage kept right on beating in my heart.

But I could—*would*—never act on my dark impulses, since that would shatter all the love and trust I had built with Leonidas over the past few weeks. During the Summit, I realized I loved Leo far more than I hated Maeven, even if it was difficult to remember at a time like this.

Grandfather Heinrich stared at Maeven, his face as cold and hard as the jet throne he was sitting on. Even the white and gray diamonds that formed the gargoyle crest in the top of the throne seemed to mirror his ire and glare down at the Morricone queen. After several seconds, his gaze flicked over to Delmira, whom he studied with a little less hostility. Delmira dipped into a deep curtsy before rising.

And finally, Grandfather Heinrich's gaze settled on Leonidas. He hadn't been happy about my bringing the Morricone prince to Glitnir, but he had relented after I'd told him how much I cared about Leonidas. I just hoped the stark, visual reminder that Leonidas was Maeven's son wouldn't damage the small inroads Leo had made with my family thus far.

The silence dragged on. Maeven, Delmira, and Leonidas remained calm and composed, their faces all carefully blank, but worry surged off all three, especially Maeven.

For the first time, I realized just how vulnerable the Morricone queen was. Sure, she was flanked by Delmira and Leonidas, and several guards wearing Mortan purple had streamed into the throne room and taken up positions on the carpet behind her, but there were far more Andvarian guards in here.

If our situations had been reversed, Maeven wouldn't have hesitated to sic her guards on me, just as she had done at Myrkvior. The remembered pain of Wexel's punches throbbed in my face, while my back burned and my hands ached again at the thought of how Milo had driven his tearstone arrows through my palms and then blasted me with his lightning. Maeven might not have laid one finger on me, but she had still let others hurt me.

My fingertips tingled for a third time, and temptation zinged through me, as bright and hot as the sun shimmering in the summer sky. I *should* scream for the guards to seize Maeven. I *should* have her chained to a table like I had been in Milo's workshop. And I absolutely *should* do a dozen horrible things to her, even more than what had been done to me. I should hurt her so bloody badly that even if she survived, even if she were healed, she would *never* recover from the trauma. Just like part of me would never recover from the Seven Spire massacre, or all the horrible things that had happened in the Spire Mountains afterward, when Xenia, Alvis, and I had been fleeing from Bellona.

The desire for vengeance bubbled up like lava in my chest, but I forced myself to look up at the dais. After all, I wasn't the only one here whom Maeven had gravely wounded.

Images flickered off Grandfather Heinrich and erupted in my own mind, like fireworks exploding one after another. Uncle Frederich smiling and waving goodbye as he boarded the train that would take him to Bellona, to Svalin and the Seven Spire massacre. Dahlia Sullivan fixing my grandfather's tea at a formal dinner, smiling sweetly at him even as she slipped a poisoned sugar cube into the hot brew. Dahlia again, slumped in the gazebo in the Edelstein Gardens, dead from the amethyst-eye poison she'd drunk rather than be captured. Uncle Lucas crouching over his mother's body, tears and pain shimmering in his blue eyes that were so much like Grandfather's and Father's and mine . . .

Jewels pricked my palm like thorns, jolting me out of my grandfather's memories. My right hand was fisted so tightly around my gargoyle pendant that my knuckles had turned white and my red starburst scar had welled up, as though it was going to burst open and spew blood everywhere. The tearstone embedded in the silver disc chilled my skin, as though I were clutching shards of ice, but I didn't mind the intense cold. The frosty sensation helped me to further extricate myself from my grandfather's memories, along with the similar ones flickering off my father. Rhea was also upset and remembering her own father, Lord Hans, who had been killed at the Seven Spire massacre.

Even as the chill, anger, and memories faded away, another emotion pinched my heart tight—regret.

I looked over and found Leonidas staring at me. His eyes were dim, a frown tugged down his lips, and his shoulders drooped with despair. He too must have seen my family's memories.

I'm sorry, Gemma, his voice whispered through my mind. *So sorry. If I could change any of it, I would.*

Even more anger sparked in Grandfather Heinrich, along with his lightning magic, making his eyes burn a bright, crackling blue. Maeven tensed, as did Delmira. The princess's hand crept over to the liladorn dagger on her belt, and a small bit of power surged off her, making my fingertips tingle again. Despite all the awful things Maeven had done, Delmira would defend her mother to her dying breath, just as Leonidas would defend Delmira.

Rhea's eyes narrowed, tracking the princess's protective motion, and her own hand curled a little more tightly around her ruby-studded sword. The Andvarian guards also snapped to attention, their hands falling to their own weapons.

The Morricones had come here in peace, but they could very easily leave dead.

The silence continued to drag on and on and on, and tension clouded the air like a freezing fog. Everyone remained locked in place, and I held my breath, wondering what my grandfather would choose—and what I would do if he lumped Leonidas and Delmira in with Maeven.

Father stepped forward and placed his hand on Grandfather Heinrich's shoulder. My grandfather's head snapped up, and his eyebrows raised in a clear question. Father shook his head, just the tiniest bit, but his message was crystal clear.

No. Don't do it.

Grandfather Heinrich shifted on the throne, as though he was going to shrug off Father's hand and yell for the guards. I stepped forward, and his gaze landed on me.

No. I sent the thought to him. *You are a good, just king. Don't let Maeven and Dahlia twist you into something you are not.*

He stared at me for several seconds, and the anger slowly dimmed in his eyes.

Grandfather Heinrich settled himself back against the throne and waved his hand at the three Morricones. "We will have plenty of time to talk later. But for now, enjoy some refreshments."

"Of course," Maeven murmured. "Thank you, Heinrich."

He ignored her reply and started whispering to my father. Rhea tilted her head to the side, listening to their quiet conversation, although she kept her hand curled around her sword, and she never took her wary gaze off Maeven. The Andvarian guards also remained at attention, as did the Mortan guards still clustered on the carpet.

Delmira threaded her arm through Maeven's. "Come!" she chirped in a loud, cheery voice, as though everyone still wasn't staring at her mother. "The food looks delicious, and of course we should greet all the Mortan gladiators who will be competing in the tournament . . ."

The princess kept chattering, even as she tugged the queen away from the dais and over toward the refreshment tables along the wall. Leonidas nodded at me, then trailed along behind them.

Maeven went willingly, but she glanced around, an icy glower on her face. The nobles, merchants, servants, guards, and gladiators all wilted under her cold, challenging glare, and no one dared to step in her way.

Delmira, Maeven, and Leonidas reached the first refreshment table, and the princess shoved a crystal goblet of cider into her mother's hand. Maeven looked over her shoulder, and her gaze locked with mine. The Morricone queen's lips drew back into a razor-thin smile, and she toasted me with her goblet.

A shiver swept down my spine. Maeven might be in the heart of Glitnir, might be surrounded by Andvarian guards and enemies on all sides, but I still felt as though my friends, my family, and my entire kingdom were in more danger than ever before.

CHAPTER EIGHT

All eyes remained on the Morricones, as Delmira escorted Maeven around the throne room, with Leonidas and the Mortan guards still trailing along behind them. Dirty looks and snide whispers abounded, but no one directly confronted the enemy queen.

"Is it going better or worse than you expected?" a familiar voice asked.

Lord Eichen stepped over to me, along with Lady Adora. Like everyone else, the two of them were clutching goblets of cider and watching the Morricones.

"No threats have been uttered, and no blood has been spilled, so I would say that things are going remarkably well so far," I drawled, not bothering to keep the worry and sarcasm out of my voice.

Matching grins spread across Eichen's and Adora's faces, and I forced myself to focus on them. Despite the fact I was in the same room as Maeven, I still had to play my part as Princess Gemma.

"Are you eager for the tournament to begin?" I asked.

Adora's eyes lit up with excitement. "Oh, yes! I think the Gray Falcons will do quite well."

Eichen's chin lifted with pride. "Not only is Adora acting as the ringmaster, but she will also be competing in the tournament."

A laugh bubbled from her lips. "I can always count on you to sing my praises, Grandfather. Although I was a bit more hopeful about winning until *he* showed up."

A rueful look filled Adora's face, and she jerked her head to the side. Kai was standing a few feet away, surrounded by a bevy of admirers who were smiling and laughing at some story he was telling. Reiko was standing in the shadows of a nearby column, watching Kai with a sad, resigned expression.

"Kai Nakamura will most likely win, just as he won the Tournament of Champions at the Regalia Games last year," Adora said. "He is one of the best gladiators I have ever seen. The tournament is his to lose, especially since the Black Swans are off touring through Vacuna."

The Black Swan troupe was the most successful and famous group of gladiators in Bellona and quite possibly all of Buchovia, thanks to its leader, Serilda Swanson, as well as Queen Everleigh Blair, who still competed with the troupe from time to time.

Eichen harrumphed. "Yes, Kai is quite formidable, but so are you, my darling."

Adora grinned at her grandfather, and the two of them started debating the merits of the Crimson Dragons versus the Gray Falcons. I glanced around, searching for the Morricones. Delmira was now pointing out the gargoyles carved into the columns to Maeven, who looked supremely bored. Leonidas was still hovering nearby, his gaze moving from one face to another, wary of threats.

"I befriended Prince Leonidas yesterday," Eichen said, a speculative note in his voice. "Perhaps I should do the same with Queen Maeven. After all, I never did thank her for the gift she sent me."

Adora frowned, clearly confused. "Queen Maeven sent you a gift? What was it?"

"Oh, just a cutting for my gardens that I had requested from Myrkvior." The lie tumbled smoothly from the lord's lips.

A noble lady approached Adora and asked for an autograph, and she moved away to sign the offered piece of paper, leaving me standing alone with Eichen.

"What would it cost me if you were to speak to Maeven and Delmira?" I asked in a low voice. "To welcome them to Glitnir as you did Leonidas yesterday?"

He shrugged, although a shrewd smile spread across his face. "Another cutting of liladorn. I was quite pleased with the one you sent to my chambers this morning."

"And?"

Eichen's smile widened. "An invitation for the Gray Falcons to perform in the final showcase of the season after the tournament ends."

My eyebrows shot up. "Only the tournament winner and the top three troupes perform in the final arena showcase."

"Adora and the Gray Falcons will be among those troupes," Eichen said in a confident voice. "I'm only asking for something I'm certain will happen. Why, it's hardly a favor, if you look at it that way."

Despite the fact he was blackmailing me into helping his granddaughter's troupe, I still laughed. "I do admire your boldness, Eichen. Very well. I will speak to Rhea about the Gray Falcons performing in the showcase, since she is overseeing the tournament security."

He tipped his head to me, then drained the rest of his cider. He grabbed another glass from a passing servant and drained it as well, then grabbed a third glass.

"One must be properly fortified for such things," Eichen murmured at my questioning look.

He winked at me, then went over to the Morricones. Delmira's face lit up, and she immediately engaged him in conversation. Maeven seemed as bored as before, but Leonidas glanced over and tipped his head to me.

"Grandfather is good at wresting favors out of people, isn't he?" Adora said, having finished with her impromptu autograph session.

We watched the lord chat with Delmira. A few more nobles circled around them, and Eichen started introducing them all to the princess.

I stared at first one person, then another, studying everyone gathered around the Morricones. I recognized all the faces, except for one woman who was standing on the edge of the crowd.

She was tall and muscled, with bright hazel eyes, tan skin, and golden hair that was wound on top of her head in a series of intricate braids. She was wearing a gorgeous white sleeveless dress that flowed around her body like a river of silk, although the scars on her hands and arms indicated she'd been in more than one fight.

Adora tracked my gaze over to the other woman. "That's Bridget DiLucri, another one of the favorites to win the tournament. She's an impressive fighter with strength magic."

"As in the DiLucri family?"

She nodded. "One and the same. Bridget splits her time between being a gladiator and helping her extended family run the Fortuna Mint. She's one of their top geldjagers."

Geldjagers did a little bit of everything, from collecting on outstanding debts owed to the Mint, to tracking down rare items for the DiLucris' infamous auctions, to participating in kidnappings, assassinations, and other dark deeds that people contracted through the wealthy family and their dangerous institution.

Suspicion filled me. Maybe Bridget wasn't here just for the tournament. Maybe she had a lead on where Milo and Wexel might be hiding—and wanted to collect the enormous bounty on the two men.

"Bridget usually floats around from troupe to troupe," Adora continued. "Although right now she's taken up with the Storm Clouds."

I remembered the note she'd sent me. "I read your letter last night. You mentioned the Storm Clouds, although you didn't seem to know much about them."

Adora shrugged. "I didn't, and still don't. From what I gather, most of the fighters are from Fortuna Island. They followed Bridget to Glanzen and decided to form their own group to compete in the tournament."

I frowned. Something about her words bothered me, although I couldn't quite put my finger on what.

"Bridget and the rest of the troupe only arrived yesterday. The main fairgrounds around the arena are already full of gladiators, along with all the nearby inns and taverns, so they've pitched tents at the old fairgrounds up on Rockslide Mountain," Adora continued.

Several decades ago, one of my Ripley ancestors carved out part of a nearby mountain and built fairgrounds where the citizens of Glanzen could gather and enjoy events. But, as the name suggested, the area was prone to rockslides, especially during the spring rains, and those fairgrounds had eventually been abandoned.

When I was a child, Grandfather Heinrich had overseen the relocation of the fairgrounds, as well as the construction of an enormous arena, on the outskirts of Glanzen. During our meeting yesterday, Rhea had reported that so many gladiators had flocked to the city for the tournament that some of them had been forced to stay at the old fairgrounds up on the mountain.

"How uncomfortable for them," I replied. "Bridget and the rest of her troupe better hope it doesn't rain or snow before the tournament is over, or they'll find themselves buried in rocks and mud."

Adora nodded. Another noble lady came up and asked her for an autograph, and she turned to oblige the woman, who engaged her in flirty conversation.

I reached out with my magic, trying to skim Bridget's thoughts, but all I heard was silence—complete, utter silence. My frown deepened. Even with this many people in the throne room, I still should have been able to hear *some* of the gladiator's thoughts, or at least get a sense of her emotions instead of all this . . . *nothingness*.

Bridget's hand crept up to the large gold pendant hanging from a matching chain around her neck. The DiLucri crest of a woman's face glimmered in the gold—only, instead of the usual coins, round pieces of dark blue tearstone formed her eyes and mouth.

My own eyes narrowed. Well, that explained the strange silence that cloaked Bridget—the tearstone in her pendant was deflecting my mind magier power. Clever.

Bridget realized that I was watching her, and she released the pendant, lifted her chin, and mockingly toasted me with her goblet, much like Maeven had done a few minutes ago. Then she downed her drink, marched over, and inserted herself in the group of people gathered around Kai.

Bridget kept her face turned toward Kai, as though she was as caught up in his story as everyone else was, but her gaze kept skittering back over to the Morricones, who were still talking to Eichen and some of the other nobles.

Even more suspicion filled me than before. Bridget might ostensibly be here for the tournament, but I was willing to bet she had another agenda in mind.

My gaze focused on Maeven again. Maybe Bridget DiLucri was doing the same thing I was—hoping that Milo would show himself by snapping at the bait I'd brought to Glitnir.

More and more nobles came up to Adora. I left the gladiator to her fans and did several laps around the throne room, smiling and talking to as many nobles, merchants, guilders, and gladiators as possible. Now that the shock of Maeven's appearance had worn off, everyone was eager to discuss the tournament, and I overheard more than a few bets being made on the outcome. Most folks were wagering on Kai, although some were putting their money on Bridget.

". . . would dearly love it if you would make me a piece of jewelry . . ."

A familiar voice caught my ear. Delmira was standing in the shadows behind one of the columns talking to Alvis. Curious, I headed over to them.

"Name your price," Delmira said. "I just want a piece from you. To add to my collection."

She gave Alvis a pleasant smile, but a wave of desperation surged off the princess, strong enough to make me sway. Even more telling, a thought rippled off her and echoed through my own mind.

Please say yes, please say yes, please, please, please . . .

I frowned. Odd. Due to the strange magic that protected her, I could rarely feel Delmira's emotions, much less hear her thoughts, but this one blasted through my mind as loudly as a trumpet, telling me exactly how important she considered the request. Delmira's jewelry collection was even more impressive than my own. So why would she be so eager to have a piece from Alvis?

The metalstone master gestured at her hand. "But you already have one of my pieces. Or at least, the next best thing. Gemma told me about that ring she made for you at Myrkvior. May I see it?"

Delmira bit her lip, clearly frustrated, but she slid the ring off her finger and passed it over to him. Alvis held the ring up to the light, turning it this way and that, studying the black jet vines and thorns and tiny amethyst spikes of lilac from all angles. I'd seen him do the same thing a thousand times in his workshop, whether he was critiquing a piece I had made, one of his own creations, or a design by a visiting jeweler.

"Gemma did a wonderful job," Alvis said, returning the ring to the princess. "This piece is as fine as anything I could make for you. Even better, the liladorn design suits you."

Delmira jammed the ring back onto her finger. "But it's not the same," she muttered. "You *know* it's not the same."

Alvis arched a bushy eyebrow. Frustration surged off the princess, twisting my own stomach into tight knots.

Delmira drew in a deep breath, then slowly let it out, clearly trying to calm herself. "You probably don't remember, but I wrote you a letter a long time ago, when I was a girl."

Alvis nodded. "Oh, yes. I remember your letter—and exactly what it said."

Her face brightened with fresh hope. "Then you know why I want a piece made by you—why I *need* it."

He shook his head. "You don't require any tools or tricks from me. You already have everything you need. You always have. You just have to dig it out of yourself, the same way a miner would chip a chunk of tearstone out of a cavern wall."

Delmira frowned, and several emotions flickered across her face. Puzzlement, curiosity, wariness, more frustration. She sucked in a breath, as if to keep arguing, but Alvis's gaze moved past her and landed on me.

"Gemma! There you are!" he said. "I was just admiring the ring you made for Princess Delmira. It's just as fine as anything I could craft."

Pride filled me. I had spent years working as Alvis's informal apprentice, and it was good to know that I could measure up to his masterful work on occasion.

"Alvis is right. It truly is a stunning ring." Delmira's words were kind, although more than a little bitterness colored her voice. "I was trying to convince him to accept a commission from me, perhaps to make a companion piece to your ring, but it seems as though I'm wasting my breath."

"I truly am sorry, Your Highness," Alvis murmured. "But I can't give you what you want—only you can do that."

Sadness gusted off Delmira, along with weary resignation. Both emotions were strong enough to make hot tears prick my eyes, even as a cold, aching numbness filled my chest.

"Then it seems I am truly out of luck," she murmured, her voice raw and raspy. "Please excuse me."

Delmira tipped her head to us, then stalked away. She vanished into the crowd, although her sadness and resignation lingered in the air, like a chilly wind chapping my cheeks over and over again.

"Care to tell me what that was really about?" I asked.

"Delmira wanted me to make a piece of jewelry for her, like I made Everleigh's bracelets." He gestured at my chest. "And your gargoyle pendant."

My hand crept up, and my fingers curled around the pendant. "But why?"

"Delmira thinks it will . . . *fix* her, and somehow repair whatever is wrong with her magic."

And just that like, everything made sense. During my time at Myrkvior, I had spied a testing table in Delmira's chambers, as though she was still trying to figure out what power she might have, if any, even though her magic should have manifested years ago. Later on, during the queen's birthday dinner, Milo had snidely claimed his sister didn't have enough magic to fill a teacup, and everyone else at the Mortan palace had regarded the princess as weak in her power, something Delmira had echoed with her own thoughts.

But I suspected Delmira Morricone had far more magic than she realized. My fingertips only tingled in the presence of powerful magic, something they'd done on more than one occasion around her. Plus, the Morricone princess had a special connection to the liladorn. She was the only person I knew of who could shape the vines and thorns into daggers, baskets, and the like, and the liladorn often mirrored her emotions, even as it did its best to protect her.

I wondered if Delmira's seeming lack of power was Maeven's doing. Perhaps *that* was the awful, mysterious thing the queen had done to her daughter, the one Leonidas had speculated about last night. Perhaps Maeven had realized Delmira's magic might rival—or even exceed—her own and decided to muffle her daughter's power so that she could remain queen for as long as possible.

If so, that had been a particularly cruel and heartless thing to do, even for Maeven.

Delmira walked over to Leonidas and joined in his conversation with Eichen and Adora. She laughed and smiled and played the part of the perfect princess, just like I always did, just like I was doing right now.

But Delmira Morricone wasn't perfect, and neither was I. Maeven had once said that her daughter's kindness would probably get her killed someday. If Delmira didn't discover whatever magic she truly had, then that day might come far sooner than anyone expected.

I made a few more laps around the throne room, talking and joking with everyone I encountered, but the throngs of people made my gargoyle pendant burn like a red-hot brand against my chest. The pieces of black jet simply couldn't hold back so many thoughts and feelings, and everyone's silent musings whined like mosquitoes in my ears, even as their emotions sloshed around in my chest, making my tiny internal ship careen wildly from side to side. I needed a break, so I slipped out of the throne room and moved into the hallway beyond.

Several groups of people had congregated out here, but I smiled, nodded, and hurried past them all. I didn't allow myself to be stopped and engaged in conversation, and I quickly left that hallway behind and stepped into another one. Everyone's thoughts and feelings slowly faded away, the annoying whine of their silent musings vanished, and that turbulent sea of emotion smoothed out inside my chest. My gargoyle pendant also cooled down, and a relieved sigh escaped my lips.

I couldn't stay gone for long, especially since the Morricones were here, but I needed a few more minutes of peace and quiet, so I meandered down the hallway, admiring the statues, weapons, and tools that were displayed in the various alcoves.

This section of Glitnir always reminded me of the hedge maze in the Edelstein Gardens, since these narrow corridors turned, twisted, and snaked back on each other much like the maze's evergreen paths. When I was younger, I used to sneak away from my tutors and hide in this part of the palace. No matter how hard and long they searched, the tutors could never find me, which had given me an odd sense of safety, especially after I'd returned home from the Seven Spire massacre.

I kept walking until I reached the hidden nook that was my favorite spot. A wooden bench was positioned in the center of the small room so that visitors could sit and study the paintings that adorned the walls. This area was devoted to notable women in Andvarian history, including Armina Ripley—and my mother.

I stopped in front of a painting of Merilde. Dark blond hair, rosy skin, pretty features. This painting was a much larger version of the portrait on the bookshelf in my study, and the bigger size let me see just how dim her blue eyes were and how many lines of pain bracketed her mouth. My mother looked like a candle that had burned down to the end of its wick and was in danger of being extinguished at any moment. A fitting sentiment, since she had died a few weeks after she posed for this portrait. Bittersweet longing swirled through my heart again, stronger and more intense than it had been last night, as if the larger portrait was somehow drawing more emotion out of me than usual—

My fingertips tingled in warning, and footsteps scuffed behind me, but I didn't turn away from the painting. "We really have to stop meeting like this."

Maeven stepped up beside me and studied the portrait with sharp narrowed eyes. The slight tilt of her head and the critical pucker of her lips reminded me of the last time we had viewed art together—when we had both been staring at a painting of the Seven Spire massacre that was hanging in Myrkvior.

"Your mother was pretty enough, but every time I see this portrait, Merilde somehow looms larger and uglier in it, as though her smug smile is sucking up all the other paint on the canvas and leaving nothing behind but her exceeding arrogance."

I stiffened with shock and anger.

"It's not an insult, Gemma, merely how *I* see the piece," Maeven drawled. "And isn't beauty—or the lack thereof—in the eye of the beholder?"

I ignored her insults and focused on her disturbing revelation. "You've seen my mother's portrait before? When?"

She shrugged. "You forget that today isn't the first time I've been inside your precious palace."

Of course not. Maeven had been here sixteen years ago, when she had been the leader of the Bastard Brigade and tried to kill Everleigh Blair in the gardens. And who knew how many other times she had slunk around Glitnir before then, secretly supplying Dahlia Sullivan with amethyst-eye poison to sicken Grandfather Heinrich.

Even more anger exploded in my chest. "Well, it could quickly be your last time in the palace, especially if Rhea realizes you're wandering around unsupervised."

Purple lightning crackled in Maeven's eyes. "I can handle Captain Rhea and her guards."

"It should go without saying, but I will say it anyway. If you harm Rhea or the guards or anyone else in even the slightest way, then I will make you regret it."

Maeven laughed, the sound bouncing off the walls and slapping me across the face. "Why, Gemma. I almost think you mean that."

I gave her a razor-thin smile. "I do mean it. Every single word. More than you know. Please, give me an excuse."

Wariness filled her face. "And what about Leonidas? He won't like you hurting me."

"No, he won't. But Leonidas understands who and what you are. You might ostensibly be here in peace, but we all know you are always planning for war. Especially since Milo hasn't been found yet."

I fully expected Maeven to put some grand scheme into motion during the tournament, some vile thing she thought would benefit her and Morta and whatever other ambitions she was harboring in her cold, black heart.

"Yes, so far my son has eluded all the bounty hunters and mercenaries, but I knew he would. Milo is far too clever to be caught by such greedy simpletons." She tilted her head to the side again and studied me the same way she had the portrait of my mother. "But you, Gemma . . . Well, you might actually succeed in your little gambit."

"I have no idea what you're talking about—"

A bitter laugh spewed from her lips, drowning out my denial. "Please. You can spout empty platitudes about peace, improving relations, and the like until you're blue in the face. You can even claim you're doing it for Leonidas's benefit, to show your love for him or some such nonsense." She speared me with a hard look. "But you and me? We both know that the only reason—*the only reason*—you invited Delmira and me to attend the Sword and Shield Tournament and stay at Glitnir was to use us as bait."

The rest of my denial died on my lips—because she was right.

Maeven's right hand drifted over to her left wrist, and a small, odd shape bulged against the fabric of her gown there, as if she had something tucked up her sleeve. I tensed, wondering if she was going to palm a dagger and stab me in the heart like she had done to Emperia Dumond, but Maeven merely adjusted her sleeve, then dropped her hand and started circling around the room. I put my back to my mother's portrait so that I could keep an eye on her.

"It seems I'm not the only one who learned how to play the Bellonan long game from Everleigh Blair," she said. "You invite me and my daughter here under the guise of friendship, peace, and all that blather, but really, you're just dangling us in front of Milo like a couple of fat worms, hoping he'll act like a strix, gobble down your oh-so-tempting bait, and try to kill us again."

"Absolutely," I replied, my voice just as cold and cutting as hers. "And when he does, I'll be ready. And then I will kill him *and* Wexel *and* whoever else might be aligned with them."

Maeven raised her hands and clapped them together several times. The harsh, steady *slap-slap-slap* of her palms made me flinch. "Once again, you have shown yourself to be far more cunning and ruthless than I expected. Bravo, Gemma. You might actually be worthy of the love Leonidas has for you."

My eyes narrowed. "But?"

She shrugged again. "But your plan is still going to fail. Milo is not stupid. He'll see my visit here exactly for the trap it is, and he won't come anywhere near me, Delmira, or Leonidas."

"No, Milo is not stupid," I agreed. "But he *is* arrogant. He was arrogant enough to think he could kill me in Blauberg and seize the city's tearstone mine, and he was arrogant enough to think he could murder me, you, Leonidas, and all the other royals during the Summit. So he'll be arrogant enough to try to kill you again, whether it's here at the palace, or at the fairgrounds during the tournament, or somewhere in between."

Her hands plummeted to her sides, and agreement flickered across her face before she could hide it.

"Since you're so interested in my long game, let me tell you how I see it playing out."

I started circling around the room, and this time, Maeven moved to put her back to my mother's portrait, making it look as though Merilde were peering over the queen's shoulder.

"What happens if—or rather *when*—Milo tries to kill you again?" I asked the question, then answered it myself. "Well, if he succeeds, you'll be *dead*. Delmira and Leonidas might shed some tears for you, but I certainly will not."

Maeven flinched and visibly recoiled, as if she didn't want to contemplate her potential murder at the hands of her own son.

"On the other hand, Milo *might* fail, and you *might* live to see another day," I continued. "But he'll still expose himself in the assassination attempt. Even if he escapes, I'll still be closer to Milo than I have been in weeks, and I'll eventually track him down."

I stopped and held my hands out wide. "Either way, I've lost *nothing*. Even more important, I've gained another chance to find Milo. You're right. My long game might be simple, but sometimes, the simplest traps are the most effective ones."

Maeven lifted her chin. "I don't have to stay here. I don't have to be part of your long game."

"No, you don't have to stay," I agreed. "But if you try to warn Milo, if you try to help him in any way, then you will suffer his same fate. No matter how much I love Leonidas."

Maeven's lips puckered into that familiar, unhappy expression, but after a few seconds, her chin dropped, and her shoulders sagged. "I'm not helping Milo. I haven't heard a word from him since he tried to kill us all during the Summit."

I studied her closely, but she seemed sincere. Even more telling, sorrow, hurt, and anger zipped off her and pierced my own heart like arrows. Even though he had tried to murder her, Maeven still cared about her eldest son. Perhaps she had more motherly love and instincts than I'd thought. Or perhaps Milo's betrayal was the one that stung the most, out of all the horrible things she had suffered over the years.

"So you haven't heard from Milo, and you still don't know exactly what he's plotting to do with his tearstone arrows?" I shook my head. "I find that hard to believe, given how you knew every little thing that was going on at Myrkvior."

Maeven shrugged. "Believe what you want. You Ripleys always do. You're as stubborn as the gargoyles you ride. Then again, I suppose that's fitting, especially for you, Gemma Ripley, the great gargoyle queen."

Frustration spiked through me. She had called me *the gargoyle queen* after the Battle of Blauberg and tormented me with the same phrase in the Caldwell Castle library during the Summit, but I still had no idea what she meant by the words.

"*Why* do you keep calling me that?" I snapped.

"Still haven't figured it out, Gemma? How sad. It seems your

mother was wrong about what the future had in store for you."
Maeven glanced up at my mother's portrait. "I wish Merilde was
here right now. It would be so delightful to watch her watch you
floundering about like a fish out of water, desperately trying to
decipher a few cryptic words from me."

My hands clenched into fists, and that storm of emotion
surged up inside me again. During the Summit, Maeven revealed
that she had known my mother far better than I'd realized—and
that Merilde had told the Morricone queen things about *me*,
about my supposed *future*. Things, of course, that Maeven would
never willingly share. Once again, she was mocking me, especially by calling me the gargoyle queen, as though the title held
some special meaning that I should instinctively know, recognize, and understand.

"Gemma?" Leonidas's voice floated through the air. "Where
are you?"

"In here!" I called out.

Footsteps scuffed, and he rounded the corner. His steps faltered, slowed, and then stopped altogether when he caught sight
of me facing off with Maeven.

Leonidas sighed. "What has she done now?"

Maeven stiffened. A surprising amount of hurt surged off
her and shot through my own heart, but she didn't defend herself. We all knew Leonidas's assessment was all too true. She was
always up to *something*, even if it was just trading insults with me.

"Your mother and I were catching up, but we're done now," I
replied. "You're just in time to escort us back to the throne room.
Isn't that right, Maeven?"

Magic flickered in the queen's eyes, and her fingers twitched,
as though she wanted to blast me with a bolt of purple lightning.

"Mother?" Leonidas asked, his soft voice full of tension.

The magic snuffed out of Maeven's eyes. "Gemma's right,"
she muttered. "We're finished."

She smoothed her hands down her skirt, lifted her head high, and marched past us.

Leonidas raised his eyebrows in a silent question, but I shrugged in return. Compared to some of my previous encounters with the Morricone queen, this one had been rather benign.

Leonidas offered me his arm, and we fell in step behind Maeven. Just before we rounded the corner, I glanced back over my shoulder at that painting of my mother. And once again, I couldn't help but wonder why Maeven kept calling me the gargoyle queen—and why my mother had told my enemy far more about my future than she'd ever shared with me.

CHAPTER NINE

Maeven, Leonidas, and I returned to the throne room. By this point, the welcome event was winding down. The Sword and Shield Tournament started at noon, and the gladiators had already left to trek to the fairgrounds on the outskirts of the city.

Leonidas promised to keep an eye on Maeven and Delmira, along with the rest of the Mortans. We said our goodbyes, and I also left the throne room to get ready for the tournament.

A few minutes later, Yaleen, my thread master, bustled into my chambers, along with several servants. They all fluttered around, outfitting me in a tight, sleeveless shirt, along with a matching, knee-length kilt and sandals with straps that wound up past my ankles. The traditional gladiator fighting leathers were a dark gray, and the Ripley snarling gargoyle crest stretched across my chest in glittering black thread. More black-thread gargoyles adorned the kilt's leather strips, and the symbol was also stitched into my sandal straps.

I grimaced. Perhaps Maeven was right. Perhaps I truly *was* the gargoyle queen, at least when it came to my tournament costume.

My dark brown hair was pulled back into three knots and

dusted with silver powder, adding an ethereal shine to my locks. More silver powder was dusted onto my face, while a black gargoyle was painted in the center of my forehead, and my lips were stained a deep, flat black. My dagger dangled from my belt like usual, and my gargoyle pendant was nestled underneath my shirt, resting close to my heart.

I stared at my reflection in the vanity mirror and ground my teeth to hold back a shudder. The outfit was eerily similar to how I had been dressed for the third and final Gauntlet challenge during the Summit—right before Corvina Dumond had snuck into my chambers and shot me with a poisoned arrow.

Of course, I had survived the fool's bane poison and eventually killed Corvina, but wearing another gladiator outfit so soon seemed like a bad omen, as though I were inviting even more trouble into my already troubled life. Then again, when *wasn't* I in trouble? There were many perils in being a princess, especially with Milo and Wexel still out roaming around, plotting against me and Andvari.

"You look wonderful, Gemma," Yaleen said in a soft voice, as if picking up on my dark thoughts. "Everyone will think so."

I smiled at her in the mirror. "Only because of your skills and designs."

The thread master smiled back at me. She squeezed my hand, then left my chambers along with the other servants.

I stared at my reflection a moment longer, worry still churning in my stomach, then got to my feet and stepped into the sitting room.

Instead of napping on the rug like usual, Grimley was standing upright in front of the fireplace, with Violet perched in between the two horns on top of his head.

"Ready . . . set . . . go!" Grimley called out.

Violet cheeped, waggled her wings, and ran down the back of the gargoyle's neck. She zoomed past his wings, across his spine, and up the curve of his long tail. Then she leaped off the arrow on the end, throwing herself out into the air and furiously fluttering her wings. Her entire body vibrated with the hard, fast motions.

"That's it!" Grimley encouraged, spinning around to watch her progress. "You're doing it! You're flying—"

Violet let out a startled squeak, and her eyes widened in panic. Her wings fluttered again, and again, but she lost her momentum, and gravity took over. The baby strix crashed down onto the floor, landing with a loud *thump* on the rug.

Violet let out a much louder, sadder cheep than before, then hunkered down on the rug and fluffed out her feathers, clearly disheartened. I went over and dropped to my knees beside her and Grimley.

"The flying lessons aren't going as well as you'd hoped?" I asked, stroking the strix's soft feathers.

Grimley shook his head. "She almost has the hang of it. She'll get there sooner or later. Won't you, Violet?"

The baby strix cheeped again, but it was a small, quiet sound. She was still disheartened, so I kept stroking her wings. After a few seconds, she shook off her melancholy, popped up, and rubbed her tiny head against my fingers.

Grimley eyed my costume. "Off to the tournament?"

"Unfortunately."

"Want me to come with you?"

I started to say no, that I wouldn't need him at such a tedious event, but at the last second, I changed my mind. "Why don't you fly around the fairgrounds and see if you can spot anything unusual?"

"You really think Milo and Wexel are here? In Glanzen?"

I shrugged, trying to hide my worry. "Well, they haven't been anywhere else that we've looked over the past few weeks. I wouldn't put it past Milo to sneak into the city in hopes of unleashing some horrific new scheme against us."

Especially now that Maeven was here, although I didn't mention that to the gargoyle.

Grimley's face creased into a frown. "You really think Milo is bold enough to launch an attack here in the capital?"

"Absolutely."

The gargoyle shook his head. "He would have to have a lot of men, creatures, and weapons to even attempt such a thing. Even if Milo had an army of soldiers and strixes, it would still most likely be a suicide mission, especially given all the guards that Rhea has patrolling the fairgrounds, along with the rest of the city."

"If I've learned nothing else over the past few months, it's that I should *never* underestimate Milo Morricone," I replied. "He is smart, sly, and capable of immense cruelty. There is *nothing* he wouldn't do, *nothing* he wouldn't risk, if he thought he could successfully attack me, kill my family, and destroy Andvari."

More words bubbled up inside my chest, and my tongue itched to release them, to give voice to my deepest, darkest fear, to finally share something I had never told anyone before. I drew in a deep breath, then let it out, along with the thought that had been haunting me for the last sixteen years.

"The Blairs thought they were safe in Svalin, that they were secure in Seven Spire palace, and look what happened to them. Vasilia, Maeven, Nox, and their turncoat guards assassinated almost an entire royal family in the space of a few hours—without even using something as dangerous as Milo's tearstone arrows."

Understanding, sorrow, and pity radiated off Grimley and pinched my own heart tight. "Oh, Gemma. Is that why you didn't leave your room for days at a time after you returned from the massacre? Because you thought we would all be murdered like the Blairs were at Seven Spire?"

I dropped my gaze and focused on petting Violet, who scooted even closer, as if she knew I needed a distraction. But the lilac color of her feathers reminded me of the lightning bolt Maeven had hurled at Xenia as the ogre morph had been spiriting me to safety during the massacre. This time, I couldn't stop a shudder from rippling through my body.

That storm of emotion boiled up inside me, along with my magic, and the sitting room vanished. Suddenly, I was hunkered down under a table on the royal lawn at Seven Spire, watching the turncoat guards slaughter the Blairs, along with the Andvarians who had been visiting the palace. Screams wailed in my ears, the stench of blood flooded my nose, and one person after another *thumped* to the ground, already more dead than alive from their gruesome wounds—

"Gemma?" Grimley's low, gravelly voice penetrated my memories.

I blinked several times. The lawn slowly faded away, and a few seconds later, I was back in the sitting room with both Grimley and Violet watching me with concerned expressions.

I petted the strix again, then stood upright. More screams wailed in my ears, and I had to lock my knees to keep from swaying.

Grimley nuzzled against my legs, while Violet did the same thing to my feet.

The gargoyle peered up at me, his face serious. "Glitnir is *not* Seven Spire, and the Ripleys will *not* end up like the Blairs. You and I will make sure of that. And so will Dominic, Heinrich, Rhea, Reiko, and even Leonidas and Lyra."

I forced myself to smile at him. "You're right."

I bent down and scratched the top of Grimley's head as though I truly believed the lie I had just uttered—and that I wasn't still deeply worried Milo Morricone was going to find some way to slaughter everyone I loved.

I opened one of the balcony doors for Grimley, who leaped up onto the railing, flapped his wings, and took off. I watched him sail up into the sky, wishing I could fly away from all my troubles as easily as he soared over the palace rooftops.

Violet let out another sad little cheep as she watched him vanish. Her wings waggled, then drooped in disappointment.

"Don't worry, little one," I said. "Soon you'll be flying right alongside Grimley."

Violet cheeped again, although it sounded more like a disbelieving snort. Yeah, that was pretty much how I felt right now too—disgusted and disheartened about everything.

I settled Violet on one of the cushioned settees in front of the fireplace. An idea occurred to me, and I went into my study. I returned with the crystal bowl that contained the liladorn, which was still lounging in the water as though it were a pleasant bath.

I set the bowl on a nearby table, and Violet hopped over to it and peered at the liladorn with a curious expression. I might not be able to distract myself from my troubles, but perhaps I could help the baby strix ignore hers for a while.

Violet stretched her beak out toward the vine, and one of the thorns whipped out in warning, making her scuttle back.

We are not a common worm to be gobbled down, that familiar voice chided.

I had no idea if Violet could hear the liladorn talking to her like I could, but she drew back and gave the vine a wary look.

Be nice, I told the vine. *She just wants to play with you.*

A haughty sniff sounded in my mind. *We do not play, Not-Our Princess.*

Violet leaned forward, staring at the liladorn again. Then, without warning, she darted forward as fast as a ball of fluffy purple lightning. Somehow, the strix avoided all the thorns, and an instant later, she was nuzzling her head up against the vine.

The liladorn vibrated with surprise, and the thorns bristled outward, like arrows about to be fired from the vine. I reached for my magic, ready to stop the liladorn if it lashed out at Violet again.

A grumpy but resigned sigh echoed through my mind. *Very well. Let us . . . play.*

The vine arched up and patted the top of Violet's head. The strix chirped with happiness and snuggled even closer to the liladorn.

Smiling, I threw a dark gray cloak on over my gladiator leathers and went to my grandfather's study.

Leonidas was waiting outside the open doors, staring at a painting of the Glanzen cityscape. He was dressed in his usual black cloak and riding coat.

He turned at the sound of my footsteps, studying me as I approached. "You look wonderful, Gemma. Like the gladiator, the warrior, you truly are."

I huffed and held my arms out wide. "I look ridiculous."

A wry smile stretched across his face. "Now you know how I felt during the second Gauntlet challenge." The smile slipped off his face, replaced by a worried expression. "You don't actually have to fight, do you?"

"No, mine is merely a ceremonial tradition. I go out to the middle of the arena floor, say a few words, and open the tournament. Then my job is done."

Leonidas snaked an arm around my waist and pulled me close. My hands rested on his chest, and my fingertips tingled as the warmth of his body soaked into my own.

"Good," he murmured. "Perhaps we can sneak away from the tournament early. Because seeing you in those fighting leathers makes me want to do all sorts of wicked things."

The tingling in my fingertips intensified. "What did you have in mind?"

Leonidas gripped my waist a little tighter. Magic flared in his eyes, and his power brushed up against my body, flowing across my cheek and down my neck, as though he was trailing his fingertips along my skin. The memory of him doing the same thing—and more—last night made a delicious shiver sweep through my body.

"Ahem!" Someone loudly, deliberately cleared her throat.

The magic snuffed out of Leonidas's eyes, and the feel of his power vanished. "Later," he whispered, a low, husky promise in his voice.

"Definitely," I replied, grinning back at him.

"Ahem!" Once again, someone demanded attention.

I turned around to find Reiko standing in the hallway. The dragon morph was wearing her usual emerald-green cloak and tunic. Her gaze flicked back and forth between Leonidas and me, and the dragon on her hand gave me a sly, knowing smirk.

"I should go make sure Mother and Delmira are ready to leave," Leonidas said.

He winked at me, nodded at Reiko, and then strode down the hallway, rounded the corner, and vanished from sight.

"You and Leo seem to be getting along remarkably well," Reiko purred. "Even if Maeven is here now."

I shrugged. "Like it or not, Maeven is part of his family. Nothing I do will ever change that, just like nothing she does will ever change how I feel about Leonidas. I just hope for his sake that the two of us can refrain from trying to kill each other during her visit."

"I wouldn't bet on that," Reiko replied.

"Me neither," I muttered.

She shifted on her feet, and my gaze snagged on the small red paper box she was clutching.

"What's that?"

Reiko's fingers curled a little tighter around the box. "Nothing."

"If it were nothing, then you wouldn't be carrying it."

She huffed at my logic. "Fine. If you must know, it's a box of sweet cakes."

"Are you ill?" I stepped forward and placed a hand on her forehead. "Are you running a fever? Do I need to fetch a bone master?"

Reiko swatted my hand away. "No! Of course not! Why would you even ask such silly questions?"

I gestured at the box. "Because you're not actually *eating* those sweet cakes, which means something must be seriously wrong with you."

Still clutching the box in one hand, Reiko huffed again and crossed her arms over her chest. "If you must know, the sweet cakes are for Kai. He likes them just as much as I do."

"Really? How interesting you know *exactly* what Kai likes," I drawled. "And how very *thoughtful* of you to take him some sweet cakes. Why, it's almost like you care about him or something."

"Or something," Reiko muttered.

"Did the two of you get a chance to talk privately this morning?"

"No. We kept getting interrupted by his adoring fans." A long, tired sigh escaped her lips. "Which was probably for the best."

"What do you mean?"

Reiko's gaze dropped to the box of sweet cakes in her hand. She jiggled it, and the treats rustled back and forth inside the paper. "After the tournament, Kai will return to Ryusama with the rest of the Crimson Dragons."

"You could always ask him to stay."

She shook her head. "No, I can't do that. Being a gladiator is as important to Kai as being a spy is to me. It's who he *is*. I would never ask him to sacrifice that for me."

Reiko kept jiggling the box of sweet cakes, while her inner dragon puckered its lips, as though it had tasted something bitter. Sadness radiated off them both, dousing me like a bucket of cold water. Despite all her protests to the contrary, Reiko truly did care about Kai.

I slung my arm around her shoulders, giving her a quick hug. "I'm sorry. I wish things weren't so . . ."

"Complicated?" She sighed again. "Me too. But these are the lives we have chosen, and we have no one to blame for our difficulties but ourselves."

Reiko jiggled the box of sweet cakes a final time, then stepped out from under my arm and headed into my grandfather's study.

Instead of following her, I stayed in the hallway, trying to get my own emotions under control. Reiko wasn't the only one with a ticking clock on a complicated relationship. Even though Leonidas had been at Glitnir for the past few weeks, we had been so busy chasing after Milo and Wexel that we hadn't talked about what future—if any—we might have together.

After the tournament was over, Leonidas might decide to return to Morta with Maeven and Delmira. Despite our relationship, he hadn't received a warm welcome from my family, the nobles, or anyone else at Glitnir, and I didn't know how long it might take for things to get better. And the cold, hard truth was that things might *never* get better.

Leonidas had spent so much of his life being used in others' courtly games. First, King Maximus had tortured Leonidas to try to take his mind magier magic when he was just a boy. Then, as he grew older, Maeven had used him as her own personal spy, to help ferret out plots against her by Milo, the Mortan nobles, and everyone else who coveted the Morricone throne. More recently, the queen had forced Leonidas to go along with her scheme to reveal my true identity at her birthday ball so she could hang on to her crown. Then, just a few weeks ago, Maeven had invoked the Gauntlet challenge and thrust her son into the spotlight yet again at the Summit.

And now, here I was, subjecting Leonidas to others' hate, anger, mockery, scorn, derision, and prejudices just so we could be together at Glitnir.

Such things were all part of being a royal, but sometimes I wondered if enduring all the Andvarians' hot glares and snide words was worth it—if our relationship was truly worth suffering through such personal, prolonged misery.

Leonidas loved me, and I loved him, but I knew better than anyone that sometimes love simply wasn't enough. All the kingdoms, from Flores and Bellona to Vacuna and Ryusama, had their share of stories about star-crossed lovers, most of whom ended up separated or heartbroken—or dead.

Was my love for Leo strong enough to survive such trials and tribulations? And how long would his love for me help him endure the slings and arrows my countrymen and -women constantly hurled his way?

I didn't know, but I felt as though the two of us were dancing along a sword's edge—and that when the music finally stopped, we would both topple off the side and be sliced to ribbons.

CHAPTER TEN

I shook off my worry and went into the study. Grandfather Heinrich was waiting inside, along with Father, Rhea, and Reiko. We quickly reviewed the security plans for the tournament a final time, then headed outside.

Several nobles, including Lord Eichen, were waiting in one of the courtyards, while servants were fetching horses and directing carriages along the wide drive that circled the gargoyle fountain in the center of the open area. A low whistle sounded, and the guards went on high alert and turned toward one of the archways.

Snap-snap-snap-snap.

Even given all the hustle and bustle of the courtyard, I could still make out the distinctive sound of heels striking stone. Even more telling, my fingertips tingled in warning. A dark figure appeared in a nearby archway, quickly growing closer and larger.

Maeven Morricone stepped into the morning sunlight.

The Mortan queen looked out over the courtyard. A sneer curled her lips, while a wave of disdain washed off her and curdled my own stomach. Many of the nobles, servants, and guards shot her angry glares, just as they had inside the throne room earlier, but just as many looked away, not wanting to draw her attention—or potential ire.

Delmira also stepped into the courtyard, along with Leonidas and several Mortan guards, and the Morricones climbed into a carriage. Even though she was sitting back in the shadows, Maeven's disdain for my people still filled my mind, as sharp and painful as a rotten tooth throbbing in my mouth.

Once again, I wondered if I had done the right thing by inviting the enemy queen to Glitnir, but her presence might be the only way to draw Milo and Wexel out of hiding. Besides, I couldn't change what had already happened, and if I asked Maeven to leave, she would probably insist on staying just to spite me.

The time for doubting my long game was over, and all I could do now was see how things played out—and kill Milo if he took the bait and tried to murder his mother again.

Grandfather Heinrich, Father, and Rhea climbed into a carriage, while Reiko and I got into a different one. The horses surged forward, and the vehicles rattled out of the courtyard, past the palace walls, and through the streets of Glanzen.

In many ways, Glanzen was a typical Andvarian city. Homes and shops lined open-air plazas, and fountains gurgled around every corner. But everything was a little bit larger, a little bit brighter and bolder in the capital, from the gold leaf that trimmed the stained-glass windows, to the silver caladriuses that adorned the columns, to the bronze weather vanes shaped like gargoyles that topped practically every building.

Throngs of people crowded into the plazas, shopping, eating, and going about their daily business, and many folks waved and cheered at the carriages rattling over the cobblestones.

Eventually, the carriages slowed, then stopped. Excitement filled me, and I threw the door open and leaped down to the ground. Reiko followed at a more sedate pace, still clutching that box of sweet cakes for Kai.

An enormous plaza—one of the largest in the entire city—stretched out before me. The cobblestones glinted a dull gray in the late morning sunlight, as did the gargoyle-shaped fountains lining the area. Another, much bigger fountain of Queen Armina clutching a sword high overhead and riding Arton, her gargoyle, into battle bubbled merrily in the center.

People were spilling into the plaza from the surrounding streets, and many folks carried pennants featuring the crests and colors of their favorite gladiators and troupes. Hundreds of conversations filled the air, and even more silent musings trilled through my mind, the sounds as light and cheerful as songbirds.

My gargoyle pendant heated up against my chest, but for once, I didn't mind the continued burn. Everyone was eager for the tournament to begin, and their excitement surged over me again and again, as though I was standing in a deliciously warm ocean. Despite all my worries, I found myself smiling and nodding at everyone I passed.

Grandfather Heinrich and Father walked through the plaza, flanked by several Andvarian guards carrying dark gray banners featuring the Ripley royal crest done in glittering black thread. The king and crown prince smiled and waved to the cheering crowd, while Captain Rhea stalked back and forth, alert for threats. Archers were also stationed on the rooftops of the surrounding buildings, ready to shoot down anyone who rushed forward and tried to harm my grandfather and father.

Maeven, Delmira, and Leonidas trailed after them, surrounded by their own much smaller group of Mortan guards carrying purple banners with the Morricone royal crest—that fancy cursive *M* surrounded by a ring of strix feathers—done in silver thread. Reiko and I brought up the rear, with neither guards nor banners announcing our presence.

People gasped, and mouths gaped at the sight of the Mortan queen, but Maeven tilted her chin up a little higher and swept right on by, as though she didn't even see the folks staring at her—or hear the angry curses many of them were muttering.

I scanned the crowd, looking for Milo, Wexel, or anyone else who might be a threat to either my family or the Morricones, but so many folks were crammed into the plaza that it was difficult to pick out individual faces. Despite the hostility toward the Mortans, the procession went smoothly, and we went through an enormous stone archway that marked the entrance to the fairgrounds.

Dozens and dozens of freestanding carts were lined up in neat rows on the cobblestones, and merchants were hawking everything from tunics bearing the crests of various gladiator troupes, to rings, bracelets, and necklaces engraved with the same symbols, to toy wooden swords and shields so children could pretend to be their favorite fighters. Other carts featured darts, ring tosses, and more games of chance, and the scent of fried funnel cakes and sticky-sweet cornucopia filled the air, along with the richer, darker aromas of hot chocolate and other brews designed to warm people up on this chilly November day. Despite the cloak covering my body, I still shivered in my gladiator leathers. Perhaps I could sneak away from the festivities and down a spiced apple cider later on.

In addition to the carts, massive canvas tents also filled the fairgrounds. Flags topped each one of the tents, the bright colors and gleaming crests denoting which gladiator troupe was calling that space home during the tournament. I glanced around, but I didn't see any flags boasting a red dragon on a gold background, the symbol of the Crimson Dragons.

"Do you want to find Kai before the tournament starts?" I asked.

Reiko chewed on her lower lip, then shook her head. "No. I don't want to distract him. I'll see him later."

I doubted Kai would consider her a distraction, but Reiko marched forward, so I followed her.

Given how many more people were inside the fairgrounds, my gargoyle pendant erupted with fresh heat, and both audible and silent conversations droned on and on like clouds of bees buzzing in my ears. The deeper we went into the fairgrounds, the more thoughts popped up in my mind one after another, like dolphins leaping up out of the sea of emotion that constantly churned around and inside me.

This cornucopia is so good. Must get another bag before the tournament starts . . .

Hope my fighter does well today. Can't afford to lose any more money gambling . . .

Fools. Let them enjoy their little tournament. This will all be destroyed by morning . . .

That last thought stabbed into my mind like a sword, and a wave of malevolence crashed over me, as though I'd cracked through the thin ice on a winter pond and taken a plunge in the cold water below. My hand dropped to my dagger, and I stopped in the middle of the main thoroughfare, searching for the person who had thought such a vile thing. My gaze snapped back and forth, but I didn't see anything unusual. Just carts, tents, and people scurrying around like ants, eager to experience all the attractions the fairgrounds had to offer—

A glimmer of gold caught my eye, but it wasn't the bright, metallic sheen of a ring or a bracelet or even a sword. No, this gold was softer and higher, more like the glint of the late morning sun bouncing off someone's hair. A threat of destruction, icy malevolence, and distinctive golden locks. All those things added up to mean only one thing.

Milo Morricone was here.

I looked around and around, even as my heart leaped up into my throat. Where was he? Where was he?

There.

My gaze snagged on that glimmer of gold again, and I spotted a man wearing a black cloak ducking behind a cornucopia cart. My hand clenched even tighter around my dagger, and I rushed in that direction—

Several people stepped out from behind a tent, cheering and waving banners and blocking my path. A frustrated growl escaped my lips, but there were simply too many people for me to push my way past them all.

"Gemma? What's wrong?" Rhea stepped up beside me.

"I saw Milo."

The captain's face hardened. "Are you sure?"

I opened my mouth to say yes, of course I was sure . . . except I wasn't sure. Dozens of people with golden hair and black cloaks were crowded along this thoroughfare. As for the threat and malevolence, well, that could have been any number of things, including one gladiator thinking about besting a hated rival.

"No, I'm not sure," I muttered. "It could have been Milo, or it could have been someone else. Either way, they're gone now."

Rhea scanned the crowd, just as I was still doing. "Well, I'm not going to take the chance that it *wasn't* Milo. Don't worry, Gemma. I'll find him. You keep heading toward the arena with the others. If Milo is here, then the last thing we want to do is act like anything is wrong and scare him off."

She moved over to talk to one of the guards stationed along the thoroughfare, and I forced myself to follow the rest of the procession. Grandfather Heinrich and Father were surrounded by guards, as were Maeven, Delmira, and Leonidas. If Milo was lurking around, then his assassination attempt would fail, and Rhea and her men would capture him.

I kept telling myself that over and over again as I walked along, once again playing the part of Princess Gemma. I smiled and waved to the crowd as though I were as light and carefree as a butterfly on a breeze, but worry pounded through my body with every step I took.

Even though I had been hoping to lure Milo to Glanzen, even though Rhea and the guards had prepared for such a thing, if the Morricone prince truly was here, then anything could happen.

That was the problem with playing a Bellonan long game. Sometimes, your scheme paid off, and you toppled your enemies. But sometimes, the game went against you, allowing your enemies to triumph and leaving you broken, bloody, or dead.

✦

I kept a close watch on the people lining the thoroughfare, but I didn't see either Milo or Wexel. No arrows zipped out of the crowd, no men with swords rushed forward, and nothing untoward happened at all. The lack of an attack made me even more concerned, as though I had invited a hungry greywolf into my house and was just waiting for it to pounce on me.

The main thoroughfare led straight to the arena in the center of the sprawling fairgrounds. The arena was one of the few structures in Glanzen that wasn't adorned with precious metals and jewels. Instead, images of gargoyles, gladiators, and weapons were carved into the enormous stone columns that supported the structure, while similar figures could be found over the archways, along the walls, and even in the flagstones underfoot. A few caladriuses also peeked out of the stone here and there, although the tiny owlish birds were dwarfed by the other, larger artistry.

It was hard to tell from the ground, but the arena itself was shaped like the Ripley crest, just like the hedge maze in the Edelstein Gardens. Grimley and I had flown over the arena more than once, and I had always thought the gargoyle looked like it was going to erupt out of the ground and swallow us whole.

Grimley? I sent the thought out. *Any sign of Milo or Wexel?*

No, he replied a few seconds later. *I've done several loops around the arena and the fairgrounds, but there are too many people for me to pick anyone out of the crowd. But I can keep circling, if you like.*

I thought about telling him about the mysterious figure I'd spotted earlier, but he wouldn't be able to find that person either, and I didn't want to needlessly worry him. *No, there's nothing you can do here. Rhea has things under control. Head back to the palace. I'll see you later. Be careful.*

You too, runt.

His voice and presence faded away, and I kept walking along with Reiko and the others.

Our procession moved through an archway and then a long tunnel that opened out into the arena. A four-foot stone wall studded with black wrought-iron gates shaped like gargoyle faces separated the walking track from the arena floor, while steps led up to the wide, flat stone bleachers that served as seats. Thousands of people had already crammed inside, and raucous cheers rang out at the sight of Grandfather Heinrich and Father.

They both smiled and waved to the crowd, then started climbing the steps to the royal terrace, which was situated about halfway up the bleachers. Everyone in our procession fell in line behind them, with Reiko and I bringing up the rear.

We were about halfway up the steps to the terrace when the shouts started.

"Morricone scum!"

"Death to the Mortans!"

"Kill Maeven! Kill the queen!"

Audible shouts rang out, along with an even louder chorus of boos, and similar thoughts flooded my mind. My gargoyle pendant grew even hotter against my chest, the intense, continued burn making sweat prickle on the back of my neck. Above me, Grandfather Heinrich and Father started climbing the steps a little faster, trying to get everyone to the relative safety of the royal terrace, while the Mortan guards closed in around Maeven, Delmira, and Leonidas.

"Kill the queen! Kill the queen! Kill the queen!" Someone started that awful chant, and thousands of people quickly joined in, punching their fists and pennants into the air in sharp stabbing motions.

Maeven slowed and turned her head, as if to glare at whoever had started the chant—

A bag of cornucopia flew out of the crowd and smacked straight into her face. The paper split apart on impact, showering the Morricone queen with popped corn, honey cranberries, and dried bits of bloodcrisp apple. More cheers rang out, along with snide laughter.

Maeven stiffened, and her shock sliced through my mind like a razor. Her lips puckered, but she lifted her chin and kept trudging upward, as though she wasn't literally dripping cornucopia with every step she took.

I glanced in the direction the bag had come from, wondering if Milo might have tossed it. I didn't see anyone with golden hair in that section of the crowd, but even more unease filled me than before. Just because I didn't see the crown prince didn't mean he wasn't here—or that he wouldn't try to incite a riot if he couldn't get close enough to murder his mother himself.

Milo wasn't the only person who wanted to murder Maeven, but someone else killing the queen could be just as disastrous for Andvari. With Maeven out of the way, Milo could try to seize the

Mortan throne again, and if he succeeded, then he would have all the men, money, and resources he would need to declare war on my kingdom.

As much as I despised the Morricone queen, as much as I sometimes longed to kill her myself for everything she'd done to me and my family, Maeven needed to live—at least until Milo was eliminated. After that, well, I didn't know what might happen between Maeven and me, or Morta and Andvari.

But right now, I felt very much like the gladiator I was dressed up as—bracing myself for the next brutal blow and hoping it wouldn't be the one that killed me while an arena full of people looked on, heartily cheering with every drop of blood that was spilled.

CHAPTER ELEVEN

We finally reached the royal terrace. No more bags of cornucopia came flying out of the bleachers, and the crowd's chants and boos slowly died down.

Delmira ushered Maeven off to one side of the terrace, brushed the last of the popped corn off the queen's gown, and picked the bits of dried fruit out of her hair. Maeven stood stiff and tall through her daughter's ministrations, although anger burned in her cheeks, as well as in my own.

Delmira finished picking the cornucopia off Maeven, who moved over to the railing and looked out over the crowd below. The princess dusted off her hands and joined her mother, as did Leonidas. The Mortan guards took up a position in the closest corner, their hands on their swords, and their eyes on the Andvarian guards, who were standing in the opposite corner, gazing right back at them.

No more chants or boos sounded, but the Andvarian nobles were once again shooting angry looks at Maeven, Delmira, and Leonidas. Despite their calm expressions, unease rippled off the Morricones, especially Leonidas. With his mind magier magic, he could sense exactly how much the Andvarians despised his mother and sister—and him too.

Worry burrowed into my heart, and doubt crept in like a thief in the night. Perhaps Leonidas and I weren't strong enough to weather this particular storm. Perhaps Maeven's visit was the beginning of the end for us. Perhaps our love would be crushed by the weight of my people's anger and then brushed aside as easily as Delmira had dusted the cornucopia off the queen's gown.

No, I vowed to myself. Leonidas and I had gone through too much to let angry looks and hateful thoughts derail our relationship, and I was wasting time and energy worrying about such things when I should be trying to fix the problem. So I squared my shoulders and marched over to the Morricones. The nobles might not accept Leonidas and his family, but I would treat them the same as I would any other royal guests.

"Delmira, Maeven," I greeted them. "I hope you both enjoy the tournament festivities."

The princess's face glowed with excitement. "Gemma! Did I ever tell you that I've always longed to be a gladiator? The costumes, the crests, the clashing weapons and epic battles. I adore them all. I frequently attend tournaments in Majesta. Why, I've even thought about investing in a gladiator troupe, although I haven't found one exactly to my liking yet."

She glanced out over the arena floor, and a thought surged off her and whispered through my mind. *Perhaps I'll find a troupe to call my own during the tournament.*

I blinked in surprise. I never would have imagined Delmira as a gladiator enthusiast, but I wished her luck. Perhaps investing in a troupe would help the princess finally discover her true power, whatever it might be.

Maeven sniffed and peered down her nose at me. "I didn't realize you were playing dress-up today, Gemma. Gladiator garb doesn't suit you."

"I'm sure you think the only thing that would suit me would be a coffin," I replied, matching her snide drawl with one of my own. "I certainly harbor similar sentiments about you. But alas, I doubt either one of us will get our wish fulfilled during the tournament."

Maeven opened her mouth to snipe back at me, but I deliberately turned my back to her and went over to Leonidas, who was standing a few feet away. To the casual observer, the Morricone prince probably looked completely relaxed, but his fingers kept clenching around the railing as though he wanted to rip the stone apart with his bare hands.

I thought about squeezing his fingers in a show of support, but instead, I rested my hand on the railing right next to his.

A small smile curved a corner of his mouth. "You don't have to do that anymore."

"Do what?"

"Be so careful about touching me."

"I will always be careful with you."

His smile grew a little wider, but it didn't banish the unease radiating off his body, and it didn't come close to erasing the dark, haunted look in his eyes. I wondered if he was remembering all the times people had touched him without permission, all the times King Maximus had hurt, abused, and tortured him. But I didn't ask, and I didn't skim his thoughts. I respected Leonidas far too much to go rooting around in his memories without his consent, just as I knew he would never try to force his way into mine.

But I did need to tell him what had happened during our walk through the fairgrounds, so I stepped a little closer and pitched my voice low. "I thought I saw Milo earlier."

Leonidas's hands clenched the railing even more tightly. "Where?" he growled.

"In the crowd in the fairgrounds." I hesitated. "I'm not sure it was him, though. I just got a glimpse of a man with golden hair."

"But you thought it was him."

"Yes."

Leonidas straightened up. Magic flared in his eyes, and his gaze swept over the crowd of people filing into the arena. His mind magier power zipped out in a dozen different directions, like arrows streaking toward their targets. After the better part of a minute, the feel of his power vanished, and his eyes cleared.

He shook his head. "If Milo is here, I can't pinpoint him. There are just too many people for me to pick him out of the crowd. I don't sense Wexel either. But Captain Rhea has implemented an excellent security plan, not just for King Heinrich and Prince Dominic, but for my mother and sister as well. The two of them are far safer here on the royal terrace than they have ever been at Myrkvior."

I shook my head. "I'm not worried about Milo attacking the terrace. He might be bold, but that's a battle even he knows he could never win."

Leonidas frowned. "Then what *are* you worried about?"

I gestured out at the arena. "I don't know what Milo has planned, but it's something big. I feel this . . . *tension* in the air. Like he's already set and coiled his trap, and now he's just waiting to spring it—and crush us all in its jaws."

Leonidas placed his hand on top of mine and gently squeezed my fingers.

This time, a wry smile curved my lips. "You don't have to be so careful with me either."

He grinned back at me, and some of the worry trickled out of my body. Leonidas was right. Even if Milo was here, even if he had already put his plot into motion, it was still doomed to fail. And once the crown prince finally showed himself, we would catch him and end this threat once and for all.

Father walked over to us. "Gemma, it's time for you to open the tournament."

I nodded. "Of course."

I expected Father to take his usual seat next to Grandfather Heinrich, but instead, he moved past me and went over to Delmira and Maeven.

"Maeven," my father said, his voice civil, if cold. "Please take your seat as the guest of honor. You too, Delmira."

The Morricone queen sniffed again. "I was wondering if you were going to make us stand here all day like commoners, Dominic. Or worse, sit in the bleachers with the rest of the riffraff."

"Don't tempt me," Father muttered.

Maeven brushed past him, then stalked over and dropped into the empty chair next to Grandfather Heinrich. Father held out his arm to Delmira and escorted her over to another chair. She sat down and gestured for Leonidas to join them.

"Does one of your Andvarian troupes need an extra gladiator?" Leonidas asked in a hopeful tone. "Because I would much rather fight in the tournament than sit with your family and mine."

A laugh bubbled out of my lips. "Sadly, no. All the tournament slots are full, and it's far too late for either one of us to run away and join a gladiator troupe. But good luck to you anyway."

Leonidas squeezed my hand again. "And to you."

He walked over and took the chair in between Delmira and my father. Despite the smile on my lips, even more worry flooded my heart than before.

I had a bad, bad feeling we were going to need all the luck we could get just to make it through the tournament alive.

Everyone on the royal terrace took their seats. I wound my way past the tables filled with nobles, forcing myself to smile and nod at the guests as though I wasn't still deeply concerned that Milo and Wexel might both be lurking in the arena.

I passed by Lord Eichen, and he leaned forward, his gaze locking with mine.

"You'll be wonderful, Gemma," he murmured.

This time, my smile was a bit more genuine, and some of the tension in my chest eased.

Reiko was waiting by the terrace exit, along with Captain Rhea.

"My men haven't seen any sign of Milo or Wexel," Rhea said in a low voice. "We'll keep looking. But for now, just concentrate on the opening ceremonies. Okay, Gemma?"

I forced myself to smile again. "Of course."

Rhea remained on the terrace, but Reiko joined me, and together, we went down the steps, then ducked into an archway where Lady Adora was waiting, along with several female gladiators, wire walkers, magiers, and acrobats. Eichen might have lobbied for the Gray Falcons to take part in the final showcase at the end of the tournament, but as the top-performing Andvarian troupe so far this season, the Gray Falcons already had the honor of staging the opening ceremonies.

Adora was still wearing the short, tight, light gray tailcoat and black leggings and boots she'd had on at breakfast, but she'd added a few things to her ringmaster's uniform. A small, jaunty black hat was now perched on her head, and she was clutching a silver cane topped with an enormous gray diamond.

"You look marvelous," I said.

Adora grinned, then swept her hat off with an elaborate flourish. "Thank you. As do you." She returned her hat to her head. "Now let's get on with the show."

Reiko touched my arm. "Good luck."

"You too."

She nodded at me, then slipped out of the archway and melted into the crowd to keep searching for Milo and Wexel.

"Places!" Adora called out. "Places, everyone!"

All the chatter stopped, and the gladiators and others snapped to attention, as though they were soldiers who had just been called to battle. Adora drew in a deep breath, then let it out, plastered a wide smile on her face, and walked forward.

The crowd roared at the sight of her. The excitement was contagious, and despite my worries, I joined in with the raucous cheers. Adora stopped in the center of the arena floor, swept her hat off her head, and bowed low to the crowd before snapping upright again. She stabbed her cane up into the air, encouraging people to cheer, yell, clap, and whistle even louder. Then, with another elaborate flourish, she returned her hat to her head and twirled her cane around, asking the crowd for silence.

"Lords and ladies! High and low! Welcome to the opening of the Sword and Shield Tournament . . ." Adora launched into the typical welcome speech, thanking the crowd for supporting the gladiator troupes from all the kingdoms over the past season.

"And now, to kick things off, please welcome my troupe, the Gray Falcons!" she called out, her voice booming through the arena.

Everyone else in the archway rushed forward. More cheers exploded, the traditional calliope music cranked up, and the show began.

The Gray Falcons treated the crowd to a marvelous performance. Wire walkers did elaborate flips and dips on the thin metal wires strung high in the air, while magiers juggled balls of fire and ice, and acrobats tumbled back and forth on the arena floor.

But all too soon, the wire walkers climbed down from their platforms, the magiers snuffed out their magic, and the acrobats popped upright again.

My turn.

I stripped off my cloak and handed it to a waiting servant. Then, at Adora's cue, I lifted my chin, squared my shoulders, and stepped out of the archway and onto the arena floor.

As soon as I appeared, an expectant hush dropped over the crowd, and the weight of everyone's gazes fell on me, like boulders sliding down a mountain to pile up at the bottom. People scrutinized and critiqued every little thing about me, from the black gargoyle painted on my forehead to my dark gray gladiator leathers to the way my hand flexed around the hilt of my dagger over and over again.

My gargoyle pendant exploded with heat, and thousands of thoughts flitted through my mind, the voices and sentiments streaking by like strixes zipping through the sky. All those thoughts, as well as the feelings that came along with them—good, bad, and ugly—crashed over me like a tidal wave, and I had to grit my teeth and brace my legs to keep from toppling over from the sheer invisible force and mass of them all.

Despite being in the spotlight since the moment I was born, I had never felt such immense, crushing, suffocating pressure to play the part of Princess Gemma—to be absolutely *perfect*—as I did right now.

I drew in one slow, steady breath after another, focusing on my own thoughts and emotions, rather than those of everyone around me. Slowly, that sloshing sea inside my chest smoothed out, although my own storm of emotion kept churning and crackling.

Somehow, despite the distance and people between us, my gaze found Leonidas's steady stare. Unlike everyone else on the royal terrace, he was on his feet, standing by the railing again.

You are magnificent. His voice filled my mind, and his warm pride swirled around me, along with his love. Both emotions further steadied me.

You're not so bad yourself, Leo. I grinned back at him, then turned my attention to the crowd.

"Hello, Andvarians and honored guests!" I called out, my voice loud and strong as I greeted my people. "Welcome to the Sword and Shield Tournament!"

Cheers erupted all around the arena again. The audible noise alone was deafening, and I once again had to grit my teeth and lock my knees to keep from being bowled over by the accompanying thoughts and emotions. Slowly, the crowd quieted down, but the calliope music cranked up to take its place, and I began my part of the show.

Since the season ending tournament was being held in Andvari this year, the opening ceremonies served as a tribute to my kingdom's history. So, with the help of the Gray Falcons, I reenacted one of the most famous moments in Andvarian history—Queen Armina Ripley leading her gargoyle army into battle against the Mortans.

I stalked back and forth, brandished my dagger, and recited the rousing speech Armina had given to rally her gargoyles, along with her human army. Then, with the Gray Falcons behind me, we marched across the arena floor, as though we were heading toward that long-ago battle.

The drama ended with me climbing a ladder and then perching atop an enormous, three-story stone gargoyle sitting on a wheeled, wooden platform, both of which had been constructed just for the opening ceremonies. I finished Armina's speech and stabbed my dagger high into the air, and the crowd erupted into even more raucous cheers than before. Everyone's excitement filled up my chest like air expanding in a balloon, and I found myself grinning, tilting my face up to the sun, and soaking it all in, even as my own storm of emotion raged inside me, fueled by all the raw feelings flooding the arena.

My gaze caught on the life-size stone gargoyles that ringed the walkway at the very top of the arena. Perhaps it was my imagination or the crowd's continued, frenzied energy, but each gargoyle seemed to nod its head in approval, as though I had done our queen and history proud. The longer I stared at the statues, the more I noticed the colors in the stone, all those bits of sapphire blue, jade green, and opal white that mirrored the tiny veins of color that ran through the bodies of the actual gargoyles, like Grimley, Fern, and Otto.

All those colors started glowing like jeweled shards embedded deep in the statues. Perhaps it was crazy, but in that moment, I felt like I could reach out and *touch* all those tiny jewel-toned shards and *hear* all the gargoyles' whispered thoughts, even though I knew that was impossible. I might be strong in my magic, but that would take a level of power and finesse I simply didn't have. Besides, those gargoyles didn't even *have* thoughts, much less actual, tangible feelings. Those statues were as dead as the much larger stone gargoyle I was currently perched on, and I was simply overwhelmed by the crowd's cheers, along with my own pride, relief, and satisfaction at how well I had played the part of Queen Armina—

Fools. Let them cheer and clap and whistle. Most of them will be dead by midnight.

That thought rose above all the others in the crowd, and the sheer viciousness of it punched into my heart like a spear and almost knocked me off the gargoyle's back.

It took me a few seconds to shove the emotion away and regain my balance, along with my breath. Then I started searching for the source of that horrible thought.

The one good thing about being up on the oversize statue was that the high perch gave me a view of the entire arena, and I glanced around, my gaze zipping from one section of bleachers to another—

A glimmer of gold caught my eye, and I once again spotted the sunlight glinting off someone's distinctive hair. A man was standing in the center of the steps on the opposite side of the arena, just level with my perch on the stone gargoyle.

He was wearing a long black cloak over a purple tunic, along with black leggings and boots, and a sword with a gold hilt dangled from his black leather belt. He was tall and muscled, and his hair kept glimmering in the sunlight, as though he were wearing a golden helm. His skin was tanner than I remembered, and bordering on sunburned, as if he had spent far more time outdoors recently than he was used to, but his angular cheekbones, sharp nose, and pointed chin were as familiar to me as my own features. Red, mottled, puckered scars adorned his hands from where I had injured him with his own lightning, and the marks looked eerily similar to the scars on my own hands.

Crown Prince Milo Maximus Moreland Morricone sneered at me, his amethyst eyes burning into mine.

My mortal enemy was here, right in the heart of Andvari, just as I had hoped—and feared.

CHAPTER TWELVE

The crowd kept cheering, yelling, clapping, and whistling, but I just sat there atop the stone gargoyle, frozen in place, staring across the arena at Milo.

The sight of him so casually standing on the bleacher steps, as though he were just another spectator, sent shock zinging through my body, as if Milo had just blasted me with one of his purple lightning bolts. Even though I had been hoping to lure the crown prince out of hiding, some small part of me hadn't thought he would be bold or stupid enough to come here. That he would actually risk *himself* instead of getting someone else to do his dirty work, like he had enlisted Corvina Dumond to try to murder Leonidas and me during the Summit. But I should have known better. Hate was a powerful motivator, and no one hated me, my gargoyles, and my kingdom as much as Milo Morricone did.

My shock vanished, replaced by a mix of anger and determination. The crown prince had been bold and stupid enough to come here, and I was going to make him pay for his arrogance—with his life.

I slammed my dagger back into its scabbard, then threw my right leg over to join my left, took hold of the gargoyle's neck, and dropped down onto the platform below. I used my magic to slow and cushion my fall, but my sandals still slammed onto the wooden planks hard enough to jolt my entire body.

I staggered forward and latched onto one of the gargoyle's legs to right myself. My head snapped up, and I looked at Milo again. He grinned, then started running down the bleacher steps. I growled, pushed away from the gargoyle's leg, and leaped off the platform down onto the arena floor.

"Gemma?" Adora asked, peering over the side of the platform. "What are you doing? This is not part of the show!"

Instead of answering her, I looked up at the royal terrace. Leonidas was still standing by the railing, staring down at me, a frown creasing his face. Father and Rhea were also standing by the railing, as if they too realized that something was wrong.

Milo is here! I sent the thought to Leonidas. *In the arena. I just saw him. Tell the others. I'm going after him.*

Leonidas's frown deepened. *He wanted* you *to see him. It's a trap, Gemma.*

I know, but I'm going after him anyway.

He gave me a sharp nod, then turned to speak to Father and Rhea.

I glanced back over at Milo, who had reached the bottom of the bleacher steps. He sneered at me again, then started running around the outside of the low wall that separated the walking track from the arena floor. He ducked into an archway and vanished from sight.

"Gemma! What are you doing?" Adora yelled at me again, although the crowd's cheers largely drowned her out.

"Keep going!" I yelled back at her. "Don't worry about me!"

I started running across the arena floor, sprinting toward the closest iron gate. As I ran, I threw my right hand up, waving at the crowd again as though this was all part of the show. Behind me, Adora barked out orders to the gladiators, wire walkers, magiers, and acrobats, and the calliope music cranked up again, blaring so loudly that I couldn't even hear my sandals slapping against the hard-packed dirt.

Reiko! I sent the thought out as far and wide as I could, since I had no idea where she was right now. *Milo is here! In the arena! He just ducked into an archway! I'm going after him!*

Surprise ripped through me, like dragon talons slicing across my stomach, and I hissed at the phantom pain.

Gemma! Be careful! Reiko's warning echoed through my mind, but I still couldn't tell where she was.

I sucked down another breath, pushed the pain away, and picked up my pace, pumping my arms and legs and running even harder and faster than before. All that mattered right now was cornering Milo before he escaped.

It seemed to take me forever to cross the arena floor, although it couldn't have been much more than a minute. I stopped and pushed on an iron gate, but it didn't budge. Locked. A curse spewed out of my lips at the delay, but I twisted my fingers and blasted the gate with my magic, and the metal padlock screeched open and dropped to the ground. I grabbed my dagger off my belt, then shoved the gate aside and kept going, now running along the outside of the low wall.

Once again, my gaze darted around, zipping right, then left, and back again. I scanned all the people on the walking track in front of me, but I didn't see the telltale golden glint of Milo's hair anywhere, indicating that he was still in the archway he'd ducked into earlier. But why had he shown himself to me? Why now, in the arena?

It was most likely a trap, just as Leonidas had said. Perhaps Milo was hoping to lure me away from Captain Rhea and the guards so he could try to shove a sword into my back. If so, he had certainly succeeded at the first part, but I wasn't going to turn back or wait for help to arrive. Catching Milo before he hurt anyone else was worth any risk—including gambling with my own life.

Still, I wasn't angry, stupid, or reckless enough to blindly rush into whatever trap Milo might have set, so I forced myself to slow down to a fast walk. I kept looking around, but I still didn't see the crown prince. I also scanned the crowd for Wexel, but I didn't spot the captain either. I even reached out with my magic, searching for the hot, caustic burn of Milo's lightning, along with Wexel's hard, brute strength, but there were simply too many people in the arena for me to latch onto the invisible strings of the Mortans' power and track them that way.

A frustrated growl spewed out of my lips, but I hurried over to the archway where I'd last seen Milo, which led into a short tunnel that branched off left and right. I didn't have time to search both sections, but if I were Milo and trying to escape, then I would take the most direct route out of the arena, not circle back around underneath the bleachers. So I headed left and moved through that tunnel, along with another one, before finally reaching a third tunnel.

Shadows cloaked the inside of this much longer tunnel, which ran for several dozen feet before opening up into the back of the fairgrounds in the distance. Perhaps I was too late, and Milo had already fled from the arena. Only one way to find out.

I tightened my grip on my dagger and stepped through the archway. Unlike the tunnel that I'd waited in with the Gray Falcons earlier, no fluorestones were embedded in the ceiling to light the passageway, which was probably why no one was using it. Except for the archway behind me, and the one up ahead, darkness cloaked the tunnel from top to bottom, as though someone had coated the walls with black paint. I scooted to my left and put my hand up against the wall to better orient myself—and so that no one could leap out at me from this side.

I crept through the tunnel, stopping every few feet to look and listen, as well as peer up ahead and glance back over my shoulder. Out in the arena, people were still cheering, and the music was still playing, although the sounds were faint and muffled in here, as though I were deep underwater instead of just several hundred feet removed from the crowd. No one was sneaking up behind me, so I faced forward again. Through the other archway, I spotted a few gladiators strolling along in the distance, although they didn't notice me.

To my right, a glint of silver caught my eye. What was that—

A figure launched itself at me from the opposite side of the tunnel, and a sword whistled through the air. I ducked, spun away, and raised my dagger. I squinted, but the figure was clothed in a long black cloak, and all I could really see was the glint of their sword, along with the faint glimmer of their eyes.

The figure snarled and swung their sword at me a second time. Once again, I spun away, although this time I was close enough to get the sense that a man was attacking me, one who was roughly Milo's size. Fresh anger and determination erupted in my heart, and I whirled back around to face my enemy.

The man lashed out with his sword over and over again, but to my surprise, he kept trying to knock my dagger out of my hand, as if he was attempting to capture rather than kill me. Strange. Perhaps Milo wanted me alive so he could torture me later at his leisure. Whatever the attacker's scheme, he wasn't leaving this tunnel alive, and I met all his blows with even harder and fiercer ones of my own.

Our blades *bang-bang-banged* together like cymbals, and our growls, snarls, and curses echoed through the tunnel. Out in the arena, the crowd's cheers got louder and louder, indicating the first gladiator bout had begun, in an odd, eerie mirror of this fight. The gladiators might only be seeking first blood, but this battle would be to the death—either mine or Milo's.

My world shrank to the cloaked man in front of me. How he moved from side to side, trying to find a weakness in my defenses. How high he raised his sword. How fast he swung the weapon at me. Attack, parry, dodge, spin. My enemy and I went around and around, neither one of us able to gain a real advantage over the other and deliver a debilitating strike.

Until he tripped.

One of the flagstones was jutting up from the tunnel floor just a little bit higher than all the others. My sandals had scraped across it more than once, and I had almost tripped over it myself three attacks ago. Even though I couldn't physically see that flagstone, I could still feel the string of energy attached to it, and I had marked that spot in my mind with my magic and sidestepped it ever since.

My enemy was not as observant—or lucky.

He lunged forward, trying to knock my dagger out of my hand again, but one of his boots must have punched into the uneven flagstone, because he stumbled to the side. He hit the wall and bounced off—right back into my blade.

"Die, you bastard!" I hissed, shoving my dagger deep into his chest.

The man screamed, the sound as loud as a crack of thunder inside the tunnel. I ripped my dagger out and swiped it across his stomach. The man screamed again and staggered away. He tripped over the flagstone a second time, and his feet flew out from under him.

Thump!

He hit the ground as loudly as a sack of potatoes. He moaned a few times, and I got the sense that his arms and legs were thrashing around. Then—

Silence and stillness.

I loomed over him, my bloody dagger still clutched in my hand. Sweat slid down my neck, and my breath puffed out in ragged gasps, matching the frantic beat of my heart. As much as I longed to charge forward and punch my blade into his body over and over again, I held my position. Milo had already lured me in here, and he might have more tricks planned, like flipping over and blasting me with his lightning the second I crouched down beside him.

But Milo didn't move, and the coppery stench of blood quickly grew sharper and stronger. I reached out with my magic, but I didn't sense any thoughts or emotions, just more of that eerie, utter silence and stillness that indicated my enemy was really, truly dead.

Still, I was careful as I eased forward. Instead of touching Milo with my hands, I used my magic to latch onto his legs and drag him toward the closest archway, which opened up into the back of the fairgrounds. I hauled him all the way out into the light, then flicked my fingers, flipping him over onto his back.

He was still swathed in that black cloak, and a hood was hiding his face, although a bit of golden hair stuck out from beneath the edge of the fabric. Anticipation surged through me, and I sent out another wave of magic, ripping the hood off his head.

A man's face appeared, his eyes bulging wide and his mouth gaping in pain and surprise. He had golden hair and tan skin, but his eyes were brown instead of amethyst, and his bushy eyebrows, round cheeks, and hooked nose were utterly unfamiliar.

Shock zipped through me. This man wasn't Milo Morricone.

I had just killed a stranger.

I stood over the dead man, a sick, sinking sensation sloshing around in my stomach. How could I have made such an awful, deadly error? How could I have been so careless as to mistake this man for Milo? Even in the dark, I should have known better, should have realized that this person didn't have the crown prince's lightning magic.

Then another thought crowded into my mind—where was Milo?

I scanned my surroundings, but there wasn't much to see. Even though I wasn't that far removed from the arena, I might as well have stepped through a Cardea mirror into a completely different realm. Gone were the overwhelming plethora of goods, boisterous games, and excited crowds that populated the front of the fairgrounds. Back here, only a few tents and merchant carts lined the main thoroughfare, most of them off to my left, while the area to my right was cordoned off into training rings.

The training rings ran for several hundred feet before giving way to the woods, and the land quickly sloped upward, with several sets of wide, flat steps zigzagging up the side of Rockslide Mountain. From this vantage point, I could just make out the dozens of tents that had been pitched at the edge of the old fairgrounds, which were about three-quarters of the way up the mountain. Not surprising. Far better to be up on the slope and have a chance to avoid the unpredictable, tumbling boulders than down here at the bottom, where you were more likely to be crushed by them—

Footsteps scuffed on the flagstones, drawing my attention. A couple of gladiators had stepped out of one of the tents and were heading toward the training rings. The two women slowed down and gave me curious looks, but the dead man at my feet and a dark glower from me sent them scurrying on their way. Even gladiators weren't immune to crime and violence. Thieves and cutthroats were known to populate this part of the fairgrounds, and more than one murder had occurred here over the years.

I glanced around again, but no one else was in sight, so I curled my fingers into a tight fist and used my magic to drag the dead man off to one side of the tunnel entrance. Then I crouched down and riffled through his pockets, hoping to find something that would tell me who he was, what he had been doing in the tunnel, and why he had attacked me.

A couple minutes later, boots slapped against the flagstones, and Reiko and Leonidas sprinted out of the passageway, both clutching swords.

I dug my hand into the last pocket in the dead man's cloak, but it was as empty as all the other ones had been. My attacker hadn't been carrying anything, not so much as a stray coin. I let out a frustrated sigh and got to my feet.

"Gemma?" Reiko asked, skidding to a stop. "Are you okay?"

"Fine."

"What happened?" Leonidas asked.

"I saw Milo duck into a tunnel, so I ran across the arena floor and followed him." I gestured down at the dead man. "I was moving through this last tunnel, searching for Milo, when this man leaped out of the shadows and attacked me. Of course, it was dark in there, and I didn't get a good look at him while we were fighting, but I thought . . ." My voice trailed off, and it took me a moment to force the words out past the hard knot of guilt clogging my throat. "I really thought he was Milo."

Leonidas studied the dead man with a sharp, critical gaze. "He does look a bit like Milo. Anyone could have made that mistake, Gemma, especially in the dark."

"You're just saying that to be kind," I muttered.

He shrugged, but he didn't disagree with me. He couldn't, since it was so clearly, painfully obvious that I had killed the wrong man.

Reiko also gave the dead man a critical once-over. "He wasn't carrying anything? No coins, no notes, no clues of any kind?"

"Nothing," I muttered again. "Not so much as a piece of candy."

"Then why did he attack you?" She frowned, as did her inner dragon. "He *did* attack you, right?"

"Of course he attacked me," I snapped. "I don't go around killing strange men for no reason."

Reiko stared at me, as did Leonidas. Neither one of them said anything, but doubt flickered off them both, the sensation poking into my gut like a cold, accusing finger.

"He *did* attack me," I repeated. "As to why . . . Well, maybe he thought I was targeting him for some reason, instead of chasing after Milo."

"If Milo was even here to start with," Reiko said.

Hurt bloomed in my heart at her obvious doubt. I stared at her in surprise, and she shrugged back at me.

"We all know your mind magier magic, especially your ghosting ability, can make you see things that aren't really there. Or at least things that aren't really there *right now*, but rather, back in the past, back in your memories."

Anger spurted through me. "So you're saying what, exactly? That my magic conjured up some old, random memory of Milo and showed it to me in the middle of an arena full of people? That I chased after that memory, that mirage, and followed it all the way over here? That I killed a man, *this man*, just because he had golden hair and vaguely resembled Milo?"

Reiko remained silent, but her inner dragon winced in confirmation. That was exactly what they thought had happened.

Even more anger spurted through me, and a harsh, bitter laugh tumbled out of my lips. "I might not always be able to control my magic, especially my ghosting ability, but my power is not *that* out of control—and neither am I."

"Then why did this man attack you?" Reiko countered.

I flung my hands up in the air. "I have no idea! Perhaps he was a thief lying in wait to rob whoever walked through the tunnel. Things like that often happen on this side of the fairgrounds."

"Maybe you're both right," Leonidas suggested. "Maybe Milo *was* here—and maybe he paid this man to attack Gemma."

Reiko frowned. "But why would he do that? Why not just hide in the tunnel and attack Gemma himself? Or get Wexel to do it?"

Leonidas shrugged. "Milo delights in playing mind games. Maybe he showed himself to Gemma in the fairgrounds earlier, and then again in the arena to make her chase after him, to make her come here and kill this man. All to get Gemma to doubt herself and the rest of us to doubt whether she had really seen Milo at all."

"That's a pretty sick and twisted game, even for a Morricone," Reiko replied.

Leonidas shrugged again. "Trust me. My brother loves torturing people however he can, whether he is messing with their minds, their hearts, or their physical bodies."

I rubbed my head, which was pounding in time to my roiling emotions. "Well, he's certainly doing a good job of torturing me—*again*."

Perhaps Reiko was right. Perhaps my magic had veered wildly out of control and shown me what I wanted to see. It wasn't out of the realm of possibility, especially given all the people, thoughts, and emotions that had been filling the arena at the time.

I closed my eyes and recalled the moment when I had seen Milo standing on the bleacher steps. The sun glinting off his golden hair, his purple tunic peeking out beneath his black cloak, the sneer on his face and the hate burning in his amethyst eyes.

No, I hadn't imagined *any* of that, not one little bit of it. Perhaps Leonidas was right. Perhaps Milo had paid this man to pretend to be him, lie in wait, and attack me. Or perhaps this man had simply been a cutthroat looking for a purse to steal and had gotten more death than he had bargained for by targeting me.

Either way, I might not know exactly what was going on, but I was still certain I'd seen Milo, both out in the main fairgrounds earlier and then in the arena a few minutes ago. The question wasn't *if* I had seen the crown prince, but rather *why* he had revealed himself to me.

Milo might love to play games, but he never did anything without a reason. So what did he possibly hope to gain by showing himself to me, then seemingly vanishing into thin air? Sure, he might be trying to make me doubt myself, as Leonidas had suggested, but that seemed like a petty, pointless thing to do, as well as a huge risk for Milo to take—unless it was all part of some larger, deadlier scheme.

More and more questions sprang up in my mind, as fast and vicious as weeds choking a garden. Where had Milo gone? What was he really doing in Glanzen? Was he here to murder Maeven like I had anticipated? Or did he have some other foul plot in mind?

Only one thing was for certain, Milo was here to do *something*, and if I didn't figure out what it was, then far more people were going to die than the stranger I had just killed.

CHAPTER THIRTEEN

I trudged back into the arena, flagged down the first guard I saw, and showed him where the body was. Then Reiko, Leonidas, and I returned to the royal terrace.

I drew Rhea aside and told her what had happened, and she dispatched some more guards to deal with the body, as well as to ask around and see if anyone knew who the dead man might be. Rhea didn't openly question whether I had truly seen Milo, but doubt flickered off her the same way it had Reiko and Leonidas earlier.

"Gemma?" Father asked, coming over to us. "What's going on?"

I repeated everything that had happened. Instead of doubt, worry gusted off my father, and his gaze darted over to where Maeven was still sitting next to Grandfather Heinrich.

I should kill Maeven. Father's thought whispered through my mind. *Before she and Milo murder us all, before they destroy Andvari and everything and everyone that I love. I could make it look like an accident—or blame it on Milo. No one would question that.*

Shock zinged through me. Not that my father would think such a thing. I had dreamed about killing Maeven more than once myself. No, what truly startled me was the cold calculation gusting off him, indicating just how seriously he was considering the idea.

I glanced over at Leonidas, wondering if he'd also heard my father's murderous thoughts, but his face was calm, and no strong emotion blasted off him. I let out a quiet sigh of relief. The last thing we needed was to start fighting with each other.

"Is something wrong?" Maeven stepped forward, shouldering her way into the circle of me, Father, Rhea, Reiko, and Leonidas. "I do hope nothing unpleasant has happened. I was quite concerned when Leonidas rushed away earlier."

The Morricone queen looked at Father and Rhea, then focused her sharp, searching gaze on me. She wasn't the only one staring. The nobles, servants, and guards had all taken note of our impromptu gathering, and even Grandfather Heinrich and Delmira were turned around in their seats, wondering what was going on.

I forced myself to smile as though nothing was wrong. "Oh, there was a small incident out in the fairgrounds. Nothing you need to concern yourself with, Your Majesty."

"Mmm." Maeven made a noncommittal sound that was dripping with disbelief. "I find that concerning myself with everything, no matter how small, is the key to being queen."

No one responded, and tension gathered around us, like storm clouds swiftly filling up the sky.

No matter what happens with Milo, Maeven herself will always be a threat to us. I should definitely kill her. Once again, Father's murderous thoughts whispered through my mind. Even more cold calculation blasted off him than before, the emotion strong enough to chill my cheeks like a bitter winter wind.

Leonidas's face remained calm and blank. He gave no indication he had heard my father's malicious musings, but I had to grit my teeth to keep my smile fixed on my face.

"Come, Mother," Leonidas said in a smooth voice. "Let us

return to our seats. Kai Nakamura is fighting soon. He is one of the top gladiators competing in the tournament, and he should put on a marvelous show."

"Mmm." Maeven made another noncommittal sound, but she let Leonidas lead her away.

Leonidas helped his mother to her seat, then dropped into the chair next to Delmira again. The princess started chattering about the opening ceremonies, as well as the bouts that had taken place so far, but her words spewed out in a nervous torrent, as if she thought that the faster she talked, the quicker she might defuse the tension still lingering in the air.

Grandfather Heinrich joined in her conversation, as did Leonidas, but Maeven remained stiff and silent in her seat.

Rhea laid her hand on my shoulder. "I should go help the guards deal with the body. I also want to increase the number of people on duty, especially around Glitnir. Milo might have slipped into the city, but he won't be able to get anywhere near the palace."

"I'll go with you," Reiko chimed in.

The captain squeezed my shoulder, then left the terrace with the dragon morph trailing along behind her. That left me standing alone with Father.

"Don't worry, Gemma," he said. "Now that we know Milo is here, we can redouble our efforts to find him, and Wexel, and whoever else might be helping them. Milo won't escape. Not this time. I promise you that."

"Thank you, Father." I forced myself to smile again, even though the expression felt as sharp as a shard of glass digging into my face.

Father returned my smile with one of his own, but worry darkened his eyes. Sometimes, I forgot that Crown Prince Dominic had to play his part just like Princess Gemma did. Not just as a concerned father, but also as the protector of his kingdom.

Still, we both knew his was an empty promise at best. Milo had already snuck into Glanzen, and I doubted some extra guards would stop him from breaching Glitnir. No, the crown prince would find some way around our defenses, just as he had found a way to kill our gargoyles with his cursed tearstone arrows.

I just wondered how many people Milo would hurt when he finally showed himself again—and how I could possibly stop my enemy when I couldn't even bloody *find* him.

Despite the tunnel attack, and my intense desire to join the search for Milo, I had no choice but to remain on the royal terrace. As Princess Gemma, I put on a grand show, cheering for all the Andvarian gladiators, including Adora and the rest of the Gray Falcons, as though I was greatly enjoying the bouts. But every *bang* of a sword hitting another sword made me flinch, as did the continued *crash-crash-crash* of weapons striking shields, as though they were all cracks of thunder heralding the arrival of a severe storm—and the start of Milo unleashing his ultimate plot.

Despite my unease, the rest of the afternoon passed by uneventfully, except for a few upsets in the tournament. Bridget DiLucri drew first blood in a matter of seconds, and I could tell why Adora considered her one of the favorites to win. Kai also easily advanced, then did an elaborate spin move and flourish with his sword that made everyone in the arena leap to their feet and start cheering. Reiko was right. Kai Nakamura was a gladiator through and through the same way that she was a spy. I just hoped the two of them could work out their differences and find some way to be together, just as I hoped the same thing for Leonidas and me.

Time would tell what would happen—and who might get their hearts broken.

Around four o'clock, the tournament wrapped up for the day, and we left the royal terrace, moved through the fairgrounds, and returned to Glitnir. We reconvened in my grandfather's study and settled ourselves in chairs around the fireplace, while the servants set out platters of sweet cakes. Grandfather Heinrich thanked the servants, who left and shut the doors behind themselves. Then all eyes turned to Rhea.

"The guards searched all afternoon, but there was no sign of Milo or Wexel anywhere in the arena or the fairgrounds," Rhea said. "They must have slipped away and returned to wherever they are hiding in the city."

Reiko's eyebrows creased together in thought. "Are you sure Milo and Wexel aren't hiding in the fairgrounds somewhere?"

"Why do you say that?" Leonidas asked.

She shrugged. "If I were Milo, and I truly wanted to blend in, then I would stay as close to the fairgrounds as possible, since they are the busiest and most crowded part of the city right now. Milo is far less likely to be noticed when he is one person among thousands, rather than one person among dozens, as he would be in other, less populous parts of the city."

Rhea drummed her fingers on the hilt of her sword. "I suppose it's possible. Milo and Wexel could certainly stay in the fairgrounds during the day, but only the gladiators and other troupe performers are allowed there at night. Someone would be sure to spot them then, especially given the flyers my men have been passing around for the last few weeks, ever since Dominic announced the bounty on them."

Father leaned forward and clasped his hands together. "What about the man who attacked Gemma?"

Rhea shook her head. "No one knows who he is or where he came from, but that's not unusual, given how many people are in the city for the tournament."

"So we don't know where Milo and Wexel are hiding, and we don't know who or how many people might be working for them." Frustration filled me. "Which means we won't find out what they're plotting until *after* they decide to attack us again."

"I'm sorry, Gemma," Rhea replied. "I know that's not what anyone wants to hear, especially you."

No, it wasn't, but it wasn't Rhea's fault we were in this mess. It was *mine*, because I hadn't managed to find Milo in all the weeks I had been chasing after him.

"What about the ball tonight?" Grandfather Heinrich asked. "That would be a tempting target for any of Andvari's enemies, but especially for Milo and Wexel."

As was the custom with other major events, such as the Regalia Games, a royal ball was scheduled at Glitnir every night after the Sword and Shield Tournament wrapped up for the day. Such balls gave gladiators, nobles, and merchants from other kingdoms a chance to visit our court, as well as make deals, inroads, and connections with Andvarian gladiators, nobles, and merchants, and promote trade and the like between all the kingdoms. Similar parties would also be held throughout the city, including at the fairgrounds, that anyone could attend, no matter their wealth, station, or status.

"I've posted extra guards all around the palace, and we are checking everyone's invitation as they arrive for the ball," Rhea replied. "There's no way Milo and Wexel could sneak inside the palace, much less make it all the way to the throne room. Glitnir is secure."

"And what about Maeven?" Grandfather Heinrich asked in a snide voice, his gaze zooming over to Leonidas. "Is she also secure?"

The Morricone prince stiffened in his seat. "If you're asking if my mother is helping Milo, then the answer is no," he said in a cold, flat voice. "He tried to depose her at Myrkvior and murder her at the Summit. Whatever Milo is plotting, Maeven is *not* a part of it."

"Not anymore." The words slipped out before I could stop them, and I silently cursed my runaway tongue.

Leonidas gave me a sharp look. "What's that supposed to mean?"

Everyone stared at me, and I had no choice but to answer him.

"During the Summit, I discovered Maeven knew what Milo was trying to do with his tearstone arrows all along," I replied, struggling to quash the anger bubbling up inside me. "She bloody *knew* he was trying to figure out a way to kill our gargoyles, and yet she said and did nothing about it. *Nothing.*"

A stunned silence dropped over the study, and Grandfather Heinrich, Father, and Rhea looked at me with shocked faces. I had never told them about my conversations with the Morricone queen in the library at Caldwell Castle, although I had mentioned them to Reiko. Leonidas didn't seem particularly surprised by my revelation, but then again, he knew exactly what Maeven was capable of—and just how much she enjoyed twisting others' schemes around to her own advantage.

I drew in a breath, then let it out, struggling to keep my voice calm and even. "Maeven said she wanted to see if Milo would succeed in his tinkerings with the tearstone and dried fool's bane flowers and whatever else he might be using to craft his arrows."

"What's your point?" Leonidas asked.

His icy tone made even more anger bubble up in my body. "My point is that sooner or later, Maeven will find a way to use Milo's arrows to her own advantage. You *know* she will."

Leonidas's fingers clenched around the arms of his chair, and a muscle ticced in his jaw, but he didn't dispute my words.

Father cleared his throat, breaking the tense, charged silence. "Well, since Maeven seems to be behaving herself, at least for the moment, we should focus on Milo," he said, steering the conversation back to safer, less hostile ground. "Let's go over the security protocols again . . ."

We spent the next half hour reviewing the security for the ball, as well as for the tournament tomorrow. Rhea was an excellent captain, and her plans would create a proverbial shield around Glitnir tonight. I didn't see any way Milo, Wexel, or any other assassins could even hope to get close to the palace, much less sneak inside the throne room and try to kill Maeven, Grandfather Heinrich, or anyone else.

Still, knowing Milo was slinking around the city put me on edge. Perhaps Leonidas was right, and this was part of the crown prince's plan—to make me so crazy with worry that I wouldn't see him slithering through the shadows until it was too late.

Grandfather Heinrich, Father, and Rhea had a few more things to discuss, so Reiko, Leonidas, and I left the study. Reiko took one look at our angry faces, murmured an excuse about getting ready for the ball, and vanished.

Even more anger filled Leonidas's face. The same emotion rolled off him, joining the ire that was smoldering in my own chest like a wildfire about to start burning out of control.

"I know you and your family think Maeven is helping Milo, but I can assure you that she is not," he snapped.

"Why? Because she would tell you if she was helping him?" I snapped right back at him. "Please. Maeven never tells you or anyone else her plans. She didn't tell you that she was going to expose my true identity at her birthday ball at Myrkvior, just like she didn't tell you that she was going to invoke the Gauntlet challenge during the Summit and make you risk your life for her whim. Not to mention all the other times she's used and manipulated the both of us in recent weeks."

"My mother isn't always the villain, Gemma," Leonidas snapped again. "Just like your father isn't always the hero."

I reared back in surprise. "What does that mean?"

His eyes glittered like chips of amethyst ice. "You heard the same things I did on the royal terrace earlier. Namely, how Crown Prince Dominic Ripley thought he could murder my mother and frame Milo for the crime."

Damn it. I'd been hoping those thoughts had escaped his notice, but Leonidas was just as strong in his magic as I was in mine, so of course he had heard them too.

"Aren't you going to deny it?" Leonidas asked in a cold voice. "Aren't you going to claim your father would *never* do anything like that? That your family would *never* eliminate an enemy in cold blood? That the good, honorable Ripleys would *never* be like the cruel, conniving Morricones they hate so very much?"

"Of course I can't deny it," I replied, my voice just as cold as his was. "Just like you can't deny Maeven isn't still plotting against my family."

"Well, in this case, Mother's actions are justifiable, especially since you brought her to Glitnir to be killed."

I froze. Despite how close we had become over the past few weeks, I hadn't told Leonidas or anyone else that part of my plan. I didn't know how he would feel about it, and I hadn't wanted him to have to choose between protecting his mother and killing Milo.

I opened my mouth to deny it, but Leonidas arched an eyebrow, looking eerily like Maeven in this moment, and the lies died on my lips.

"You might have spouted platitudes about bringing Maeven here to improve relations between Morta and Andvari. Maybe that truly was part of your plan."

"But?" I challenged.

"But we both know the *real* reason you asked Mother to come to Glitnir was so that Milo might try to murder her again, and you could finally kill him in return." A harsh laugh spewed out of

Leonidas's mouth, and the cold, caustic sound splattered all over me like sleet on a winter day. "I'm a Morricone, Gemma. I've seen enough long games at the Myrkvior court to recognize yours."

Once again, I opened my mouth, and once again no words came out. I couldn't deny his accusation. No, scratch that. I *wouldn't* deny it. Because I would play a dozen, a hundred, a thousand bloody long games if it meant protecting my people and gargoyles from Milo and Maeven and anyone else who might be targeting my kingdom.

"You're right. I *did* invite Maeven here to use her as bait, and I won't apologize for it. Why, I would snap a bear trap around your mother's leg and stake her out in the middle of the arena for everyone to see if it meant catching Milo."

Leonidas's eyes narrowed, and his lips puckered, as though he had just tasted something rotten. I lifted my chin and glared right back at him.

After a few seconds, the anger leaked out of his face. He blew out a breath, and weary resignation rippled off him. "Perhaps you were right at the Summit."

"About what?" I asked in a wary voice.

"That nothing will ever truly *change*," he said in a flat, toneless voice. "That no matter what happens between us, our families will *never* stop fighting. That we'll always be caught in the middle of that royal trap. That we'll always have the weight and history and blood of the Morricones and the Ripleys flowing between us."

His words punched into my heart, cracking through my anger, and sadness rushed in through all those sharp, jagged chasms, making my entire body feel bruised and battered.

"I don't want it to be like this," I confessed in a low, strained voice. "I don't want to always have to worry about what Maeven is going to do next or come up with my own schemes to thwart hers in return. I truly thought . . ."

"What?" Leonidas asked in a guarded voice.

I sighed. "That if I killed Milo, the Morricone threat to Andvari would finally *end*. But it won't. Not as long as your mother is still alive."

Leonidas shook his head. "I told you before: she's not helping Milo in whatever he's plotting."

"I know that, and I believe you. Truly, I do."

He threw his hands up into the air. "Then why do I still hear the doubt in your voice?"

"Because Maeven is Milo's mother," I replied. "She will *always* be his mother, just as she will always be your and Delmira's mother. No matter what Milo has done to her, or you, or Delmira, I imagine there is still some small part of her that wants to help him, that wants to *save* him. She admitted as much to me at the Summit, after she learned about my father's bounty on Milo."

I sighed, even more of that sadness filling my body and dragging me down, down, down. "No mother should have to watch her child die, not even Maeven."

"You could ask your family to show mercy," Leonidas said, a bit of hope flickering across his face. "Convince King Heinrich and Prince Dominic that Milo be captured instead of killed. Then let my mother deal with him. Let her be the one who decides if he's imprisoned—or executed."

"You know I can't do that." Anger and determination surged through me. "No, that's a lie. I *won't* do that. Not after everything Milo has done to me. I will *never* show him mercy, just as he would never show me any."

Leonidas's lips puckered into that sour expression again. "It's so ironic."

"What?"

"Just yesterday, you said you would do anything for me, and I claimed I would do anything for you in return." He shook his head. "But that's not the case when it comes to our families, is it?

We're both still trying to protect them as much as possible. I suppose we were both lying—to ourselves."

His words punched into my heart again, widening all those sharp cracks and chasms, until my entire chest felt as hollow and empty as a canyon. Perhaps he was right. Perhaps we *had* been lying, especially to ourselves. Leonidas might want Milo dead as badly as I did, but he didn't want Maeven to experience the pain of losing her son, even if that son had turned on her long ago. I could appreciate his dilemma, but I wasn't going to change my mind about Milo. Not when my kingdom was at stake.

Not even if it broke my heart.

I didn't know what to say, so I just stared at Leonidas, wishing I could cross the space between us, draw him into my arms, and rewind time to last night in my room, when we had lost ourselves in our magic and each other, and the rest of the world and our worries had ceased to exist.

But I couldn't do that, and neither could he, no matter how much we both might want to.

Leonidas dropped his head. When he straightened up again, his face was schooled back into that blank, icy mask that had so often coated his features at Myrkvior. "I should go check on Mother and Delmira."

Once again, I wanted to *do* something, say something to bridge this sudden gulf between us, and once again, I remained silent. Back during the Battle of Blauberg, I thought I had finally gotten rid of Coward Gemma, finally drowned her for good, but she kept right on bubbling back up to the surface of my mind and especially my heart, like a kraken that refused to die.

Leonidas whirled around and stalked away, his cloak snapping around his legs like a nest of coral vipers, as though the fabric were as angry as the prince himself.

I watched him go with a heavy heart, wishing I could call him back, and knowing I couldn't.

He was right about one thing, though. Our families were slowly but surely tearing us apart, like greywolves sinking their teeth into our love and gobbling it down one bloody, shredded chunk at a time. Even worse, I had no idea how to stop the assault and stanch the bleeding, and I wasn't sure we could survive the damage being done to us on all sides.

chapter fourteen

I trudged back to my chambers. Grimley had returned from the fairgrounds, and he and Violet were napping in front of the sitting-room fireplace. Even the liladorn was sleeping in its crystal bowl on the table, so I tiptoed past them all and headed into my study.

I closed the door behind me, then sat down at my desk. More letters were piled up on a silver platter, waiting to be opened and read, but I just stared dully at the colorful envelopes, my heart still aching over all the harsh words and ugly truths Leonidas and I had hurled at each other about our love, families, and duties to our kingdoms—and my thirst for revenge against Milo.

Ever since Leonidas had come to Glitnir, I had been wrapped up in a soft, lovely dream, and I had lost myself in him night after night. But that dream was as fragile as a soap bubble, and today, it had finally popped. If I was being brutally honest with myself, even the dream had been an illusion. In the back of my mind and the bottom of my heart, I had always been worried about what would happen next between us. Happy for now was *not* the same as happily ever after, if such a thing even truly existed.

Right now, I had serious doubts about that.

But even if our families stopped plotting against each other, even if they could find some way to peacefully coexist, that still wouldn't solve the other mountain of a problem towering over Leonidas and me, one that was shaped like the sharpest crown.

If Milo was captured or killed, then Leonidas would officially be Maeven's heir—and the future king of Morta.

Leonidas would be an excellent king. He would rule justly and fairly, improve relations with the other royals, and encourage trade with the other kingdoms, both on the Buchovian continent and the ones beyond. He would do everything in his power to protect his people and strixes and make sure they all prospered during his reign.

At Myrkvior, during the queen's birthday dinner, Leonidas had revealed how he invited minstrels, poets, paint masters, and other artisans to the Morricone palace, how he thought the beautiful music, writing, art, and goods they created were the future of Morta. As king, he could make that future a reality—and do so much *more*.

Reiko said she couldn't ask Kai to give up being a gladiator for her. Well, I couldn't ask Leonidas to give up being king of Morta for me. It was his birthright, the same way the Andvarian throne was mine, and our hallway fight had been a painful reminder of that.

But perhaps it was for the best. Perhaps all these sly schemes, harsh words, and ugly truths were necessary to finally sever this connection Leonidas and I had had ever since we first met in the Spire Mountains as children. Perhaps knowing the good he would do as king of Morta would make it easier to let him go.

Perhaps my heart would only break a little bit when he left, instead of completely shattering into shards.

I sighed and rubbed my temples, trying to massage away the ache building in my brain, as well as ignore the even stronger pricks of worry needling my heart, but it didn't work. Of course not. Well, if I couldn't get rid of the head- and heartaches, then I would do what I'd done to my magic, memories, and emotions for so long.

Bury them as deep as they would go, and hope they would never rise again.

I sighed again, then plucked the top letter off the tray. Perhaps I would get lucky, and one of the missives would contain a clue about where Milo and Wexel were hiding. I might not be able to solve the problems between myself and Leonidas, but I still needed to eliminate Milo Morricone—before it was too late.

An hour later, I growled with frustration and tossed the last letter aside. None of the notes had contained any information that would lead me to Milo or Wexel, and I was sorely tempted to take the lot of them into the sitting room, throw them into the fireplace, and watch them burn.

A soft knock sounded on the sitting-room door, and I felt Yaleen's presence outside the chambers.

I glared at the letters again. "You're lucky I have to get ready for the ball."

Of course the papers just sat there, but I still felt like the colorful inks and envelopes were mocking me all the same. I rubbed my aching head again. As a mind magier, I had always worried my magic and memories might one day drive me mad, and here I was, not using a lick of power, yet still threatening pieces of paper.

Perhaps Reiko had been right earlier. Perhaps I was so desperate to find Milo that I was seeing enemies in everyone and everything around me.

Yaleen knocked again, a little louder and more insistent than before. I bit back a groan, then left the study and went out into the sitting room to admit her and the other servants.

The thread master outfitted me in a simple but stunning silver dress. Midnight-blue thread shaped like gargoyle faces circled the cuffs and ran down the deep V neckline, which also showcased my pendant. More snarling gargoyle faces dotted the long, billowing skirt, and my dagger dangled from the midnight-blue velvet belt that was cinched around my waist. Flat silver sandals with blue gargoyle-studded straps, similar to the ones I had worn in the arena earlier, covered my feet.

The paint masters covered my eyes with dark blue shadow and liner, then painted my lips the same deep color. Waves were set into my dark brown hair, which was left loose around my shoulders, while silver glitter was dusted over the top of my head, in lieu of a tiara.

Yaleen dismissed the other servants, then frowned at me in the vanity mirror in my bedroom. "Gemma? Is the gown not to your liking? You haven't said anything in the last five minutes."

"I adore it," I chirped in a bright voice. "Your designs are always lovely, but this one is truly special. I just . . . have a lot on my mind."

A sly grin crept across her face. "Wondering how many times you can dance with Prince Leonidas at the ball?"

After our earlier fight, I would be lucky if Leonidas even spoke to me, but I forced myself to smile at her. "Something like that."

Yaleen winked at me in the mirror, then left my chambers. I trudged out into the sitting room, where Grimley and Violet were still stretched out in front of the fireplace.

"Finally, some peace and quiet," Grimley grumbled. "I thought they were *never* going to finish primping you."

I rolled my eyes. "So sorry my getting ready for an important event interrupted your evening nap."

He harrumphed, but Violet waggled her wings at me.

"So pretty!" the baby strix trilled in her high singsong voice. "You sparkle like a star!"

I bent down and petted the strix. "Thank you, Violet. I'm glad someone appreciates all of Yaleen's hard work."

Grimley harrumphed again. "I appreciate it plenty . . . when it doesn't interfere with my sleep schedule."

Who can sleep when the gargoyle's snores are louder than fireworks exploding?

A familiar voice filled my mind, and I laughed and glanced over at the liladorn, which was still curled up in its crystal bowl.

"What's so funny?" Grimley asked, shooting the vine a suspicious look.

"Our guest wishes you would enjoy your naps a little more quietly."

The gargoyle glared at the liladorn, which flipped around, pointedly ignoring the other creature.

"Stupid vine," Grimley muttered.

Beside him, Violet waggled her wings again and cheeped her agreement.

The gargoyle peered up at me, and his face softened. "You do look lovely, Gemma. Despite how worried you are."

I opened my mouth to deny it, but Grimley narrowed his eyes at me.

"Fine," I muttered. "I am worried."

"About what?"

"My father plotting to kill Maeven, her plotting to do the same thing to him and Grandfather Heinrich, Milo and Wexel somehow sneaking into the throne room tonight and murdering us all." I flung my hands out wide. "Take your pick."

"And what about your fight with Leo?" Grimley asked.

My hands dropped to my sides. "How do you know about that?"

He shrugged. "Fern was flying around that wing of the palace earlier. She overheard the two of you arguing. So did Otto. I suspect Lyra and all the other creatures know by now too."

"Gossiping gargoyles," I growled.

Grimley shrugged again. "It helps to pass the time." His face turned serious. "Don't worry, Gemma. Rhea has dramatically increased the security around the palace, and I've told all the gargoyles to be on high alert. Fern and Otto are out there right now, studying all the guests as they arrive for the ball. Otto will spot Milo and Wexel if they try to sneak inside the palace."

Yes, he would. Given how brutally Milo had tortured him when he was young, Otto was as familiar with—and despised—the crown prince just as much as I did.

"What are you going to do?" I asked.

Grimley got to his feet, let out a loud, jaw-cracking yawn, and stretched like an oversize cat. "I'm going to fly around the rooftops with Lyra and make sure Milo and Wexel don't use strixes to breach the palace walls. Milo might be in the city, but he won't get close to Glitnir. We'll make sure of that."

My heart swelled with love and appreciation for him and all the other creatures, and I scratched his head in between his two horns, just how he liked. "I know you will do your best, and I'm so proud of you and everyone else for protecting the palace."

Grimley nuzzled closer and licked my hand. His rough tongue scraped against my skin, but not unpleasantly so. I petted him again, and he trotted over to the balcony doors. I opened one of them, and he padded outside, hopped up onto the railing, flapped his wings, and shot up into the evening sky.

The gargoyle sailed away, as light as a feather floating on the breeze, while I remained on the balcony, firmly grounded in my worry.

I closed the balcony door, fed Violet, and made sure the liladorn had plenty of water in its bowl. Then I left my chambers and went down to the main level of the palace, where throngs of people were streaming through the corridors.

The nobles, merchants, and guilders were dressed in beautiful gowns and formal jackets, and they glided past me like glittering butterflies, with sapphires, diamonds, rubies, and other jewels flashing around their necks, wrists, and fingers. I also spotted several gladiators who had triumphed in the tournament earlier today. They too sported gowns and jackets, with the colors and crests denoting their respective troupes. Along the walls, the royal guards stood at attention, their hands on their swords, keeping watchful eyes on the crowd.

People waved, called out, and chattered to each other as they headed toward the throne room. The audible conversations were just as loud as they had been in the arena earlier in the day, and of course, dozens of silent musings flew through the air and droned in my ears like clouds of bees.

Can't wait to see what desserts the cook masters have made for the ball . . .

Hope I get to dance with Lord Fleming . . .

Perhaps I can convince one of the gladiators to warm my bed tonight . . .

My gargoyle pendant heated up against my chest, straining to hold back the waves of thoughts and feelings, but for once, I didn't mind the uncomfortable sensation or the mundane babble filling my brain. They told me the people here had no murderous intentions and that the palace was secure—for now.

Still, the crowd reignited my headache, so I turned a corner and stepped into another hallway, taking a less crowded route to the throne room—

"You look beautiful tonight," a low, familiar voice murmured. "Then again, you always look beautiful, whether you are covered with sweat and dust in the gladiator arena or silently skulking through the shadows."

I stopped and peered through a pair of open doors into one of the palace libraries. Reiko was standing in front of a fireplace along with Kai.

He was right. She did look beautiful in a long, tight gold gown patterned with tiny emerald-green dragon faces. Her hair flowed down past her shoulders like silky black ribbons, while smoky shadow and liner brought out her green eyes and crimson berry balm stained her lips. A gold dragon pendant hung from the gold chain around her neck. Emeralds glittered as the dragon's eyes, while rubies and diamonds spewed out of its mouth, as though it were breathing jeweled fire and smoke. A gold ring shaped like a flying dragon, complete with matching jewels, stretched across all four fingers of her left hand, as was the popular Ryusaman style.

Kai was wearing a long, formal crimson coat studded with ruby buttons. Dragon faces done in a slightly lighter red paisley pattern shimmered all over the fabric, making it seem as though he was about to morph into his larger, stronger form. The glow from the flickering flames accentuated his black hair, along with his golden eyes, adding to his handsome aura. The red dragon on his neck was peering down at the green one on Reiko's hand, which was admiring it in return.

Reiko let out a low, sultry laugh. "You're just saying I'm beautiful because you want to repeat what we did at the Summit."

A wicked grin spread across Kai's face. "Absolutely. Is it working?"

Reiko stepped closer to him and laid her hand on his heart. "Why don't you kiss me, and we'll find out?"

Kai's grin widened, and he bent down and lowered his lips to hers. Reiko's fingers dug into his coat, and passion erupted off them both, burning even more fiercely than the flames crackling in the fireplace.

Equal parts happiness and sorrow flooded my heart. I was glad the two of them had found their way back to each other, but their light, playful teasing was a stark contrast to my earlier argument with Leonidas, and more than a few swords of jealousy stabbed into my chest.

Voices sounded, and some nobles appeared farther down the hallway. I didn't want them to disturb Reiko and Kai's private moment, so I flicked my fingers and the library doors silently swung shut. Then I continued to the throne room.

The long gray carpet from this morning's gladiator introductions had been removed, and the stone floor had been polished to a shiny gloss. To my right, people were meandering along the refreshment tables, filling plates with sweet cakes and other treats. To my left, several musicians were playing violins, flutes, and other instruments, while other folks whirled around the dance floor, matching their steps to the soft, dreamy music. Servants carrying platters filled with goblets of cider, sangria, and other spirits circulated through the crowd, while guards were spaced along the walls, ready to spring into action at the faintest hint of trouble.

Father and Rhea were among the dancing couples, although Rhea kept looking around, as if she were using their waltz to scan the throne room for potential threats, rather than truly enjoying the music and motion. Grandfather Heinrich was standing at the bottom of the royal dais, sipping sangria and talking to Lord Eichen and Alvis, although a couple of guards were lurking nearby, staying much closer to the king than normal, in case they needed to leap to his defense.

A loud, boisterous laugh near the refreshment tables caught my ear, and I spotted a group of Andvarian nobles, all men, clustered around a central figure—Delmira.

The front of her black hair had been transformed into a crownlike braid that arched across her head, while the rest of her locks hung in soft, loose waves. Lilac-colored shadow and liner rimmed her eyes, brightening their dark amethyst color, and the same pale shade of berry balm stained her lips.

Delmira was lovely enough all by herself, but her gown was truly a thing of beauty. Thin bands of black velvet had been woven together with lilac-colored ribbons to form the cap sleeves and tight, fitted bodice, as if Delmira had somehow shaped the garment out of liladorn vines. Tiny pieces of black jet glittered all over the silky lilac skirt, winking like dozens of eyes and further adding to the liladorn illusion. Her only jewelry was the liladorn ring I had made for her, which glinted on her finger like usual. I was starting to wonder if she ever took it off.

One of the Andvarian nobles let out another boisterous laugh, and Delmira chuckled along with him. Then another man stepped forward, elbowed the first noble aside, and presented her with a plate of sweet cakes. Delmira chose one, sank her teeth into it, and gave the second man a serene smile.

Despite the angry, hostile reception the Morricones had received this morning, Delmira's popularity tonight didn't surprise me. She might be a Mortan and the daughter of the most notorious person in all of Buchovia, but she was still a princess. Funny how things like titles, thrones, and money could make people overlook centuries of hostilities.

Maeven was standing a few feet away, sipping sangria and watching the admirers flutter around Delmira like bees buzzing over a particularly heady blossom. The queen was wearing a dark purple gown, and the Morricone crest—that fancy cursive *M* surrounded by a ring of strix feathers—stretched all the way across her chest in glittering silver thread. Her golden hair was sleeked up into its usual bun, while dark purple berry balm stained her lips. A gorgeous crown of diamond vines, jet thorns, and amethyst spikes of lilac rested atop her head, looking like a tangle of liladorn that she had somehow tamed to make herself queen.

Maeven's lips puckered, as though she wasn't particularly pleased by the attention her daughter was receiving. Knowing Maeven, she probably already had someone picked out back in Myrkvior for Delmira to marry. Some wealthy noble or merchant whom she could control as easily as she did everything else in the Mortan court.

To my surprise, Eichen stepped out of the crowd, bowed to the Morricone queen, and gestured over at the dance floor. Maeven gave him an icy glower, but instead of wilting like a rose in the summer sun, Eichen grabbed a glass of sangria from a passing servant and stayed by the queen's side, not-so-covertly pointing at the nobles still gathered around Delmira. Knowing Eichen, he was probably sharing everything he knew about each man. From my recent visit to Oakton Manor, I knew Eichen enjoyed gossiping about the other nobles almost as much as he did recounting famous gladiator bouts—

My fingertips tingled, and a jolt of awareness skittered down my spine. I spun around, as though I was one of the people whirling across the dance floor, and my gaze landed on Leonidas.

The Morricone prince was standing beside one of the columns, as still, fierce, and beautiful as the gargoyles carved into the stone. His black hair gleamed like polished onyx, and the tips of his locks pointed slightly out and upward, reminding me of the feathers on a strix's wings. He was more in the shadows than the light, and his cheekbones and nose seemed sharper and more angular than usual. He was wearing a long, formal coat in the traditional Mortan purple, and a small Morricone crest was stitched in silver thread right over his heart.

Leonidas must have sensed my stare because he turned in my direction. His face was carefully blank, his eyes unreadable. Several weeks ago, at Maeven's birthday ball at Myrkvior,

Leonidas had danced with me in front of all the Mortan nobles, but tonight, he made no move to approach me—just as I made no move to approach him.

My heart ached, but I remained on my side of the throne room. With each passing second, Leonidas seemed farther and farther away, even though neither of us was moving, and the space between us might as well have been as wide and deep as the Cold Salt Sea.

Leonidas held my gaze a moment longer, then went over to Delmira, who was still surrounded by her flock of admirers. A couple of the men scattered at the prince's presence, but the majority held their positions. Marrying a princess could improve even the wealthiest lord's status, and a few dark, angry scowls from Leonidas weren't nearly enough to make the fortune and title hunters give up their prey.

Delmira nodded and laughed at everything the men said, but her smile kept slipping off her face, as though it were a loose screw she continually had to tighten to hold in place. She was no fool. Like me, she had heard this music many, many times before, and she knew the lords were far more interested in what she could do for them than who she was as a person. Another peril of being a princess.

And now it was time for me to play the same part. So I plastered a smile on my own face and made a lap around the throne room, speaking to Father and Rhea, then Grandfather Heinrich and Alvis, and then some of the wealthier, more important nobles, merchants, and guilders. I even danced with a few of the lords, most of whom peppered me with questions about Delmira. I should invite more princesses to Glitnir, as it was quite refreshing *not* to be the focus of everyone's attention and calculated interest for a change.

Eventually, I ended up standing beside the same column that Leonidas had earlier. He was on the other side of the throne room now, dancing with Lady Darot, an extremely wealthy—and beautiful—Andvarian merchant who owned several diamond mines. I wasn't the only one who noticed them dancing, and a group of nobles over at the refreshment tables kept glancing back and forth between me and the whirling couple.

If Darot smiles any wider at the prince, her lips are going to pop off her face . . .

Poor Glitzma. She's not half as pretty as Darot is . . .

Darot has enough diamonds in her mines to buy anything, even a marriage to a Morricone prince . . .

I gritted my teeth and managed to block out the rest of the snide thoughts, but my gargoyle pendant kept burning against my chest, and the throne room suddenly became unbearably hot and stuffy. Even worse, my magic bubbled up, stirred to life by the nobles' pettiness, as well as my own jumbled emotions.

I gritted my teeth again, trying to shove my magic down, but it kept squirting out of my grasp. I didn't want to risk having a ghosting or some other unwanted episode in the middle of the ball, so I slipped behind the column and hurried out of the throne room.

Throngs of people were crowded in the hallway outside, gossiping, laughing, and drinking. I forced myself to smile and nod to everyone who called out or toasted me with their goblets, but I didn't slow down, and I didn't stop to speak to anyone. Right now, I just needed to escape from everyone and everything inside Glitnir.

I moved from one hallway to another, my sandals *slap-slap-slap-slapping* against the floor. Eventually, I broke free of the people flocking around the throne room, wrenched open the first door I saw, and stepped outside. The chilly night air gusted over my cheeks, bringing some relief, but I kept going until I reached the Edelstein Gardens. By this point, the only other people around were the guards patrolling the perimeter, but my gargoyle pendant was still burning, and my emotions were still boiling, so I plunged into the hedge maze and followed the twists and turns to the most deserted part of the gardens—the gargoyle's right eye.

I stalked over and plopped down on my mother's memorial bench. Even through the thick fabric of my gown, the silver slats felt as cold as ice, but I welcomed the chill. Slowly, my pendant cooled against my skin, my emotions smoothed out, and my magic settled back down. I sighed with relief, my breath frosting out in a cloud before wisping away. If only the problems and obstacles between Leonidas and I would vanish as quickly and easily. But even Princess Gemma couldn't make that wish come true.

Now that my magic had calmed down, I should return to the ball, but the thought of smiling, dancing, and enduring more inane chatter further soured my mood. But I was too worried and restless to just sit here, so I got to my feet and reached out with my magic.

Grimley? Where are you? Any sign of trouble?

He answered me a few seconds later. *I'm on one of the rooftops with Lyra. No signs of trouble. All the guests have arrived, and everyone is either in or around the throne room, enjoying the ball.*

I asked the same questions of Fern and Otto, and they gave me similar reassuring responses. Everything was proceeding as normal, and Milo and Wexel didn't seem to be anywhere near Glitnir.

Frustration filled me, and I started pacing back and forth. Eventually, my steps led me over to the mausoleum, which was glittering like a gray star in the moonlight. My thoughts turned to the vision I'd had of my mother standing here and staring at the mausoleum doors. Had that only been last night? It seemed like a lifetime ago.

Still, the longer I stared at the structure, the more worry bubbled up inside me. Had that been a true vision of my mother?

One brought about by my own time magier magic? If so, then what, if anything, had Merilde been trying to tell me? Or had it just been a mirage and wishful thinking on my part?

Either way, brooding about questions I would most likely never get the answers to was pointless. I sighed again. Like it or not, it was time to return to the ball—

A gust of wind zipped through the gardens, and one of the mausoleum doors slowly swung open.

I froze, wondering if this was part of another vision—or mirage—but the door slowly creaked open a little wider. Why wasn't it locked?

My fingertips tingled in warning, and a shadow slithered up beside mine on the grass. I whirled around and dropped my hand to the dagger on my belt.

A man stood in front of me.

For a moment, I thought he was one of the royal guards, since he was wearing a dark gray cloak over a matching tunic, along with black leggings and boots. But a second, closer look revealed that his tunic was missing the Ripley royal crest and the hilt of the sword clutched in his hand was gold instead of silver. Plus, a royal guard would never skulk around the gardens with the hood of his cloak up, since that was an excellent way to be mistaken for an intruder.

As if hearing my thoughts, the man tossed back the hood and lifted his head. His short black hair glinted like ebony needles embedded in his scalp, while heavy stubble darkened his square jaw. His skin was a muted bronze in the moonlight, although his hazel eyes burned with hatred.

"Hello, Glitzma," Captain Wexel growled, then swung his sword at me.

CHAPTER FIFTEEN

I grabbed my magic, curled my hand into a fist, and yanked on the string of energy attached to Wexel's sword. The weapon flew out of the captain's hand, zipped over, and *thunked* into the pear tree close to my mother's bench, vibrating back and forth like a clock pendulum.

I growled and reached for the strings of energy around Wexel so I could toss him into the side of the mausoleum and snap his bloody spine—

The sharp point of a sword pressed into my back, making me stiffen in surprise.

"Don't move." A low, sinister voice snaked through the air. "I would hate to kill you before I'm ready."

I turned my head to the side so I could see the man standing behind me. Golden hair, tan skin, smug sneer, amethyst eyes glittering with disgust and loathing.

"Milo," I snarled. "I knew that was you in the arena earlier. I *knew* it!"

"Of course it was me. I *let* you see me, first when you were walking through the fairgrounds, and then later on, when you were sitting atop that ridiculous gargoyle monstrosity."

"Why?"

He shrugged, and the point of his sword dug a little deeper into my back. "Because I knew you would rush after me like a reckless fool. Unfortunately, you bested the man I sent to fetch you. Oh, well. You saved me the effort of killing him myself for his failure."

Fetch me? I thought of how the man in the tunnel had tried to knock my dagger out of my hand, rather than gut me with his sword. So Milo had been trying to kidnap instead of kill me. But why?

Wexel wrenched his sword out of the pear tree and stalked over to me. His eyes still burned with hatred, and an image flickered off him and filled my mind—my stabbing Corvina Du-mond with my gargoyle dagger during the Summit battle in the Caldwell Castle gardens. His rage blasted over me, heating every part of my body, as though I were standing in front of a roaring wildfire that was about to char me to ash.

Wexel's arm twitched, and his sword tipped upward, as though he was thinking about lunging forward and driving the blade into my chest. I gathered up my magic, although I didn't know if I would be able to hurl the captain away before Milo rammed his weapon into my back.

"Remember the plan," Milo warned. "We sneak in, we sneak out. Quietly, and with no bodies left behind to reveal our presence. So Gemma gets to live—for now."

Wexel kept staring at me, a muscle *tic-tic-ticcing* in his jaw as though it were a clock counting down the seconds to my death. The captain had cared about Corvina, perhaps even loved her, and he clearly wanted to murder me here and now.

"Wexel," Milo said, far more bite in his voice than before. "Don't make me regret bringing you along."

A breath hissed out between the captain's teeth, and he slowly lowered his sword to his side. "You're right. We should follow the plan—and make the bitch suffer before she dies."

My stomach clenched with dread. What plan?

"Exactly," Milo replied. "Finding Gemma here was a marvelous surprise, and we should take full advantage of this unexpected boon."

His brows creased together in thought. "Although . . . why *are* you out here? Instead of being at the ball with everyone else?"

I wasn't about to admit I'd been brooding about Leonidas and the ghostly image of my dead mother. But before I could spin some lie, he cut me off.

"It doesn't matter," Milo said. "Get the chains on her."

Wexel shoved his cloak aside, revealing a pair of dull black shackles dangling from his belt. More dread filled me. Coldiron, a metal that dampened magic. Milo had used similar shackles to restrain me in his Myrkvior workshop.

Wexel stepped forward and clamped the shackles around my wrists. The metal circles were as cold as the night air and yet strangely sticky at the same time, like leeches sucking at my skin. My stomach roiled with disgust, and even worse, my magic instantly iced over, as though it were trapped beneath the surface of a frozen winter pond. I tried to grab it, tried to punch through that ice to reach it, but it was like pounding on a gladiator shield that had absolutely no give.

Grimley! I called out in my mind. *Milo and Wexel are here! In the palace! In the gardens!*

An eerie, empty buzzing filled my ears, and the gargoyle didn't answer me. I tried calling out to Reiko and Father and even Leonidas, but no one responded.

Wexel grinned at me, then removed my dagger from my belt and slid it into a slot on his own. More frustration filled me at being left weaponless, and I struggled to remain calm and not give in to my boiling anger. That would only get me killed quicker.

Milo dropped his sword from my back and moved to stand in

front of me. "Dried fool's bane flowers have all *sorts* of uses," he said. "For example, they can greatly increase the effectiveness of coldiron. So much so that I don't need to snap a matching collar around your neck to snuff out your magic. Pity, Gemma. I would have enjoyed seeing you even further humiliated."

I ground my teeth and swallowed down an angry growl. He was right. I *was* humiliated at how quickly and easily he had taken me prisoner—and deeply worried about what he was going to do next.

Milo pursed his lips and let out a low whistle. The mausoleum door opened even wider, and three other men stepped into the gardens. Like Milo and Wexel, they were all wearing dark gray cloaks over matching tunics, mimicking the uniform of the royal guards.

"You used the Ripley tombs to sneak into the palace," I accused in a harsh voice.

"Of course," Milo replied. "My man at the arena was supposed to bring you to me, so that you could lead us through the tunnels, but we managed to find our own way here. Your familial burial grounds are quite fascinating—and extensive. Did you know the Ripley tombs feed into a series of old mines and caverns that run underneath much of Glanzen?"

"Of course I bloody know that," I snapped. "The question is, how do *you* know that?"

Another smug smile curved his lips. "I can't reveal all my secrets at once, Gemma. What would be the fun in that?"

My hands curled into fists, and my entire body hummed with the desire to punch him in the face. Wexel sidled forward, his fingers flexing over the hilt of his sword, and I forced myself to rein in my violent urges.

The other three Mortans moved forward, and several soft *tink-tink-tinks* rang out from the bulging knapsacks strapped to each man's back. They must all be mutts with strength magic to carry such heavy loads. Wexel went over and fished a similar knapsack out of the shadows around the mausoleum.

Tink-tink-tink.

Tink-tink-tink.

Tink-tink-tink.

Wexel and the three other men drew closer, and the noise grew louder, morphing into a distinctive sound, one that reminded me of the first time I had seen the captain several weeks ago in Blauberg.

Dread swept over my body like an icy rain, chilling me to the bone. "You brought tearstone arrows here. Why? To kill more gargoyles?"

A merry laugh tumbled out of Milo's lips. "Is that what you think I'm doing with my arrows?"

I shrugged, and he laughed again, the sound even more mocking than before.

"Don't get me wrong. Killing gargoyles is quite amusing. At first, they're so confident, so certain that nothing can penetrate their stone skin." Milo smiled, and his teeth glinted like white spears in the moonlight. "But they quickly learn that my tearstone arrows are the exception to the rule. It's fascinating to watch the gargoyles thrash around, trying to escape the pain I inflict on them."

I had to dig my nails into the scars in my palms to keep from lunging forward and trying to choke him to death with my bare hands.

"But no, Gemma," Milo continued. "I'm not planning to kill any of your gargoyles. Not tonight, anyway. Tomorrow, though, well, that will be a different story—for everyone in Glanzen, gargoyle and human alike."

Milo jerked his head at Wexel and the other three men. "Let's go. I want to be in position before the evening's speeches start in the throne room."

The three men nodded and headed toward the hedge maze. Milo followed them.

Wexel clamped his hand on my upper arm and snapped his sword up. I jerked back, but I wasn't fast enough to keep the blade from grazing my left cheek and opening up a deep cut. I hissed with pain, and he tightened his grip, his fingers digging into my skin.

The captain glared at me, his hazel eyes still hot with hate. "You try to run or whisper so much as the smallest sound, and I will cut out your tongue—before I remove your head from your shoulders." He stepped even closer, and his breath—warm, sour, and rotten—brushed up against my face. "Give me a reason, any reason at all, and I'll be more than happy to send you to join your dead ancestors in that fucking tomb. Understand?"

The wound in my cheek throbbed, and warm, wet blood slid down my face. I nodded.

"Good," Wexel hissed. "Now move."

The captain tightened his grip, and I had no choice but to march forward toward my own death.

Not only did Milo somehow know about the Ripley tombs, but he also knew each path to take in the hedge maze, and he never hesitated or wavered, not even for an instant.

I frowned. Who had told him so much about the inner workings of Glitnir? Was there a traitor among the nobles at court? Had Milo—or even Maeven—planted a Mortan spy among the servants or guards? Those questions and a dozen more flitted through my mind, but given Wexel's threat, I kept quiet.

We exited the hedge maze. Once again, Milo seemed to know exactly where he was going, and he took a shadow-cloaked path that ran by a balcony that led into the throne room. Even more people were crowded inside than before, talking, eating, drinking, and dancing. Music and laughter trilled through the air, punctuated by the soft *tink-tink-tinks* from Wexel and the other Mortans' knapsacks.

Milo stopped and peered in through the glass doors lining the balcony. "Look at them," he purred, smug satisfaction coloring his words. "Laughing and drinking and gossiping like they're truly *safe* here. Fools. In less than an hour, they'll all be dead."

A shiver swept down my spine, but I made my voice as strong as I could. "Even with me as a prisoner, you still won't get into the throne room, much less murder everyone inside. There are too many guards."

Milo chuckled. "Whoever said I wanted to get into the throne room? I have a far more interesting destination in mind."

He moved on, and once again, Wexel forced me to follow, with the other three men closing ranks behind us.

Eventually, Milo reached another door and slipped inside the palace. From there, he quickly moved from one corridor to another. Everyone was at the ball, so this section of the palace was empty, even of guards. How was he going to kill everyone when they were all still in the throne room? Where was he bloody *going*?

A few minutes later, Milo started down a set of steps—the same steps I had come down last night—and a horrible suspicion filled my mind. Sure enough, the crown prince didn't stop until he reached the doors to the Ripley royal treasury.

He tilted his head to the side and stared at the double doors, his gaze lingering on the gargoyle crest that stretched across the stone. "Excellent. They're just as Dahlia described them."

Shock zipped through me. "Dahlia? As in Dahlia Sullivan?"

He cocked a mocking eyebrow at me. "Yes, Dahlia Sullivan. Unless King Heinrich had some other Mortan mistress that I don't know about?"

I glared at him, but Milo ignored my dirty look and turned back to the doors.

"Uncle Maximus wasn't the only one who wrote journals," he said. "All the members of the Bastard Brigade recorded their exploits. All the journals are in my mother's private library in Myrkvior—except for this one. I stole it several months ago. I don't think Mother ever realized that it was missing."

He reached into one of his cloak pockets and pulled out a small book with a light purple cover. He thumbed through a few pages, which were filled with notes and drawings. I recognized the handwriting, as well as the images. The mausoleum, the hedge maze, the royal treasury. Dahlia Sullivan had written about all those things and much more.

"I always thought Dahlia's journal was the most important one," he continued. "After all, she was the only member of the Bastard Brigade who actually managed to infiltrate the Glitnir court and stay there for decades. Why, Dahlia probably knew just as much about the palace as you do, Gemma. Time to find out."

Milo snapped the book shut and slid it back into his pocket. I tensed, thinking he was going to order me to open the doors, which I would *never* do, but to my surprise, he stepped up to them himself.

A bit of hope flared in my heart. He couldn't possibly know the correct sequence of jewels. As soon as he tripped the venom trap in the glass teeth, I would wrench free of Wexel, bowl over the other three men, and run. With any luck, I could scream loudly enough for one of the guards to hear me—

Left horn. Right eye. The center tooth. Right horn. Left eye.

Milo pressed in on the various parts of the crest. He hesitated a moment, then hit the gargoyle's nose to complete the sequence. He scuttled back, but the locks *click-click-clicked* one after another, and the doors opened as easily for him as they had for me last night.

Smug triumph filled his face. "I was right. Dahlia's journal *was* the most important one."

"You did it," Wexel said in a low, reverent voice. "You got us into the Ripley royal treasury."

The other three men were just as stunned as the captain, and they all kept blinking and blinking, as if they weren't sure this was actually happening. But for me, it was all so painfully real—a nightmare come to life.

"Of course," Milo replied, his voice dripping with arrogance. "I always do *exactly* what I promise. I've told you all along I was going to destroy Andvari, and now I can finally put my plan into action."

He smirked at Wexel and the other three men, then focused on me. "But first, it's time for a tour, and we have the perfect person to guide us." He swept his hand out to the side. "Lead the way, Gemma."

Once again, I had no choice but to do as commanded, so I swallowed my rising dread and stepped into the royal treasury, wondering what new secret Milo would reveal next—and how he was going to use them all to destroy my kingdom.

CHAPTER SIXTEEN

I walked through the front part of the treasury. The crowns, tiaras, necklaces, rings, and bracelets were still perched on their velvet pillows, and they all glimmered just as brightly as they had when I'd been in here last night.

Wexel let out a low, appreciative whistle, while the other three men looked around with wide eyes. Despite the coldiron shackles dampening my magic, I could clearly feel the greed blasting off all three of them. The Mortans *whooped* with excitement, then rushed forward, smashed several cases, and pocketed the jewels inside.

Milo also glanced around at the dazzling displays, but instead of greed, his nostrils flared in disgust. "Useless trinkets."

A ball of purple lightning popped into his hand, and he reared back and threw it at a crown that had belonged to Queen Armina Ripley. The glass case shattered, the stone pedestal cracked into chunks, and the crown dropped to the floor and tumbled away in a swirl of silver and sapphires. The soft, distinctive *tink-tink-tinks* of the metal and jewels striking the flagstones eerily echoed the sounds of the tearstone arrows still rattling around in the Mortans' knapsacks.

I flinched at the noise, along with the destruction, but Wexel brandished his sword, forcing me to move forward. Milo fell in step beside me. The three Mortans grabbed a few more jewels, then followed us.

We quickly moved through the first few sections of the treasury. Milo barely glanced at the ceremonial robes, statues, paintings, and cases filled with books, although his interest piqued when we reached the armory. He meandered around that section, studying the swords, shields, and daggers, as did Wexel and the other three Mortans. This time, greed blasted off all five men. Milo eyed a sword made of solid gold and crusted with rubies as though he wanted to slip it into his pocket and hope no one would notice he had swiped it.

Wexel was far more discerning. He released my arm, sheathed his sword, and roamed around the armory, muttering *no-no-no* before finally stopping in front of a collection of weapons, jewels, and other objects. He glanced over his shoulder at Milo, who was still lusting after that gold sword, then plucked something off a shelf and stuffed it into his pocket, although I couldn't make out what it was.

"Going from murder to thievery seems like a big step down for you, captain," I drawled.

Wexel growled, surged forward, and punched me. Pain erupted in my jaw, and white stars exploded in my eyes. The force of his mutt strength knocked me back, and I blindly reached out, trying to break my fall.

My hands landed on something cold and hard, and I latched onto the object and used it to steady myself. I blinked, and Queen Armina's armor came into focus. The silver breastplate was still posed on its wooden mannequin, along with the two matching gauntlets.

Wexel dug his hand into my hair, yanking me away from the armor. He spun me around, forced me up against the wall, and drew back his fist to punch me again. I grabbed the long chain connecting my shackles, determined to smash it into his throat—

"Enough!" Milo's voice rang out in a clear command. "I have a far more delicious death in mind for Gemma than you merely pummeling her into a bloody smear."

Wexel's fist hovered in the air, waving back and forth like a flag in a stiff breeze. Then all the wind went out of the captain, and he lowered his hand to his side. "You say one more fucking word, and I'll cut out your tongue," he growled.

"No, you won't," I snarled back. "Not until your master lets you off your leash—if he ever does."

Wexel glowered at me, even more hate burning in his eyes than before, but he made no move to attack me again. We both knew I was right and that he wouldn't dare do any real, lasting damage without Milo's consent.

Unfortunately for me, that consent was coming sooner rather than later.

Milo stepped up and sneered at the armor, which was still wobbling back and forth on its mannequin. "I still can't believe Armina Ripley defeated the Morricones and all their men and strixes wearing what amounts to a tin can on her chest. Another useless trinket."

More purple lightning flared on his fingertips, and he blasted the armor the same way he had Armina's crown. The wooden mannequin flew backward and slammed into the wall. The arms cracked off, but the chest slowly slid down to the floor, as though it were a real person who had just been mortally wounded.

Milo's magic scorched the wood, and the resulting smoke blackened the silver breastplate, but those tiny bits of blue embedded in the armor grew darker and darker, until they were gleaming like sapphire stars amid the rest of the ruined display.

Matching bits of blue also gleamed in the gauntlets, which had landed nearby and were still attached to the mannequin's broken arms.

My eyes narrowed. Those weren't sapphires—they were shards of tearstone.

Despite all the times I had studied the armor, I had never realized what the bits of blue truly were. Then again, I had never seen them blasted with magic before either. But Milo's lightning had brought out all those flecks, and the tearstone had deflected his power, keeping the three pieces of armor from being damaged, like the wooden mannequin had been.

Strange. Tearstone was often crafted into swords, shields, daggers, and other weapons, but it also had a tendency to shatter, which is why I'd never heard of it being used to make armor. But if you were going to make tearstone armor, then why use such small shards? Why not craft the entire breastplate out of the ore instead of just adding slivers of it to the silver? The whole thing seemed extremely odd.

"Aw, are you upset Milo ruined another one of your precious treasures?" Wexel said in a mocking voice. "I'd be much more worried about him doing the same thing to *you*, Glitzma."

I eyed the broken, smoking mannequin, and I couldn't stop myself from shuddering. As much as I hated to admit it, the captain was right. Milo could easily do the same thing to me, especially given the coldiron shackles still dampening my magic. If I had any hope of surviving, then I needed to find some way to escape from the Mortans and remove the shackles, or at least get my hands on a weapon. My gaze dropped to my gargoyle dagger, which was still dangling from Wexel's belt.

He grabbed my arm and pulled me forward. I slammed into his chest, bounced off, and fell to my knees. Several wooden splinters from the mannequin sliced through my gown and pricked my skin, making me hiss.

"Quit fumbling around," Wexel snapped.

"Then quit yanking me around like a bloody rag doll," I snapped back.

He rolled his eyes, clamped his hand around my arm again, and hauled me upright. Once again, I stumbled forward and plowed into his chest. At the same time, I kicked out, driving the toe of my sandal into his left ankle as hard as I could. He growled and hopped around, although he didn't release his grip on my arm.

"Whoops," I chirped. "Clumsy me."

"Enough!" Milo barked out again. "We have a schedule to keep."

The crown prince strode away, with the other three men following behind him. Wexel's face darkened with anger, but he tightened his grip and pulled me along.

My hands were still chained in front of me, but the captain didn't seem to realize I'd plucked my dagger off his belt the second time I'd gotten close to him. A little trick Xenia had taught me years ago.

I quickly flipped the weapon around and slid the blade in between the shackle and my right wrist. To my surprise, the tearstone blade pressing against my skin lessened the effects of the coldiron, and a bit of my magic bubbled back up, although it was as weak, thin, and fragile as a strand in a spiderweb. Still, even that faint thread of power lifted my spirits and hardened my resolve.

Milo took the lead and swiftly moved through the rest of the treasury until he reached the section filled with the metal carts and wooden pallets piled high with tearstone. Once again, Wexel let out a low, appreciative whistle, although the other three men gave the ore bored looks. They weren't nearly as impressed with the tearstone as they had been with the jewels in the front of the treasury.

Milo drifted forward. His eyes lit up with delight, and a wide smile stretched across his face as he looked out over the thousands and thousands of pounds of raw ore. His fanatical expression made another shiver ripple down my spine.

"There's even more tearstone here than I imagined," he purred. "Excellent. It will cause even more destruction than I anticipated."

I frowned. "What are you talking about? Didn't you come here to *steal* the tearstone? That's what you've been doing for months now. Killing Andvarians and stealing all the tearstone in their possession."

Another merry laugh slithered out of Milo's lips and splattered all over me like coral-viper venom. "That's your problem, Gemma. You never think *big enough*. It's going to be the death of you, tonight, as a matter of fact."

He snapped his fingers. "Start with the arrows."

Wexel slung his knapsack down onto the floor. The other three Mortans did the same thing, then started pulling arrows out of the bags. Razor-sharp tips, oversize arrowheads lined with hooked barbs, short shafts. These weapons looked exactly the same as the tearstone arrows Milo had tortured me with at Myrkvior and equipped Corvina Dumond's fighters with at the Summit.

Wexel shoved me over to one of the other Mortans, who clamped his hand around my upper arm to hold me in place. Then the captain and the other two men grabbed fistfuls of arrows and spread out. One by one, they used their mutt strength to drive the arrows into the biggest chunks of tearstone in the carts and on the pallets. It didn't take long, and by the time they were done, at least one arrow glinted in every single section.

"Now the wire," Milo ordered.

One of the men plucked a fat spool of wire out of his knapsack and handed it to Wexel. The captain circled the room, hooking the wire to the end of first one arrow, then another, then another, as though the weapons were pieces of popped corn being strung up on a yule tree. More confusion filled me. If Milo wasn't here to steal the tearstone, then what was he doing? What was the point of all this?

Wexel finished with the arrows, then backed up, feeding out the rest of the wire and letting it fall to the floor. The captain tossed aside the empty spool, walked over, and handed Milo the very end of the wire.

Milo admired the wire for a moment, then held it out where I could see it. "In case you were wondering, this is firewire."

My stomach clenched with fresh dread. Firewire was just what its name implied—a special kind of thin black wire that had been coated with a magier's fire. It was mostly used to ignite fireworks or blast through thick seams of rock in mines. Some thieves and bandits also used it to break into vaults, destroy train tracks, and the like.

"Tell me, Gemma," Milo purred. "Have you ever seen lightning in a bottle?"

I shook my head, not sure what he was really asking.

"It's an experiment my mother showed me when I was a boy. Back when she used to call me her little prince of lightning." Memories darkened Milo's eyes, and a strange, almost wistful look filled his face. After a few seconds, he shook his head, as if flinging off whatever soft thoughts had invaded his mind and heart.

"But I always had much more fun conducting the experiment with Uncle Maximus. He would get me to put a spark of my lightning magic into a glass bottle and stopper it up tightly. Then we would sit the bottle on a table in his workshop and watch while the lightning inside grew and grew."

I frowned. "What does that matter? Your arrows are made of tearstone, not lightning."

Milo snapped his fingers. "Exactly my point! For years, I wondered how I could amplify my magic, just like we did with the bottle experiment. And I finally figured it out, with the help of some of Maximus's old journals."

I flashed back to all the journals, papers, and notes in Milo's workshop. I hadn't understood much of the information, but King Maximus's signature had been scrawled across many of the pages.

"You already know my tearstone arrows conduct magic," Milo said. "Especially since I tortured you with some of them and my lightning in Myrkvior."

Hot sparks of phantom pain erupted in my fingertips, while the sounds of my own screams rang in my ears.

"Then, at the Summit, Corvina told you how I also coated the arrows with dried fool's bane, in order to make them conduct as much magic as possible."

"What are you going to do?" I asked, that sick, sick feeling flooding my stomach again.

"The same simple experiment I did as a boy—just on a much, much larger scale," Milo replied, his smile even wider and far more chilling than before. "When you put lightning in a bottle, it bounces back on itself almost faster than the eye can follow. Each strike against the glass adds more energy, more power, more strength to the lightning. It's quite beautiful to look at, until . . ."

His voice trailed off, and he smirked at me.

"Until what?" I asked, wanting to know and yet fearing the answer.

He waggled his fingers, and purple lightning danced across his knuckles. "Until the bottle breaks."

My gaze snapped from one arrow to another, along with the firewire strung between the weapons, all of which circled the carts and pallets filled with tearstone. That chill intensified, morphing into an icy river of worry snaking down my spine.

"The royal treasury is your glass bottle," I whispered.

"Exactly!" Milo beamed at me, then flung his hands out wide. "King Heinrich did me a grand favor, storing all this tearstone here. Even better, it's all sitting right underneath the throne room where that insipid gladiator ball is taking place."

My head snapped up, and I studied the high ceiling, thinking about where we were in relation to the rest of the palace. He was right. This part of the treasury *was* under the throne room, directly beneath the dais where my grandfather was probably sitting right now, delivering his remarks for the evening.

"Do you know what the quickest way to conquer a kingdom is, Gemma?" Milo sneered at me again. "Crush its heart. Another lesson Uncle Maximus taught me. After tonight, you and the rest of the Ripleys will be dead, along with your precious gargoyles, and Glitnir will be nothing more than a smoking crater."

CHAPTER SEVENTEEN

Milo's words echoed in my mind over and over again, booming as loudly as the raucous calliope music had blasted through the arena earlier today. Horror bloomed in my heart, even as that icy chill sank into my bones.

Despite the coldiron shackles still clamped around my wrists, another bit of my magic bubbled up. The treasury around me flickered, and suddenly, I was standing at the edge of the Edelstein Gardens. Piles of cracked, scorched stones stretched out in front of me, smoke wisping off them and filling my nose with an acrid stench. The smoke slowly dissipated, revealing hands and feet, and arms and legs, and heads and chests sticking out from beneath the rubble like tombstones marking the graves of everyone who'd been in the throne room.

My gaze snapped from one body part to another, and my stomach roiled as I recognized pieces of all the people I loved. The crown that had been on Grandfather Heinrich's head. The matching signet ring on Father's hand. The ruby-studded sword still clutched in Rhea's fingers. The dark gray jacket Alvis had been wearing. Reiko's gold dragon pendant nestled in the center of Kai's crimson coat. The long purple coat Leonidas had been sporting, the silver Morricone crest spattered with his blood—

No! I screamed in my own mind, and shoved the vision away with all my might. The weak flare of magic snuffed out, and the treasury solidified around me again, but my heart continued to pound with fear, horror, and dread. For once, my time magier power had shown me a vision of the future—one I had no idea how to prevent from becoming a reality.

"Once Glitnir is reduced to rubble, it will be easy for my men to slip out of their hiding place and take the city," Milo said, dark satisfaction rippling through his voice. "And once I have Glanzen and all its wealth, I can buy even more mercenaries. First, I'll conquer the rest of Andvari, then turn my attention to the other kingdoms."

He paused, and another smug smile stretched across his face. "I'll conquer Morta last. Assuming my mother somehow manages to survive the explosion, I'll let her sit on her throne for a little while longer and then I'll take it from her, with some help from my new friends."

New friends? What did he mean by that? I had no idea, but it didn't really matter right now. All that did was stopping Milo's experiment before he destroyed everything and everyone I loved.

The crown prince gave me another evil grin, then turned to Wexel. "Are you ready?"

Wexel nodded and patted his pockets. "Don't worry. I've got the matches here somewhere . . ."

The man guarding me focused on the captain, and his grip on my arm loosened, just a bit. I slowly, carefully dropped my hands down in front of me as far as they would go and slid my dagger out from between the shackle and my wrist. Then I flipped the weapon around into its natural position in my hand, still hiding it from sight.

"A-ha!" Wexel called out in triumph, and yanked a small box out of one of his pockets. "Here they are—"

I yanked my arm free of the guard's grip, whirled around, and stabbed my dagger into his throat.

The man's eyes bulged, and a scream spewed out of his mouth, although it abruptly cut off as I ripped the dagger out of his throat. The Mortan gurgled and dropped to the floor. I jammed the tip of the dagger into the simple lock on the shackle on my left wrist, trying to pop it open and free myself from the coldiron—

My fingertips tingled in warning, and I spotted a bright flare of purple out of the corner of my eye. On instinct, I threw myself down onto the dead Mortan, then grabbed him and rolled over so that his body was in front of mine.

Crack!

A bolt of purple lightning slammed into the man's back, making him thrash against me, even though he was already dead. I shuddered, but I jammed the dagger tip into the lock again.

"Kill her!" Milo yelled. "Before she gets free!"

Screech!

The lock opened, and the shackle dropped from my left wrist. I quickly repeated the process on the other shackle and was rewarded with another satisfying *screech*. The instant the coldiron fell away from my skin, the rest of my magic came rushing back. Anger and determination filled me, and I grabbed the shackles; shoved the dead, scorched guard away; and scrambled to my feet, my dagger still in my other hand.

The other two Mortans drew their swords and rushed forward. I waited until the closest one was in range, then reared my hand back and tossed the shackles at him. As soon as the coldiron left my hands, I took hold of it with my magic and slammed it into the first man's face, making him howl with pain.

The shackles started to fall to the ground, but I took hold of them with my magic again. I curled my fingers into a tight fist, and the attached chain snaked up and wrapped around the man's throat like a ribbon on a yuletide present. A twist of my hand tightened the chain, crushing his windpipe, and the Mortan fell to the floor, his face turning blue as he gasped for air he was never going to get.

The second man swung his sword, but I ducked his attack and sliced my dagger across his stomach. He howled and tumbled to the floor, clutching his guts, which were more outside his body than in it now. A flick of my fingers and a blast of my magic cracked his head against the stone floor, and his cries abruptly cut off, even as blood oozed out from beneath his body.

Something whistled in my direction, and I spun away from it. Wexel's sword slammed into a chunk of tearstone sitting atop one of the pallets. Shards flew up out of the ore and stung my cheek like tiny bees, but I twirled my dagger around in my hand and surged toward the captain to kill him too—

A bright flare of purple once again caught my attention. I stopped and whirled to my left.

Sometime during the fight, Milo had stretched the firewire out as far as it would go, and he was now standing at the opposite end of the room. The firewire was lying at his feet, and Milo held his right hand up, showing me the purple lightning dancing along his fingertips again.

"Nice try, Gemma," he crowed. "But once again, you're too late."

He flicked his fingers, and his lightning hit the end of the firewire. With a loud, sickening *hiss*, the wire turned a hot, molten purple and started to burn, heading straight for the tearstone in the center of the treasury.

I froze, more horror filling my body, and my magic chose that moment to bubble up again. The air around me shimmered, morphing back into that scene of ruined rubble and broken bodies, that awful vision of the future that was oh so close to becoming a reality. Once again, I gritted my teeth and shoved the image away.

I charged forward, determined to cut the firewire before it reached the first tearstone arrow—

A hand dug into the back of my gown, and I was lifted up off my feet and tossed aside. My back slammed into one of the pallets, and the jagged chunks of tearstone punched into my spine like spiked hammers. I groaned and stumbled forward, my knees cracking against the floor.

A shadow fell over me, and I looked up to see Wexel raising his sword, ready to keep his promise to separate my head from my shoulders—

"Leave her!" Milo ordered. "She can't stop it now! We have to get out of here before the treasury explodes!"

Wexel hesitated, clearly torn between killing me and escaping. An angry snarl spewed out of the captain's lips, but he turned and sprinted toward Milo.

"Goodbye, Glitzma!" Milo called out. "How very appropriate you're going to die down here in the middle of the wealth you Ripleys love so much. But your jewels won't save you from this. Nothing will!"

He snapped off a mocking salute to me, then he and Wexel both ran, leaving me alone to watch the firewire burn.

I scrambled to my feet, but I didn't bother chasing after Milo and Wexel. I also didn't run away like they had. Even if I could somehow get all the way up to the throne room, I would never be able to evacuate everyone from the ball in time. Milo's plot was far more ambitious than I had ever imagined, and he was going to destroy the palace—unless I found some way to stop his horrific experiment.

Leo! Reiko! Grimley! Delmira! Lyra! Can you hear me?

Father! Rhea! Alvis! Grandfather! Milo has set a trap in the treasury! Get everyone out of the throne room! Now!

I called out again and again, but no one answered my frantic cries. Of course not. I was too far away, too deep underground, and surrounded by too much tearstone for them to hear me.

I was on my own.

So I sucked in a breath and ran over to where the firewire was still burning. The purple lightning was snaking along the black strand like a coral viper, quickly slithering closer and closer to the first pallet of tearstone. My best chance—maybe my only chance—was to cut the wire before it reached the first arrow.

As if sensing my plan, the lightning zipped along the strand, moving even faster than before. Once again, I lunged forward and stretched out with my magic—and once again I was too bloody late.

The lightning hit the first tearstone arrow.

For an instant, everything went dark. The lightning, the firewire, the arrow. They were all cold and still, and hope surged up in me that Milo's magic had fizzled out—

Whoosh!

A light flared, so bright, hot, and intense that I had to squint to see what was happening. For a moment, the light gray tearstone arrow turned a wicked purple—the same purple as Milo's lightning magic and the dried fool's bane flowers.

Then it ignited.

The purple arrow burned even brighter, hotter, and more intensely than before. Then, in the next heartbeat, its color deepened to midnight blue—the same midnight blue as the arrow Alvis had showed me in his workshop yesterday. Milo's lightning spread from that arrow into another chunk of tearstone, and soon, it too was glowing the same dark, dangerous blue and vibrating with ominous intent, like a rattlesnake about to strike. Even worse, the magic kept going, infecting another piece of tearstone.

And another piece . . . and another piece . . .

Meanwhile, Milo's purple lightning continued to snap, crack, and sizzle around the first arrow it had touched. The arcing bolts of magic clipped the next two adjoining strands of firewire, igniting them, and sending the power shooting over to the next arrows attached to the black strings.

Horrified, my gaze zipped past those arrows to all the other ones Wexel and his men had embedded in the chunks of tearstone. Milo was right. With just the arrows, the firewire, and his lightning magic, he had transformed the supposedly indestructible treasury into a fragile glass bottle—one that was bound to shatter sooner rather than later.

The purple lightning would just keep going and going, igniting all the firewire, and spreading Milo's magic into each and every piece of tearstone. The power and the pressure would build and build and build, until the tearstone couldn't contain it anymore. The magic would have to go *somewhere*, have to be released in some way, and the firewire would ensure that release was as violent as possible.

The treasury would explode.

And that was only the beginning of the damage. Not only would the explosion incinerate everything in the treasury—including me—but the walls and ceiling would also collapse, and everyone in the throne room above would either be killed in the initial blast or would tumble down here. If the fire and the fall didn't kill them, then they would either be cut to pieces by the shrapnel or crushed by the debris. Hundreds, potentially thousands, of people would die.

Unless I found some way to save them.

Fear and panic cascaded over me like an icy blizzard, threatening to freeze me in place, but I forced myself to look around, trying to figure out some way to defuse Milo's gruesome experiment—or at least lessen its deadly impact.

Whoosh!

Another arrow burned purple, then blue, and Milo's lightning zipped a little faster along the next strand of firewire. Suddenly, the answer came to me.

The arrows—I had to get rid of as many arrows as possible. I couldn't stop the magic that had already ignited, but maybe, just maybe, I could keep the amount of power to a minimum. So I sprinted over to the far side of the treasury. Given the enormous room, it took me far longer than I would have liked, but I finally reached the last arrow in the last chunk of tearstone on the last pallet.

I reached for my magic, curled my fingers into a tight fist, and yanked. That arrow flew out of the chunk of tearstone and dropped to the floor. I sucked down a breath, then started running again, yanking each arrow I came to out of the surrounding tearstone and sending them all clattering to the floor. Every few arrows, I stopped long enough to use my dagger to sever the firewire from the strands that were still ominously burning in this direction.

I repeated that process over and over again, and I managed to pry dozens of arrows out of the tearstone—but it still wasn't enough. With each arrow that ignited, the firewire burned a little hotter, brighter, and more quickly than before, and it was rapidly outpacing me. For each arrow I yanked out of the tearstone, the firewire lit up two, sometimes three more. I didn't even make it back to the middle of the room when the remaining firewire and arrows ignited all at once.

WHOOSH!

Purple lightning blasted over all the carts and pallets and boiled up into the air like a massive storm cloud. The lightning zoomed out, the bolts zigzagging from one piece of tearstone to another and turning them all that dark, ominous midnight blue. Some of the bolts bounced off the ore and zinged deeper into the treasury, like sharks zipping through the water, hungry for more fish to gobble down.

Hot sparks flew through the air like raindrops, and several of the wooden pallets started smoking. In the distance, one of the bolts slammed into a shelf filled with jewelry, making the metal slabs glow with heat. All the glass cases shattered, and several gems *pop-pop-popped!* like fireworks, the magic inside them bleeding into what was already filling the room.

My heart sank. I might have disarmed part of Milo's trap, but there was still enough lightning, enough fire and power and heat, to punch through the treasury ceiling. Not only was the tearstone absorbing Milo's magic, but it was also deflecting it onto other pieces, both attracting and repelling the lightning at the same time and adding even more magic to this already catastrophic mix.

So how could I stop it? How could I keep the treasury from exploding? How could I save everyone in the throne room? How could I save my palace, my home?

My gaze snapped back and forth, but all I saw was more and more magic, building toward an inevitable, violent conclusion like the final note in a loud, frantic symphony.

Have you ever seen lightning in a bottle? Milo's snide voice whispered through my mind. *It's quite beautiful to look at . . . until the bottle breaks.*

Until the bottle breaks . . .

Until the bottle breaks . . .

Until the bottle breaks . . .

The treasury was Milo's bottle, his way to trap all his horrid lightning in a confined space, and the carts and pallets full of tearstone were only adding to the problem, creating more and more magic with each passing second. I might not be able to extinguish the magic, but at the very least, I could remove the fuel from the fire, as Alvis had said in his workshop yesterday.

Oh, I couldn't move the tearstone away from the lightning. There was far too much of it, and it was far too heavy. But maybe, just maybe, I could move *the lightning* away from the tearstone.

Several weeks ago, during the Battle of Blauberg, I'd grabbed hold of the lightning bolts Milo had tossed at me. I'd stopped his magic from killing me, and I'd even managed to throw it all right back at the crown prince, severely injuring his hands in the process. Maybe I could do the same thing again now—or maybe the effort would kill me.

Either way, I had to try.

Still, as I stared out over the growing mass of magic, I realized I needed something to shield me from the burgeoning power or it would burn me to a crisp before I took three steps with it. I needed . . . *armor.*

An idea popped into my mind. I shoved my dagger back onto my belt, then ran past the tearstone pallets and out into the area beyond. It took me less than a minute to reach the armory and the wooden mannequin Milo had blasted with his magic earlier—the one that featured Armina's silver breastplate.

I fell to my knees, tore the breastplate off the mannequin, and dropped it down over my own head. I tied the straps as tightly as they would go, then pried the two matching silver gauntlets off the mannequin's broken arms and shoved them onto my own. Once that was done, I scrambled to my feet and sprinted back into the other room.

Even though I'd been gone less than two minutes, the magic had doubled, tripled in size, painting the treasury in an eerie purple glow. Once again, I wondered if I could actually do this, but I was out of options and time. So I drew in a breath, then let it out and walked straight into the heart of Milo's magic.

As I moved forward, I dove into that storm of emotion deep inside me, going down, down, down as though I was a kraken streaking toward the bottom of the sea. That sea was impossibly deep, and so was the well of magic inside me. At least, that's what I told myself, even if I didn't truly believe it.

Then, when I was ready, and I had gathered up as much of my own power as possible, I stopped, stretched my arms out and up, and took hold of the mass of magic crackling in front of and above me.

In an instant, my fingertips burned, sweat covered my body, and my legs trembled, threatening to buckle. I'd corralled Milo's magic in Blauberg, but a hundred—a thousand—times more power was spitting, hissing, and writhing in the treasury right now. Each and every bolt of lightning licked up against my own magic, trying to burn right through it, trying to burn right through me.

But I kept going, reaching for both the magic inside myself and the dark purple storm that was still gathering strength in front of me.

When I was younger and first learning how to use my magic, Alvis had told me to think of my power as something I could control, some small action or task that I could complete. So I did the same thing again now. I imagined taking each lightning bolt and looping it back onto itself, as though they were all part of an enormous string of purple thread I was winding back up onto a giant invisible spool suspended in between my hands.

I ignored the bright flashes, booming cracks, and acrid stench of Milo's magic. If I looked at that storm of power, if I thought about its overwhelming size and scope, then I would get distracted, waver, and lose the tenuous control I had over my own magic. So instead, I focused on one individual lightning bolt at a time. I caught one string of magic, looped it onto my invisible spool, and then moved on to the next one.

Just one more . . . just one more . . . just one more . . .

I chanted that to myself over and over again, matching my movements to my words. Grab a bolt, loop it onto the spool, then search for another one.

Grab, loop, search . . . grab, loop, search . . . grab, loop, search . . .

The seconds ticked away and bled into minutes, but I had no real sense of how much time passed. My entire world had been reduced to plucking those lightning bolts out of the air and wrestling them into submission with all the others I was already holding. I reached for yet another bolt . . . and . . . and couldn't find one.

I blinked and blinked, coming out of my self-imposed trance, and the treasury slowly came into focus around me. Every piece of tearstone was still glowing that dark, dangerous midnight blue, but without the fuel of Milo's purple lightning, the chunks of ore were no longer rattling around and ominously vibrating, as though they were going to explode at any moment.

One problem solved. A relieved sigh escaped my lips, and I dropped my gaze and examined my second, much larger worry.

I had managed to grab all the lightning bolts bouncing off the floor, walls, and ceiling and condense them down to the space between my hands. I had imagined creating a spool of thread, and that's exactly what it looked like I was holding—an oversize, misshapen spool of glowing, crackling purple threads that were writhing around like a nest of coral vipers. A strange fascination filled me, momentarily overcoming my worry, fear, and dread, and I stared straight into the heart of all that magic, all that power.

Milo was right—it *was* beautiful, one of the most beautiful things I had ever seen.

But it was also one of the deadliest, and if I didn't get rid of it soon, then it would escape my grasp, burn right through me, and explode. Hundreds of people and creatures would be killed. Father. Grandfather Heinrich. Rhea. Reiko. Kai. Grimley. Lyra. Fern. Otto. The liladorn. Delmira. Leonidas. Even Maeven.

I had to get Milo's magic out of the treasury, out of the palace, without losing control and blowing it and myself sky high. I stared down into the beautiful, writhing mass for a heartbeat longer.

Then I let out a breath and moved forward.

chapter eighteen

Once again, I focused on a small, simple task—walking.

I put one foot in front of the other, taking only one step at a time. Then I shoved the mass of magic and my body forward so that I could move my other foot and take another small step. More seconds ticked by and bled into minutes, but once again my world shrank to containing Milo's magic and moving it out of the treasury, along with my own body.

The weapons in the armory, the paintings on the walls, the books on the shelves, even the crowns and tiaras gleaming on their velvet pillows. They all seemed dull, dim, and distant compared to the power spitting, hissing, and crackling between my hands.

Sometime later, I reached the double doors that led out of the treasury. To my surprise, they were standing wide open. Milo and Wexel must not have wanted to stop long enough to lock the doors behind themselves. A relieved sigh escaped my lips. I didn't know what I would have done if the doors had been closed, and the Mortans' haste was my salvation. At least when it came to actually getting out of the treasury.

Still clutching the spool of magic, I tiptoed forward and peered out into the corridor beyond, but it was empty. Of course it was. Milo thought his plan was foolproof, and he and Wexel weren't stupid enough to stick around and risk being blown up with everyone else.

I started walking again, slowly moving from one corridor to the next. I made it through several hallways before I encountered another serious problem.

The stairs.

I chewed on my lower lip, my own salty sweat stinging my mouth. I hadn't thought I would make it out of the treasury, but now that I was here, I had no choice but to keep going. So I raised one foot and eased it forward, climbing up onto the first step—

The slight change in elevation made my head spin. My sandal slipped on the slick stone, but I locked my legs and managed to right myself. The spool of magic wobbled dangerously in front of me, like a wet glass bowl that was trying to squirt out of my grasp, but I gritted my teeth and tightened my grip on it. The burning sensation in my fingertips spread up into my hands, and even more sweat streamed down my face than before.

But I had made it onto the first step, so I put my back up against the wall, wincing at the loud scrape of the silver breast-plate against the stone. Then I sidled forward and slowly, carefully climbed onto the second step. The magic wobbled again, although not quite as wildly as before, so I kept going.

Somehow, I made it up that first flight of steps, although my heart sank as I stared at a second staircase looming in front of me. A low, frustrated growl spewed out of my mouth, although the crackling magic quickly drowned it out.

Why were there so many bloody *stairs* in the palace? I was going to have a serious conversation with Father and Grandfather Heinrich about installing more metal lifts in Glitnir.

A crazy, hysterical laugh bubbled up out of my lips. How very Glitzma of me to be thinking about installing metal lifts at a time like this. While I was at it, maybe I should consider putting a fountain in my chambers, even though all the misting water would ruin the furniture. Or perhaps I could build Violet her very own rookery, for when she finally learned how to fly. Or even give the liladorn strand in my room its very own flowerbed in the Edelstein Gardens . . .

The odd, nonsensical thoughts helped me ignore the pain burning through my hands and arms and climb the rest of the stairs. By the time I made it up the last step, I had remodeled the entire palace in my mind. Perhaps I would even implement a few of my changes—if I survived this.

Now that I had reached the ground level, another problem presented itself. Where could I go to release the magic without blowing up either the palace or myself? But I really had only one choice—the Edelstein Gardens. That was the largest open-air space in the entire palace and the only spot where I could potentially direct the magic up into the sky, where it might safely dissipate.

So I headed in that direction, slowly moving from one corridor to the next and taking the quickest route to the gardens. Eventually, I rounded a corner, and two guards standing at the far end snapped to attention. The guards drew their swords and took up defensive positions, although they quickly frowned with recognition.

"Princess Gemma?" one of the guards asked, his eyes widening in commensurate measure to how quickly his face paled. "What—what are you doing? What *is* that?"

"Open the door!" I snarled. "Now!"

The first guard continued gaping at me, but the second man darted forward and threw open a glass door.

By this point, the spool of magic hovering between my hands was lumpy and uneven, as though the threads were badly frayed. I tightened my grip on it, but one bolt of lightning slipped free, peeled off the spool, and blasted into another nearby door, shattering the glass. The two guards yelled in surprise, but I grimaced and stepped outside.

While I'd been down in the treasury, it had snowed, and a thin layer of white powder covered the flagstones. I wanted to weep as the cold wind blasted against my sweaty cheeks and flowed over my hands, relieving a tiny bit of the pain that was now burning through my entire body. A few flakes of snow fluttered down from the night sky and landed on the lightning, hissing away into nothingness. I drew in a deep breath, sucking as much air down into my lungs as I could. The crisp chill gave me the strength to keep going.

Behind me, the guards yelled at each other, but I didn't dare look back to see what they were doing. If I wavered, even for an instant, then I would lose my tenuous grip on the magic, and this entire section of the palace would still be destroyed, killing everyone inside.

So I moved away from the open door and walked across a terrace. At the edge, I ran into yet another problem—more bloody stairs. Going down the wide, flat steps was even more of a challenge than coming up the ones in the lower part of the palace had been, especially since I couldn't see where I was putting my feet. But I managed it, and I sighed with relief as my sandals landed on flat ground again.

The Edelstein Gardens loomed up in front of me. Once again, I hesitated, wondering where to go, but I still needed to get the magic as far away from the palace walls as possible, which left me with only one choice—the hedge maze.

Right, left, straight, two more rights, another left. I followed the route I had memorized long ago, and soon I ended up in the gargoyle's nose in the center of the maze. I skirted around the pond with its cattails and water lilies and finally stopped in the open space in front of the gazebo.

A breath escaped my lips and frosted away into the chilly

night air, but my relief was short-lived. I might have gotten out of the treasury, out of the palace, and away from all the people inside, but I didn't know what to do now. I didn't know how to release the spool of magic without all the lightning blowing back and immediately killing me, as well as roaring through the gardens unchecked.

All this effort, all this energy, all this bloody *pain*, and I was still going to fail, even though I was finally outside, with the night sky arcing over my head like an ebony crown studded with diamond stars.

Tears of anger and frustration streamed down my cheeks, mixing with the sweat still soaking my body, even as my magic started to wane. Another bolt of lightning slipped out of my grasp and slammed into a nearby bench, reducing the wood to splinters and spewing purple sparks, ash, and smoke up into the air.

I gritted my teeth, trying to corral the rest of the lightning, but another bolt squirted free. This one slammed into the center of the pond, turning the water an eerie, electric purple and instantly frying the water lilies and cattails.

In the distance, shouts rose up, booming even louder than the lightning strikes, but all I could see and feel was that cursed ball of magic hovering in between my shaking hands. The lightning was fighting back, desperately trying to get free, and it lashed out like a nest of yellow jackets, stinging my fingers over and over again.

Sometime during my trek, the starburst scars on my hands had split wide open and were now dripping blood, but that was a small misery compared to the other agony burning through my body. I'd always thought of my mind magier magic as a deep, endless sea, but Milo's lightning was quickly boiling away all of my power. Even if I somehow survived this, I didn't know if there would be anything left of that sea—if there would be anything left of *me*.

I took a step forward to try to physically shove the magic away and release it into the sky, but my sandal slipped on the snow-dusted grass. This time, I wasn't able to catch myself, and my right knee slammed into the ground. Pain spiked through my leg, and I listed to the side, like a ship about to sink. Try as I might to hold on, I was seconds away from toppling over, losing my grip on the magic, and dying—

A light, feathery presence brushed up against my mind, a shadow fell over me, and strong, sure hands grabbed my waist. Those hands kept me from hitting the ground, and two amethyst eyes appeared through the magic sparking and swirling between us.

"Gemma!" Leonidas yelled above the crackling lightning. "I've got you!"

"No!" I yelled back. "Let me go! Get away! Save yourself!"

His hands tightened around my waist. *Never.* His voice sounded in my mind. *I will never let you go. I will never let you fall. I will never let you fail.*

Once again, I wanted to weep, but I forced that emotion back down into the rapidly dwindling sea inside my own body. "I don't know how much longer I can contain the lightning," I rasped, my voice raw and hoarse. "It's too powerful to release by myself. I won't be able to control where it goes . . . or who it hurts."

A stubborn look filled Leonidas's face. "Then we'll do it together."

If I could have, I would have shaken my head. "No. I don't want to risk you."

"You're not risking me. I told you before that I would do anything for you."

"I don't want you to die with me!" I snapped. "I couldn't bear that."

A small smile curved the corners of his lips. "And I couldn't bear having to live without you. So let me help you, Gemma. Please."

It was that bloody *please* that did me in. I could never deny Leonidas anything he asked for, anything that was in my power to give, especially not now, when I could feel his love for me mixing and mingling with all of mine for him.

Suddenly, the fight we'd had earlier seemed so silly, so trivial, so inconsequential. I didn't tell him that I was sorry, though. I didn't have to. I knew he could feel my regret, just as I could feel his regret washing through my own body.

"Let me help you," Leonidas repeated. "Please, Gemma."

"Okay," I rasped.

Leonidas slowly released my waist, making sure I wouldn't topple over, then brought his hands up so they were level with mine.

Give me some of the lightning, his voice whispered in my mind. *Let me take some of the bolts from you. Let me ease your burden however I can.*

For the third time tonight, I focused on a small, simple task—unwinding all the magic I had gathered up in the treasury. I pictured plucking the end of one of the lightning bolts off the spool of thread and slowly unwinding it from all the others. Then, when I felt steady enough, I imagined handing that thread, that bolt, over to Leonidas.

I wasn't certain it would work—but it did.

Leonidas grabbed the bolt like it was a ribbon he was plucking out of my hair, and the magic jumped from the space between my hands to the open air in between his. Leonidas hissed, and his pain bloomed in my mind, merging with my own.

I'm so sorry, I said. *I never meant to hurt you.*

He shook his head. *It's okay. It doesn't sting nearly as badly as other things.*

I thought of all those layers of scars on his back, each one a vivid reminder of all the times Maximus had tortured him when he was a boy. Sorrow filled me, and I wanted to weep again.

It's okay. We've both been hurt, but we won't let it happen to anyone else. Not tonight. Leonidas gave me another crooked smile. *Besides, this doesn't hurt half as much as losing you would.*

My heart swelled with love for him—so much love that I thought it would burst wide open, just like the scars on my hands had. But the surge of emotion steadied me and gave me the strength to keep going, to keep fighting to save him and myself and everyone else who was counting on us, whether they knew it or not.

Leo nodded at me, as if sensing my jumbled thoughts and feelings, as well as my determination and resolve. *Give me another bolt, Gemma.*

I carefully unwound a second thread of lightning from the spool and passed it over to him. Then another one, then another one, then another one . . .

I repeated that process over and over again, until the bolts were evenly spread between us, as though we were children building a cat's cradle. I was still holding on to an incredible amount of magic, as was Leonidas, but my breath came a little easier than before, and the burning pain in my body simmered down to a more manageable level.

More and more shouts sounded, and several people rushed out of the hedge maze, although they skidded to a stop at the sight of Leonidas and I kneeling on the grass and holding the magic between us.

Father. Grandfather Heinrich. Rhea. Reiko. Kai. Alvis. Lord Eichen. Adora. Delmira. Maeven. They were all here. Several shadows swooped down from the sky and landed on the grass. Grimley. Lyra. Fern. Otto.

Father broke free of the crowd and slowly approached us,

with Reiko, Maeven, and Delmira trailing along behind him. Grimley and Lyra also loped forward.

My father stopped a few feet away. A thought flickered off him, and I saw myself through his eyes—singed hair, blackened gown, tense body. The flecks of tearstone glimmered like blue stars in the breastplate and gauntlets I was still wearing, while the silver armor itself gleamed against my red, burned, blistered skin. I shuddered. Right now, I didn't look like Princess Gemma, but rather a wax doll that had been left out in the sun and partially melted. I felt that way too, like I was just barely keeping myself from oozing down and liquefying into a puddle.

Anguish and worry rolled off Father in strong, bitter waves. Grandfather Heinrich's face was deathly pale, and he looked as though he might faint, while Rhea had her hand clapped over her mouth, as though she was trying not to vomit. Alvis, Eichen, and Adora wore similar horrified expressions. Even Kai looked stunned, as did Fern and Otto.

Reiko kept glancing back and forth between Leonidas and me, while Delmira twisted her liladorn ring around and around on her finger. Grimley and Lyra crept a little closer, their wings twitching with worry. Maeven's lips puckered, but she seemed more thoughtful than concerned, despite the obvious danger.

Determination filled my father's face, and he shoved up his jacket sleeves and stepped forward. "Give me the magic."

Maeven grabbed his arm, stopping him. "No."

Father jerked out of her grasp. "Don't try to stop me."

"You're not strong enough to control that much magic," she replied in a cold, flat voice. "But I am."

Father opened his mouth to argue, but Maeven cut him off.

"For once in your miserable life, trust me," she snapped.

"And why should I do that?" Father growled.

"Because I don't want my son to die any more than you want your daughter to perish," Maeven snarled right back at him.

Father stared at her with narrowed eyes. "If this is some trick—"

"If this is a trick, then we will *all* die," Maeven replied. "Now get out of my way, Dominic. We're wasting time."

Father glared at her, but he jerked his head in agreement and stepped aside.

Grimley growled at Maeven, and his tail lashed from side to side, the arrow on the end pointed straight at her, as though he wanted to stab her with it. Lyra trilled out a sharp warning note and nudged him with one of her wings. Grimley growled again, but his tail slowly dropped down.

Maeven ignored the two creatures and circled around Leonidas and me, examining the mass of magic still spitting, hissing, and crackling between us, as though it was an angry kite we were trying to wrestle into submission.

"Milo . . . did this . . ." I rasped between the waves of pain surging through my body. "He snuck . . . into the treasury . . . and used firewire . . . and his arrows . . . and his lightning . . . to try to make all the tearstone explode."

Understanding filled Maeven's face. "Lightning in a bottle," she murmured, appreciation rippling through her voice. "That was the very first experiment I ever showed him."

Bittersweet longing surged off her, although I couldn't tell if it was for those simpler days gone by or the fact that Milo's experiment hadn't killed me yet.

Maeven stepped forward and held out her hand to Leonidas. "Take my hand."

He shook his head. "I can't. I'll lose my grip on the lightning."

"No, you won't," she replied. "The lightning will flow to me. Magic always seeks out like magic. Trust me."

Leonidas stared up at her, the same doubt on his face that my father had shown, but he nodded and slowly climbed to his feet. The threads of magic stretched out between Leonidas and me, growing thin and taut, like strings about to snap from too much pressure. That same pressure built inside me, and I almost buckled under the force and weight of it.

The magic dipped and bobbed between us. Leonidas sucked in a breath, as did Maeven, and the two of them froze.

I gritted my teeth, shoving back against the pressure, and the ball of power slowly steadied.

"Take my hand," Maeven repeated.

Leonidas latched onto her hand. The second his skin touched hers, the magic swung around, veering away from the prince and hovering in the air in front of the queen. Not only that, but all those threads of energy brightened, as though Maeven's lightning magic was giving them even more strength and power.

Maeven held out her other hand to me. "Take my hand, Gemma."

Doubt filled me, so much bloody *doubt*, but I didn't have a choice. My own magic was almost exhausted, and I was seconds away from losing my grip on the lightning. So I forced myself to climb to my feet. Once again, those threads of magic stretched out, this time between Maeven and me, and that immense pressure settled over me again, even heavier and more painful than before. A snarl spewed out of my lips, and with the last of my strength, I reached out and grabbed Maeven's hand.

This was the first time I had ever physically touched the Morricone queen, the first time I had ever laid so much as a single finger on her. I wasn't sure what I was expecting. Perhaps for her skin to start smoking against my own given how much the two of us despised each other. But her hand was warm, strong, and certain. Even more important, some of the magic in front of me skipped over to her, easing the pressure on and around me.

As with Leonidas, the magic brightened as it hovered in

front of Maeven, and the glow of it was reflected in her amethyst eyes, as though she was made of the same pure purple lightning. Maybe she was.

The three of us stood there, hands linked, with the magic still hissing, spitting, and crackling in front of us. If I'd had the strength, I would have laughed at the irony of the situation. Despite all the times we'd tried to hurt, kill, and otherwise destroy one another over the years, Leonidas, Maeven, and I were still all twisted, tangled, and bound together, just like the threads of lightning I'd captured.

"Now what?" Leonidas said through gritted teeth, sweat dripping down his face. "How do we get rid of it without killing ourselves?"

"On my command, push the magic up, then let it go," Maeven said. "I'll do the rest. On three. One . . . two . . . three . . . push!"

Together, with my fingers still intertwined with Maeven's, I snapped both my hands up as high as they would go and shoved the mass of magic with all my might. Maeven did the same thing, along with Leonidas.

Slowly, the ball of magic rose up into the air in front of us. I kept shoving and pushing and straining with all my might. Maeven and Leonidas did as well, and the magic quickly floated higher and higher. The farther away it moved from us, the less contained it became, and bolts of lightning unraveled from the spool and shot out, heading straight toward Grandfather Heinrich and everyone else gathered on the grass—

Father stepped up and hurled his own blue lightning at the purple bolts, knocking them away from the people and creatures, and sending them shooting into the hedges. The evergreen bushes caught fire, but Eichen waggled his fingers, causing the bushes to clap together like thorny green hands and snuff out the flames.

"That's it!" Maeven yelled over the loud, continuous cracks

of thunder that were now rumbling through the air. "One final push, then let it go. On three. One . . . two . . . three . . . now!"

With a final blast of power, I shoved the lightning as far away as I could. Maeven and Leonidas did the same thing, and the mass of it shot up into the sky faster than a strix taking flight.

The magic kept rising and rising and rising, even as more and more and more bolts slipped off the spool of power. Maeven watched it with a critical expression. Then, at the last second, just before the spool of magic would have completely unraveled, she snapped up her hands and shot her own bolts of lightning at it.

BOOM!

The mass of magic exploded.

In an instant, the entire sky turned that eerie, electric purple that had been filling my eyes and burning my body for so long. Somehow, I could see every wicked bolt, every sharp fork, every jagged shard of power. Most of the bolts zipped harmlessly away in the night sky, but a few zinged downward, and several *crack-crack-cracks* rang out, as the lightning slammed into some of the palace walls and towers.

A few minutes later, the last of the lightning dissipated, although the sky remained that bright, eerie purple, and an electric charge filled the air, along with a smoky, acrid scent. Or perhaps that was the stench of my own fried flesh filling my nose. I couldn't quite tell.

Either way, it was finally over.

The magic was gone—and so was I.

I didn't feel my legs buckle, but they must have, because I suddenly found myself down on the ground, flat on my back, wondering how I had gotten there.

"Gemma! Gemma!" Leonidas's voice drifted over to me, but he seemed far away.

I rolled my head to the side. Leonidas was on his knees beside me, but my gaze skipped past him and focused on Maeven, who was towering over me. I stared at the queen, struggling to focus on her face, although her features quickly blurred, and all I could really see were her amethyst eyes.

They glinted like stars for a moment, then the color shrank to pinpricks. Even that little bit of light vanished, and I tumbled headlong into the darkness that had been trying to claim me for so very long.

PART THREE

THE GARGOYLE QUEEN

CHAPTER NINETEEN

One moment, I was drifting along in the soothing black void of unconsciousness. The next, I was right back in the Edelstein Gardens.

I blinked, and suddenly, I was standing next to the gazebo, staring down at my own body lying on the grass. I sighed. Even though I didn't feel so much as a trickle of magic in myself right now, I was still ghosting. It sometimes happened when I was severely injured—or dying, like I was right now.

My gaze roamed over my still form, and the sight made me grimace. I looked even worse than the vision I'd gotten off my father a few minutes ago. The ends of my brown hair were singed and uneven, as were the sleeves of my gown. Large holes dotted my skirt where the lightning had scorched through the fabric, and I looked like a cinder maid from some old fairy tale who had just crawled out of a hot fireplace and was covered with soot and ash.

But the worst part was the burns.

Red, puckered burns and blisters dotted my face, along with what I could see of my arms and legs through my ruined gown. But those injuries were mild compared to the ones on my hands.

Oh, my poor, poor hands. Not only had my starburst scars

split wide open from the strain of trying to hold on to so much magic, but they were still weeping blood. At least, I thought they were still weeping blood. It was hard to tell given the purple burns that covered my hands from my wrists to my fingertips. Even my fingernails were a dark, ugly purple. My hands didn't even really look like hands anymore, but rather grotesque balloons that had somehow been attached to my arms.

I'd thought my hands had looked pretty horrific after Milo had driven his arrows through them at Myrkvior, but this was so much *worse*. My stomach roiled, and I had to look away to keep from vomiting. Or at least trying to vomit. I wasn't sure whether I could actually do that in this ghostly form, but I didn't want to find out.

The only parts of me that were relatively unscathed were my chest and forearms, which were still covered by Armina's breastplate and gauntlets. A dark purple patina had stained the silver armor, but the bits of tearstone were still that clear, rich midnight blue, and they twinkled like tiny stars in the metal, as though I had somehow draped the night sky across my chest and forearms like a velvet blanket.

I'd been wrong before. I wasn't a half-melted wax doll. No, I was a candle that had been burned down to the very last wisp of its wick. A small, distant part of me wondered if this was the end, if I would die where I lay on the grass, but the thought didn't fill me with panic. If nothing else, I'd saved Glitnir from Milo's cursed experiment. My only regret was that I hadn't managed to kill the crown prince before he'd snuck out of the palace.

"Gemma! Gemma!" A frantic voice intruded on my musings, and Leonidas leaned forward, staring down at my unconscious body.

His face and hands were burned almost as badly as mine were, but his amethyst eyes were clear and bright, and he was still the most beautiful thing I had ever seen. My gaze roamed over his body, but other than the burns, I didn't see any more injuries. Relief flooded my heart. He would live, even if I wouldn't.

Maeven stared down at me with a dispassionate expression. "Is she . . ."

Leonidas ignored his mother, leaned down a little closer to me, and gently laid his fingertips on the back of my right hand, as though I was made of ash and he didn't want me to crumble to nothingness at his light touch. He closed his eyes, and his magic brushed up against my body. The light, feathery, electric presence still tickled my skin, even in my ghostly form.

Gemma? Leonidas's voice sounded in my mind. *Gemma, you have to hold on. You have to keep fighting.*

I sighed and sat down on the steps that led up into the gazebo. *But I'm so tired. I want to rest now. I want to rest forever.*

He didn't seem to hear me, though. *Gemma*, he kept repeating. *Please come back to me. Come back to me. Come back to me . . .*

Leo's voice and magic washed over me again and again, like a high tide that stubbornly refused to be dragged back out to sea. Every time he reached out, I felt a little stronger than before, and every time he said my name, I realized how much I wanted to go back to him. We'd only had a few weeks together, and I wanted *more*—more time, more smiles, more love and laughter and adventures.

But his magic and my longing weren't quite enough to overcome the numb weariness creeping through my body, and I slowly listed to the side. My shoulder hit one of the gazebo columns, and the snarling gargoyle carved into the stone dug into my arm, as though it was trying to hold me upright.

A slither of movement caught my eye, startling me out of my dreamlike state. One of the liladorn strands I'd seen during yesterday's garden party was twining around my right wrist. Even though I could see it happening, I couldn't actually *feel* the vine snaking along my skin, which told me exactly how badly I was burned—and how very close I was to dying.

Going to scratch me yet again? I asked in a snide voice.

No, Not-Our-Princess, that familiar voice replied. *We know you saved us—and our future. We want to save yours in return.*

What future? Once again, I had no idea what the mercurial plant meant. The liladorn remained twined around my wrist, but it didn't sink its black thorns into my flesh. Maybe it couldn't, since I was ghosting, and this form of mine wasn't really here.

Delmira rushed over and dropped to her knees beside the plant. She plucked the liladorn dagger off her belt, then leaned forward and took hold of one of the vines.

The instant she touched it, I felt something *move* through that strand, through all the liladorn in this tangle of vines, and all the others in the gardens, and all the way up into my own body. Something old, something powerful, something that made a thousand visions flash before my eyes all at once.

We see everything.

The liladorn had said that to me during the Summit, and now I knew exactly what it meant. People, creatures, places. Balls, battles, gladiator bouts. Blizzards, droughts, monsoons. They all flickered through my mind almost too fast for me to follow, but I spotted a familiar face in that rushing river of memories.

I lunged forward and grabbed hold of that memory. I tried to yank it out of the river, but the image sucked me in like a whirlpool, and Delmira, Leonidas, and even my own burned body vanished. I was still sitting in the same spot in the gazebo, but now only one other person was here.

My mother.

Much like Delmira was doing in the real world, Merilde was kneeling in front of me with a gardening spade in her hand and a potted strand of liladorn sitting on the ground next to her. My mother looked pale, thin, and sickly, but she drove the spade into the ground again and again, creating a sizable hole. Once she was finished with that, she removed the liladorn from the pot and stuck the vine deep into the soil, where it would be sure to take root.

Then she started filling in the dirt all around the liladorn, her movements fast and furious, as though this were a race, and she was rapidly running out of time. But she finished, and her soil-stained hands stilled, as if just planting the vine had exhausted what little strength she had left.

"One final gift for my daughter," she whispered.

Merilde patted the soil a final time, then set down her spade and slumped against the opposite side of the gazebo, just like I was still doing. For a moment, her tired blue eyes met mine, and I felt as though she was *really* seeing me, even though this was just a memory, and not even one of my own. Mother stretched her hand out, and it came to rest next to mine on the gazebo step. Then she smiled, closed her eyes, and went utterly still.

A sob rose in my throat. This was the spot where she had died—the exact spot where I had found her. Even though the bone masters had told her to stay in bed and rest, Mother had snuck out of her chambers. When I'd realized she was gone, I'd come to the gardens to search for her. I'd always wondered what she had been doing here that day, and now I knew. She'd been planting the liladorn in hopes of saving this future version of me—

Delmira shifted forward, and her hand tightened around the strand of liladorn. Weary and heartsick, I looked over at her—and found her staring right back at me. Her eyes widened in surprise. Even though I was in my ghostly form, she still saw me, the same way I was seeing her.

"Gemma," Delmira whispered.

Her gaze flicked past me, and her eyes widened again, as if

she was seeing Merilde too, still slumped against the side of the gazebo.

"Gemma," Delmira said in a stronger, more confident voice.

Determination flared in her eyes, along with magic—much more magic than I had ever sensed from her before. So much magic that my fingertips tingled in warning, despite how dead and burned they were. The intense sensation confirmed something I had suspected for weeks now, ever since the Summit.

Maeven Morricone was one of the most powerful magiers I had ever encountered, but Delmira was even *stronger* than her mother.

Delmira's lips puckered in thought, much like Maeven's always did, and she bent down and used her dagger to lop off a thick strand of liladorn from the other vines. Then she got to her feet and hurried back over to where my unconscious body was still stretched out on the grass.

"Move!" Delmira snapped at my father.

Father was standing beside my body, with one arm wrapped around Grandfather Heinrich and the other one wrapped around Rhea, and tears were running down all their faces.

Father frowned at her sharp tone, but he stepped out of her way, as did Grandfather Heinrich and Rhea. Delmira glanced over at Alvis, who gave her an encouraging nod. She flashed him a small smile, then dropped to her knees beside me.

"Lift up her head, and open her mouth," Delmira ordered.

Leonidas's eyebrows drew together in confusion, but he did as she commanded. Delmira leaned forward, held the liladorn up over my mouth, and squeezed on the vine. Several large, fat drops of sap oozed out of the cut end and dripped into my mouth, as though I was catching snowflakes on my tongue.

With each drop, my mind became a little clearer and sharper, and some of that bone-deep weariness faded away. I slowly pushed my shoulder away from the column and sat upright again.

"Come on, Gemma," Delmira muttered. "Don't you dare give up."

She squeezed and squeezed that vine until she had wrung every last drop of sap out of it. Even though I was in my ghostly form, I could still feel the sap soothing my burned, cracked lips, filling my mouth, and trickling down my throat. Strangely enough, it tasted like lilac-flavored water, and I found it utterly delicious.

Delmira set the used vine aside and cut two more. She squeezed more sap into my mouth from the second vine, then spread the sap from the third one on my many burns, starting with the ones on my ruined hands.

On its own, the liladorn sap was cool and soothing, but Delmira's magic was much, much stronger, and her power flowed over me like a river, taking all my pain along with it, and leaving me floating in a quiet, peaceful place.

Delmira finished with those two strands, then laid them aside and sat back on her heels, looking as exhausted as I still felt. She glanced up at Maeven. Warm pride filled the queen's eyes, even as a small, knowing smile curved her lips.

"Well done, my darling," Maeven said in a soft voice. "Very well done."

Delmira nodded and wiped the sweat off her forehead with a shaking hand.

Maeven stared at her daughter a moment longer, then looked over at the gazebo. She didn't seem to see me, but her gaze locked onto the remaining strands of liladorn. Maeven touched her right hand to her left wrist, and her fingers stroked over a small bulge there, as if she had some sort of weapon tucked up her sleeve. A thought whispered off her and filled my mind.

Merilde finally kept her promise. Perhaps I will keep mine too.

I frowned. What did that mean? I had no idea, and I was too tired to puzzle it out—

Footsteps sounded, and a couple of the palace bone masters rushed into the gardens, along with several guards.

"Over here!" Father barked out. "Heal Princess Gemma! Help my daughter!"

The bone masters hurried forward. Delmira moved out of their way, but Leonidas stayed put, still kneeling on the grass and cradling me in his arms.

As the bone masters' magic flowed over my body, fixing everything that was burned and blistered, Leo's voice echoed in my mind again.

Gemma, come back to me.

I didn't go back to Leonidas, but I didn't fall back down into the black void of unconsciousness either. Instead, I blinked, and from one moment to the next, the gazebo, the hedge maze, and the rest of the Edelstein Gardens vanished, replaced by a tree-lined clearing atop a rocky ridge deep in the Spire Mountains . . .

I glanced around, recognizing the clearing and the campsite from the vision I'd had last night when I was in the royal treasury. I sighed. I might have burned through almost all my power corralling Milo's lightning, but the dregs of my magic had still found a way to toss me back into the past. Wonderful.

Well, at least my magic had picked a good memory for this ghosting episode—one of the best memories of my entire life.

I walked over and sat down at the edge of the canyon, with my legs dangling off the side. The scuff-scuff of my sandals scraping against the rocks reminded me of another memory—being trapped in the Blauberg mine after Conley, the treacherous foreman, had shoved me into a chasm and left me for dead. I glanced back over my shoulder, hoping Leonidas might appear in his own ghostly form, as he had back in the Blauberg mine, but I was all alone here.

Except for Gems.

The twelve-year-old version of myself was using the rope she'd tied around a nearby boulder to lower herself down the cliff face to the ledge where the baby gargoyle was still trapped.

Gems's left boot slipped, sending a shower of rocks and dirt tumbling downward. One of the rocks hit the gargoyle's head and bounced off. The creature let out a low, annoyed growl and lifted its head, revealing its bright, sapphire-blue eyes. Gems froze, staring down at the gargoyle, and her heart soared with wonder. The gargoyle stared right back at her, its eyes narrowing, studying every little thing about the girl.

Gems shook her head, flinging off her daze, then picked up her pace, until she was sliding rather than climbing down the cliff face. Rocks scraped her hands, but she didn't pay any attention to the shallow slices, and she kept going, moving even faster than before.

Less than a minute later, Gems reached the small ledge. Still clutching the rope, she slowly shifted her body from side to side, making sure the ledge was sturdy enough to hold her weight. When she was certain the rocks weren't going to crumble, she released the rope and eased toward the creature.

Most baby gargoyles were shy, skittish things, but not this one. Curiosity creased its face, and the same emotion radiated off the creature, as though it had never seen anything like her. Few people ventured this deep into the Spire Mountains, and it was quite possible the gargoyle had never seen a human before.

"It's okay, little one," Gems said, still easing closer. "I'm here to save you."

The gargoyle snorted, as though it didn't believe her words. Gems carefully sat down next to the creature and tucked her legs underneath her body, so that she wouldn't accidentally topple off the side of the ledge to her death.

She studied the gargoyle, and the creature did the same thing to her, its—his—eyes still glowing with that bright, fierce light.

"Is it okay if I pet you?" Gems asked. "Because I would very much like to do that."

The gargoyle let out a sound that was somewhere between a snort and a huff, but he didn't pull away when Gems stretched her hand out toward him.

Her fingertips touched down on his forehead, and blue sparks erupted, making her, my, our whole hand, arm, and body tingle. The sparks showered over the gargoyle like hot, hissing raindrops, and all the tiny blue flecks in his dark gray stone skin lit up, just for an instant, before winking out like stars giving way to the approaching dawn. I frowned. Odd. I had never noticed that before, back when this had actually been happening.

Gems didn't shy away from the sparks. Instead, she started scratching the creature's head, right in between his two small horns. The gargoyle's eyes widened in surprise, then a low, pleased rumble erupted out of his throat, and he leaned into her touch.

A loud, happy laugh burst out of Gems's mouth, the first real, genuine laugh that had come out of her mouth since before the Seven Spire massacre all those weeks ago. She laughed again, and a thought filled her mind and whispered through my own.

I'm going to be okay.

Even stronger than her thought was the feeling that radiated off her. All those tight, heavy knots of worry, fear, tension, and dread that Gems had been carrying around ever since the massacre slowly unraveled. She drew in a full, deep breath and tilted her face up to the sun, like she was a flower that was finally ready to bloom after being in the dark for so long.

The baby gargoyle growled and headbutted her side, demanding to be petted again. A third laugh tumbled out of Gems's lips, and the light, happy sound warmed me from head to toe.

"You're a grumpy little thing, aren't you?" she asked. "Maybe that should be your name—Grumpy. Do you like that?"

The gargoyle shook its head and let out another displeased growl. Truth be told, it wasn't the most original or inspired name, but I had only been twelve at the time.

"Okay, how about . . . Growly?" Gems suggested.

The gargoyle snorted, and his tail lashed from side to side in a clear no-no-no.

Gems chewed on her lower lip, and her face scrunched up in thought. Then her features smoothed out, and she snapped her fingers. Even now, all these years later, the sharp sound made me flinch, although I wasn't quite sure why.

"I know! I'll call you Grimley, after the hero in one of the stories my mother used to read to me. What about Grimley? Do you like that name?"

The gargoyle cocked his head to the side, and I heard him test out the name in his own mind. Grimmm-leeey. Grim-ley. Yes, I am Grimley.

He licked Gems's hand in approval. She laughed again and petted him for a few more seconds before carefully climbing back to her feet.

"All right, Grimley. Let's get off this ledge. What do you say?"

The gargoyle scrambled to his feet.

Gems studied the cliff face, the rope, and the baby gargoyle. Then she undid the rope from around her waist and tied it around Grimley, creating a crude sort of harness.

When she was finished, she crouched down so that she was eye level with him. "I'm going to climb back up the cliff. Then I'll grab the rope and haul you to the top. Okay?"

Grimley grumbled his agreement and rubbed up against Gems's legs. She scratched his head again, right in between his two horns, then straightened.

Gems started climbing. Once again, the rocks scraped her hands, but she smiled through all the small stings. This was the best thing that had happened to her—us—since before the Seven Spire massacre, and her excitement bubbled up like a geyser in my chest, making an answering smile stretch across my own face.

She quickly reached the top of the cliff and took hold of the rope. Grimley was staring up at her, his tail once again lashing from side to side. A scared whine rumbled out of his throat.

Gems pulled and tugged and yanked on the rope, but Grimley was much heavier than he looked, and she just didn't have the physical strength to haul him up the cliff. Frustrated, she released the rope. Once again, Grimley looked up at her, his whine more pleading and desperate than before.

This was it, I realized. This was the moment when I decided I would never leave Grimley behind, no matter what happened or how much danger it put me in.

Determination flared in Gems, burning as bright and hot as the summer sun, and she swung her legs down over *the side of the canyon, so that she was sitting right next to me, even though she didn't realize it. Even though I wasn't really here and this had all happened years ago.*

Magic sparked in Gems's eyes, turning them the same bright sapphire blue as Grimley's gaze, and she leaned down and focused on the gargoyle. I'm going to get you off that ledge. No matter what I have to do.

Her thought whispered through my mind, and Grimley heard it too. The gargoyle nodded, then went very, very still, almost as if he realized what was coming next. Perhaps he did.

Gems stretched her hand down and out and reached for her magic. Her eyes narrowed, and she bit her lip in concentration. The power sluiced off Gems, dropped down, and wrapped around Grimley, gripping him just as tightly as the rope still tied around his tummy. Gems took hold of all those invisible strings of energy and clenched her hand in a tight fist. Then she clenched her other hand in a fist and pulled on all those strings.

Grimley rose an inch up off the ledge. Then two, then three, five, seven, ten . . .

Gems dug her heels into the rocks, leaned back, and kept going, pulling on all those invisible strings of energy and slowly hoisting the gargoyle up off the ledge. Sweat poured down her face, her breath puffed out in ragged gasps, and her entire body trembled. More than once, she almost lost her grip on her magic, and on Grimley too, but she gritted her teeth and held on to it along with the gargoyle.

Finally, just when Gems had reached the end of her strength and magic, Grimley's head appeared at the edge of the cliff. The gargoyle flapped his wings, and he surged up and over the side and back onto solid ground.

Gems shuddered out a breath and released her magic.

All the energy drained out of her body, and she slumped forward, like a rose that had wilted in the scorching sun.

Grimley yipped with delight, wiggled out of the rope, and bounded forward. He ran straight into Gems, knocking her down onto the ground, then leaned forward and licked her cheek. Gems let out another delighted laugh, wrapped her arms around the gargoyle's neck, and hugged him tight—

"Lookee here, boys," a voice drawled. "We finally found our runaway princess."

Gems froze, her arms still wrapped around Grimley, who let out a low, angry growl. Then she released him, scooted away from the edge of the canyon, and lurched to her feet.

Several turncoat guards were standing in the clearing, all clutching swords. Gems's gaze darted from one face to another, but she didn't recognize any of the men. Desperate, she looked past the guards, scanning the trees that lined the far side of the clearing.

I knew exactly who she was looking for—Leonidas.

Young Leo had been with the guards who had first found Gems, Alvis, and Xenia in the woods a few weeks ago. Gems fully expected him to be with this group as well, since he had been using his mind magier power to track her down per King Maximus's orders, but Leo didn't appear.

One of the men stepped forward. He was tall, with a thin, lean, muscled body. His dark brown hair was slicked back from his forehead, and his eyes were a pale blue against his ruddy skin.

Going to make captain for finally catching this brat. *His thought whispered through Gems's mind, and mine too.* Captain Arlo. I like the sound of that.

"What's wrong, princess?" Arlo sneered. "Did that gargoyle rip out your tongue?"

Gems didn't respond, but Grimley sidled closer to her and let out another low, angry growl.

"King Maximus only said we had to bring you in alive," Arlo continued. "He didn't say that you had to be . . . undamaged."

"So what?" Gems asked in a wary voice.

An evil grin split his face. "So I, for one, am in the mood to damage you quite a bit, given the merry fucking chase you've led us on these past several weeks. What do you say, boys?"

Answering grins twisted the guards' faces. Anger and other horrid things surged off the men, and their combined malevolence hit Gems like an invisible tidal wave, almost knocking her down. Her gaze darted around, but the guards had her trapped up against the edge of the canyon, and there was nowhere to run.

The men sheathed their swords and advanced on Gems, who clenched her hands into fists and reached for her magic, determined to fight them off for as long as possible . . .

A series of *scrape-scrape-scrapes* rang out, shattering my memories. My eyes snapped open, and I found myself staring up at the carving of Queen Armina that adorned the ceiling over my bed. In this image, Armina was clutching a sword in her hand and sitting atop her gargoyle, Arton, as they engaged in a fierce battle against their enemies.

Some people might have found the carving violent, but it had always comforted me, ever since I had first returned home from the Seven Spire massacre. If nothing else, the image had always assured me that I was safe in my own bed.

Another series of *scrape-scrape-scrapes* sounded. I pushed myself up to sitting.

Scrape-scrape-scrape.

I frowned. That sounded like it was coming from . . . the floor. I peered over the side of the mattress.

Grimley was sleeping right next to the bed. His paws were twitching, and his long black talons were dragging across the flagstones, hence all the *scrapes*.

I skimmed his thoughts and an image of Milo filled my mind. In his dream, Grimley was chasing down Milo, then using his talons to rip the crown prince to shreds. Low, angry growls rumbled out of the gargoyle's mouth, and he tore into Milo over and over again, as if he couldn't kill the crown prince enough times.

My heart swelled with love and gratitude. Even in his dreams, the gargoyle was protecting me, just as I would always protect him.

I leaned over and placed my hand on his forehead, right in between his two horns. "It's okay, Grims," I whispered, scratching that spot. "Sleep well."

I didn't know if he heard me, but some of the tension drained out of his body, his talons stopped scraping against the flagstones, and his growls died down to smoother, softer breaths.

Keeping one hand resting on Grimley's head, I lay down and let his snores lull me back to sleep.

CHAPTER TWENTY

Sometime later, I woke up again. According to the clock on the nightstand, it was late afternoon, and sunlight filled my bedroom. Crimley was gone, but Violet was curled up on a cushioned chair in the corner. The baby strix was napping in a sunspot, and squeaky little snores fluttered out of her open beak.

A glimmer of silver caught my eye. Armina's armor—the breastplate and two matching gauntlets—was propped up in a chair in the corner, also gleaming in a sunspot. Someone had scrubbed the ugly purple patina off the metal, but I still shuddered and looked away from it.

I pushed myself up to sitting. I reached for the edge of the blankets to shove them aside and froze when I caught sight of my hands. Thick white bandages covered my hands from my wrists all the way down to my fingertips. Worry filled me, and I tossed the blankets back. A nightgown covered my body, and my gargoyle pendant was hanging around my neck like usual. I patted myself down from head to toe, but the burns on my face, arms, and legs had all been healed, and only my hands were bandaged.

A breath hissed out between my teeth, but my relief evaporated along with it. Just because the rest of me was fine didn't mean my hands were. Despite the dread rising in my stomach,

I held my hands up and cautiously reached for my magic. To my surprise, my power came to me easily, indicating that it too was fine, and I used it to slowly unwrap the bandages.

With every loop of fabric that loosened around my fingers, an answering knot tightened around my heart. Milo had almost destroyed my hands when he had tortured me with his tearstone arrows in Myrkvior, and I had injured them even more badly last night by holding on to so much of his lightning for so long.

The first layer of bandages dropped away, and I moved on to the second layer, then the third. Impatience overpowered my dread, and I used my magic to rip the final bandages off in one long piece. The white fabric fluttered down onto the bed, revealing my hands.

My whole, intact, healed hands.

Oh, they weren't completely healed, since those red starburst scars still covered them, front and back, but my skin was whole, intact, and free of the gruesome purple lightning burns. I wiggled my fingers. Sparks of pain ignited in my fingertips, and the familiar dull aches were stronger and more pronounced than before, but my hands flexed, stretched, and moved normally. Another relieved breath hissed out of my lips.

The soft, sweet scent of lilacs flooded my nose, and I took a closer look at my hands. A thin layer of salve was still glistening on my skin—the same sort of liladorn salve Delmira had used to heal my hands at Myrkvior. Once again, the Morricone princess had saved me. I wondered if she had finally realized how powerful she truly was—and just how much control she had over the liladorn.

Either way, I had slept long enough, and I needed to see if my friends and family had found Milo and Wexel, so I used my magic to rewrap the bandages on my hands. Then I snagged a robe from the foot of the bed, slipped it on, and stood up. The room spun, but I gritted my teeth and started moving. I grabbed for the nearest bedpost, but I misjudged the distance and started falling—

A pair of hands caught me around the waist. I looked up, and Leo was there.

"Gemma!" he said, alarm in his voice. "What are you doing out of bed? You should be resting!"

Instead of answering him, I curled my fingers into his black riding coat. Well, as much as they could curl through the bandages. That small motion caused more hot sparks and dull aches to ripple through my hands, but I ignored the pain and tightened my grip. My gaze swept over his face and down his body, but his burns had also been healed, and he was whole again, just as I was. More relief rushed through me, even stronger than before. Leo was here, and so was I, and that was all that mattered right now.

"You should get back in bed," Leonidas said.

Over on the chair, Violet woke up, lifted her head, and let out a loud, agreeing cheep. The strix was staring at me with bright, concerned eyes, just like Leonidas still was.

I shook my head. "No. I've already been asleep far too long. I need to get out of this room."

Leonidas loosened his grip on my waist. "Okay. But you are going to sit down somewhere."

I raised one hand and snapped off a mock salute. "Yes, sir, Your Highness!"

He rolled his eyes, but my teasing must have convinced him that I was truly okay because some of the tension drained out of his body. Before I could protest, Leondias bent down and scooped me up into his arms.

"Come on, Violet," he called out.

The strix waggled her wings and lifted herself up off the cushion. She was hovering more than flying, so I reached out with my magic, and she floated over to my outstretched palm.

Once I had Violet nestled against my chest, Leonidas carried us into the sitting room.

Grimley was stretched out on the rug in front of the fireplace, while Reiko was sitting in a nearby chair, eyeing a platter of sweet cakes on the low table like she wanted to eat every single one of them. Delmira was perched on a settee, clutching a goblet of lemonade and eyeing the strand of liladorn, which was still lounging in its crystal bowl on one of the tables.

"She's awake," Leonidas announced, setting me down in the chair closest to the fireplace. "And as stubborn as ever."

"Good," Reiko drawled. "That means she's feeling better and not dying anymore."

Leonidas froze, and Delmira gave the dragon morph a sharp look. Reiko shrugged, plucked a sweet cake off the platter, and popped it into her mouth. She was never one to sugarcoat things, and I was glad she was treating me normally. It helped lessen the impact of everything I'd gone through last night—and just how very close we had *all* come to dying, along with everyone else in the palace.

Grimley yawned, stretched, and padded over to me. The gargoyle rubbed up against my legs, and I scratched his head.

Don't you ever scare me like that again. His stern voice filled my mind. *The floor in your room is far too hard and cold for me to sleep beside your bed with any regularity.*

I'll do my best. I threw my arms around his neck, hugging him tight. *I love you, bruiser.*

Grimley's wings came around and stroked down my back, and his love flowed through my body with each light touch. *I love you too, runt. And just so you know, all this worrying about you is ex-*hausting. *Why, I haven't been able to take a proper nap all day.*

I drew back and grinned at him. *Oh, no. We can't have that.*

No, we cannot. Naps are one of the great joys of life. He nuzzled up against my legs again. *Now help the others find Milo and Wexel so I can rip them to pieces.*

Your wish is my command.

Grimley snorted and turned his attention to Violet, who was still cuddled in my lap. "Come along, little one. It's time for your next flying lesson. Otto, Fern, and Lyra are waiting outside for us."

Violet cheeped in excitement, waggled her wings, and hopped down to the floor. Delmira laughed, got up, and opened one of the doors for the baby strix.

Grimley followed Violet out onto the balcony. The afternoon sun gilded the gargoyle in a beautiful golden sheen and brought out the tiny blue flecks in his dark gray stone skin. I frowned. For some reason, those flecks reminded me of the bits of tearstone embedded in Armina Ripley's armor. Not only that, but the flecks in Grimley's skin seemed larger and brighter than before, almost like they were a map of stars embedded in his skin and connecting all the different parts of his body. I blinked, and those stars glimmered even more brightly, their colorful glow stretching out into the air all around Grimley and far beyond—

The gargoyle scooped Violet up in his paw and set her on his back, then flapped his wings and shot up into the sky. The baby strix let out a high singsong *cheep-cheep* of happiness. Delmira closed the door and returned to her chair, but I kept staring at those blue stars still hovering on the balcony.

"Gemma?" Reiko asked. "Are you okay?"

I blinked. The stars snuffed out, and Grimley flew past a tower and vanished, with Violet still riding on his back.

"Gemma?" This time, Delmira asked the question.

I forced myself to smile at her, as well as Reiko and Leonidas, who were also staring at me with concern. "I'm fine. Pass me some sweet cakes before Reiko eats them all."

She scowled at me, as did the dragon on her neck, and popped another sweet cake into her mouth.

Leonidas cleared his throat. "Actually, I had one of the cook masters make something special for you."

He picked up a silver platter from another table, set it on my lap, and removed the cover with a dramatic flourish. This time, a genuine smile spread across my face.

"A toasted cheese-and-jam sandwich!" I squealed with delight.

"Of course," he replied. "I know it's your favorite."

Leonidas smiled, but he couldn't quite hide the worry in his face and voice. Neither could Reiko or Delmira, and concern and tension blasted off all three of them and hung in the air like a wet blanket.

To distract myself, I grabbed a triangle of the sandwich and sank my teeth into it. The delicious combination of crunchy, toasted sourdough bread, ooey, gooey melted gruyère cheese, and sweet, tangy apricot jam filled my mouth, and suddenly I was too ravenous to think about anything else. Leonidas poured me some cranberry lemonade with a tart bite of apple, and Reiko even let me eat most of the chocolate-raspberry sweet cakes.

Reiko and Leonidas didn't say much while I gobbled down the food, but Delmira kept up a steady stream of chatter about how much she adored the fine furnishings in my chambers, how delicious the sweet cakes were, and other inane things. But eventually, even the ever-cheerful Delmira ran out of things to say, and silence dropped over us again.

"So . . ." Reiko said after I finished eating. "What happened last night?"

I drew in a breath and told them everything, from my wandering out to the gardens, to Milo, Wexel, and the other Mortans sneaking into the palace through the old mining tunnels, to the crown prince constructing his lightning-in-a-bottle experiment in the treasury and leaving me to die, along with everyone else inside Glitnir.

When I finished, a stunned silence dropped over my friends, and no one moved or spoke for several long, tense seconds. Finally, Delmira shook her head.

"I've always known Milo was capable of horrible, evil, despicable things. I've witnessed his cruelty many times over the years, and I've often borne the brunt of it myself. But to create such a wretched experiment, to try to destroy an entire palace and murder all the innocent people inside . . ." Her voice trailed off, but anguish surged off her and wrenched my own stomach. "Well, no wonder everyone hates the Morricones."

"It's not your fault," I replied. "Milo made his own choices, his own decisions. This is the path *he* chose—not you."

Delmira nodded, but her lips puckered, and anger and disgust burned like ice-cold flames in her amethyst eyes. In that moment, she looked like a mirror image of Maeven, a dark and dangerous enemy, instead of a kind and gentle friend. On the table beside her, the liladorn straightened up in its bowl, standing tall and proud, as though it was a loyal captain awaiting its queen's command.

"Either way, Milo needs to be stopped," Delmira continued. "He needs to be killed."

Reiko gave her an admiring look. "I didn't think you were capable of such murderous urges."

Delmira laughed, but the harsh, brittle sound reminded me of glass breaking. "In case you've forgotten, I'm a Morricone too. We're *all* capable of such murderous urges. Why, if Milo was here right now, I would slit his throat with my liladorn dagger and watch him bleed out all over Gemma's rug while I sipped my lemonade."

The hard set of her lips, as well as the determination rippling off her, indicated that she meant every single word. Maeven had

once said that Delmira's kindness would get her killed someday, but I thought the Morricone princess was very much like the
liladorn in the crystal bowl. Seemingly soft, gentle, and flexible—
but with a hard, unbreakable strength and plenty of razor-sharp
thorns to rip her enemies to pieces.

A knock sounded, and a door opened. Father and Rhea
stepped into my chambers, along with Grandfather Heinrich and
Alvis. To my surprise, Maeven also entered. The queen looked
around curiously, although she stood in the corner, as though she
was afraid to venture any farther into the room lest she burst into
flames just by being here.

I got to my feet. Father came over and enveloped me in a tight
hug, his love and relief washing over me and warming my body
from head to toe.

"You scared me so much," he whispered.

"I scared myself," I whispered back. "But I'm okay. I'm alive,
and Glitnir is still in one piece. That's all that matters right now."

He nodded, but he hugged me even more tightly than before.
Rhea, Grandfather Heinrich, and Alvis also hugged me. I looked
over at Maeven, who was still standing in the corner by herself.

Her sharp gaze roamed over my body before lingering on my
bandaged hands. "You're looking well, Gemma. All things considered."

I looked her over in return, but if she felt any ill effects from
helping Leonidas and me get rid of Milo's lightning last night,
she wasn't showing them. Then again, Maeven Morricone *never*
showed any hint of weakness, not even to Leonidas and Delmira.

A needle of sympathy pricked my heart. How sad that the
Morricone queen thought she always had to be so strong, that she
could never lean on anyone else, that she could never show even
the smallest hint of vulnerability, not even to her own children.

Maeven must have seen the pity on my face, because her eyes
narrowed and her chin lifted in that haughty, arrogant gesture I

knew all too well. She tilted her head to me, then swept out of the room. Delmira murmured an excuse and followed her mother. Grandfather Heinrich, Rhea, and Alvis also left, claiming they needed to check on various things.

That left me alone with Leonidas, Reiko, and Father.

"Tell me what happened," Father asked.

We all sat back down, and I repeated my story to him. The longer I talked, the more his face darkened, especially when I mentioned the journal Dahlia Sullivan had written, which had revealed so many of Glitnir's secrets to Milo.

Father surged to his feet and started pacing back and forth. "Since Glitnir isn't a smoking crater, Milo knows his experiment failed. No doubt he's already preparing another attack, and if he knows about the Ripley tombs and the adjoining mining tunnels . . ."

He grimaced, and his voice trailed off, as if he didn't even want to speculate about how much more damage Milo could do to the palace—and us.

Father stopped pacing and looked at Leonidas. "What do you think Milo will do next? Will he finally retreat?"

This was the first time my father had sincerely asked Leonidas for his opinion or advice since he had come to Glitnir. Surprise flickered across Leonidas's face, although his expression soon turned serious again.

"No. Milo won't retreat. He's spent *years* planning this. Gemma stopping him from destroying the palace is a serious blow, but Milo will consider it only a temporary setback." Leonidas shook his head. "My brother wants to do the one thing that King Maximus never could, which is conquer all the other kingdoms, starting with Andvari. He thinks it will make him the greatest king, the greatest Morricone, in history. Milo will *never* give up on that goal—not until he's dead."

Father nodded and resumed his pacing. He didn't ask

Leonidas any more questions, but the worry and dread surging off them both matched what was relentlessly beating in my own heart.

Eventually, Father stopped his pacing, hugged me again, and told me to get some rest. Then he left my chambers to check in with Grandfather Heinrich and Rhea about the new security measures that were being implemented in and around the palace. By this point, the sun was setting, streaking the sky with crimson rays.

Reiko also got to her feet. "I should go too and see how Kai did in the tournament."

I frowned. "The tournament?"

She nodded. "Yes, the bouts and other events went on today as scheduled, as per King Heinrich's orders."

Of course. No doubt gossip was running rampant through the Glitnir court about last night's attack, and Grandfather Heinrich would want to show the nobles and everyone else that he was still in complete control of his kingdom. Letting the tournament proceed as planned was the quickest, easiest, and most visible way to do that.

"From what we've heard, the crowds at the fairgrounds today were even larger than the ones yesterday," Leonidas added.

"Who told you that?" I asked.

He shrugged. "Fern. She and Otto flew over the arena earlier, searching for Milo and Wexel, although they didn't find them."

Reiko snorted. "Gemma, sometimes, I think your gargoyles love to gossip even more than the nobles do. Still, I wonder . . ."

Her voice trailed off, and a thoughtful look filled her face. Her inner dragon also narrowed its eyes in concentration.

"What is it?" I asked.

"Oh . . . just a little something I want to check on." Reiko gave me a bright smile, clearly lying. "Anyway, I should go tell Kai that you're feeling much better. He was worried about you too. He was going to dedicate all his victories today to you."

Before I could protest or tell her to thank Kai for his concern, Reiko surged to her feet and rushed out of my chambers. That left Leonidas and I alone in the sitting room.

He stood up. "I should let you get some more rest."

I grabbed his hand. "Stay with me. Please."

Leonidas stared down at me, more concern creasing his face. "Are you sure?"

I gripped his hand even tighter. "Yes."

He nodded, then leaned down, scooped me up into his arms, and carried me back into the bedroom. He set me down on my feet beside the bed and started to step back, but I grabbed his hand again and tugged him forward, so that his body was brushing up against my own. Leonidas's breath hitched in his throat. His gaze locked with mine, and the growing heat in his eyes made me shiver with anticipation.

I undid the silver strix pin that held his cloak around his throat and placed it on the nightstand, right beside my gargoyle dagger. Then I removed the cloak from his shoulders and tossed it over onto the chair Violet had been sleeping on earlier. I held out my hand, which Leonidas took, and tugged him over to the bed. Together, we both lay down on top of the blankets.

Leonidas wrapped his arms around me, and I rested my head on his chest, listening to the reassuring *thump-thump-thump* of his heart beating under my ear. I closed my eyes, drinking in the soft, soothing sound, as well as his honeysuckle scent. Twenty-four hours ago, I thought I would never experience this again, and I was going to enjoy every single second of our quiet time together.

We lay there in silence for several minutes before Leonidas shifted on the bed beside me.

"I don't know exactly when I realized you were in danger," he said in a low voice. "Sometime during the ball, my fingertips started tingling. At first, I thought it was all the people, thoughts, and emotions in the throne room. But now I think it was my magic, trying to find yours."

"Magic always seeks out like magic," I murmured, repeating Maeven's words in the gardens last night.

Leonidas nodded. "I started searching the throne room for you, but it was so crowded, and so many people came up to me, wanting to gawk at the Morricone prince. I should have realized what was happening sooner, should have found you sooner, helped you sooner. Maybe if I had, you wouldn't have almost died."

My bandaged fingers dug into his riding coat, and I raised my head so that I could look at him. "The palace walls and the tearstone blocked my power. I called out with my magic, but I couldn't reach you or Grimley or anyone else. There was nothing you could have done to help me."

Leonidas sat up, pulling me along with him. An anguished look filled his face, and guilt surged off him. "I should have been there with you, Gemma. If only we hadn't argued before the ball, maybe I would have been. Then I could have helped you with the lightning sooner."

His face darkened, and a hot rush of anger drowned out his guilt. "Or perhaps one of us could have finally killed Milo and Wexel."

I shook my head. "No, you can't think like that. None of us realized the enormous scope of what Milo was planning, much less that he had Dahlia Sullivan's journal and knew how to slip into the palace undetected, as well as open the treasury doors."

Leonidas tipped his head, acknowledging my points. "Perhaps not. But when I sensed your pain, your suffering, when I thought I might lose you . . ." He had to stop and clear his throat.

"This cold, cold dread filled my heart—more dread than I have ever felt before in my entire life."

"I felt that same dread too—that I might never see you again."

He took my hand in his, gently stroking his thumb over the white bandages. Despite the fabric separating his skin from mine, I felt his touch all the way down in my bones.

"I ran out of the throne room and followed the feel of that dread like it was an arrow leading me straight to you. I passed some guards yelling and running in the other direction, but I ignored them and kept going." Leonidas drew in a breath, then slowly let it out. "Eventually, I found my way through the hedge maze. When I saw you clutching that ball of lightning, I couldn't believe you were still upright. All that power, all that energy, all that raw force . . ."

He shook his head in wonder. "I still don't know how you kept it from burning right through you, Gemma."

My gaze darted over to Armina's armor, which was still propped up in a chair in the corner. The breastplate and gauntlets had certainly shielded my chest and arms from the lightning, and the bits of blue tearstone embedded in the silver had deflected some of Milo's magic, just like my gargoyle pendant had. But I still felt like the armor had done something else, something *more*, although I couldn't puzzle out exactly what it might be.

Leonidas shifted on the bed, and I dragged my gaze away from the armor and focused on him again.

"I'll never forget the sight of you in the gardens, holding that pulsing ball of lightning in between your hands, with the snow dusting the ground all around you," he continued. "Is it strange to say it was one of the most beautiful things I have ever seen?"

Images flickered off him and filled my mind. His fingertips tingling in warning the same way mine so often did. Him sprinting out of the throne room, knocking people aside in his haste, then rushing through the hedge maze. And then, finally, him spotting me in the gardens, my dark brown hair wild and singed, my blue eyes wide in my burned face, my jaw clenched tight as I tried to contain the spitting, hissing, crackling mass of magic.

Emotions also surged off Leonidas. All the surprise and wonder and horror as he realized exactly how much raw energy I was struggling to contain. Then the cold, sickening knowledge that if I failed, if I let it go, if it overpowered me, the force would kill me and him and everyone inside the palace.

I shuddered. "I thought the magic was beautiful too. Milo's trap, his experiment, his design. All his talk of lightning in a bottle. It was so simple and yet so elegant, in a twisted, terrifying way."

Leonidas nodded, and we fell silent again for several minutes, both of us lost in our own thoughts.

Finally, he blew out a breath and raised his gaze to mine again. "I'm so sorry, Gemma," he said in a low, strained voice. "For fighting with you before the ball. It was stupid."

I shook my head. "No, you were right. Your mother isn't always the villain, and my father isn't always the hero. I was a fool to let my own worries about Milo and Maeven take over and get in the way of everything else, get in the way of *us*. I'm not going to let that happen again. I love you, Leo, and I trust you. That will never change, no matter what might take place between our families."

He nodded, and some of the tension trickled out of his face. "I love you too, Gemma. I always have, and I always will."

I cupped his face in my hands, then leaned forward and pressed my lips to his. Leonidas's arms snaked around me, and he pulled me closer. I melted into the warm, solid strength of his body and deepened the kiss, my tongue licking at his lips.

Leonidas pulled back. "Your injuries—"

"Are completely healed," I replied. "Even my hands."

He stared down at my bandaged fingers, which were resting against his chest. "Are you sure?"

"Absolutely."

His worry vanished, and a wicked grin spread across his face. Once again, Leonidas scooped me up into his arms. This time, he carried me into the bathroom and kicked the door shut behind us. He set me down on my feet, then turned on the faucets, running hot water into the oversize porcelain tub.

I eyed the tub. "I had something a bit more invigorating in mind than a bath."

Another wicked grin spread across Leonidas's face. "Oh, I find that baths can be extremely invigorating—when you share them with the right person."

He started unfastening the buttons on his riding coat. I leaned back against the counter and watched the show, which was much, much better than any gladiator bout.

Leonidas set his riding coat aside, then lifted his tunic and stripped it off as well. His boots were next, followed by his socks, leggings, and undergarments. In less than a minute, he stood naked before me. My gaze traced over his body, from his gleaming black hair to the hard, defined muscles of his chest and stomach. My mouth went dry, and my fingertips itched with the urge to explore every delicious inch of him.

Leonidas turned off the faucets and stepped into the tub. He dunked under the water, then surfaced, slid over to one of the seats that was built into the porcelain, and rested his arms on the side of the tub. Hypnotized, I watched the glimmering droplets drip out of his hair, streak down his face, and then slide along his chest before vanishing back into the rest of the water.

"Are you going to stand there and just look?" he teased. "Or are you going to join me?"

I never could resist a challenge, so I sauntered over to the tub, putting an extra swing in my hips. Heat filled Leonidas's eyes, and his fingers clenched around the side of the porcelain, as though he was having a hard time keeping himself from reaching for me.

Now it was my turn to strip. I took my time, opening my robe and letting it fall to the floor, before undoing the laces on the front of my nightgown. I also removed my gargoyle pendant, then unwrapped the bandages on my hands and set them aside. With every part that I revealed, that heat burned a little hotter and brighter in Leonidas's eyes. Hunger blasted off him and curled around my body, mixing and mingling with my own growing desire for him.

I kicked my clothes out of the way, went over, and got into the tub. Then I dunked myself under the water the same way he had. When I surfaced, Leonidas was right in front of me. He took hold of my hands and lifted them up and out of the water. He studied first one hand, then the other, as if making sure they were whole—that *I* was whole.

I flexed my fingers, watching the red starburst scars ripple across my skin. "Delmira and her liladorn salve saved my hands yet again."

"I'll be sure to thank her for that—later," Leonidas said. "Forgive me if I don't want to talk about my sister right now."

I arched an eyebrow. "Then what *do* you want to talk about, Your Highness?"

He focused on my right hand, gently pressing his fingers into my skin and massaging away the dull aches. I hummed with pleasure. Leonidas pressed a kiss to my palm, then grabbed my other hand and massaged it the same way before pressing a kiss to it as well.

I leaned forward and kissed the side of his neck, inhaling his honeysuckle scent, which was even more pronounced and heady in the warm water. I drew back, then leaned forward again and kissed the other side of his neck.

"There are other parts of me that you could kiss," he suggested.

"Oh, you mean like this?" I scooted closer and pressed a chaste kiss to the center of his forehead.

His eyes darkened at my teasing, and a growl rumbled out of his throat. "I was thinking of something more like this."

His lips descended on mine, and his tongue stroked against my own. Fire exploded in my veins, the liquid desire making me feel even hotter and more weightless than the water did. I tangled my fingers in his wet hair and deepened the kiss, drinking in the taste of him, as well as his slick body sliding up against my own. Every single chiseled inch of him molded perfectly to my slightly softer curves.

Sometime later, we broke apart, both of us breathing hard. I pushed Leonidas back so that he was sitting in one of the tub seats again. He reached out, and I curled my hand into his and floated over to him. I wrapped my fingers around his hard cock and stroked him up and down, making my movements as fluid as the water around us. Leonidas hissed, and his pleasure spiked through my mind, adding to the ever-increasing ache in my own body.

This time, he leaned forward. His tongue licked at the hollow of my throat, while his hands caressed my breasts. I sighed and arched back, and Leonidas curled one arm around my waist and lifted me partially up out of the water. Then he put his mouth where his hands had been, licking, nipping, and sucking on my right breast, then my left one. That ache between my thighs coalesced into sharp, throbbing need, and my fingers dug into his shoulders, pulling him even closer.

Leonidas lifted his head, and we kissed again and again and again, until all I could feel, see, smell, taste, and touch was his body against my own. He drew me back down into the water, and I straddled him.

Leo.

Gemma.

We stared into each other's eyes, our thoughts and desires flowing back and forth just like the water sluicing over our bodies. Then, with one thought, one need, we came together. I moved forward, even as Leonidas thrust upward into me. We both groaned, adjusting to the feel of each other. Leonidas's hands fell to my hips, and I rocked forward, meeting his next thrust.

And the one after that . . . and the one after that . . . and the one after that . . .

Our movements became quicker and harder. We kissed again and again, our lips and tongues crashing together, even as water arched up over the rim of the bathtub and splattered down onto the floor.

Leonidas thrust into me again and shuddered, an orgasm ripping through his body. I rocked forward a final time, reaching my own climax, and every single nerve ending in my body exploded with the pleasure of that sweet, electric release.

Even though we weren't moving anymore, the water around us continued to rock back and forth, mirroring the passion and love we had just shared.

CHAPTER TWENTY-ONE

eonidas and I relaxed in the tub until the water cooled, then got out, dried off, and went to bed. I woke the next morning feeling happy, sated, and refreshed. Smiling, I stretched, rolled over, and reached out, but my hands met only empty blankets. My eyes popped open. Leonidas was gone, but he'd left a note on one of the pillows.

Meet me on the balcony.

Still smiling, I got dressed in my usual tunic, leggings, and boots, and headed out onto the balcony. A round table covered with silver platters squatted in the middle of several large, square warming stones that had been spaced around the balcony to ward off the early morning chill.

Leonidas was sitting at the table, using a charcoal pencil to sketch something in a small black journal—the same journal that had fallen out of his cloak pocket the night we'd returned from Allentown. At the sound of my footsteps, Leonidas shut the journal, set it and the pencil aside, and stood up. Curiosity filled me, but I decided not to pry. I'd meant what I'd said about trusting him, and he would reveal his secret when he was ready.

Grimley and Lyra were lazing on the warmed flagstones, while Violet was hopping around and cheeping in hopes they would abandon their naps and play with her. So far, the baby strix was fighting a losing battle. Grimley used the flat side of the arrow on the end of his tail to push Violet toward Lyra, who used one of her wings to nudge the baby strix right back toward the gargoyle. Violet let out another enthusiastic series of *cheep-cheep-cheeps*, clearly enjoying the odd game.

Leonidas leaned down and kissed my cheek. "I thought breakfast in bed might be a bit crowded." He jerked his head at the three creatures. "So I had the servants set it up out here."

"This is perfect," I said, and dropped into one of the chairs.

In addition to the numerous covered platters, several carafes of cranberry, apple, and other juices covered the table, along with a surprising guest—the strand of liladorn, which was relaxing in its water-filled bowl much the same way Leonidas and I had in the tub last night.

Ahh. The liladorn's contented sigh whispered through my mind, and it turned its thorns up to the early morning sun.

"And now, please allow me to present my lady with her breakfast." Leonidas leaned down, took hold of the cover, and plucked it off the platter in front of me, revealing . . .

A merry laugh tumbled out of my lips. "Blackberry pancakes?"

He grinned. "Of course. It's one of our traditions now. You had them at Myrkvior, and I had them at the Summit, so I thought we could have them together at Glitnir."

I laughed, even as hard fingers of sorrow and worry pinched my heart tight. I loved having a favorite breakfast food with Leonidas, and I wanted to make so many more traditions with him—but I didn't know if we would ever get the chance. Despite everything that had happened between us last night, and all the love we'd shared, nothing had really changed, and we hadn't made any promises to each other about the future.

"Gemma? Do you not like the pancakes?" Leonidas asked, a frown creasing his face.

I forced myself to smile. "I love them. Now let's eat before they get cold."

He grinned and took his own seat.

In addition to the blackberry pancakes, the cook masters had prepared a scrumptious spread of scrambled eggs, fried ham, bite-size spinach-and-cheddar quiches, and raspberry sweet cakes drizzled with a vanilla-bean-sugar glaze that were bursting with tart flavor and yet still melted in my mouth. The food was delicious, and I polished off several servings of everything, along with a couple of glasses of cranberry juice.

Leonidas speared the last pancake with his fork, cut it, and took a bite. "Mmm. Don't tell anyone I said this, but these blackberry pancakes are even better than the ones at Myrkvior."

The mention of the Morricone palace made the smile slip from my face, and more fingers of sorrow and worry pinched my heart. I might have stopped Milo's plot to destroy Glitnir, but he was still lurking in Glanzen somewhere, and I was running out of time to find him. The Sword and Shield Tournament would end soon, and Milo might decide to slip out of the city along with the crowds. But whether he was caught or not, once the tournament ended, Maeven and Delmira would return to Morta, and Leonidas might feel duty-bound to go with them, to protect his family in case Milo decided to attack them again at Myrkvior.

I set down my fork, and Leonidas raised his eyebrows in a silent question. As much as I wanted to pretend everything was fine and enjoy this time with him, I still had work to do. So I drew in a breath to ask him how we might go about tracking down Milo—

Gemma! A frantic voice filled my mind.

I froze. *Reiko?*

Gemma! Gemma!

Her voice filled my mind again. I closed my eyes and reached out with my magic, trying to locate her soft, smoky presence, but I didn't sense her anywhere nearby.

What I did sense was her extreme dread and worry.

The emotions raked across my chest, sharp, pointed, and vicious, as though her dragon talons were slicing through my skin and plunging into my heart. My eyes popped open, and I sucked in a strangled breath.

"Gemma?" Leonidas asked. "What's wrong?"

Reiko's voice didn't echo through my mind again, and I still couldn't tell where she might be, but her dread and worry continued to rip into me, as though her talons were gouging deeper and deeper into my heart with each passing second—

It stopped.

The talons, the dread, the worry. It all abruptly ceased, as if Reiko was no longer feeling anything herself, as if she was unconscious . . . or dead.

"Gemma?" Leonidas asked again. "Why are you clutching your pendant like that?"

I glanced down. My hand had fisted around the gargoyle pendant, and I tightened my grip, using the sharp pricks of the jewels against my skin to help banish my own fear.

Then I released the pendant and surged to my feet. "Reiko's in trouble."

Leonidas's eyebrows knit together in worry, and he also surged to his feet. "Milo?"

I shook my head. "I don't know, but whatever is happening, it's bad. We need to find her—now."

I asked Grimley and Lyra to fly around the palace to see if they could spot Reiko anywhere. Grimley promised to get Fern and

Otto to help, then he and Lyra took off. Violet let out a disappointed cheep that she couldn't go with them, but Leonidas took her back inside, along with the liladorn, and settled them both in the sitting room.

I hurried into my chambers and grabbed my dagger off the nightstand. I started to go back into the sitting room when my gaze landed on Armina's armor, which was still on a chair. I hesitated, then changed direction and went over to it. I pulled the breastplate on over my head and tied the straps, then yanked the silver gauntlets onto my arms. On my way out of the bedroom, I grabbed a dark gray cloak and settled it around my shoulders to help hide the armor.

I had just stepped into the sitting room when a soft knock sounded on the door. Hope filled me, and I rushed over and flung it open to find . . .

Delmira standing in the hallway, her hand poised to knock again.

She took one look at my face and frowned. "What's wrong?"

"Reiko's in trouble."

"Then we will find her and get her out of it," Delmira declared.

I opened my mouth to argue that it wasn't her problem, but Delmira speared me with a hard look, and my protests died on my lips. "Thank you."

She nodded. "Tell me what happened."

I told her and Leonidas about Reiko calling out to me, along with the harsh emotions I'd sensed from the dragon morph. I had just finished my story when Grimley's voice filled my mind.

There's no sign of Reiko in the gardens or anywhere else in the palace, but Fern flew Reiko over to the fairgrounds yesterday afternoon.

Reiko had said she was going to visit Kai and see how he had done in the tournament yesterday. Maybe she had spent the night with him and was still at the fairgrounds. Maybe Milo had seen her there and sent someone to attack her, just like he had targeted me during the tournament's opening ceremonies.

Gemma? Grimley asked. *What do you want to do?*

Leonidas and I need to fly over to the fairgrounds—right now. Come back to the balcony, please. And ask Lyra, Fern, and Otto to come too.

On my way.

A few minutes later, all four of the creatures landed on the balcony. I scrambled up onto Grimley, while Leonidas did the same thing to Lyra, and Delmira hopped onto Otto's back. Then, together with Fern, we all took off. The creatures pumped their wings hard and fast, zipping toward the fairgrounds on the out-skirts of the city.

A couple other gargoyles were flying out into the countryside to hunt, but most of the creatures were lazing on the rooftops, soaking up the early morning sun and watching the people mov-ing through the streets below.

I glanced down, but I didn't see anything unusual. Just folks eating breakfast and going about their morning chores. Throngs of people were already heading toward the fairgrounds, even though the tournament wouldn't resume until this afternoon. Everything was calm, quiet, and normal, but a cold finger of un-ease still snaked down my spine.

Something was wrong—I just didn't know what it was yet.

As we neared the main plaza in front of the fairgrounds, I pointed out a deserted alley to Grimley.

Put us down over there, please. I don't want to get too close to the plaza or the fairgrounds. I don't want anyone to realize that we left the palace and came here.

Why not? Grimley asked.

I'm not sure, exactly. I just . . . have a bad feeling, and I want to find Reiko as quickly and quietly as possible.

Grimley veered in that direction and dropped down into the

alley. Lyra did the same, and Leonidas and I both dismounted. Delmira slid off Otto, while Fern plopped down on her haunches.

"Where did you leave Reiko last night?" I asked the gargoyle.

Fern glanced around. "A couple of streets over, in an empty alley just like this one." Her face scrunched up with worry. "Was I not supposed to bring Lady Reiko here? She asked so nicely. She even gave me some of her sweet cakes. I thought it would be rude to say no."

I scratched Fern's head. "Don't worry. You didn't do anything wrong. We'll find Reiko. You stay here and keep watch from one of the rooftops with Grimley, Lyra, and Otto. We'll call if we need you."

Fern nodded, then flapped her wings and shot up into the sky. The other creatures followed her.

I raised the hood of my cloak to hide my face, and Leonidas and Delmira did the same thing. Together, the three of us left the alley, crossed the plaza, and entered the fairgrounds. Several merchants had already opened their carts, and the delicious scents of fried funnel cakes, caramel apples, and other sticky-sweet treats seasoned the air. Other merchants were setting out pennants, jewelry, and swords to sell, while some folks were setting up dart boards, ring tosses, and other games.

Even though it wasn't quite midmorning yet, the fairgrounds were still far more crowded than the plaza and the surrounding streets had been, and I reached out with my magic, skimming the thoughts of everyone around us.

Wonder how many funnel cakes I can eat today. Three seems like a good start . . .

Need to get rid of these apples before they spoil . . .

Hope my bet on Kai Nakamura to win the tournament pays off . . .

The usual sort of chatter filled my mind, but the mundane

thoughts did little to ease my worry. I quickened my pace, and Leonidas and Delmira hurried along beside me.

Several gladiators were sitting outside their tents, wolfing down eggs, bacon, potatoes, and more to fuel their bodies for their bouts later in the day.

"Where is Kai's tent?" Leonidas asked.

I glanced around, but I didn't see any flags that bore the troupe crest of the Crimson Dragons. Frustration filled me. "I don't know."

Delmira pointed to her right. "Let's go this way. I see something that might help."

Leonidas and I followed her through a couple of narrow lanes that ran in between the tents. A few hundred feet later, Delmira stopped in front of a gray-and-white-striped tent topped with a white flag featuring a gray falcon—the symbol for the Gray Falcons.

Just like many of the other gladiators, Adora was sitting outside her tent. An empty plate perched on the chair beside her, and she was sharpening a sword. She glanced up at the sound of our footsteps and did a double take when she caught sight of me.

"Gemma?" Adora asked. "Is that you?"

I lowered the hood of my cloak. "Hello, Adora."

She frowned. "What are you doing here?"

"I'm looking for my friend Reiko. She came to visit Kai Nakamura last night. Do you know where his tent is?"

Adora nodded, sheathed her sword, and got to her feet. "Sure. Follow me."

The gladiator stuck her head into the tent and told whoever was inside that she'd be back soon. Then she led us through the fairgrounds. A few minutes later, Adora stopped and pointed to a large tent at the end of a lane.

"There it is."

I started to head in that direction, but Adora stepped in front of me. The gladiator touched my arm and stiffened in surprise as she felt the silver gauntlet through my cloak. She released my arm, her eyes narrowing as she looked first at me, then Leonidas, then Delmira.

"What's wrong?" she asked. "And does this have anything to do with the attack at the palace two nights ago?"

I bit back a curse. I'd forgotten Adora had been in the gardens with Eichen and had seen Leonidas, Maeven, and me shove Milo's lightning into the sky.

Adora crossed her arms over her chest. "I thought we were friends, Gemma. True friends. But apparently, I was mistaken."

I frowned. "Of course we're friends. Why would you say that?"

She arched an eyebrow. "Because a true friend would accept help from another friend."

I bit back another curse. I hated her logic, but she was right. We *were* friends, and even though I didn't want to worry the gladiator, she deserved to know what was going on. Besides, maybe she had seen something that would tell me where Reiko might have gone.

So I told Adora everything I'd heard and sensed from the dragon morph. "Have you seen Reiko this morning?"

Adora shook her head. "Not this morning, but I did see her and Kai last night. They were strolling through the fairgrounds arm in arm. They looked quite happy together."

"Thanks for the information. I'll go see what Kai says."

Adora nodded and started to walk away, but this time, I reached out and touched her arm. She stopped and faced me.

"If you would, just . . . be on the lookout," I said. "And please tell the royal guards if you see anyone or anything suspicious."

Her eyes narrowed in thought. "You think there's going to be another attack. Maybe during the tournament?"

I shrugged, more frustration filling me. "I don't know. But

you saw what happened in the gardens, and I don't want something similar to happen here at the fairgrounds."

Adora's hand curled around her sword. "You can count on me and the rest of the Gray Falcons. I'll alert the others, and we'll keep an eye on the fairgrounds."

"Thank you."

She flashed me a smile, then walked down the lane, rounded a tent, and disappeared.

I headed toward Kai's tent, with Leonidas and Delmira still following along behind me. The closer I got, the more my steps quickened, and my cloak started snapping against my legs, as though the fabric was feeling the same worry that I was right now.

Kai's tent was smaller than I expected, especially given his enormous success as a gladiator, but a couple of guards were posted outside. No surprise there. Despite their own fighting prowess, the most popular gladiators often employed guards to help deal with overenthusiastic fans, along with threats from other gladiators. Some of the fighters and ringmasters were more than happy to stick a dagger in a competitor's back—literally—if it meant winning more bouts, riches, glory, and applause.

"Sorry," one of the guards said, and held his hand out. "But no fans are allowed inside."

I stepped forward and lifted my chin, letting the guards get a good look at my face. Their eyes widened in surprise.

"Are princesses allowed inside?" I drawled.

"Um, well . . ." the first one stammered.

"Move," I ordered. "I wish to speak to your master."

The guards looked at each other again, then eased away from the entrance. I swept past them, shoved the flap aside, and stepped into the tent. Leonidas and Delmira followed me.

The inside of the tent was much larger than it looked from the outside. Thick rugs covered the hard flagstones, while fine tables, chairs, and settees squatted here and there. A corkboard featuring today's tournament bouts, along with the names of the competing gladiators, was propped up on a wooden stand in one corner, while a bed with rumpled sheets took up another corner.

"It's about time you returned, my spy," a low, teasing voice called out. "I thought I was going to have to track you down again."

Kai stepped out from behind an ebony dressing screen next to the bed. A pair of black leggings was slung low on his hips, while his bare chest was an impressive wall of muscle, although small white scars cut across his skin here and there. Kai might be a fearsome champion, but he had paid the price for his success in the arena, as all gladiators did.

He froze at the sight of us standing in his tent. His golden gaze flicked from Leonidas to Delmira before finally landing on me, and the red dragon on his neck frowned.

"Reiko's in trouble," I said.

"What kind of trouble?" he asked in a sharp voice.

"That's what we're here to find out. Where did she go?"

He shook his head. "I don't know. We walked around the fairgrounds for a bit last night. Then we came back here and . . . talked."

An image flickered off the dragon morph—him and Reiko tangled up in the rumpled sheets in the bed. Of course they had *talked* last night. The two of them felt the same way about each other as Leonidas and I did, and Reiko would want to make the most of however much time she had left with the fierce gladiator.

"What happened after that?" I asked.

"We talked some more."

I arched an eyebrow.

"We really *did* talk," Kai said. "About the attack at Glitnir and where Milo and Wexel might be hiding in Glanzen. And about . . . us, and what might happen next."

I opened my mouth to keep questioning him, but Delmira

laid her hand on my arm and shook her head, telling me to calm down. She was right. My snapping at Kai wouldn't help Reiko, so I forced myself to draw in a deep breath and let it out.

"When did you last see Reiko?" I asked, my voice far less tense and hostile than before.

"She kissed me goodbye and slipped out of bed early this morning. She said she was going to investigate something. I offered to go with her, but she told me to get some more sleep and that she would be back in time for my first match." Kai glanced over at a clock sitting on a table. "That was more than two hours ago."

Concern surged off him and moved through me. Icy spikes of fear jabbed into my heart, while those talons of worry and dread dug in a little deeper. Reiko had gone out on another spy mission—alone. But why? And where?

Oh . . . just a little something I want to check on, Reiko's voice whispered through my mind. She'd said that in my chambers yesterday afternoon when we'd been talking about Milo and Wexel. Something in our conversation must have sparked an idea or given her some clue as to where the Mortans were hiding. I thought back, trying to remember everything we'd said, but nothing important popped into my mind.

Frustration filled me, but I forced myself to remain calm and keep asking questions. "Did Reiko bring anything with her last night? Or leave anything behind? Anything that might tell us where she went this morning?"

Kai ran a hand through his hair in obvious frustration, and his gaze darted from one thing to another. After a few seconds, he gestured over at a small red paper bag sitting on one of the tables. "Just some sweet cakes."

"Do you care if we look around?" I asked.

"Go ahead," he replied, more concern rippling off him. "I'll help you look."

Kai started roaming around the tent, as did Delmira and Leonidas. The three of them opened drawers, peered behind the furniture, and even lifted the rugs up off the ground, but I doubted they would find anything. Reiko Yamato was an excellent spy—the best—and she was far too smart to pick such obvious hiding places. If she had left a clue behind, it would be something small, something subtle, something most people would overlook.

I backed up until I was standing in a corner, then studied everything inside the tent. Where would I hide something as a spy? What sort of clue would I leave behind?

My gaze landed on the small red bag. I went over and peered inside, but only a few cakes littered the bottom of the paper. Odd, that Reiko hadn't eaten them all. Frustrated, I started to turn away when I realized the bag was sitting on something—a map.

The thick parchment featured a gargoyle's-eye view of Glanzen, from the surrounding Spire Mountains to the main streets and plazas to Glitnir sitting in the heart of the city like the center diamond in an elaborate engagement ring. My gaze snapped from one side of the map to the other and back again. Reiko could have gone anywhere in Glanzen or even out into the forests and mountains beyond, but she'd had some idea about where Milo was hiding, and I needed to figure out exactly what it was—before it was too late for her.

So I bent down and studied the map from every angle, looking for stray letters, ink stains, or anything else Reiko might have used to mark where she had gone. But I didn't see anything like that, and the only thing on the table beside the map was the bag of sweet cakes—

My gaze locked onto the bag again. Maybe Reiko *had* left a clue behind after all. I snatched up the bag and stared down at the spot that was revealed on the map.

Old Fairgrounds stretched across the parchment, along with a few drawings of tiny tents and cabins flanked by much larger rocks.

Of course.

I could have smacked myself for not seeing it sooner. All along, I'd been worried Milo and Wexel would use the crowds associated with the Sword and Shield Tournament to slip into Glanzen. I just hadn't thought they would be able to hide among the gladiators, especially given how well known and recognizable some of the fighters and troupes were.

I thought back, trying to remember everything I knew about the old fairgrounds. The area was about two-thirds of the way up Rockslide Mountain and featured several wooden buildings, along with the abandoned arena. It was the perfect place for Milo and Wexel to hide. Not only was it free of the scores of guards that Rhea had patrolling the city streets, but it was close enough to the main fairgrounds for the Mortans to slip in and out of the crowds. It was also close to an entrance to one of the old mining tunnels that ran underneath the city and eventually led to the Ripley tombs.

I set the bag of sweet cakes aside and tapped the map. "Reiko went here—to the old fairgrounds."

Kai hurried over and stared down at the map. "Why would she go there?"

"Because that's where Milo and Wexel are hiding."

Worry filled his eyes and creased the face of his inner dragon. "Are you sure?"

I pointed at the red paper bag. "Reiko loves sweet cakes more than just about anything else. There's no way she would leave them uneaten—unless something else, something more important caught her interest."

I looked at Leonidas and Delmira. "Let's go."

Kai stepped in front of me. "I'm coming with you."

I shook my head. "Reiko left you behind for a reason. She

didn't want you to get hurt, just like she didn't want me or anyone else to get hurt."

Determination filled his face, and his hands clenched into fists. "I know that, but I'm still coming with you."

I gestured over at the corkboard where his name was spelled out in big, black, bold letters. "But what about the tournament? Your match is the first one of the day. It's already after ten o'clock. We won't be back in time for it, and you'll forfeit your spot."

Kai moved past me and grabbed a red tunic that was draped over the dressing screen. "I care much more about Reiko than I do about winning another tournament."

The worry and concern gusting off him matched what was beating in my own heart. I wished Reiko could have heard what he'd just said, but Kai could tell her himself when we found her.

When—not if.

Because I didn't know what I would do if it was already too late, and Reiko was already dead.

CHAPTER TWENTY-TWO

K ai quickly dressed and buckled a weapons belt around his waist. Then he stuck his head inside another tent and told the Crimson Dragons ringmaster that he was leaving the fairgrounds.

"What? You can't leave now! We can't win the overall troupe championship for the season unless you win the tournament . . ." The ringmaster's protests rang out loud and clear.

Kai murmured something I couldn't hear. The ringmaster fell silent, and Kai stepped out of the tent, a determined look on his face. "Let's go."

I headed toward the arena, with the others walking alongside me. "Milo probably has people watching the main steps that lead to the old fairgrounds, so we'll have to take another route up the mountain."

Delmira gestured at the sky. "Don't you want to call for the creatures and fly up there? It will be much faster than hiking."

The image of Milo's arrows glowing with magic in the royal treasury filled my mind, and I had to suppress a shudder. "No, it's too risky. Milo is sure to have guards posted, and he's probably told them to watch for Grimley and Lyra. The last thing we need is for Milo to spot us flying up the mountain and use whatever tearstone arrows he has left to shoot us out of the sky. As much as I hate the delay, hiking up there on foot is our best option."

Worry pinched Delmira's face, but she nodded.

Once again, I drew up the hood of my cloak and lowered my head, as though I was protecting myself against the morning chill. Leonidas, Delmira, and Kai all did the same thing. We circled around the arena and headed toward the back of the fairgrounds. Only a few folks were out and about here, and no one gave us a second look as we moved past the gladiator training rings and slipped into the trees beyond.

In addition to the wide, flat steps, several parallel trails ran through the forest, but I ignored them all in favor of a faint, narrow path that veered sharply to the right, then zigzagged up the mountain. The path was littered with boulders, some so massive that we had to skirt around them, and it was so steep in some places that we were crawling upward more than walking.

"I feel like a bloody goat," Delmira grumbled, grabbing onto a tree branch to pull herself up a particularly steep section.

"I wish I were a goat right now," Leonidas replied, his boots churning up dirt and leaves as he followed her. "That way, I would be far less worried about falling and hitting every single rock on my way down the mountain."

"How do you know where to go?" Kai asked, glancing over at me. "I wouldn't think a princess would spend much time out here in the forest."

I smiled, memories filling my mind. "Oh, my mother used to bring me out here all the time to pick wildflowers, herbs, ramps, and the like. Years ago, before the new arena was built, we would pack a picnic lunch and hike up the mountain. My mother always took me to this plateau above the fairgrounds where we could sit and eat and watch the gladiators train below. She called it one of our secret spots, just like . . ."

My voice trailed off. Just like the spot where her memorial bench stood outside the Ripley mausoleum in the Edelstein Gardens. My smile vanished as I thought back over everything that had happened the past few days—and all the visions I'd had of my mother.

First, I'd spotted Merilde staring at the mausoleum doors that Milo, Wexel, and their men had used to infiltrate the palace. Then I'd seen her planting the liladorn by the gazebo, as if she'd known I would someday need its healing power to overcome Milo's lightning. And now here I was, following in her footsteps yet again. Had all those childhood trips to the old fairgrounds been innocent adventures? Or had they been meant to prepare me for this day, for this moment, when I so desperately needed to find Reiko?

If my mother had foreseen all of that, if she had *known* all these events would happen, then Merilde Ripley had been a far more powerful time magier than I had ever realized—and I owed her a debt I could never, ever repay.

Eventually, the steep slope leveled out, and we reached the wide plateau I remembered from all those childhood jaunts. The trees gave way to a stone ridge that jutted outward. I held my finger up to my lips, warning everyone to be quiet, then went down onto my hands and knees. Leonidas, Delmira, and Kai did the same thing, and we all crawled forward, then dropped onto our bellies and peered over the edge.

Just as I remembered, the ridge overlooked the old fairgrounds, which ran for more than a mile before following the curve of the mountain and disappearing from view. To the right, a few old wooden barracks crowded together like dull brown teeth, with the walls of the abandoned arena rising up behind them in the distance. A blur of movement caught my eye, as though something was dropping down into the arena. I squinted against the sun, but I couldn't tell what it was. Perhaps a rock or a dead tree sliding down the steep slope.

Besides, I was far less worried about whatever might be in the arena than I was about what filled the rest of the old fairgrounds. I'd expected the area to be mostly deserted, except for some gladiators, but I was wrong.

People, tents, and weapons stretched out as far as I could see.

Dull brown canvas tents topped with a variety of crested flags were lined up in neat rows, with narrow lanes running between them, just like down in the main fairgrounds. Some of the lanes opened into large circular areas, where men and women wearing black cloaks were sitting around fire pits, talking, laughing, and eating. Beyond the fire pits, wooden racks bristling with swords, spears, and other weapons stood at the ends of the lanes.

To a casual observer, this probably looked like a normal camp, a natural extension of the gladiators and tents crowding the main fairgrounds at the base of the mountain. But no merchants were hawking their wares, no minstrels were singing or playing music for coins, and no spectators were roaming around in search of their favorite fighters. Even more telling, tension hung in the air, as thick as the clouds of fog that still cloaked the very tiptop of the mountain.

Beside me, Leonidas let out a soft whistle, while Delmira chewed on her lower lip, worry creasing her face. A soft, muttered curse escaped Kai's lips.

"What's wrong?" I asked.

The dragon morph pointed to a spot near the center of the fairgrounds. "That's Bridget DiLucri's tent. I recognize her colors and crest from other tournaments."

My gaze landed on a large white tent with gold stripes that was topped with a white flag that featured a woman's face done in gold thread. Two coins formed the woman's eyes, while another coin served as her mouth. Kai was right. That was definitely the DiLucri crest. The flag rippled in the wind, making the woman's face glimmer like . . . a gold coin.

Like the same kind of gold coin I had found in the cargo hold of *The Drowned Man* a few days ago.

I'd thought Milo and Wexel had been trying to book passage on the ship to escape Andvari, but that had *never* been Milo's plan. He hadn't gone to Allentown to escape—he'd gone to get what he'd paid for.

What kind of passengers? From where? My own voice whispered through my mind, followed by Captain Davies's reply.

Gladiators, from the looks of them. From Fortuna Island. This is the fifth load of them I've hauled up the river in the last few weeks. Going to the Sword and Shield Tournament in Glitnir like everyone else.

Then Adora's voice whispered through my mind. *Bridget splits her time between being a gladiator and helping her extended family run the Fortuna Mint. She's one of their top geldjagers.*

Adora had mentioned that the morning of the gladiator introductions in the throne room. I hadn't given much thought to her words at the time, but now I couldn't stop thinking about them, along with something Milo had said when he'd broken into the treasury.

Once Glitnir is reduced to rubble, it will be easy for my men to slip out of their hiding place and take the city.

Now I knew where that hiding place was, and more important, what he was planning. All these men and women might look like gladiators, and some of them might even be competing in the Sword and Shield Tournament, like Bridget DiLucri was. But really, they were DiLucri fighters, bought and paid for by Milo.

An army of mercenaries was camped out at the old fairgrounds—and they were getting ready to invade my city.

For several seconds, all I could do was stare out over the people, tents, and weapons. With every mercenary I looked at, and every tent, and every sword glinting in the sun, more and more icy worry invaded my body. Desperate to focus on something else, I dug my fingers into the edge of the ridge. The stone scraped against my palms, and those dull aches rippled through my hands again, but the uncomfortable sensations helped me push down that growing tide of worry.

"So this is Milo's plan," I murmured. "Clever. Very, very clever. If nothing else, you have to admire his audacity."

Kai frowned. "What do you mean?"

I swept my hand out, gesturing at the encampment, along with all the mercenaries moving around below. "First, Milo creates tearstone arrows to kill gargoyles. Then he breaks into the royal treasury and uses those same arrows to fuel his lightning-in-a-bottle experiment in hopes of killing me and my family, along with most of the Andvarian nobles. If he had succeeded, he would have marched these mercenaries into Glanzen while Glitnir was still a pile of smoking rubble. In one fell swoop, he would have killed the Ripleys and anyone else who might have stood against him and taken control of the city. After that, it would have been easy for him to conquer the rest of Andvari."

As I said the words aloud, the full weight and impact of them hit me like a spear slamming into my chest. Milo's plan had almost worked, but the most frightening thing was that it could *still* work.

Oh, Milo might not have killed my family and the nobles, or destroyed the palace, but he had enough mercenaries to do major damage to Glanzen. And if some of the mercenaries were equipped with his tearstone arrows . . . Well, Milo could use the weapons to shoot his own lightning through the streets and sky. The crown prince and his mercenaries could slaughter dozens, hundreds, perhaps even thousands of Andvarian guards, along with innocent citizens and gargoyles.

Milo could still seize the city, just like he'd planned.

I shivered, but I forced myself to push my concern aside. First, we needed to find Reiko. Then we could worry about thwarting Milo and his mercenaries.

My gaze flicked from one face and tent to another. I didn't recognize anyone or see anything that would tell me where Reiko might be, so I reached out with my magic.

These eggs need more pepper . . .

Wonder when Bridget will give the order to march down the mountain . . .

Hope we don't have to fight until after the tournament wraps up . . .

I moved past the mercenaries and all their thoughts and stretched out even farther with my power, searching for that sly presence that was uniquely Reiko—

A thin, familiar thread snaked through the air, as soft and fragile as a wisp of smoke. I started to move past it, but it made my fingertips tingle, just the tiniest bit. So I grabbed hold of that thread and followed it, as though it were a trail of breadcrumbs leading me through the forest of mercenaries . . .

From one instant to the next, the camp below me vanished, and I found myself standing inside a large tent. The tent itself was a dull brown, but a large purple banner with a gold Morricone crest hung on one of the walls. My magic had led me to Milo's tent. Now I just needed to find Reiko.

I turned around in a slow circle, not wanting to move too fast for fear of losing the thread, the connection I had to the dragon morph. A bed, a desk, and some chairs crowded into the tent, along with a table that featured a map of Glanzen that was even larger and more detailed than the one in Kai's tent. My gaze landed on a small book with a light purple cover that was open on the corner of the table—Dahlia Sullivan's journal.

As much as I itched to go over and see what Milo had been looking at in the journal, I kept turning in that slow circle, still searching for Reiko—

A familiar bit of green caught my eye. I froze and looked to my right. A hand was peeking out from behind the thick, wide post in the center of the tent—a hand that featured a dragon face with emerald-green scales.

"Reiko," I whispered, even though I knew she couldn't hear me in this ghostly form.

My caution evaporated, replaced by another surge of worry, and I hurried forward and rounded the post, dreading what I would find on the other side.

It was even worse than I'd feared.

Coldiron chains wrapped around Reiko's chest, binding her to the post. She was hunkered down on the ground, with her legs curled up beneath her and one of her hands shackled high above her head, leaving her in a twisted, awkward, painful position.

And she had been severely beaten.

Blood and bruises covered Reiko's face like red, purple, and blue paint. She had two black eyes, her nose was broken, and both of her lips were swollen and split wide open. Her knuckles were also battered and bruised, as though she had repeatedly punched someone—or several someones. Blood also flecked her hands and rimmed her fingertips, as though she'd partially morphed and sunk her talons into an enemy. At least, I hoped that was an enemy's blood, and not her own.

I went down on my knees and started to reach out to her, but my hand fell to my side. It was no use. She wouldn't feel anything, not with me in this ghostly form, and I certainly couldn't remove her chains, much less get her out of the tent.

Guilt and anguish filled me, but those emotions were

quickly replaced by a far more chilling realization—Reiko hadn't moved or stirred the whole time I'd been in here. Hadn't opened her eyes, or shifted on her knees, or moaned with pain. My gaze dropped to the dragon on her right hand, but its eyes were closed, and it seemed as limp and lifeless as the rest of her body did.

Fear and dread gripped my chest like a pair of icy talons, squeezing my heart tight and tearing into it at the same time. No, she couldn't be . . . she wasn't . . . she couldn't be *dead*.

Not Reiko, not my friend, not the best spy I had ever known.

Those talons of fear and dread clamped down even tighter, shredding a little more of my heart. The seconds ticked by in quiet, eerie silence as I waited for Reiko to twitch, to blink, to do something, *anything*, that would indicate she was still alive—

The dragon on her hand slowly cracked its black eyes open and looked around with a weary, bleary gaze, as though it was utterly exhausted. Some of the fear and worry in my heart eased, and I could finally breathe again.

I leaned forward so that my face was level with her bloody, battered features. "Don't worry. We're going to get you out of here. So hold on, just a little while longer. Okay?"

Reiko's eyes fluttered open, as if she had heard my whispered plea. A few tears streamed down her face, revealing just how much pain she was in, but she straightened up the tiniest bit.

Her gaze flicked back and forth, and her inner dragon frowned. "Gemma?" Reiko rasped. "Are you here?"

"Yes! Yes, I'm here! Can you hear me?"

This time, I did reach for her, although my hand wisped right through hers, since I was still in my ghostly form. Reiko flinched, as though she had sensed my touch. I froze, not wanting to cause her any more pain. She glanced around again and wet her split, bloody lips, making herself wince this time.

"Gemma," Reiko whispered in a low, urgent voice. "If you're here, listen to me. Don't come into camp. Milo knows you'll realize that I'm missing and eventually find this place. I left you a clue in Kai's tent in case I didn't make it back. But don't be stupid and try to rescue me."

Her green gaze darted back and forth again, as though she was trying to find me even in my ghostly form. "For once in your life, listen to me. Don't come here. Don't put yourself in danger. Don't be a hero. Be a spy instead and save your people and gargoyles—"

The canvas flap rustled, and Reiko bit off the rest of her words. I shot to my feet and whirled around, my hands balling into fists, even though it wouldn't do me any good, since my fists—and I—weren't really here.

Milo strode into the tent, along with Captain Wexel and Bridget DiLucri.

The crown prince was dressed in a short, formal purple jacket, along with black leggings and boots. Gold buttons marched down the front of his jacket, while the Morricone crest, done in shimmering gold thread, stretched all the way across his chest. A gold sword dangled from his belt.

Wexel was also dressed in a short, formal purple jacket, although his lacked the royal crest. He too was carrying a sword, along with a dagger. Jewels sparkled on another object hanging from his weapons belt, although I couldn't quite make out what it was. Perhaps it was the mysterious item he'd stolen from the royal treasury.

Worry surged through me. The crown prince and the captain weren't hiding who and what they were anymore, which meant Milo was much closer to unleashing his mercenaries than I'd realized.

Unlike the two Mortans, Bridget wore a white tunic, along with sandy brown leggings and boots, and a brown cloak rippled around her shoulders. She too was armed with a sword, and a couple of daggers also dangled from her belt.

Milo and Wexel went over to the map on the table, but Bridget eyed Reiko, as if making sure the dragon morph was still securely chained to the post. Reiko glared up at the other woman, hate and disgust blazing in her eyes.

Bridget eyed Reiko a moment longer, then went over to Milo and Wexel. "Are you certain your plan will still work?"

Milo flapped his hand in a curt, dismissive gesture, not even bothering to look up from the map. "Of course. The Ryusaman spy wandering into camp changes nothing."

Bridget didn't look convinced. "You should have let me kill Yamato the second I spotted her sneaking around camp. She might have used her magic to reach out to her friends, especially Gemma Ripley. According to that prophecy you mentioned, the Ripley princess is far more powerful than anyone suspects."

I frowned. What prophecy? And what, if anything, did it have to do with me?

Milo flapped his hand again, this time gesturing at the purple journal on the corner of the table. "Just because Dahlia Sullivan and my mother believe some moldy old prophecy doesn't mean it's true."

Bridget looked at Wexel, who shrugged back at her.

"Besides, you and your men captured the spy before she could do anything other than look around my tent," Milo continued. "Reiko Yamato is no threat to us now, and she didn't have time to tell her friends anything. From the rumors I've heard, Glitzma is still holed up in the palace, recovering from her ordeal. And if she's not, and she does wander up here . . ." He gestured at Reiko. "Well, every trap needs bait."

Reiko glared at the crown prince, and her hands flexed, as though she wanted to strangle him, despite her severe injuries.

Bridget harrumphed. "Yes, well, Gemma Ripley recovering from her ordeal is another failure on your part. *You* didn't destroy the palace as you promised, much less kill any of the Ripleys or Andvarian nobles. So far, your plan has been one massive disappointment after another."

At her sharp words, Milo lifted his head, and magic crackled in his eyes. Wexel grimaced and sidled to the left, moving out of the dangerous space in between the crown prince and the gladiator-turned-geldjager.

Bridget stared right back at Milo, anger blazing in her hazel eyes, completely unafraid of him. Magic swirled around the gladiator, and her fingers clenched into a tight fist, as though she wanted to use her strength power to punch the crown prince right through one of the canvas walls.

"My plan remains on track," Milo said in a cold voice. "The mercenaries will slip down the mountain and take their positions around the arena. Then, when Heinrich Ripley arrives for the start of the tournament this afternoon, Wexel and I will use my tearstone arrows and lightning magic to assassinate him, along with everyone else on the royal terrace. After that, my soldiers will join forces with the mercenaries and march through the streets, killing anyone who gets in their way, until we reach the palace."

Bridget shook her head. "Forget about making a spectacle of the Ripleys in the arena. After the tournament ends for the day, everyone will be too busy drinking and celebrating to be on the lookout for trouble. We should delay the attack until late tonight or early tomorrow morning when everyone, including the royal guards, are either drunk, exhausted, or asleep."

This time, she gestured over at the purple journal. "You said that book contains information about all the secret passageways that lead inside the palace. The Andvarians might have blocked the mausoleum entrance, but they couldn't have possibly gotten to all the other ones yet. We should let the tournament proceed as planned, then march straight to Glitnir under the cover of darkness tonight and use one of the secret passageways to slip inside the palace."

"You're just saying that because you want to win the tournament," Wexel said in a snide voice. "Didn't Kai Nakamura beat you in the final bout in the Tournament of Champions last year at the Regalia Games?"

Anger stained Bridget's cheeks. "Of course I want to win the bloody tournament. And yes, Kai Nakamura did beat me last year, which is why I want to face him in the final bout." Her hand drifted over to her sword again. "Since you seem so uncertain about my skills, perhaps I should show you just how good a gladiator I am."

Wexel's face paled, and he sidled back a little farther at her threat.

Bridget gave him a disgusted look, then focused on Milo again. "Tournament aside, we should still wait until tonight to strike. I don't want to waste men just because you want the Ripleys to die in some grand, theatrical fashion."

Milo stared down his nose at her. "The last time I checked, they were *my* men, bought and paid for, and thus, mine to do with as I please."

"Bought and paid for with Corvina's money," Wexel muttered, although neither Milo nor Bridget paid any attention to him.

"Or is the Fortuna Mint reneging on our deal?" Milo asked.

Bridget stiffened as though he had slapped her. "Of course not. The Mint *always* keeps its promises."

"Good," he replied. "Then we will move out this afternoon as scheduled while everyone is distracted and inside the arena."

More magic crackled in Milo's eyes, and an evil grin curved his lips. "Besides, I'm going to enjoy using my tearstone arrows and lightning to take Glitnir by force."

Bridget harrumphed again. "Just don't forget who is backing your plan—and especially what you promised the DiLucris."

Milo flapped his hand yet again. "Yes, yes. When I am king, I will elevate the DiLucris and make Fortuna Island its own kingdom."

The deal they'd struck didn't surprise me. The DiLucris had long wanted to be recognized as a royal family and have Fortuna declared an official kingdom, even though they already controlled the island.

"Good," Bridget replied in a deceptively pleasant tone. "Because my family does *not* condone failure—or especially betrayal. Either one will immediately void our deal."

Milo opened his mouth to protest, but Bridget cut him off.

"And just in case you were thinking of stabbing me in the back and trying to force my men to follow yours, let me remind you that the Fortuna Mint takes such matters extremely seriously. My family has an entire legion of geldjagers dedicated to tracking down and killing those who try to double-cross us." She gestured over at Reiko. "Those geldjagers will make the beating Wexel gave this spy seem like a pleasant dream compared to what they will do to the two of you."

Bridget gave the Mortans a sweet, venomous smile. Wexel had the good sense to look worried, but Milo rolled his eyes.

"Your concerns are noted." He arched an eyebrow at her. "But you would do well to remember that *I* am the one who managed to invade Glanzen *and* Glitnir right under the Ripleys' noses, which is far more than you and your lauded geldjagers have ever accomplished."

Bridget stiffened again, and anger blasted off her, the emotion hot enough to make my own cheeks burn, despite my ghostly presence.

Milo sneered at Bridget again, then turned back to the map,

but Wexel kept eyeing the gladiator, as did I. More anger blasted off Bridget, and her fingers clenched around her sword, as though she wanted to gut Milo with the weapon.

After several seconds, Bridget huffed out a breath and removed her hand from her sword. "If you are still determined to go through with this, then I will go ready my men."

Wexel nodded. "I will do the same."

Milo waved his hand, not even bothering to look at them. Bridget left the tent, along with Wexel—

"Gemma?" Kai's voice intruded on my thoughts. "Gemma? What are you doing?"

I tried to stay in the tent, but his voice broke that thin thread connecting me to Reiko, and my magic and essence snapped back into my own body.

I sucked in a breath and opened my eyes. Kai was staring at me, a worried look on his face. Delmira also seemed worried and confused, but Leonidas reached over and gripped my hand.

"What did you see?" he asked.

I jerked my head, and we all slithered away from the edge of the ridge, got to our feet, stepped back into the protective screen of the trees. I told my friends everything I had seen and heard in the tent, including Reiko's injuries and Milo's plan to attack my family and the nobles during the tournament, then march on the palace.

Delmira cursed, as did Leonidas. Only Kai remained silent, his gaze moving from one tent to another, as if he could stare through all those canvas walls and see Reiko just as I had.

"I'm going to get Reiko," Kai announced. "The rest of you can do whatever you want about the impending attack."

He drew his sword and spun around. I bit back a curse. Bloody Ryusamans. Why did they always want to take on their enemies alone? Maybe it was the solitary nature of being a gladiator and a spy, or perhaps it was sheer stubbornness. Either way, it was a wonder that both Kai and Reiko hadn't been killed long ago.

I darted in front of the dragon morph.

"I don't have time to argue with you, Gemma," Kai snarled. "Milo and Wexel won't risk leaving Reiko behind in camp, and they'll kill her as soon as they are ready to march out. If she dies, if I lose her . . ." His voice trailed off, and the face of his inner dragon scrunched up with worry.

Kai shook his head, as if trying to fling his fear away, then moved to the side. He started to barrel past me, but I stabbed my finger into his muscled chest.

"Stop!" I hissed. "*Think.* Because that's exactly what Reiko would do right now. Not go rushing down into a camp full of mercenaries like a reckless idiot. You do that, and you'll only get yourself killed, along with Reiko and the rest of us."

An angry glower filled Kai's face, as well as that of his inner dragon, but he didn't try to move past me again. "And what do *you* suggest we do, princess?"

He hurled my title around as if it were an insult, but I ignored his harsh tone. He was just worried about Reiko, the same as I was. But we needed a plan, so I glanced down at the camp again. Most of the mercenaries were still eating, talking, and sharpening their weapons, and I couldn't really tell which ones were standing guard, since they were all wearing those black cloaks—

An idea popped into my mind, and a smile curved my lips.

"Gemma? What are you thinking?" Leonidas asked.

"We're going to do what Reiko always does."

"What's that?" Delmira asked.

My smile widened. "Hide in plain sight."

CHAPTER TWENTY-THREE

I told the others my plan. No one particularly liked it, especially not Leonidas, but we all agreed it was our best chance to save Reiko.

"I should go with you," Leonidas said. "My mind magier power could be more useful down there than Kai's morphing ability. It's not like he can shape-shift into another person."

I shook my head. "No, you need to stay here precisely because you *are* a mind magier. If the worst happens, and we get captured or killed, then you and Delmira need to summon Grimley and the other creatures, fly back to the palace, and tell my family what Milo is plotting. Otherwise, this will all have been for nothing, and Glanzen will still fall. Promise me that you won't come try to save us. Promise me, Leo."

His jaw clenched, and a stubborn look filled his face, but I stared him down.

"I promise." He ground out the words. "But the second your family knows what's going on, I'm coming back to help you."

"I know."

Leonidas cupped my cheek in his hand and stroked his thumb over my skin, making me shiver. He pulled me toward him, and his lips crashed into mine. I tangled my fingers in his hair, drawing him closer and kissing him back just as fiercely. All too soon, we broke apart, both of us breathing hard. His thumb stroked over my skin again, then he dropped his hand from my face and stepped back.

"See you soon," he murmured.

"Count on it."

Leonidas stared at me a second longer, then whirled around and stalked away. Delmira nodded at me, then followed her brother deeper into the woods. That left me standing alone with Kai.

I closed my eyes and reached out with my magic. *Grimley. We've found Reiko. She's in the middle of a camp of DiLucri mercenaries . . .*

I told the gargoyle everything that had happened, and what Kai and I were going to do. He didn't like my plan any more than Leonidas did, but he too agreed it was our best chance to save Reiko.

When I finished talking to Grimley, I reached out with my magic again, trying to tell Father, Grandfather Heinrich, and Rhea what was going on, but I got only faint flickers off them, and they were simply too far away for me to communicate with them.

A frustrated sigh escaped my lips, and I opened my eyes to find Kai staring at me, a thoughtful expression on his face, as well as that of his inner dragon.

"You're different than how I'd thought you would be," he said.

I arched an eyebrow. "And how did you think I would be? Spoiled? Pampered? As dumb and worthless as a box full of fool's gold?"

He shrugged. "Something like that. I assumed people called you *Glitzma* for good reason. But I can see why your friendship means so much to Reiko." A rueful smile tugged at his lips. "You're just as smart, sly, and stubborn as she is."

"I take that as the highest compliment." I drew my dagger from my belt and twirled it around in my hand, so that the blade was resting up against my wrist and hidden from sight. "Now let's go get her back."

Kai and I left the ridge behind and crept through the trees and down the slope toward the old fairgrounds. Just like Reiko, Kai moved through the woods as easily and silently as a cloud of smoke, and I strived to match his stealthy steps. For the most part, I managed to be almost as quiet, and we reached the edge of camp without anyone seeing or hearing us approach.

Two men wearing black cloaks were sitting around a fire pit, stretching their hands out over the crackling flames. No one else was moving through this area, and a row of tents blocked this section off from the rest of the camp.

I looked at Kai, who nodded and slipped back even deeper into the trees. I gave him a few seconds to get into position, then squared my shoulders, lifted my chin, and strode out of the woods. I was no longer trying to be quiet, so I scuffed my boots through some dead leaves, making plenty of noise. The two men drew their swords, stood up, and stepped forward, blocking me from going any farther.

"Sorry," one of the guards said. "But this camp is for gladiators only. No fans allowed."

"Oh, I'm not a fan any more than you're a gladiator," I replied in a breezy tone. "But I am the person who's going to kill you."

The two guards glanced at each other, then they both started laughing. I tightened my grip on the dagger still hidden in my hand and waited for their chuckles to fade away.

The second man jerked his thumb over his shoulder. "You want to keep her here while I fetch one of the captains?"

"Nah," the first guard drawled. "I have a much better idea of what to do with her."

His gaze trailed down my body, lingering on my breasts and hips, even though they were covered up by my cloak. A cruel grin split his face, and his lust blasted over me, as sharp as a razor dragging along my skin.

"Oh, yeah," he crooned. "We should make sure she's not a threat. You know, search her for weapons before we summon a captain."

Understanding filled the second man's face, and he also grinned. "Definitely."

"Keep watch," the first guard ordered, and sheathed his sword.

The second man leered at me, but he held his position and kept his sword at the ready. The first man slowly approached me, as if he thought I was going to scream, run, or both, but I just stood there and watched him creep closer.

The idiot didn't realize he was sneaking up on his own death.

Right before the first guard would have reached me, a shadow detached itself from the side of one of the tents and sidled forward. The second guard must have seen the motion out of the corner of his eye because he turned in that direction—

Kai let out a low growl, surged forward, and raked his long black talons across the guard's throat.

The guard's sword slipped from his fingers and clattered to the ground. He opened his mouth, trying to scream, but he was already choking on his own blood. Kai whipped up his own sword and slashed it across the man's chest. The guard let out another choked whimper, then sagged to the ground, already more dead than alive.

The first guard spun in that direction. "What the—"

The second he turned away, I sank my fingers into his hair, yanked his head back, and slit his throat with my dagger. I released him, and the guard dropped to the ground without making a sound.

Kai and I both glanced around, but everything remained quiet, and no one came running over to check on the guards. Together, we dragged the two men into a tent, stripped off their black cloaks, put them on, and drew the hoods up over our heads, hiding our faces. Then we slipped out of the tent and headed even deeper into the camp.

With our stolen cloaks, Kai and I were just two more mercenaries roaming around, searching for food, drink, and warmth from the various campfires. We kept our heads up, and our strides long, smooth, and confident. A few folks gave us cursory looks, but most of the other mercenaries were too busy eating, talking, and sharpening their weapons to care what we were doing.

Kai and I went down one lane after another, quickly making our way to the center of camp. He pointed out Bridget's gold-striped tent, and we ducked behind it and peered around the side. I searched for Reiko's smoky presence, and my gaze landed on another, much larger tent about fifty feet away that had two guards posted outside.

"Reiko is in there," I whispered.

He gripped his sword a little tighter. "Then let's go get her."

I nodded and reached out with my magic, searching for a different presence, and a light, electric, feathery touch tickled my mind. *We're in position.*

So are we, Leonidas replied. *Get ready.*

Kai and I held our positions. No one was moving through this section of camp, although snatches of conversation drifted over to me, along with soft *pop-pop-pops* of firewood and the occasional *clang-clang* of pots and pans banging together.

"What is taking him so bloody long?" Kai growled.

"Don't worry. Leonidas will get the job done—"

CRACK!

The sound ripped through the air like a sharp spike of thunder, booming over the entire camp. As soon as the harsh echoes faded away, a babble of voices sounded.

"What was that?"

"Thunder, maybe?"

"Where did it come from? There's not a cloud in the sky!"

High up on the ridge, an enormous boulder broke loose from an outcropping of rocks and tumbled down the slope, gaining speed with every hop, skip, and bounce. The boulder hit another ledge and soared out into the air, as though it were a strix taking flight. Then, just as swiftly, the stone plummeted downward and rolled right into the camp, tearing through tents, smashing through weapons racks, and squishing mercenaries like bugs.

The boulder kept rolling, rolling, rolling, leaving a trail of death and destruction in its wake. Screams filled the air, and dark satisfaction rippled through my heart.

Good job. I sent the thought to Leonidas. *The mercenaries are running around like ants whose nest has been kicked to pieces.*

Just following your example. I remembered you dropping that tree on Wexel's men in the woods outside Haverton. Besides, I thought Rockslide Mountain should live up to its name.

Even though he couldn't see me, I still rolled my eyes. *Show-off.*

Leonidas's laughter echoed in my mind.

The guards in front of Milo's tent exchanged a look, then scurried away.

Kai stepped forward, but I grabbed his arm.

"Wait," I whispered. "Just wait. That's what Reiko would do."

His biceps bunched under my hand, as though he was going to pull free, but he slowly relaxed and held his position.

Even though the boulder had come to a stop, the noise and commotion went on for quite some time. Several mercenaries rushed by our position, but they were all trying to determine whether it was a natural rockslide or a calculated attack, and no one stopped and asked why we weren't doing the same thing.

Eventually, the shouts died down, and a more normal level of noise descended over the camp. Some of the mercenaries kept rushing around, but since no enemies were invading the fairgrounds, most folks had decided it was just a rockslide and nothing more.

Kai shifted on his feet, and thick clouds of black smoke boiled out of the mouth of his inner dragon and skated across his skin. More than once, he sucked in a breath, as if to demand we storm into Milo's tent, but each time, I shook my head and he pressed his lips together. But tension kept radiating off him, and his unease clamped around my body like a vise, increasing my own worry.

After about ten minutes, the canvas flap on the tent drew back, and Milo stepped outside. Kai and I both froze, and I held my breath, hoping the crown prince couldn't sense my magic the same way his lightning was making my fingertips tingle in warning.

Milo glanced around, his right foot tapping with impatience. A few seconds later, Wexel rounded the side of a nearby tent and hurried over to the crown prince.

"Well?" Milo demanded.

Wexel shrugged. "It seems to be a rockslide. The ground is still wet from the recent rains and snows. Some of the men slipped on the trail going up the slope to check it out. They didn't find any footprints or anything else to indicate it was deliberate sabotage."

Milo stared up at the ridge, his forehead crinkling, as though he could see what had really happened just by looking in that direction long and hard enough.

"Very well," he replied. "But tell everyone to be on alert. Gemma Ripley is sure to have realized her little dragon is missing by now, and sooner or later, she'll come here to fetch her friend. Tell the perimeter guards to let Glitzma sneak into the camp, all the way to my tent. If she does try a rescue mission, then we'll be waiting for her."

Milo stuck his head back into his tent and murmured something I couldn't hear. A few seconds later, Bridget DiLucri stepped outside, along with half a dozen mercenaries, all of whom were clutching swords.

Beside me, Kai let out a soft, muttered curse. "Did you know all those people were waiting inside to capture us?"

"When I was ghosting earlier, Milo said Reiko was bait, and he had her chained to the post in the exact center of the tent, like he wanted her to be the first—and only—thing someone saw when they stepped inside. So I figured he had some sort of trap planned."

Kai and I held our positions, and each minute that ticked by seemed longer and slower than the last. People came and went from Milo's tent, and I kept count of those entering and leaving. Eventually, all the mercenaries departed, and only two guards remained posted outside. Even Milo, Wexel, and Bridget wandered away to check out the damage the boulder had done.

"Now?" Kai asked, that impatient edge back in his voice.

It could still be a trap, but we wouldn't get a better chance than this.

I nodded. "Now."

Together, we left our hiding spot in the shadows and headed for Milo's tent.

"Let me handle this," Kai whispered as we approached the guards.

He tossed back the hood of his cloak, plastered a smile on his face, and swaggered over to the two men, who eyed him with obvious suspicion. Unlike many of the other people in the camp, these two men were wearing purple cloaks, marking them as Mortan soldiers instead of black-clad DiLucri mercenaries.

"Hey, fellas," Kai said, his smile widening. "We're here for the shift change."

One of the men frowned. "What shift change?"

"Yeah," the other man chimed in. "We were told to stay here and not to let anyone inside until Prince Milo returns."

"Captain Bridget told us to relieve you fellas." Kai shrugged, as if he couldn't understand the whims of the higher-ups. "Besides, don't you want to get some food in your belly before we all have to march down the mountain?"

As if in answer to his question, the first man's stomach let out a loud, hungry grumble, and he winced in embarrassment.

Kai clapped that man on the shoulder. "Good thing we came when we did. Sounds like you could use some breakfast, my friend."

The man scowled and shrugged off Kai's hand. "I'm not your friend. I'm a soldier, and you're a mercenary. Big difference, buddy."

The other Mortan muttered his agreement.

Kai shrugged again, taking the insult in stride. "Whatever you say. Anyway, we have our orders, so you fellas can go take a break, and we'll stand guard until the bosses get back and sort out who's doing what. Okay?"

The two Mortans glanced at each other again, clearly torn. No one, not even the most devoted, loyal soldier, actually *liked* guard duty. Most of the time, it was the most boring job in all of Buchovia, especially right now, when everyone else was running around, chattering about the supposed rockslide.

The first guard opened his mouth as if to agree, but then he sighed and shook his head, and the second man followed suit.

"Sorry, pal," the first guard said. "Milo Morricone himself told us to stand watch, so that's what we're going to do."

"Yeah," the second man chimed in. "You don't want to know what Milo does to guards who leave their posts."

Both men shuddered and shifted on their feet.

Frustration surged off Kai, but he grinned again and opened his mouth, still determined to convince the guards to leave their posts—

"Hey," the first man said, staring at me. "You look really familiar. Have I seen you before?"

Before I could spout some lie, the second man let out a vicious curse. "That's Gemma Ripley—"

I sprang forward, whipped up my dagger, and buried the blade in his chest, even as I used my magic to clamp his lips shut. The man's eyes bulged, and he let out a muffled scream. He raised his sword, but I slapped the weapon out of his hand, then ripped my dagger out of his chest and slashed it across his throat. He stumbled backward, hit the side of the tent, and slid down to the ground.

The first guard cursed and brandished his sword, but Kai knocked the weapon away, then raked his talons across the guard's throat. The man also dropped to the ground, choking to death on his own blood.

I glanced around, but no one else was in this section of camp, and our attack had gone unnoticed—for now. "Help me get them out of sight!" I hissed.

Together, Kai and I dragged the guards around to the back side of the tent and propped them up against one of the canvas walls, as though they were still sleeping off last night's drink. Then we headed back around to the front of the tent, raised the canvas flap, and slipped inside.

Even though we'd watched all the guards leave earlier, I still scanned the area, searching for enemies. But the tent was deserted, except for Reiko, who was still chained to the center post, just like I'd seen in my vision earlier.

Kai let out a low, angry growl, his gaze fixed on Reiko. At the last second, right before he would have charged forward and closed the distance between them, I flung my arm out, stopping him.

For a moment, I didn't even know why I'd done it, but an instant later, my fingertips started tingling in warning. "Stop. There's a magical trap in here somewhere."

Kai tensed, but he held his position. We both glanced around, and I reached out, trying to follow that invisible string of magic back to its source—

A light gray gleam caught my eye, and I looked to my left. One of Milo's tearstone arrows was loaded in a crossbow propped up on a nearby table. A thin piece of string was wrapped around the crossbow's trigger. I squinted and followed the other end of the string along the table and down to the ground. It stopped about two inches above the rugs, wrapped around one of the table legs, and then stretched across the width of the tent—right in front of Reiko.

A crude but effective tripwire. Knowing Milo, that arrow was probably coated with fool's bane, amethyst-eye, or some other deadly poison to ensure it killed whoever triggered the trap.

I pointed out the tripwire to Kai, who went over, leaned down, and used his sword to carefully sever the string, rendering the crossbow harmless.

"Any more traps?" he asked.

I reached out with my magic again, but I didn't sense anything else. "We're good."

Kai hurried over, sheathed his sword, and dropped to his knees in front of Reiko. Anguish filled his face, and his inner dragon let out a silent roar before spewing out clouds of thick, black smoke, along with red-hot flames that made his skin glow.

"Reiko?" Kai asked in a low, strained voice. "Can you hear me?"

She was in the same position as before, slumped up against the post, with her legs tucked under her body, and one arm stretched high above her head. Despite the low rumble of Kai's voice, Reiko remained completely, utterly still, and her inner dragon had its eyes closed again. Fear punched into my stomach that we were too late, that Milo and Wexel had already killed her—

A soft sigh escaped her lips. Her head slowly lifted, and Reiko peered at Kai through her swollen, blackened eyes.

"Kai?" she whispered. "Is that really you? Or is this another dream?"

He smiled at her, tears gleaming in his own eyes. "Of course it's me. I couldn't let you sneak into Milo's camp and have all the fun."

Reiko laughed, but it was a small, weak sound, more like a rasp of air leaking out of her lungs than genuine amusement. "Oh, yes. I've been having barrels of fun with Milo, Wexel, and Bridget."

He smiled at her again, although his inner dragon kept belching out clouds of smoke and fire. "Let's get you out of here."

Magic rippled off Kai, and long black talons sprouted on his fingertips again. Instead of trying to tear through the coldiron chains, he bent down, stuck one of his talons into the attached lock, and slowly wiggled his finger back and forth. A few seconds later, the lock popped open.

"Neat trick," I said.

He grinned. "Reiko showed me how to do it."

Kai unwrapped the chains from around her body and removed the shackle from her wrist. Reiko pitched forward, and Kai scooped her up into his arms.

"You're safe now," he murmured. "We're going to get you out of here, and then I'm going to come back and kill every single mercenary and soldier in this camp."

Reiko let out another raspy laugh. "Spoken like a true gladiator. We both know you couldn't possibly kill them all, unless you used poison, of course."

He grinned back at her. "Spoken like a true spy."

Reiko laughed again, then rolled her head to the side and peered at me. "Gemma? Is that you?"

I stepped forward so she could see me better. "Of course it's me. Like Kai said, we couldn't let you sneak into Milo's camp and have all the fun."

Wonder filled her face. "You heard me. When I called out to you earlier. When Bridget, Wexel, and Milo first captured me."

I gently touched her shoulder. "Of course I heard you. And now we're going to get you out of here."

Reiko lifted a hand and gestured at that enormous map spread out on the table. "But you don't know what Milo's planning."

"I know enough," I replied in a grim voice. "I've seen the camp and the DiLucri mercenaries. But right now, we need to leave before Milo returns."

I jerked my head at Kai, who moved toward the front of the tent, still cradling Reiko in his arms. Then I sheathed my dagger, went over, and grabbed the crossbow off the table. My finger curled around the trigger, and I eyed the gleaming tearstone arrow. Maybe I would get a chance to shoot Milo with it on our way out of camp.

I bloody hoped so.

But for right now, rescuing Reiko was the most important thing, so I lowered the weapon to my side and followed Kai out of the tent.

We kept off the wide main thoroughfares and instead stuck to the smaller, narrower lanes that ran between the tents. Our circuitous route took a lot longer, but we didn't run into anyone. From the few people I spotted running along the other lanes, most folks were still on the far side of camp, trying to deal with the dead, help the injured, and clean up the mess Leonidas had made with that crashing boulder.

While we skulked along, I reached out with my magic.

We have Reiko and are heading toward the edge of camp. The east side, where Kai and I first came down the slope.

Leonidas answered me. *Good. Delmira and I are back on that side of the ridge. We'll keep watch. Lyra and Grimley are flying up the mountain, along with Fern and Otto. Grimley says they can all keep out of sight of any guards that might be watching the sky.*

Okay. We'll be there soon.

I released my power and glanced back over my shoulder at Kai. "Leonidas and Delmira are waiting for us on the ridge, and the creatures are coming to help. All we have to do is slip out of camp, then we can fly back down the mountain to safety."

He nodded and hoisted Reiko a little higher in his arms. Her eyes were open, but she was gritting her teeth, and sweat glistened on her forehead. Pain jolted off her body with every step Kai took, but she remained silent. My stomach twisted with guilt and grief, even as my heart burned with rage. Torturing Reiko was just one more thing in a long list of evil deeds that Milo Morricone was going to pay for—with his life.

Kai and I kept going. We still didn't pass any mercenaries, but I could hear people talking in the distance. The confusion and excitement of the boulder crashing into camp was dying down, and everyone was returning to their previous posts and chores.

"We need to move faster," I warned.

Kai nodded, and we both picked up our pace—

Milo rounded the corner of a tent right in front of us.

I skidded to a stop, while Kai let out a muttered curse. The crown prince was flipping through a small purple book—Dahlia's journal—although his head snapped up at the sound of Kai's voice.

Milo's gaze landed on me, and anger exploded in his eyes. "Intruders!" he screamed. "Kill them!"

CHAPTER TWENTY-FOUR

Milo sucked in another breath to scream, but I snapped up the crossbow, leveled the weapon at him, and pulled the trigger.

My aim was straight and true, and the tearstone arrow zipped through the air toward Milo's chest. For one brief, shining, glorious moment, I thought I had done it—that I had finally, finally killed Milo Morricone.

But right before the arrow would have slammed into the empty space where his heart should be, Milo blasted the projectile with his lightning magic. The arrow flew off to the left and sank into the leg of a Mortan soldier who was running in this direction. The soldier screamed and dropped to the ground, but Milo didn't even glance over at the other man.

Instead, he drew his hand back and hurled some lightning at me, but I slapped it away with my own magic, and the bolt zinged into a nearby tent. The dull brown canvas ignited, spewing purple sparks and smoke up into the air, and acting like a bull's-eye telling everyone exactly where we were.

"Run!" I screamed at Kai. "Go, go, go!"

He tightened his grip on Reiko, then darted down one of the lanes that led off to the left.

"Guards! Guards!" Milo screamed. "Shoot her! Shoot the Ripley bitch!"

More and more Mortan guards and soldiers appeared, spilling out of the nearby tents, while the DiLucri mercenaries sprinted along the lanes, all of them heading in this direction. Several of the Mortans were armed with crossbows, and they stopped and pulled the triggers, sending a hail of arrows at me.

I growled, dropped my own empty crossbow, and lifted my hands. Then I clenched my fingers into tight fists, stopping all the projectiles in midair. A couple of flicks of my wrists whipped the arrows around and launched them right back at the soldiers. The projectiles punched into the men's arms, legs, and chests, making them scream and tumble to the ground.

The moment that first wave dropped, I spun around and sprinted after Kai. The dragon morph had abandoned all stealth and was running through the main thoroughfare that led through the middle of camp, trying to get to the slope where Leonidas and Delmira were waiting as quickly as possible.

I fell in step behind him and reached out with my magic. *Grimley! I need you! And the others! At the camp! Now!*

On our way! the gargoyle roared in my mind.

Shouts rose up behind us, but no more arrows zipped through the air, so we kept running. Finally, after what seemed like forever, but couldn't have been more than a minute, Kai darted past the last of the tents and started climbing up the slope, still holding Reiko in his arms.

"Put me down!" she yelled. "I can climb!"

"No, you can't!" Kai yelled back at her. "I can make it!"

But the slope was steep, and despite all his dragon morph strength, speed, and power, he was struggling. His face was red, his inner dragon looked like it was panting for breath, and his boots slipped on the slick leaves time and time again. Kai wasn't going to make it up the slope before the soldiers and mercenaries caught up with us.

Not unless I gave them something—or rather someone—else to chase.

I glanced up. Delmira was running down the slope as fast as she dared, trying to reach Kai so that she could help him with Reiko. Leonidas was still standing at the top of the ridge, magic crackling in his eyes, ready to lash out with his power and protect them.

My steps slowed. I stopped running and stared up the slope at Leonidas, memorizing the sharp, angular lines of his face, and searing the image of him into my mind and heart.

Get everyone else to safety, and tell my family what's happening, I told him. *I'll distract Milo and his mercenaries.*

Gemma? No! What are you doing? Leo's voice sounded in my mind, but I had already whirled around and started running in the opposite direction, heading back toward my enemies.

I darted down one of the lanes and skidded to a stop at the end, sucking some much-needed air into my lungs and trying to get my bearings. By this point, I was much closer to the front of the camp than the back, and I could see the steps that led down the mountain to the main fairgrounds in the distance. A few mercenaries gave me curious looks, and more shouts rose in the distance. I had a minute, maybe two, before everyone in the camp converged on my position.

Determination surged through me, along with more than a little anger. Forget being quiet. If I was going to be a distraction, then I might as well be as loud, spectacular, and destructive as possible.

So I sucked down another breath, stepped out onto the main

thoroughfare, and sprinted right through the middle of the camp. As I ran, I lashed out with my magic, overturning pots and pans, knocking over racks of weapons, and causing as much chaos and confusion as I could. More shouts and yells erupted behind me, but one voice boomed out louder than all the others.

"There she is!" Milo yelled. "Kill her! Kill the Ripley bitch!"

I glanced back over my shoulder. Milo, Wexel, and Bridget were all much farther down the thoroughfare, although the captain and the geldjager were sprinting in this direction. The crown prince's shouts finally penetrated the mercenaries' collective confusion, and they started surging to their feet and grabbing weapons.

I faced front again and picked up my pace, trying to put as much distance between me and my enemies as possible. I had only two choices: keep running or find someplace to hide. Neither one was ideal, and the only question was how long it would be before Milo and his mercenaries caught up to and then killed me.

And they *were* going to kill me.

There were simply too many of them and only one of me. Still, I had to buy my friends as much time as possible to get away, as well as to warn my family what was happening. Plus, it would take Rhea even more time to marshal the royal guards and mount a defense. So how could I distract Milo and the mercenaries long enough for all of that to happen? Where could I go where I might be able to stop and make one last stand?

My gaze snapped back and forth, but all I saw were tents, tents, and more tents. Even worse, I was literally running out of room, and the edge of camp was growing closer and closer, along with the wide, flat steps that led down the mountain to the main fairgrounds—

An idea popped into my mind about where I could lead Milo and the mercenaries. Now I just had to get there before they caught me.

So I sucked down another breath, ignored the stitch throbbing in my side, and kept going. I broke free of the mercenaries' camp and reached the steps. Behind me, more shouts sounded, along with heavy, thudding footsteps, but I focused on crossing the first step and hopping down to the next one. If I tripped, then I would fall, tumble down all the steps, and probably break every single bone in my body—

Thunk!

A tearstone arrow zipped by my head and slammed into a nearby tree, spraying wood chips everywhere. I flinched, but I kept running, sprinting down the steps as fast as possible.

Thunk! Thunk! Thunk!

More arrows zipped through the air. Some slammed into the trees, while others punched into the steps, but I ignored them all and kept going. Slowly, much, much too slowly, the bottom of the steps appeared, along with the training rings on the back side of the main fairgrounds.

I leaped over the bottom step and stumbled forward. My arms windmilled, but I managed to catch myself and skid to a stop—

Thunk! Thunk! Thunk!

Another round of arrows rained down, stabbing into the ground all around my feet. I glanced back over my shoulder. The mercenaries were streaming down the steps, their cloaks rippling around their bodies, and their swords, spears, and other weapons glinting in the sunlight. More and more of them appeared at the top of the slope and then rushed down, like a river spilling over the top of a dam one wave at a time.

My gaze snagged on two bits of color in the mass of black cloaks—Wexel in his purple jacket and Bridget in her brown cloak. The two of them were right in the middle of the mercenaries, about halfway down the steps, although I didn't see Milo among the mass of enemies.

Several of the mercenaries were mutts with speed magic, and they were leaping down the steps and quickly closing the gap between us. I wasn't where I wanted to be yet, so I curled my hand into a fist and used my magic to yank the arrows they'd fired at me out of the ground. A flick of my wrist sent the arrows shooting up the steps into the closest mercenaries.

Those men and women screamed and pitched forward. Most of them landed on the steps, creating obstacles that slowed the other mercenaries, while some of the injured bounced off the stones, hit the steep slope beyond, and tumbled away in a shower of leaves and dirt.

"Stop!" Bridget's sharp command pierced the air. "Stop shooting arrows at her! Stop giving her more bloody weapons!"

No more arrows streaked down the slope, so I whirled around and sprinted away. The back side of the fairgrounds was still largely deserted, although more people were roaming through the area than before, mostly gladiators on their way to the training rings. Their faces scrunched up with confusion as they caught sight of me.

"Move! Move! Move!" I yelled as I ran past the gladiators and other troupe members. "Get to safety! We are under attack! Glanzen is under attack!"

I didn't know if the people actually heard my words or if they simply spotted the mass of mercenaries flowing down the steps and sweeping into the fairgrounds, but most of them turned around and fled.

Most, but not all.

Arrows zipped past me and sank into the arms, legs, and chests of the gladiators. Screams tore through the air, blood sprayed everywhere, and people dropped to the ground. I skidded to a stop and spun around, determined to protect as many folks as possible.

More and more mercenaries rushed into the fairgrounds.

Some of them charged toward me, but others broke off and darted down the lanes in search of other, easier targets.

For a moment, I stood there, paralyzed. Not from the fear, panic, pain, and dread surging off the fleeing people, or the frenzied bloodlust blasting off the mercenaries, but rather from my own seething rage, bubbling anguish, and crushing disappointment. I might have saved Reiko, might have finally uncovered Milo's ultimate plot, but I had unleashed his mercenary army in the process, and now people—*innocent people*—were suffering because of me.

It was like the Seven Spire massacre all over again.

No! I vowed. I wouldn't *let* this be like the massacre. I would *not* be a coward again. Not while I still had the strength, breath, and magic to fight. With that ruthless promise beating in my heart, I ran right back toward the mercenaries.

"There she is!" one of the men shouted. "There's the princess!"

"Kill her!"

"Kill Gemma Ripley!"

The mercenaries lifted their swords in anticipation of cutting me to pieces. I skidded to a stop and watched them rush toward me, sucking as much air down into my lungs as possible. Then, when the mercenaries were in range, I reached for the strings of energy around a nearby cornucopia cart, picked it up, and flung it at them. The cart slammed into the men and drove them into the ground, crushing them to death.

That definitely got the mercenaries' attention. Many of them howled and charged at me, and I attacked them the same way I had the others. I picked up carts, pennants, candied apples, toy swords, stray rocks, broken bits of glass, and whatever else I could grab with my magic. Then I hurled all those items at my enemies, slamming the debris into their faces, throats, and chests, and killing the people who wanted to kill me. Every time

I dropped a group of mercenaries, I backpedaled a little farther down the main thoroughfare and attacked them with a fresh round of goods.

My plan worked, and most of the mercenaries focused on me, since I was by far the biggest threat. But there were far more mercenaries than carts, pennants, and rocks on the thoroughfare, and I simply couldn't kill them all with such small, simple things. One man slipped past the barrage of objects. Then another, then another. In an instant, they were all swarming toward me.

I picked up a final cart and tossed it at the mercenaries. That bought me a few precious seconds to turn and run. I just had to hope they would keep following me, rather than spreading out through the fairgrounds and attacking whoever was unlucky enough to cross their path.

Once again, I sucked down a breath and charged forward, putting one foot in front of the other. Just like Milo, I wasn't running away from my enemies so much as I was running toward something.

The arena.

The structure loomed up before me, slowly growing closer and closer with every frantic footstep. The columns gleamed like gray candles in the morning sunlight, while the gargoyles carved into the stones seemed to blink, yawn, and stretch, as though they were just waking up for the day and were looking forward to seeing my bout against the mercenaries.

If I'd had the breath for it, I would have laughed. It wasn't going to be a bout so much as it was an execution—*my* execution. But this was the plan I'd come up with, and I was too committed to stop now. Besides, just like up on the mountain, I had run out of room, and there was nowhere else for me to go. At least, not without putting even more innocent people in danger.

So I picked up my pace, veered to my right, and sprinted into one of the tunnels—the same tunnel where Milo's man had attacked me two days ago. It was still dark inside, but I focused on the sunlight shining through the other end and quickened my steps. I sprinted through that area, then the other adjoining tunnels. Less than a minute later, I raced out of an archway and into the arena proper.

It was still early, so no one was inside yet, and my footsteps echoed like cracks of thunder in the empty, cavernous space. I veered onto the walking track, darted through an open gate, and sprinted out onto the arena floor. It too was empty, except for the enormous stone gargoyle that I'd climbed up onto during the opening ceremonies. The statue was positioned on the same side as the royal terrace, and the gargoyle seemed to narrow its eyes and peer down at me as I finally staggered to a stop in the center of the arena floor.

By this point, that stitch in my side had morphed into a dagger, steadily grinding deeper and deeper into my ribs, so I concentrated on drawing as much air down into my lungs as possible. The pain in my side slowly eased, although my arms and legs kept twitching and spasming from how long, hard, and fast I'd run. I wiped the sweat off my face with a shaking hand, then ripped off my stolen cloak and tossed it aside. A gust of wind caught the fabric and tossed it skyward, and the cloak snagged on one of the gargoyle's teeth, as though black blood was dripping out of the creature's mouth.

I tilted my head to the side, listening, but all I could hear was my own quick, hoarse, raspy breaths, along with my pounding heart. So I started counting off the seconds in my mind, willing both my breathing and my heart to slow down.

One, two, three . . .

Ten . . . twenty . . . thirty . . .

Forty . . . fifty . . . sixty . . .

I dropped the count back down to one and started again. All I had to do was hang on for a little while longer. Every minute

I distracted the mercenaries was another minute that innocent people had to get to safety. Every minute I fought gave my friends more time to warn my family what was going on. Every minute I stayed alive was another minute that Rhea had to marshal the royal guards to protect our city.

Every minute counted now—more than it ever had before in my entire life.

I'd counted off a little more than two minutes when footsteps rumbled in my direction.

I drew in a deep breath, then lifted my chin, squared my shoulders, and dropped my hand to my dagger.

Shouts echoed out of one of the arena tunnels, but a familiar voice boomed out above all the others.

"She's in the arena!" Wexel yelled. "Circle around! Don't let her escape!"

More footsteps sounded, along with answering cries acknowledging the captain's orders. A few seconds later, dozens and dozens of mercenaries erupted out of the tunnel, along with some Mortan soldiers. Ten, twenty-five, fifty, one hundred . . . I soon lost count of exactly how many of them there were.

Some of them charged through the open gate and streamed out onto the arena floor in front of me, while others split off, going both left and right, circling around, and entering from the open gates behind me. In less than a minute, they had surrounded me.

But even worse than the sheer mass of enemies were their thoughts.

Finally got this bitch cornered . . .

I've never carved up a princess before . . .

Too bad there won't be anything of her left for us to enjoy . . .

On and on their thoughts went, each one more vicious, disgusting, and horrid than the last. These mercenaries and soldiers didn't want to just kill me—they wanted to humiliate, torture, and brutalize me in the most painful, horrific ways possible.

In an instant, my exhaustion vanished, all the worry, fear, and dread inside me crystalized, and that storm of emotion deep inside me stilled, as though it had been frozen in place. These people had willingly come here, to my kingdom, to my capital, to the very heart of Andvari to destroy everything the Ripley name represented, everything my family had worked so hard to build and protect so that our people might live and flourish in peace and safety. The DiLucri mercenaries and Mortan soldiers had taken money to hurt my friends, my gargoyles, and my people. And now they wanted to hurt, torture, and kill me for daring to stand in their way.

Well, they weren't going to get away with it—and they most definitely weren't going to survive *me*.

Instead of looking at the ever-increasing horde of enemies, I raised my gaze higher, to the three-story stone gargoyle looming over the arena floor. My stolen black cloak was still caught on one of the creature's teeth, and the wind pushed it back and forth, making the fabric seem as though it was being ripped to shreds. The gargoyle's face gleamed in the sunlight, and one particularly bright ray made it seem as though the creature was winking at me. Perhaps it knew what I had planned next. Either way, I thought it would approve. I stared at the statue a moment longer, then dropped my gaze back down to my enemies.

The mercenaries and soldiers finally realized I wasn't going to try to break through their ranks, and they quieted down. A tense, eerie silence dropped over the arena, although I could still hear faint screams and shouts in the distance, outside the towering walls. Each one raked across my heart like a strix's sharp talons.

I might have drawn most of the mercenaries and soldiers into the arena, but some of them were still out in the fairgrounds. Even if I killed every single person in here, I had still failed to protect my people. That sick knowledge, along with the accompanying guilt and grief, churned in my stomach and cut me up from the inside out, as though I had swallowed a mouthful of razors. An answering scream bubbled up in my throat, but I choked it down.

Screaming wouldn't help anything—but killing my enemies would.

So I held my position in the center of the arena floor and waited for them to approach.

Several of the Mortan soldiers stepped aside, and Wexel walked forward and stopped about ten feet away from me. The captain grinned, his teeth flashing like tiny white spears in the sunlight, and his bloodlust stabbed into my stomach, as sharp as the sword he was clutching.

A few mercenaries stepped aside, and Bridget moved forward. She too stopped about ten feet away, but she was standing off to the side, and there was a clear divide between her black-cloaked mercenaries and the purple-clad Mortan soldiers.

For a moment, I thought about forcing my way past Wexel's and Bridget's strength magic, grabbing the strings of energy attached to their hearts, and crushing them both with my magic. As satisfying as that would be, I discarded the idea. I had a far more important enemy to use my power on—Milo.

I glanced around, but I didn't see the crown prince. "Where's your master? I thought he would want to come here and kill me himself."

Wexel gave me an evil grin. "Oh, don't worry. Milo's on his way." He glanced upward. "Why, there he is right now."

My head snapped up. At first, I didn't see what Wexel was looking at, but then I spotted a dark spot high in the sky. The spot zoomed in this direction, growing larger and larger, before making a steep turn and streaking down into the arena like a shooting star.

A few seconds later, a strix landed on the arena floor, right in front of the Mortan soldiers.

Milo was sitting atop the creature. Sometime during my run down the mountain, the crown prince had donned a gold breastplate that gleamed as brightly as the noon sun. The tousled strands of his hair glimmered like ribbons of gold, while a gold sword dangled from his belt, right next to a couple of light gray tearstone arrows. A purple cloak flowed around his shoulders, and he looked every inch like the conquering king he so desperately wanted to be.

He sneered down at me, then puckered his lips and let out a high, sharp whistle that echoed from one side of the arena to the other and back again. A few seconds later, another shadow fell over me. Then another one, then another one, then another one . . .

The shadows swiftly descended, and more strixes landed on the arena floor. Ten, twenty-five, fifty, one hundred . . .

More and more strixes appeared, all carrying riders armed with crossbows. One of the men leveled his weapon at me, and the telltale glint of a tearstone arrow caught my eye. I flashed back to the old fairgrounds and that strange shadow I'd seen drop into the abandoned arena. Milo must have turned the space into his own rookery to secretly house his strixes.

Even more worry churned in my gut than before. But my worry wasn't for myself—it was for my city, my people, and my gargoyles. Not only did Milo have ground forces, but he also had an aerial squad, one that could rain death, terror, destruction, and tearstone arrows down from on high.

Milo dismounted his strix and strutted toward me, his hand resting on the sword on his hip. Wexel stepped to the side, and the crown prince stopped in the space between Wexel and Bridget. Milo looked me over from head to toe, studying me like a gladiator would a hated rival right before an arena bout.

A smile slowly spread across his face, as though the sun was coming out after a long, dark night. But there was no light, no warmth, no softness in his smug smirk—only the promise of pain, suffering, and death.

"I always knew you were a fool," Milo sneered. "There's no way out of here, Glitzma. Not for you. Not this time."

He was right.

I was trapped in an arena, surrounded by hundreds of enemies—and now I was going to die.

CHAPTER TWENTY-FIVE

Despite the mercenaries, soldiers, and strixes in front of me, I didn't let any of my worry show. Not the smallest flicker. Instead, I studied Milo the same way he was studying me, looking for any sign of weakness, anything I could exploit to kill him and his minions before they killed me.

These bastards might slaughter me right here in the middle of the arena, but I was going to take as many of them with me as I could.

"If you surrender now, I might not kill you," I called out, making my voice as cold as the wind swirling through the air.

Milo threw his head back and laughed, his hearty chuckles bouncing off the bleacher steps and booming through the entire arena. Wexel snickered, as did the Mortan soldiers, but Bridget remained silent. She stared at me a moment, then made a small, discreet hand gesture. She held her position, still in line with Milo and Wexel, but the mercenaries shifted on their feet and sidled back, putting some more space between them and me. Smart. Bridget and the DiLucri fighters might just live through this, although I would happily kill them all too, if I got the chance.

The crown prince spread his hands out wide. "Surrender? When I'm on the verge of sacking your city? Of taking your precious capital? Please. You should know by now that I would *never* surrender to you, not even if I was clapped in chains with an executioner's axe at my neck." Another grin split his lips. "But since you *are* about to be executed, maybe *you* should think about surrendering. What do you say, Gemma? If you bow down to me here and now, I'll have Wexel run you through and make your death quick, if not painless."

The captain twirled his sword around in his hand. Hate burned in Wexel's eyes, making them gleam like hazel coins set into his face.

I wanted to tell Milo to take his empty promise and shove it up his ass, but I swallowed the harsh words. I needed to keep the crown prince and the captain distracted for as long as possible, so I shoved my anger aside and focused on that deceptive, dangerous stillness frozen and buried deep inside me. I was in the eye of the storm, and I needed to stay there for as long as possible.

So I spread my hands out wide, much the same way Milo had done. "You might have an army of Mortans, strixes, and mercenaries, but you're still not going to take my city. You failed to destroy Glitnir with your lightning-in-a-bottle experiment, and you're going to fail to sack Glanzen too." I looked him up and down, my lips curling back with disgust. "All that fancy gold armor doesn't hide the fact that you're nothing but a fucking *failure*."

Milo's eyes bulged, and his face turned a satisfying shade of red. Wexel sucked in a breath, but Bridget remained calm and watchful.

"Face it, Milo. You fail at *everything*. You failed to catch me at Myrkvior, you failed to kill me in Blauberg, and you failed to murder me and the other royals at the Summit a few weeks ago. So why do you think now is going to be any different?"

"I didn't fail!" Milo screamed. "My plans never, ever *fail*!"

His voice boomed out again, and rage scorched off him, hot enough to make my entire body burn, despite the distance between us. Several of the strixes shied away from the crown prince, and even some of the Mortans shot him wary looks.

Milo stared at me, his eyes narrowed and his nostrils flared, but he must have realized how crazed he looked because he pinched his lips together and made a visible effort to get his emotions under control.

"Admit it, Milo. I've exposed your plan, which means you've already lost this battle," I called out, trying to dig my verbal daggers even deeper into his enormous ego and rip it to shreds. "You might have a lot of men and strixes, but you'll *never* get close to Glitnir now."

Milo shrugged off my words. "I don't need to get close to Glitnir. All I have to do is take the city, and I can surround your pretty palace. Why, it would be grand fun to lay siege to Glitnir, knowing the Ripleys are trapped inside, along with Maeven. I wouldn't even have to storm the palace. Your father and my mother despise each other. It wouldn't be long before they started tearing each other to pieces, even as they slowly starved. As far as I know, cannibalism is one thing that even the Morricones won't do, although I'm sure my mother would make an exception if it meant her own survival."

My heart wrenched. He was right. He did still have a chance to take the city, and if he managed to surround the palace . . . Well, Milo would hang on like a tick on a bloodhound's hide, and I didn't know how my friends and family would ever dislodge him from Glanzen.

"But enough about my plans," Milo continued. "Right now, I'm happy to get on with the task of finally killing you, Gemma."

He snapped his fingers. I tensed, expecting one of the Mortans to raise their crossbow and shoot an arrow at me, or perhaps hand a weapon to Milo so he could do it himself. But instead, a woman moved forward, along with the strix she'd been riding.

The crown prince leaned forward and murmured something to the creature that I couldn't hear. The strix's head swung around, and it fixed its bright amethyst eyes on me and raked its long black talons across the ground, throwing up bits of dirt.

Milo stepped back. The woman looped the reins around the saddle on the strix, tying them up and out of the way. Then she scuttled to the side.

Milo snapped his fingers again, and the strix leaned forward, its eyes still fixed on me.

"Kill her," he ordered.

The strix let out a fierce, wild *caw!* and flapped its wings. It shot straight up into the sky, and then it dove right back down, its talons stretched out toward my chest.

The creature was moving incredibly fast, but I forced myself to wait until it was almost right on top of me. Then, at the last second, I rolled to my right, diving out of the way. The strix was too committed to its attack to stop, and it plowed into the hard-packed dirt, leaving a small crater behind. The blow stunned the strix, and it wobbled around, clearly dazed by the hard, jolting impact.

I popped back up onto my feet. None of the Mortans were creeping up behind me, and the DiLucri mercenaries were still holding their position in the distance. Of course. Everyone wanted to watch the show, such as it was.

Milo snapped his fingers again. The strix whirled back around, let out another fierce *caw!*, and raced forward. Once again, I held my ground.

The strix stopped and reared up, getting ready to snap its beak down and out and bury the sharp point in my chest, but I dove forward, right in between the creature's legs. The strix squawked in surprise and started to hop away, but I grabbed my dagger off my belt and sliced the blade along the creature's side. Not a mortal wound, but hopefully one deep enough to stop the creature from attacking me again. I didn't want to kill the strix unless I had no other choice.

The creature cawed again, this time in pain, and scuttled away. Once again, I got to my feet, my bloody dagger in my hand.

Milo snapped his fingers yet again. "Kill her," he commanded. "Right bloody *now*."

But instead of obeying his order, the creature hunkered down, trying to protect itself from suffering any more blows.

Milo shot the strix a disgusted look, then gestured at Wexel. "Finish her—and make it hurt."

Wexel grinned. "With pleasure."

The captain twirled his sword around in his hand again, then advanced on me, as did several other Mortans. Only Bridget and her mercenaries remained behind, still holding their positions and silently watching with curious, wary expressions.

I tightened my grip on my dagger and backed up.

"There's nowhere for you to run, Glitzma," Milo crowed. "Not this time."

I ignored the arrogant bastard and kept backing up, watching as Wexel and the Mortans followed me. Milo was right about one thing. I wouldn't escape, but that didn't mean I was going to stop fighting.

I would *never* do that.

A grim smile curved my lips. Besides, we were in a gladiator arena, and I couldn't think of a more fitting ending to this black-ring match than slaughtering as many of my enemies as possible.

So while Wexel and the Mortans kept creeping toward me, I reached out with my magic. In an instant, I could feel the energy in, on, and around everything in the entire arena, from Wexel and the Mortans, to the swords and crossbows in their hands, to the bleacher steps, to the gargoyle statues perched on the walking track at the very tip-top of the structure.

I sorted through all those strings of energy, then reached out and grabbed the ones I wanted, holding them close to my heart, just like I would a beloved book. It was surprisingly easy, especially compared to how hard controlling Milo's lightning had been in the royal treasury. In a strange way, he had done me a favor, because I felt stronger in my magic than I ever had before. So I gathered up all those strings of energy and let the power fill me up, although I didn't let it break through that calmness still holding steady in my chest.

Not yet—but soon.

Wexel stopped in front of me. Hate flared in his eyes again, and the same emotion blasted off him, burning just as hotly as Milo's anger had earlier. The rest of the Mortans hung back a few steps, creating an odd bubble of space around the captain and me.

"You killed Corvina, and now I'm going to kill you," Wexel spat out.

I tilted my head to the side, studying him, even as I kept gathering up those strings of magic. "You really did love Corvina, didn't you?"

A muscle ticced in his jaw, confirming my words.

"I am sorry I had to kill her."

That muscle ticced in his jaw again, although he jerked his head, acknowledging my words. "But?"

"But Corvina chose her path, just as you've chosen yours."

A caustic laugh bubbled out of Wexel's lips. "Corvina didn't *choose* anything. She simply followed the path Maeven set her on years ago when Maeven started killing the people Corvina loved." He eyed me. "Just like you're following the path Maeven set you on during the Seven Spire massacre."

This time, I tipped my head, acknowledging his point. "You might be right about that. Just like you're following the path Milo set you on. And what has it gotten you? Your lover is dead, you've been outcast and exiled from your own kingdom, and now you're going to die fighting someone else's battle. We both know Milo is a coward at heart. Why, he doesn't even have the courage to come over here and try to murder me himself."

Wexel shrugged. "True. But when he takes your city, and especially your palace, he'll be the one in command. He'll seize the rest of Andvari, and then conquer the other kingdoms one by one by one."

"And what will you do?" I asked, genuinely curious.

For the first time since I'd known him, tiredness flickered across Wexel's face, and longing surged off him and tickled my heart like a cold finger. "I can finally fucking *rest*. I'll take the money Milo has promised me, and go someplace where no one knows me and there are no more enemies to kill."

A wistful note crept into his voice, and an image flickered off him and filled my mind—a small cottage deep in the woods, surrounded by trees and silence. The door opened, and Corvina appeared on the stoop, smiling wide, her auburn hair glinting in the sun. Wexel shuddered out a breath, and the image vanished.

Despite the fact he was one of my most hated enemies, a tiny needle of sympathy pricked my heart. He could have had that, the two of them could have had that, if only they hadn't let their greed and ambition get in the way. But it was too late for Corvina, just as it was too late for Wexel—and for me too.

"Goodbye, Gemma," Wexel said, his voice not unkind. "I wish things could have been different—for all of us."

He raised his sword, and I gathered up a few more strings of magic—

A low rumble rang out, sounding like thunder rolling in this direction.

Wexel stopped. "Did you hear that?" he muttered, although I wasn't sure if he was talking to himself, me, or the Mortans.

"What are you waiting for?" Milo called out. "Kill her. Now."

But instead of obeying, Wexel's eyes narrowed, and he backed away from me and turned to the side, scanning the Mortans and strixes gathered around us, as well as the mercenaries and the open, empty arena floor beyond.

That rumble came again, a little louder this time, and a familiar presence filled my mind. A grin slowly stretched across my face.

That rumble came a third time, and a pair of bright, sapphire-blue eyes appeared in one of the arena tunnels, like matches flaring to life in the depths of a dark cavern.

"If I were you, I'd get out of the way," I said.

Wexel's gaze darted around as he searched for the threat he knew was coming but hadn't spotted yet—

A shadow erupted out of the tunnel, charged through an open gate, loped across the arena floor, and smashed straight into the Mortans. Half a dozen men went down in that initial assault, and the shadow loped over and skidded to a stop right beside me.

"Gemma!" Grimley shouted. "Let's go!"

I shoved my dagger back into its scabbard, ran forward, and threw myself up and onto the gargoyle's back.

"Shoot them!" Milo roared. "Now! Before they take off!"

Several Mortans snapped up their crossbows and aimed the weapons at us. I leaned over Grimley's side and reached for my magic, ready to rip the crossbows out of their hands—

Two more creatures erupted out of the tunnel, raced across the arena floor, and barreled into the Mortans who were targeting Grimley and me.

Otto reared back on his hind legs like a Floresian stallion, then plunged down and forward and smashed his front paws into the chest of one of the archers. Atop the gargoyle, Delmira hurled a liladorn dagger at another archer, catching that man in the throat and killing him.

A few feet away, Lyra stabbed her beak into a Mortan's back, while Leonidas grabbed another archer with his magic and tossed that man into a couple more, knocking them all down to the ground.

"Let's go!" Leonidas yelled.

Lyra flapped her wings and shot up into the sky, quickly followed by Otto. Grimley flapped his wings as well, and the two of us also took off, leaving our enemies behind.

CHAPTER TWENTY-SIX

H ang on, Gemma!" Grimley yelled, pumping his wings hard and fast. "I'll get you out of here!"

"No!" I yelled back at him, "We have to stop the Mortans and mercenaries!"

Grimley nodded, then flapped his wings and veered around, heading back toward the arena.

Leonidas and Lyra zoomed through the air beside us, along with Delmira and Otto.

Gemma! Leonidas's voice sounded in my mind. *What are you doing?*

We have to stop Milo's men here and now. We can't let them leave the arena. If they make it into the rest of the fairgrounds, or worse, the city streets beyond, then they'll kill whoever gets in their way, and innocent people will die.

A grim look filled his face. *What did you have in mind?*

You and Lyra keep the archers busy. I'll take care of the rest.

Leonidas nodded, and Lyra veered off, spiraling back down toward the arena floor.

I glanced over at Delmira, who was still riding atop Otto. *Help Leonidas and Lyra. Get the archers to focus on you.*

I sent the thought to both the princess and the gargoyle, and they both nodded. Otto flapped his wings, following Lyra back down toward the arena.

Gemma? Grimley asked. *What do you want to do?*

Fly over to the walking track on top of the arena and land next to the gargoyle statues.

He headed in that direction. A few seconds later, Grimley coasted onto the walkway that lined the very top of the arena. I slid off his back and hurried over to the stone railing, staring down at the battle below.

Lyra and Otto were flying back and forth over the Mortans, who were alternating between ducking their heads and firing arrows at the creatures. Leonidas used his magic to catch the arrows, spin them around, and send them shooting right back down at the Mortans, while Delmira leaned over Otto's side, grabbed the end of a crossbow, and wrenched it out of someone's hands. Then, on the gargoyle's next pass over the Mortans, Delmira straightened up, flipped the crossbow around, and shot one of the archers.

I didn't see Milo or Wexel in the madness, and the strixes and their riders had also vanished, along with Bridget DiLucri and her mercenaries. Worry churned in my gut about where they all had gone, and the violence they might unleash on my people, but I shoved the emotion aside. Right now, I needed to focus on killing the enemies in front of me.

My gaze locked onto the three-story gargoyle statue I'd climbed onto during the opening ceremonies. It was still standing off to one side of the arena, with my stolen black cloak hanging out of its mouth. I stretched my hands out in front of me and took hold of all the strings of energy emanating from the statue, as well as the wooden platform it was sitting on.

And then I started rolling it forward.

I circled my wrists around and around, pulling, yanking, and tugging on the strings of energy attached to the platform's wheels. The platform was large, wide, and heavy, and the statue sitting atop it even more so. Sweat popped out on my forehead, and my arms and shoulders ached, even though I wasn't physically touching anything but the open air in front of me.

But I kept circling my wrists around and around and pulling with my magic, and the platform jerked forward an inch. Then another inch. Three inches. Five. Then a whole foot at once.

The harder I yanked on those invisible strings, the smoother the platform's motion became, and it kept going, rolling straight toward the Mortans.

Several Mortans stopped their attacks on Leonidas, Lyra, Delmira, and Otto and watched the platform sail toward them, clearly wondering why it was suddenly moving. A few of the Mortans even had the good sense to start running in the opposite direction. But most of them were so focused on trying to kill my friends that they didn't realize the danger gliding toward them on creaky wooden wheels.

But my friends did notice the danger, and Lyra and Otto pumped their wings harder, shooting themselves, along with Leonidas and Delmira, up and away from the arena floor.

I released my grip on the wheels, but the platform kept rolling forward, now propelled by its own weight and motion. This time, I grabbed the strings of energy attached to the gargoyle statue itself. One after another, I plucked all those invisible threads out of the air and clutched them in my hands, as though I was scooping swords up off the arena floor.

More sweat slid down my face, and the ache in my arms and shoulders intensified, but the statue slowly rose into the air, hovering over the wooden platform. In that moment, I felt like Violet. Only, instead of trying to fly like the baby strix was so determined to do, I was desperately trying to keep the thick, solid, heavy statue aloft on the invisible wings of my magic.

I reached for even more magic, even more power, and I

finally cracked through that cold, eerie stillness inside my chest. It was finally time to unleash my storm on my enemies.

I gathered up a few more strings of energy, my body shaking from the effort. Then, with a scream of determination, I shoved my hands forward, along with my magic, and hurled the gargoyle statue outward—right into the center of the arena floor.

Without the strings of my magic to hold it up like an invisible spiderweb, the stone gargoyle plummeted downward and landed right in the middle of the Mortans.

CRASH!

The statue shattered on impact, and a hard, vicious jolt reverberated through the arena, as though it had been rocked by an earthquake. The entire structure swayed from top to bottom, and I had to latch onto the railing to keep my balance. Beside me, Grimley dug his talons into the walkway flagstones to stay upright.

More jolts ripped through the arena, and all I could hear was the violent roar of the statue breaking apart and all those sharp pieces of stone banging and clapping together. Strangely enough, it sounded like applause, as though every shard of stone was approving of my violent destruction of the statue.

Slowly, the jolts and tremors faded away, the arena stopped swaying, and the shards, rocks, and other debris stopped banging together. Thick plumes of dust boiled up, making me cough, although the wind quickly wisped them away.

A massive pile of gray rubble now filled the center of the arena floor, looking like a miniature volcano. Only, instead of lava, blood oozed out of all the cracks.

Most of the Mortans had been crushed by the statue, then buried under the resulting rubble, but a few were still alive, moaning and groaning and trying to crawl to safety. The stone shrapnel had shredded their arms, legs, and chests, and their injuries left bloody smears behind in the thick layer of gray dust that now coated the arena floor.

Despite the sickening sight, a relieved breath tumbled out of my lips and drifted away, along with the dust. I had done it. I had stopped my enemies.

For now.

The last of the dust dissipated, and two figures appeared in the air over the arena. Beside me, Grimley tensed, and a low, warning growl rumbled out of his throat. I reached out with my magic, and four familiar presences filled my mind. Another relieved breath escaped my lips.

A few seconds later, Lyra and Otto landed on the walkway, and Leonidas and Delmira slid off the creatures' backs and ran over to me.

"Gemma!" Leonidas called out. "Are you okay?"

I gave him a tired smile. "I'm fine. Just exhausted."

Leonidas put his arm around my waist, and I rested my head on his shoulder, drinking in his warm, solid strength. Leonidas's arm tightened around me, and his relief washed over me like a cool balm, soothing all my own jumbled, ragged emotions.

"Where are Reiko and Kai?" I asked, pulling away from him.

"Fern flew them to the palace to tell King Heinrich and Prince Dominic what was happening," Delmira replied. "Captain Rhea should be marshaling the royal guards even as we speak."

More relief rushed over me.

Delmira stared down at the pile of rubble and the injured Mortans. "Do you think . . . do you think Milo is down there?" she asked in a low, strained voice.

Leonidas gazed down at the destruction, magic flaring in his eyes. After a few seconds, he shook his head. "I don't sense Milo anywhere. But just about everyone down there is dead, so I can't tell if he's buried under the rubble—"

A loud, harsh *caw!* tore through the air. That one sharp cry was quickly followed by another one, then another one, and a wave of icy malevolence washed over me. Leonidas and I both whirled around, as did Delmira, Grimley, Lyra, and Otto.

Dozens and dozens of dark shadows appeared, cutting through the thick clouds of dust still hovering over the arena. The shadows grew closer, morphing into strixes, all carrying archers equipped with crossbows.

My gaze locked onto the two figures leading the charge—Milo and Wexel. Somehow, the two of them had escaped from the arena and managed to regroup. No, not just regroup. This group of strixes and archers was even larger than the one in the arena had been. Milo must have had more creatures and fighters waiting up on the mountain in case he needed to call in reinforcements. And now this fresh wave of strixes and soldiers had joined all those who had escaped from the arena to form this one massive group that was barreling through the sky.

Milo hadn't just brought Bridget DiLucri and her mercenaries to Glanzen—he'd enlisted an army of soldiers and strixes to help him destroy my city and finally conquer my kingdom.

✦

I just stood there at the top of the arena, stunned and horrified, even as part of me marveled at the complexity of Milo's plot. The crown prince had set up one contingency after another, and he'd planned his attack well. Rhea and the royal guards were still miles away, and the only things standing between Milo and the city were me, Leonidas, and Delmira, along with Grimley, Lyra, and Otto.

Worry and frustration spiked through my heart as though I'd been skewered by a gladiator's spear. It wasn't enough. We weren't enough. *I* wasn't strong enough to stop Milo and his army. Not this time.

A slice of sunlight broke through the dust and hit Milo's gold breastplate, and the resulting glare stabbed straight into my eyes, making me hiss. I winced and tried to look past the glare, but my magic suddenly boiled up, sweeping me away to another place, another time . . .

The arena vanished, along with Leonidas, Delmira, and all the creatures. In an instant, I was standing on a rocky plateau at the edge of the forest, watching the turncoat guards advance on a young Gems, along with a baby Grimley.

"Damn it!" I snarled. "Not now! Let me go! Let me go!"

But once again, I had no control over my magic, and despite all my yells and screams and desperate pleas, all I could do was watch this latest ghosting episode play out.

Arlo and the rest of the turncoat guards marched forward, swinging their swords back and forth in a clear attempt to intimidate the girl and the gargoyle.

Gems stepped in front of Grimley, her hands balling into fists. "Leave now, and I won't kill you," she said in a cold voice.

Arlo stopped and let out a low, ugly laugh. "Did you hear that, boys? The little princess is offering not to kill us. How generous of her."

Anger stained Gems's cheeks a bright red, but she stood her ground. Grimley poked his head around her legs, staring at the turncoat guards.

Arlo laughed again and sauntered forward. Gems's fists squeezed a little tighter, and I felt the magic building and building all around her, like a geyser that was about to erupt.

And then it did—too soon.

Magic spurted off Gems and slammed into one of the guards, tossing him back into a couple of others. They all went down in a heap.

Arlo's eyes widened in surprise. "She's a bloody mind magier!" he hissed. "Take her down! Now! Before she uses her power again!"

He quickly closed the distance between them and swung his sword, but Gems ducked the blow and spun away. She reached for her magic again and snapped up her hand, but this time, the power wouldn't come to her, and nothing happened.

Arlo growled and swung his sword again. Gems lurched away, but she wasn't quite quick enough, and the blade sliced across her right forearm. Gems screamed and stumbled back. Her boots slipped on a couple of loose rocks, and she hit the ground hard.

Gems grunted and started to scramble to her feet, but Arlo stepped forward and kicked her in the ribs. Pain spiked through her side, and mine too, even though this had all happened long ago. Gems rocked back and forth on the ground, clutching her ribs and wheezing for breath.

Arlo towered over her. "King Maximus might want you alive, but I'm not taking any chances. Time to die, little princess!"

He raised his sword high, then swung it down. Gems flinched and threw up her hand to try to ward off the killing strike—

A low, angry growl rang out. Grimley loped across the ground, flapped his wings, zipped up into the air, and clamped his jaws around Arlo's sword arm.

Arlo screamed, but Grimley clamped down even harder, hanging off the guard's arm like an ornament on a yule tree.

Arlo's boots slipped on some loose rocks, and he tumbled to the ground just like Gems had. Grimley released Arlo's arm, then hopped up onto the Mortan and started raking his talons across the man's chest and stomach.

Rip. Rip. Rip.

The gargoyle's razor-sharp talons tore through Arlo's purple jacket, along with his flesh underneath. A spray of blood fountained up, and Arlo's guts spilled out of his stomach. Dark satisfaction filled me, along with love and admiration. Even back then, Grimley had been so brave, fierce, and loyal.

"Get off me, you beast!" Arlo roared.

He shoved Grimley away, and the baby gargoyle went tumbling wings over tail across the ground, heading straight toward the edge of the canyon.

"Grims!" Gems screamed.

She scrambled back onto her feet, stretched her hand out, and reached for her magic, frantically trying to grab hold of the strings of energy around the gargoyle.

One, two, three . . .

One after another, the strings of energy slipped through Gems's fingers, but she reached for them again, and again, and again . . .

Gems finally latched onto one of those invisible threads and snapped her hand into a tight fist. Grimley jerked to a stop right before he would have tumbled off the edge of the canyon, most likely to his death. I doubted even a gargoyle could have survived a fall that high, especially one as young as Grimley.

Gems gently released the gargoyle, then hurried over and scooped up Arlo's sword from the ground. The other turncoat guards got back onto their feet, brandished their weapons, and charged forward. Gems watched them come with an icy *expression. Then, when they were in range, she took hold of the strings of energy surrounding them. She yanked tightly on all those strings, then threw her arm out wide, repeating the motion over and over again.*

One by one, the turncoat guards flew off the edge of the canyon. Gems released the strings of energy, and the guards dropped like bricks, their screams cutting off as they smashed into the jagged rocks at the bottom.

Arlo staggered to his feet, his face as red as the blood spilling out of his stomach. "You little bitch!" he snarled.

He charged at her again, and Gems watched him come with that same icy expression. Then, when he was in range, she sidestepped him, whirled around, and slashed the sword across his back. Even more dark satisfaction filled my heart. Rhea had taught me that move.

Arlo stumbled forward, and Gems used her magic to shove him off the edge of the canyon. He screamed all the way down, just like his men had done, and the sharp crack of his body hitting the rocks pealed as loudly as a clap of thunder.

Gems eyed the woods in the distance, but no more enemies appeared. A relieved breath hissed out between her teeth, and she dropped the sword, then rushed over and fell to her knees beside Grimley. Even now, all these years later, I could feel the rocks digging into my skin, but the sensation made me smile.

"Grims!" she cried out. "Are you okay?"

The baby gargoyle grunted as Gems ran her hands over his body. A couple of scrapes and bruises dotted his face and sides from where he'd tumbled over the rocks, since his skin wasn't as tough, strong, and hard as that of an adult creature's yet, but he was in one piece. Another relieved breath hissed out of Gems's mouth. Mine too.

Cuts and scrapes also covered Gems's face and hands, but she still leaned down and scratched the baby gargoyle's head, right in between his two horns, just as he liked.

Blood dripped off her cut forearm and plop-plop-plopped against Grimley's head. As the blood slid downward, those tiny bits of blue embedded in the gargoyle's dark gray stone skin shimmered to life, as though they were stars twinkling in the night sky. I frowned. I had never noticed that back when this had actually been happening.

"Thank you for saving me," Gems whispered, throwing her arms around Grimley's neck and hugging him tight.

One of the gargoyle's wings came around and stroked down her back. "We . . . saved . . . each . . . other," he rasped, his voice low and gravelly, as though he wasn't used to talking.

Gems smiled and threw her arms around Grimley's neck, hugging him tight again, and the two of them sat there, wrapped up in each other . . .

Another slice of sunlight stabbed into my eyes, jolting me back to the here and now. I blinked, and the arena around me solidified again—as did Milo and his army of soldiers and strixes still streaking through the sky toward us.

"Gemma!" Grimley said. "Look!"

He pointed his tail to the side, and I peered in that direction. We weren't the only ones who had noticed Milo and the soldiers and strixes—so had the gargoyles who'd remained in the city for the day. Every creature who had been lounging on the nearby rooftops was now on its feet and staring up at the aerial army approaching us all.

One of the gargoyles flapped his wings and shot up into the sky, heading straight toward the strixes. A smile creased Milo's face, and he hefted the crossbow in his hand.

My eyes widened, and horror shot through my body. "No!" I screamed, even though I knew the gargoyle couldn't possibly hear me. "Fall back! Fall back! He'll kill you—"

Milo pulled the crossbow trigger, and I could have sworn I heard the soft *thwang* of the arrow releasing, or perhaps that was just my own heart wrenching in my chest. Either way, the arrow zipped through the air and slammed into the gargoyle's side.

The creature screamed with pain, and an answering scream ripped out of my own throat. The gargoyle's body dipped, but it pumped its wings and managed to remain aloft.

Milo snapped up his hand, and purple lightning zipped out of his fingertips and streaked through the air. The gargoyle banked sharply to the right, trying to avoid the bolt, but the magic snaked in that direction, as if it was . . . *drawn* to the tearstone arrow, like a magnet seeking out another magnet, despite the distance between them.

And just like the arrow, the lightning slammed into the gargoyle's side.

The creature screamed again, and its agony punched into my throat, stealing my own answering scream. Just like in the treasury, the tearstone arrow both conducted and amplified Milo's lightning, and the magic washed over the gargoyle. For a moment, the creature's body lit up like a fluorestone in a dark room, and the bits of green embedded in the gargoyle's light gray skin sparkled like the clearest, brightest emeralds.

Milo blasted the gargoyle with another lightning bolt, and the creature burst into flames. The gargoyle's screams abruptly cut off, and it plummeted to the ground. Even though I knew what was coming next, I still grimaced—

CRACK!

The gargoyle hit the flagstones outside the arena, and the creature's burned body shattered into black shards, as though it were made of fragile glass instead of solid stone and bones.

It was one of the most sickening, horrifying things I had ever seen.

Tears streamed down my face, and a sob lodged in my throat, but all I could do was stare down at the broken remains of the dead gargoyle. Perhaps it was a trick of the sun, but those bits of green shimmered a few seconds longer before slowly winking out and turning as dark and dead as the creature.

"Fire!" Milo screamed. "Fire at will! Don't stop until you reach the palace!"

My head snapped up. The Mortan archers raised their own crossbows and fired arrows at the other gargoyles that had taken to the air to try to avenge the fallen creature.

The tearstone arrows streaked through the sky one after another like a horde of angry bees, clipping wings, slicing across shoulders, and sinking deep into the gargoyles' stone skin. Then Milo shot out bolt after bolt of lightning, further torturing and injuring the creatures, and sending them spinning to their deaths on the flagstones far, far below.

More and more horror flooded my body, even as a dreadful thought hammered in my heart.

Milo had finally unleashed his attack on my gargoyles—and I had no idea how to save them.

CHAPTER TWENTY-SEVEN

Beside me, Leonidas growled, stepped forward, and lashed out with his magic. An invisible blast of his power ripped through the sky, blowing the latest hail of arrows off course and making them flutter harmlessly to the ground.

"Gemma!" Leonidas yelled. "Help me!"

I gritted my teeth and tried to shove the gargoyles' pain away, but the sheer mass of it hit me over and over again, each blow just as hard and fast as the arrows that had punched into the creatures' bodies.

Leonidas sent out another blast of magic, then another, then another, trying to knock as many arrows away from the gargoyles as he could. One rider broke away from the others and spun their strix around in our direction.

Wexel's lips drew back into a snarl as he raised his own crossbow and fired an arrow at Leonidas.

"Leo!" Delmira screamed. "Watch out!"

She rushed forward to shove him out of the way, but she wasn't fast enough. The arrow slammed into Leonidas's leg, knocking his feet out from under him. Leonidas landed in a heap on the flagstones, hissing with pain.

Milo steered his strix toward us. A cruel smile split his lips, and he raised his hand and shot a bolt of lightning at Leonidas, trying to kill his brother the same way he had the gargoyles. I still couldn't push past the gargoyles' pain and summon up my own magic, so I leaped in front of Leonidas.

Crack!

Milo's lightning slammed straight into my chest and knocked me back. Somehow, I managed to stay on my feet, and I tensed, waiting for his magic to wash over me and fry my body the same way it had the gargoyles . . .

Nothing happened

I glanced down, expecting my chest to be burned, blackened, and smoking, but all I saw was a dull sheet of silver. I'd forgotten I was still wearing Armina Ripley's armor, and the silver breastplate had absorbed the impact of Milo's lightning, keeping it from killing me.

But that wasn't all the armor had done.

All those tiny bits of tearstone were gleaming in the silver, as though I was covered with glittering drops of blue blood. I frowned. Why hadn't the tearstone shards conducted Milo's magic the same way his tearstone arrows had? Why wasn't I as charred, fried, and dead as the gargoyles he had shot out of the sky?

The longer I stared down at the glimmering bits of ore, the more I was reminded of how Grimley's skin had glowed the same color when we'd been attacked by those turncoat guards all those years ago. And Grimley wasn't the only gargoyle that glowed with hidden bits of color. My gaze darted over to Otto, who was growling and glaring up at Milo. Otto shifted on his feet, and those tiny bits of white shimmered in his skin almost as brightly as the tearstone still glimmering in the breastplate on my chest.

Why? Because they were all the *same*. The bits of blue in

Grimley's skin, and the white in Otto's, and the purples, greens, reds, and all the other colors in all the other gargoyles—they were all the same because they were all made of *tearstone*.

Just like the tiny shards of tearstone that were embedded in the silver armor on my chest and the matching gauntlets on my forearms.

For the first time, I realized tearstone wasn't just gray and blue like I'd been taught, like everyone believed. It was gray and blue and white and purple and green and red and every other color you could ever imagine. The Spire Mountains, especially those in Andvari, contained more tearstone than any other place on the Buchovian continent, just like Andvari was home to more gargoyles than any other place on the continent.

Legend claimed Armina Ripley had pried the first gargoyle out of a wall in a mine near Glanzen. I didn't know if that was true, but I was connected to the gargoyles, just as Armina had been. Maeven kept calling me the gargoyle queen for a reason. I just had to figure out what it was, and the tearstone seemed to be the key.

My mind kept whirring as I thought about everything that had happened over the past few days. The tearstone arrow Alvis had been experimenting with in his workshop had amplified his magic, just like those Milo had used in the royal treasury, and the ones the crown prince and his men were firing at my gargoyles right now. Of course, all those arrows had been coated with dried fool's bane, but during the Summit, Corvina Dumond had mentioned something else that reacted to tearstone and amplified its power.

Blood.

I grabbed my dagger off my belt and stared at the gargoyle crest glimmering in the hilt, all those pieces of black jet and midnight-blue tearstone that made up Grimley's snarling face.

Milo was using his tearstone arrows to increase his lightning, but maybe I could use the tearstone embedded in the gargoyles to amplify my own power in a different way—the way I had been *supposed* to use my magic all along.

"Gemma?" Delmira asked, a frown crinkling her face, even as she knelt beside Leonidas. "What are you doing? Help me!"

I ignored her and slashed the dagger across my left palm, opening up a deep cut. Blood welled up out of the gash and dripped down my hand.

"Gemma?" This time, Leonidas spoke up. "What are you doing?"

He propped himself up against the stone railing. Beside him, Delmira used a liladorn dagger to tear a long strip off the bottom of her cloak, then tied the fabric around his leg to slow the bleeding.

Leonidas grimaced with pain, but he kept his gaze steady on mine. "Gemma?" he asked again.

I slid my dagger back into its scabbard, then showed him my cut hand. "Saving us all. I hope."

Confusion creased his face, but he nodded at me. "Go blast that bastard out of the sky."

His firm, steady, unwavering belief made me love him even more, and I leaned down and squeezed his hand. Leonidas stared at me, and I looked right back at him, thoughts and feelings flowing between us.

I squeezed his hand again, then straightened up and turned to Grimley. "Do you trust me?"

"Always," the gargoyle replied. "What do you have in mind?"

"Something that will probably get us both killed."

A grin spread across his face. "I like those odds."

I grinned back at him. "Me too."

Before I could think about how much danger I was putting

us both in, I scrambled onto the gargoyle's back. Grimley shot up into the sky, and we headed straight for our enemies for one last battle—the most important battle of our lives.

Grimley pumped his wings hard and fast. *Now what? Shall we charge at Milo and his men?*

Not yet. We need reinforcements. Drop down and fly over some of the rooftops.

You got it.

The gargoyle veered away from Milo and his approaching army, tucked his wings into his sides, and dropped low, buzzing over the rooftops. Down below, people were crowding into the streets, staring upward while shielding their eyes against the sun. By this point, folks knew something bad was happening. As much as I wanted to yell at everyone to quit gawking and go inside where it was safer, I focused my attention on the gargoyles.

As we buzzed over the rooftops, the gargoyles took notice, staring at Grimley and me the same way the people on the streets below were. I drew in a deep breath and let it out, steadying myself. Then I pressed my cut hand against Grimley's side.

Perhaps it was my blood or my magic or something else entirely, but a jolt zinged through me, and I felt Grimley in a way that I never had before. Every single part of the gargoyle merged with every single part of me. His thoughts, his feelings, every flex of his wings and twitch of his tail steering us through the air. I felt all that and more—so much *more*.

Grimley kept flying, and I peered over his side at the other gargoyles, seeking and straining and reaching out with my magic. The longer I looked out over the gargoyles, the better I could see them, and the sharper they came into focus. Not just their horns and wings and tails, but all those tiny flecks of tear-stone in their skin.

Grays and blues and whites and purples and greens and reds . . . The colors stretched out as far as I could see, like a web of fluorestones connecting every gargoyle to every other gargoyle on all the rooftops throughout the city. I reached out with my magic again, touching one colored string after another in that eerie, electric, beautiful web only I could see. With every string and every gargoyle I touched, my magic expanded, and I felt the other gargoyles in my mind as clearly as I did Grimley.

I had always loved my connection to Grimley, but this was special in a different way. These gargoyles and all their glimmering colors lit up the dark, distant corners of my mind that I never even knew existed, and warmth filled my heart, merging with that storm of emotion that constantly crackled deep inside me. If I'd had more time, I would have marveled at the beauty and complexity of this connection, but right now, I needed to focus.

Our city is under attack! I said, sending the thought out as far and wide as I could. *Will you protect it? Will you help me and my friends? Will you fight with us?*

I sent those words out over and over again, while Grimley zigzagged over the rooftops. But all too soon, he completed his circle, flew past the last building, and headed back toward the arena, where Milo and his men were now hovering in the air.

I glanced back over my shoulder, but the sky was clear and empty. My heart sank. Perhaps my theory had been wrong, or perhaps my magic simply wasn't strong enough—*I* wasn't strong enough—to reach all the creatures at once.

A female gargoyle flapped her wings and shot up into the air. Then a male gargoyle.

Then another creature. Three more. Five more. Seven more . . .

All the gargoyles flapped their wings, shot up off the rooftops, and started hovering in the air beside and behind Grimley. I looked from one face to another. Some of the creatures had names, either ones that I or other humans had given them or monikers they had chosen for themselves. Some of the wilder creatures didn't have names. Some loved watching the humans scurry about on the streets below, while others were content to spend their days hunting in the mountains and ignoring people as much as possible.

But at this moment, I was connected to every single one of them, and their thoughts ebbed and flowed with my own.

Kill the strixes . . .

Tear down the men . . .

Murder the Morricone prince . . .

Their thoughts kept washing through my mind one after another. My gargoyle pendant heated up against my chest, making me sweat, and the creatures' thoughts and feelings threatened to overwhelm me, as human musings and emotions so often did. I grimaced, dropped my head, and focused on the blue bits of tearstone shimmering in Grimley's skin. The harder I focused on the tearstone, the easier it was to navigate the gargoyles' waves of thoughts and all the angry, protective feelings that came along with them.

And I remembered something I should have realized before, something I had known all along. Tearstone might absorb and amplify magic, but it could also *deflect* magic. So I lifted my head and looked from one creature to another, focusing on the tearstone glimmering in their bodies.

Alvis had always told me to think of my magic as some small action, something I could control, so I pretended that each color was a magnifying glass. If I wanted to hear a certain creature's thoughts, then I concentrated on that color, that glass, and the window into the gargoyle's mind opened wide, even as all the others remained shut. I did that over and over again, skimming their thoughts and still controlling my own, as well as my own power.

But I didn't just hear the gargoyle's thoughts and feel their emotions. The connection went so much *deeper* than that, and their fierceness filled me, beating in perfect harmony with the determination pounding in my own heart. The gargoyles steadied me and gave me the strength to turn around and face Milo Morricone and his aerial army.

Most of the Mortans looked stunned, including Wexel, whose mouth was gaping. An image flickered off the captain and filled my own mind—me with a legion of gargoyles spread out in the sky all around me. Wexel's worry, fear, and dread blasted over me, and he glanced around, as though searching for a way to escape this madness that Milo had created. No surprise there. The captain always ran away when a fight didn't go his way, and he was ready to bolt once again.

I pushed Wexel out of my mind and concentrated on Milo. For once, the crown prince wasn't sneering at me. Instead, he had gone pale with shock.

"How—how are you *doing* this?" he demanded. "How are you controlling all of them at once?"

His shock faded away, and speculation filled his face, along with a raw, jealous hunger that made me sick to my stomach.

I shook my head. "That's where you're wrong. That's where you've *always* been wrong. I'm not controlling the gargoyles— they came to me willingly. They've *always* been willing to fight, bleed, and die for Andvari, for their home, for their freedom. Can you say the same about your strixes?"

Milo didn't glance back over his shoulder, so he didn't see the wry, grim smile that played across Wexel's lips. It was the look of a man who knew he probably wouldn't survive the coming battle but was still determined to try. I almost felt sorry for the captain and everything he had lost by following Milo.

Almost.

"I can still kill you, Gemma," Milo hissed. "I can still take your city, destroy your palace, and conquer your kingdom."

"No, you won't," I replied in an ice-cold voice. "All you're going to do is die, and your men and strixes along with you."

Milo eyed me. For a moment, I thought he might stand down, that he might order his men to retreat, that he might actually try to flee and save lives instead of wasting them. But then his face hardened, and magic flared in his eyes.

With a scream of rage, Milo snapped his hand up, then down, and tossed a lightning bolt straight at Grimley and me.

CHAPTER TWENTY-EIGHT

The lightning streaked toward me, growing brighter and hotter with each passing second, and turning the entire sky an eerie purple. Milo had put a massive amount of power into that one bolt, and the electric charge of it made my entire body tingle in warning.

Determination roared up inside me, and I reached for my own magic. That storm of power crackled in my chest, stronger than ever before, thanks to my connection with all the gargoyles still hovering in the air around Grimley and me. I stretched my hand out and swatted the lightning away, and it rattled harmlessly through the sky.

For an instant, a faint flicker of fear surged off Milo, but he snarled, raised his sword high, and urged his strix forward. The archers on the other strixes followed him, and the mass of creatures, men, and weapons zoomed straight toward me.

Anger blasted off Grimley, along with all the other gargoyles, and some of the creatures eased forward, as though they were thinking about charging at the Mortans.

Wait! I called out to the gargoyles. *Wait.*

The creatures flapped their wings and hovered in the air. Low, violent growls spewed out of their mouths, and the rumble of their anger filled the sky just like Milo's lightning had a few seconds ago.

The archers and strixes kept streaking through the air toward us, with Milo leading the charge and Wexel close behind him. As they neared our position, the archers lifted their crossbows, and the wicked gleam of hundreds of tearstone arrows winked at me, as though I was staring at a field of bright gray stars.

More growls and anger blasted off the gargoyles, and once again, a few of them crept forward, their eyes narrowed to slits, and their lips curled back to reveal their sharp teeth.

Wait! I told the gargoyles again. *Wait.*

And so they did, all of us still hovering in the air.

"Fire!" Milo screamed.

The archers pulled the triggers on their crossbows, and tearstone arrows shot out like a sheet of pointed, deadly rain zipping in this direction.

Up, up, up! I told the gargoyles.

With one thought, the creatures flapped their wings, and they all shot even higher into the sky. The arrows zoomed by below, but I leaned over Grimley's side, reached out with my magic, and grabbed as many of those strings of energy as I could.

A single invisible thread of magic filled my hands. Then two. Three. Five. Seven. A dozen. Two dozen. Three dozen.

I quickly lost count, but when I'd snagged as many arrows as possible, I twisted my wrists and spun them all around in midair. Then, with a flick of my fingers, I sent the weapons shooting right back at the archers who'd fired them.

The arrows slammed into the Mortans, punching into their arms, legs, and chests. Some of the men slumped forward on their strixes, while others were knocked off the creatures' backs. Screams, blood, and bodies filled the air as those men plummeted, crashing into the rooftops below, before bouncing off and toppling all the way down to meet a hard, bone-shattering death on the cobblestone streets.

I'd targeted the archers, but some of the arrows plunged into the strixes, clipping their wings and sending them spinning down to the ground. Nausea roiled in my stomach at the sound of the strixes' sharp shrieks. I hated hurting, wounding, killing the creatures—I *hated* it—but it was a necessary evil to save my kingdom.

With that first wave of arrows, I knocked almost half the archers and strixes out of the sky, but the others quickly circled back around.

Attack! I shouted to the gargoyles. *Don't let them fire another round of arrows! Attack! Attack! Attack!*

The creatures growled again and then dove, their teeth bared and their talons outstretched.

The gargoyles smashed into the strixes, and the creatures tore into each other, using their teeth and talons and beaks and wings to try to drive their enemies down to the ground.

The growls and shrieks boomed out like cracks of thunder, punctuated by the solid, heavy *smacks* of the creatures' bodies slamming into each other. It was, without a doubt, one of the most awful sounds I'd ever heard.

Some of the archers and strixes fell to their deaths, but many managed to land in one piece—more or less—on the rooftops and streets below. The gargoyles had knocked down half of the remaining Mortans, and now it was my turn to deal with the rest of our enemies.

Go! I told Grimley. *Dive right into the heart of their formation. Let's end this.*

His anger and determination surged through my body, and I felt his sharp smile in my mind. *With pleasure.*

Grimley let out a fierce roar, then flapped his wings and shot downward, right into the Mortans. I grabbed my dagger off my belt and lashed out with it, slicing the blade into every rider that I passed. I also reached out with my magic, yanking crossbows, swords, and other weapons out of the Mortans' hands. If I couldn't cut someone with my dagger or wrest their weapon away, then I aimed lower, slicing my blade through the leather straps that wound around the strixes' bodies and then using my magic to rip the saddles—and riders—right off the creatures' backs.

That still, frozen eye inside me was long gone, and I was nothing but the storm now, a whirlwind of death and destruction and chaos and magic.

And Grimley was right there with me, his thoughts and power and strength still mixing and mingling with my own, until I didn't know where he ended and I began. Together, we were one, a violent force lashing out as fast and furiously as we could, and we carved a path of devastation through the sky. Enemies screamed, shrieked, and plummeted to the ground in our wake, and blood spattered through the sky like a rain cloud dousing everything with its warm, coppery, sticky wetness.

Grimley broke free of the last of the Mortans and veered around for another charge. I spotted a glint out of the corner of my eye. I looked up and had to duck right back down as Wexel zoomed by, leaning over the side of his strix and trying to lop off my head with his sword.

The captain swung his strix around. His lips drew back into a snarl, and he lifted his sword high, ready to urge his strix forward and attack me again—

Wexel screamed and arched back, his eyes bulging in pain and surprise. He stayed like that for a moment, as though he was somehow frozen in midair. Then blood bubbled up out of his lips, and his sword slipped from his grasp and went tumbling down to the ground so very far below.

The captain stared at me, blinking rapidly. His hand dropped to his belt, and he clutched some jeweled object holstered there. Then his eyes closed, his shoulders slumped, and he slipped off the side of his strix. Wexel didn't make a sound as he streaked downward. He clipped a large bronze gargoyle weather vane, bounced off it, and hit the roof below. He didn't move after that.

A blur of movement caught my eye, and my gaze snapped back up.

Lyra was hovering in midair where Wexel had been, her black beak wet and shiny with the captain's blood from where she had driven it into his back. Her eyes blazed a bright amethyst, and her satisfaction rolled over me like a dark fog.

Told you I would hurt him. Her high singsong voice filled my mind. *For everything he did to Leo—and you too.*

She hovered in midair for another moment, then flapped her wings and shot up even higher into the sky. When she was free of the fighting below, Lyra stopped and let out a sharp, wild, fierce *caw!* that boomed through the sky even louder than the screams and shrieks had.

Her cry startled everyone, gargoyles and strixes alike, and in an instant, all the creatures had paused their attacks and were staring up at her.

Strixes! Her voice rang through my mind loud and clear. *Stop wasting your lives fighting for evil, greedy men who care nothing about you, about us. Follow me, and finally be free!*

Lyra dove back toward the main plaza outside the arena. For a moment, an eerie, tense silence filled the air, and the only sounds were the rapid buzzing beating of the gargoyles' and strixes' wings.

One strix tucked its wings into its sides and spiraled down toward the plaza, following Lyra's command and course. Then another one, then another one. Soon, all the strixes were coasting down toward the ground, despite the protests of the Mortans still on their backs.

Several of the gargoyles growled and started to follow them, to attack the strixes again, but I sent out another thought.

No. The strixes aren't our enemies. They never have been. Don't hurt any more of them. Return to your rooftops and keep watch.

A few reluctant grumbles filled my mind, but the gargoyles also started spiraling downward to return to their roosts—

Another wave of icy malevolence washed over me. Grimley must have sensed it too because he tucked his wings into his sides and dove. A shadow zipped over us, and I ducked my head, barely avoiding the outstretched talons of a strix.

Grimley whirled back around, but the strix dove at him again, and he had to dart to the side to avoid the other creature, who still had a rider—Milo.

The crown prince was still wearing his golden breastplate and wielding his matching sword, but his purple cloak was gone, his golden hair was tangled, and his amethyst eyes were wide and wild in his blood-speckled face. More malevolence rolled off him and crashed into me, but underneath the bitter hatred was a sharp tang of desperation that hadn't been there before.

"You bitch!" he screamed. "You've ruined everything! This all could have been mine! It should have been mine all along!"

"Andvari will never be yours!" I screamed back at him. "Never!"

Milo urged his strix forward. I did the same to Grimley, and we all crashed together in midair.

Milo swung his sword at me over and over again, hammering me with all his might, but I gritted my teeth and used my dagger to block the vicious attacks. His strix beat its wings hard and fast, attacking then retreating, but Grimley did the same thing, keeping me as safe as possible while I battled the crown prince.

A gust of wind made Milo lurch to the side, and I ducked under his defenses and slashed my dagger across his forearm. He howled, then snapped up his hand and flung a lightning bolt at me. Grimley dove to the side, dodging the blast of magic, but Milo steered his strix right into Grimley's side. The two creatures crashed together, then bounced off each other. The hard, jostling motion almost threw me off Grimley's back, but I clamped down with my legs, and I managed to keep my seat.

Grimley snapped his teeth at the strix, forcing the other creature to disengage, and he pumped his wings and sailed even higher up into the sky. Milo and the strix both screamed with frustration and chased after us.

Grimley and the strix zigzagged back and forth through the sky, while Milo flung bolt after bolt of lightning at me. Grimley dodged some of the bolts, while I tossed the others away with my magic.

I sent another bolt spinning away and looked around, expecting another attack, but I'd lost track of Milo, and all I saw was the clear blue sky stretching out all around me.

"Where is he?" I yelled at Grimley, glancing back over my shoulder. "Where is he?"

"I don't know!" Grimley answered, also swinging his head from side to side.

Something tickled the back of my mind. Some whisper of wind, some slight change in the air. On instinct, I jerked to my side—

An arrow punched deep into my left side, right below the edge of the silver breastplate. Agony exploded in my body, and the hard jolt threatened to knock me off Grimley's back. I screamed with pain, but once again, I managed to keep my seat on the gargoyle.

A shadow zipped by overhead, and the strix dropped down in front of us. Milo was still atop the creature, although he had traded his sword for a crossbow. He stared at me, murder in his eyes, and slapped another one of his damned tearstone arrows into the crossbow. He wasn't trying to win the battle, or even escape. Not anymore. No, Milo's rage had blotted out all sense of reason, logic, and survival, and he was determined to kill me, even at the cost of his own life.

The same rage and determination roared through me.

The bastard might have shot me with one of his arrows, might have already killed me, but I was taking him down with me. So I stretched my hand out, blood dripping off my fingers, and reached for all the magic, all the power, all the strength and energy and emotion I had left.

In an instant, I felt everything around me. The sun's rays beating down on my head. The air currents gusting off the surrounding mountains. The bunch and flex of Grimley's wings as he held his position in the sky. Even the slice of the strix's feathers through the air as the creature did the same thing.

But most of all, I felt Milo Morricone.

I felt the magic that continuously crackled around the crown prince like an invisible field of lightning. The power and strength and hate flowing through his body. The anger and bitterness and frustration. I felt all that and more, so much more, but I stretched out even farther with my magic, diving even deeper into Milo and sorting through all his roiling thoughts and emotions until I found what I was looking for.

There—there it was.

For the third time, I reached out with my magic, and I finally grabbed hold of Milo's heart.

The crown prince froze, his eyes bulging, his finger still curled around the crossbow trigger. He struggled against me with all his might, and his lightning thrashed against my own power, cracking at it over and over again in hot, caustic waves. The sensation reminded me of Milo lashing my back with a coral-viper whip at Myrkvior, but his attacks were small, insignificant stings compared to the pain pounding through my side right now.

"Do you know what true power really is, Milo?" I yelled, although my voice was rapidly losing strength, right along with my body. "Having your enemies helpless before you."

An image flickered off Milo and filled my mind—him taunting me with those same exact words when he'd been torturing me in his Myrkvior workshop.

He opened his mouth, probably to scream curses at me, but I used my magic to snap his lips shut. He didn't deserve to utter another word. Milo's eyes bulged again, his silent screams ripped through my mind, and his magic thrashed against mine again. I hissed with pain and tightened my grip on him, making sure I had a firm hold on all those strings of energy radiating out from his heart, along with the rest of his body.

Then I ripped him right off the top of the strix.

Startled, the creature squawked and flew away, but Milo hung there in midair like a puppet. Right now, he was a puppet—*my* puppet, the same way I'd been his in Myrkvior.

Fear and dread and panic and frustration flashed across his face, and his emotions cascaded over me, each one adding to the pounding pain in my own body. I stared him in the eyes a moment longer.

And then I let go of all those strings.

Milo dropped like a stone.

I leaned over Grimley's side and watched my enemy fall. Milo's arms and legs flailed wildly, and bolts of purple lightning shot out of his fingertips one after another. I wasn't sure if he was still trying to kill me or attempting to use his magic to grab hold of something that would stop his rapid descent.

Either way, it didn't work.

CRACK!

Milo slammed into the flagstones right outside the main entrance to the arena.

Despite the distance between us, our gazes met and held,

and I felt every single bit of his pain. All that tremendous force, all those bones breaking, all that trauma shattering every single part of his body. His eyes flashed a bright, electric purple, and he slowly raised his hand, as if to shoot one more bolt of lightning at me . . . but then his hand dropped, his eyes dimmed, and his magic snuffed out, along with his life.

Milo Morricone was finally dead.

And so was I.

CHAPTER TWENTY-NINE

Grimley quickly spiraled down toward the arena. He landed a few seconds later, and I slid off his side. My legs buckled, and I crashed to the ground, much like Milo had done.

I glanced over at the crown prince, who was still sprawled across the flagstones. Milo's head was tilted to the side, and even in death, he seemed to be glaring at me, royally pissed I'd gotten the better of him, once and for all.

Just as he had gotten the better of me.

Pain kept pounding through my body, and tears streamed down my face, but I forced myself to examine the tearstone arrow embedded in my left side. I didn't know if Milo had poisoned this arrow, but it was still slowly killing me. The arrowhead had sunk deep into my flesh, and I didn't know how to get it—and especially the hooked barbs lining the edges—out of my body without doing even more damage to myself.

"Gemma!" Grimley said, hunkering down beside me. "Gemma!"

I braced a hand on the rough flagstones, but my bloody fingers slipped, and I ended up toppling over onto my back. Still, I forced myself to lift my hand and touch the gargoyle's cheek.

"It's okay, Grims," I rasped.

The look on his face said it was anything *but* okay. He knew the same truth that I did—I was dying.

"Gemma! Gemma!" More voices sounded, calling my name, but I didn't have the strength left to answer them.

Footsteps sounded, and suddenly, Delmira was crouching down beside me, with Leonidas hobbling along behind her. Two more shadows fell over me, and Otto and Lyra also appeared. Everyone started talking at once, although I couldn't understand what they were saying.

Hold on, Gemma! Leonidas's voice floated through my mind. *Hold on!*

His face swam into view above my own, and his hand cupped my cheek, firm, strong, and warm. But the sensations quickly vanished, and the last thing I saw was the worry in his eyes before the blackness swallowed me, and I drowned in the dark.

I kept fading in and out of consciousness. Every time someone moved me, the pain of the arrow shifting in my side would snap me awake and give me a few seconds of clarity before I blacked out again.

In a way, I felt as though I was wandering through a portrait room, seeing paintings of everything that was happening. Leonidas scooping me up into his arms and climbing up onto Lyra's back, despite the arrow still sticking out of his own leg. The strix flying us to Glitnir and landing in front of the gazebo in the Edelstein Gardens. Father, Grandfather Heinrich, and Alvis rushing forward, along with several bone masters. Maeven lurking in the background, watching everything with a cold, speculative gaze.

The bone masters gathered around me. Something wrenched in my side, making me scream, but an instant later, magic flowed over me, warm, soft, and soothing. The pain receded, but somehow, I felt even more tired than before, as though the bone masters removing the arrow from my body had also removed what little strength I had left.

I blinked, and the world slowly came into focus. Everyone was standing around me in a loose circle, except for Leonidas and Grimley, who were both kneeling beside me, with worried looks on their faces.

"We don't know what's wrong." The soft, apologetic voice of one of the bone masters cut through the air. "We've removed the arrow and healed her wound, but she's getting weaker instead of stronger. The arrow must have been poisoned, although I don't know with what. We don't . . . we don't know what else to do."

The bone master gave my father a helpless look.

Delmira perked up. "Perhaps the liladorn can help Gemma. Like it did before."

She reached down toward the stand, but the black vines lowered themselves and snaked away from her.

No, I heard the liladorn whisper in my mind. *We are not what she needs. We cannot save her. Not this time.*

Delmira stopped and blinked in surprise, as if she too had finally heard the liladorn's voice in her own mind. Her shoulders drooped, and she glanced over at my father and shook her head. His jaw clenched, and tears gleamed in his eyes. Grandfather Heinrich laid a hand on my father's shoulder. Delmira, Alvis, Lyra, Otto . . . They all looked similarly somber.

Finally, my gaze settled on Maeven, who was still lurking on the edges of the crowd. The queen stared down at me, an unreadable expression on her face.

A small, bitter laugh escaped my lips, shattering the tense silence. "Looks like . . . you're finally . . . getting your wish."

She frowned, her head tilting to the side. "What do you mean?"

If I'd had the strength for it, I would have pointed to the gazebo behind me. "You didn't . . . kill Everleigh here . . . but now . . . you get . . . to watch . . . me die instead. I suppose . . . half a victory . . . is better . . . than none . . . right?"

Maeven's lips puckered in thought, and she looked past me. An image flickered off her and filled my own mind. Not of Everleigh Blair, but of Dahlia Sullivan, dying and gasping for breath, just like I was right now. Sorrow surged off Maeven, but for the first time, I thought it had more to do with her genuine grief over Dahlia's death, rather than her failure to kill Everleigh that night. Or perhaps it was a mixture of both. Perhaps it had *always* been a mixture of both.

Either way, I pushed Maeven out of my mind and focused on Leonidas, who was still crouching down beside me.

He reached out and cupped my cheek again. "You can't die," he said in a low, strained voice. "We haven't come up with any more traditions yet."

His lips lifted into a lopsided grin, although the expression vanished, and anguish filled his face again. "Gemma, I—" His voice choked off, and tears dripped down his face and spattered onto my own.

"It's okay," I replied, my voice even raspier than before.

"I wish we'd had more time," Leonidas whispered, stroking my tangled, bloody hair.

Another wave of lethargy swept over me, and I had to force out the words through the lump of emotion clogging my throat. "I don't regret . . . a single second . . . I spent loving you . . ."

More tears streamed down Leo's face, and his hand slid down to cup my cheek again. I tilted my head to the side, leaning into his touch, even as I stared into his eyes, knowing they would be the last thing I ever saw—

Maeven let out a very loud, extremely unhappy *harrumph*. Everyone looked at her in surprise, including Leonidas and me.

"Such theatrics," she drawled. "You Ripleys can't even die without showing off one final time."

Father stepped forward and stabbed his finger at her, but before he could tell her to shut up and let me pass away in peace, Maeven plucked something out of her left sleeve and held it out where we could all see it.

Instead of a dagger or some other weapon, a small glass vial filled with a midnight-blue liquid glittered in her fingertips. Maeven rolled the vial back and forth, and several tiny bubbles of dark purple rose to the top. She stopped and stared into the depths of the vial, as though it held the final clue to a puzzle she had been trying to solve for a long, long time. Then she sighed and tossed the vial over to Leonidas, who caught it.

"What is this?" he asked in a confused voice. "Some sort of poison?"

Maeven huffed in exasperation. "Why would I give you a poison when Gemma is so obviously dying?"

"Because . . . you're . . . you," I rasped.

Maeven huffed again. "If you must know, it's crushed tearstone mixed with liladorn sap."

Delmira's face scrunched up in confusion. "I've never heard of that before. Why would you make such a thing? And carry it around in your sleeve?"

The queen stared down at me, that unreadable expression on her face again. "Because Merilde said I would need it one day—and today is that day."

I looked back at her, so many questions swirling through my mind. Those same questions also filled everyone else's faces, but Maeven ignored everyone except for Leonidas and me.

"Give it to her," she snapped. "Before I change my mind."

Leonidas plucked the stopper out of the top of the vial, then put his arm under my shoulders and helped me sit up. I opened my lips, and he tipped the liquid down into my mouth.

The first drop touched my tongue, making it tingle. In an instant, those tingles swept through my entire body, as though I was sitting in the center of a violent lightning storm. But instead of scorching me to ash, these tingles reignited everything inside me that had gone cold and numb and dead.

Dimly, I realized what was happening. That the tearstone was amplifying the liladorn's healing properties, just as the tearstone embedded in the gargoyles' skin had increased Milo's deadly lightning, as well as my own mind magier power.

The liquid was pure, undiluted magic.

I lay there, cradled in Leonidas's arms as the magic washed over me. It invaded every single part of my body, crushing, killing, and ultimately conquering whatever poison had coated Milo's arrow.

Sometime later, the magic slowed, then faded away altogether. I drew in a breath and slowly sat up, with Leonidas and Grimley still crouched down on the ground beside me.

Father, Grandfather Heinrich, Alvis, Delmira, Lyra, Otto, the bone masters. I looked at all of them in turn before my gaze settled on Maeven.

"Thank you," I said in a soft voice.

The queen's lips puckered with displeasure, the way they so often did whenever she looked at me. But after a few seconds, she nodded at me, and for once, the motion was more respectful than mocking.

"Gemma," Leonidas said, his gaze searching mine. "Are you really okay?"

I trailed my fingers down his cheek. Tears streamed down my face, but I smiled and nodded at him. "I'm really okay."

Leonidas shuddered out a breath, then gathered me up into his arms. I buried my face in his neck, inhaling his honeysuckle scent.

Gemma . . .

Leo . . .

Our thoughts and love mingled together, and I let them sweep me away. They didn't take away all the horrors of the day, or the pain of everything we'd been through over the past few months, but they made everything just a little easier to bear—together.

Despite my protests that I was fine, more or less, the bone masters carried me to my chambers, where I was given several more rounds of healing, along with a hot bath. I was too exhausted to protest, so I let the bone masters and servants do as they wished, then crawled into bed. Leonidas drew the covers up to my chin and pressed a kiss to my forehead, and I drowned in the darkness again.

The first thing I saw when I opened my eyes the next morning was Reiko sitting in a chair, her socked feet propped up on my bed and a platter of sweet cakes balanced on her lap. My friend had also been healed, and no trace of Bridget DiLucri's attack and Wexel's vicious beating marred her features. Both Reiko and her inner dragon were peering down at the cakes with critical gazes, as though they were debating which treat to eat first.

"I never thought I would be comforted by the sight of you holding a platter of sweet cakes," I drawled, sitting up in bed. "But right now, I find it oddly satisfying."

Reiko snorted, then popped a cake into her mouth. She must have liked the flavor because her inner dragon smacked its lips in appreciation. "You're just lucky you woke up when you did—and that the servants brought two platters of sweet cakes. I've already polished off the others, and I was getting ready to do the same to these. Sitting vigil by your bedside is far more boring than I anticipated."

She held the platter out to me, and I took a cake. Mmm. Cranberry-apple, one of my favorites.

We sat in silence, downing the cakes. When the treats were gone, Reiko set the platter aside, dropped her feet from the bed, and sighed.

"I suppose you want to yell at me now," she muttered.

"For what?"

"For not telling you my suspicion that Milo was hiding at the old fairgrounds. And for not telling Kai where I was going and what I was doing." She sighed again. "And especially for getting captured and having to be rescued."

"Why would I yell at you for any of that?" I countered. "You figuring out where Milo was hiding helped us stop his plot. You saved my family, my people, and my gargoyles. You saved my bloody *kingdom*, Reiko. I will always be grateful for that, more than you will ever know."

She gave me a wary look. "But?"

I leaned over and poked my finger into her shoulder. "*But* you should have told me what you were doing and where you were going. I would have gone with you. I would have *helped* you."

Reiko rubbed her shoulder, then sighed for a third time. "I know that. Truly, I do. It really was just a hunch. I didn't expect to find an army of Mortans, strixes, and mercenaries camped up on the mountain."

"I know," I replied in a softer voice. "Next time, just tell me what's going on. Promise?"

She gave me a solemn nod, as did her inner dragon. "Promise."

The tension between us eased, and I settled myself back against the pillows. "So how *did* you figure out where Milo was hiding?"

Reiko shrugged. "I kept thinking about you seeing Milo in

the fairgrounds and then again during the opening ceremonies of the gladiator tournament. And I wondered why he would show himself to you there when he was planning to sneak into the palace later that night. Why not wait until *after* he'd destroyed Glitnir to show his face?"

"Well, Milo did say he wanted to kidnap me in case Dahlia Sullivan's journal wasn't accurate, and he couldn't use it to find his way through the old mining tunnels underneath the city."

"True." Reiko tipped her head, acknowledging my point. "But I kept thinking about why he would show himself to you in the arena, especially given the number of guards that were patrolling in and around the structure. And I realized Milo was doing exactly what I would in his situation—hiding in plain sight. I just wasn't sure exactly where he might be until Leo said something about the crowds at the fairgrounds the afternoon after the treasury attack. Then later that night, I saw a map of Glanzen in Kai's tent, and I realized the old fairgrounds were the perfect place for Milo and his men to hide."

She grimaced. "I just didn't realize exactly *how* many men he had until I was up at the camp. I was in Milo's tent, trying to find out when he was going to order his men to attack when Bridget DiLucri came in and spotted me. She managed to knock me out, and when I woke up, Wexel started beating me."

Anger flared in her eyes, and smoke boiled out of the mouth of her inner dragon. If I were Bridget, I would not want to meet Reiko again in the future.

My friend shook her head, as if flinging off her anger, and focused on me again. "So what happened after you heard me call out to you?"

I told her everything that had happened, from going to the fairgrounds to find Kai, to figuring out where she had gone, to rescuing her from the mercenary camp. I also told her about my part in the battle and how I'd flattened many of the Mortans with the gargoyle statue in the arena before taking to the skies on Grimley's back and asking all the other gargoyles to fight with us.

When I finished, Reiko's face turned thoughtful. "I still can't believe Maeven actually saved your life."

"Me neither," I muttered. "Although I'm sure she'll find some way to make me pay for it later."

Reiko laughed. "Probably."

Once again, her face turned serious. "I'm so glad you found me," Reiko said in a soft voice. "I thought I was going to die in that tent, that Wexel was going to beat me to death, that I was never going to see you or Kai again . . ."

Her voice trailed off, and she cleared her throat. "But you found me, Gemma. I might have saved your kingdom, but you saved me in return. And that—and especially your friendship—means more to me than you will ever know."

She reached out and gripped my hand, and I gripped hers back just as tightly. We sat like that for a long, long time, drawing what strength and comfort we could from each other, and trying to ignore the collective horrors still rattling around in our minds and raking their cold, sharp talons across our hearts.

CHAPTER THIRTY

Even though I wanted nothing more than to remain in bed, I got up, got dressed, and got on with the business of being alive.

I spent the rest of the day in meetings with Grandfather Heinrich, Father, and Rhea, discussing everything that had happened over the past few days. Despite our victory, I was still tense, as was the rest of my family.

We all knew how very, very close we had come to losing our lives, along with our kingdom.

But we couldn't afford to show our worry, so that night, a royal ball was held in my honor to celebrate my victory over Milo and his would-be invaders. I stood outside the closed double doors that led to the throne room, with Leonidas by my side.

"How do I look?" I asked, running my hands down my skirt.

"Marvelous," Leonidas replied. "A true gargoyle queen in every sense of the word."

Despite the time crunch, Yaleen had whipped up a truly spectacular design. My dark gray velvet gown featured tiny shards of midnight-blue tearstone, along with bits of jet, that combined to form the Ripley snarling gargoyle crest, as though Grimley's face had been stamped all over the fabric. A small jet-and-sapphire tiara was nestled in my dark brown hair, and Yaleen had even made silver wings shot through with veins of midnight-blue thread that hooked to the back of my gown. According to the thread master, the wings were supposed to make me look like the human version of a gargoyle, but I felt more like a butterfly—one that had barely escaped getting crushed by the events of the last few days.

"Well, if I'm a gargoyle queen, then you are a shadow knight," I teased, gesturing at Leonidas.

The Morricone prince looked exceptionally handsome in a short formal black jacket with amethyst buttons shaped like flying strixes. For once, no royal crest dotted his jacket, although I hadn't gotten up the courage to ask Leonidas what, if anything, the lack of symbols meant. I didn't want to ruin this quiet moment between us, especially not when part of me still couldn't believe I was here with him and the horrors of the past few months were finally over.

That Milo was dead, and we had won—although not without great cost.

I had destroyed the gargoyle statue in the arena, killing dozens and dozens of Mortans in the process, and even more Mortans and mercenaries had died in the main fairgrounds, thanks to Adora and the rest of the Gray Falcons. Adora had taken my warning to watch out for trouble to heart, and she had rallied her gladiator troupe as soon as she realized that enemies had invaded the fairgrounds. Thankfully, no innocent bystanders had been killed, although dozens of people had been injured, some of them quite severely. Dozens of gargoyles had also been injured or killed, along with even more strixes.

I grieved the loss of so much life, of so much useless pain, anguish, and destruction, and I was trying to figure out a way to help everyone who had been injured, including the gargoyles and strixes.

"I'm sorry," Leonidas said in a low voice, picking up on my turbulent thoughts. "That we didn't stop Milo sooner. That your people and creatures had to suffer because of his greed and ambition."

I gave him a sad smile. "Me too. But all we can do now is move forward—together."

Leonidas nodded and held out his arm. Inside, the Ripley royal march started playing. I threaded my arm through his, and we both faced forward.

"And now, announcing Her Royal Highness, Gemma Armina Merilde Ripley!" the announcer's voice boomed out.

The doors slowly opened, and I plastered a smile on my face as though nothing was wrong, my heart wasn't brimming with sorrow, and I was absolutely delighted to be here.

It was time for me to play the part of Princess Gemma yet again.

The ball went exactly as I expected it to. People gathered around me in droves, like bees buzzing around a particularly attractive flower, and I was the center of attention, much more so than I had ever been before. Everyone wanted to speak to the person who had saved Glitnir and Glanzen from ruination.

Everyone except for Maeven.

The Morricone queen kept her distance from me. According to Rhea, Milo's body had been retrieved from outside the arena and was being taken back to Morta so that he could be buried at Myrkvior with the rest of the Morricones.

Curiously enough, Wexel's body had not been found, and no one had been able to determine what object he'd swiped from the royal treasury. I couldn't help but think that the mysterious item had somehow helped the captain survive. As for what Wexel would do next, well, perhaps it was foolish after everything he'd done, but part of me hoped he finally found that rest he so desperately craved.

Despite all the awful things Milo had done, and all the times he had tried to depose and kill her over the past several months, Maeven was still a mother who'd lost her son. Every time she looked at me, pain, anger, and regret shimmered in her eyes, and the same emotions gusted off her, overpowering everyone else's joy, triumph, and relief, including my own.

Eventually, the music and dancing started, and I was finally able to escape my pack of admirers and slip out of the throne room. I dug my fingers into my cheeks, and it took me several seconds to unlock my jaw and massage the fixed smile off my face.

Then I went in search of Maeven.

She too had slipped out of the throne room, telling my father that she had a headache and wanted to rest. Lies, of course, but I couldn't fault her for leaving a ball where everyone was celebrating her son's death.

I reached out with my magic, and I sensed her presence at once. An aggravated huff escaped my lips. Of course she would go *there* again. It was the scene of so much Andvarian and Mortan history, as well as so many of the things that bound the two of us together.

So I opened a door, crossed a terrace, and slipped into the hedge maze. It didn't take me long to follow the twists and turns to the open space in the gargoyle's nose.

Maeven was sitting on a cushioned bench in the gazebo, staring out over the pond in the distance. She didn't seem surprised to see me, just as I wasn't surprised to see her here.

Sometimes, I felt as though this was the spot where my life had truly begun. Oh, sure, I had survived the Seven Spire massacre and all the horrible things that had happened after that in the Spire Mountains, but this was where Everleigh Blair had been attacked by the Bastard Brigade all those years ago. This was the place where I had finally decided to be brave, instead of afraid. This was the place where I had finally decided to act, instead of react. And this was the place where I had realized just how much danger my kingdom was in and had almost given my life to save it a few days ago.

As strange as it was, Maeven was a large part of all those memories, all those actions and decisions and sacrifices on my part.

I stepped into the gazebo, went over, and sat down beside her on the cushioned bench. We didn't speak for several minutes, but for once the quiet was companionable instead of hostile, and the only sound was the steady *slap-slap-slap* of water in the pond.

"I've always thought this was a lovely spot for an ambush," Maeven murmured.

"Oh, yes. It *is* an excellent spot for an ambush," I agreed without a trace of sarcasm. "And for a rendezvous too. Lovers used to sneak out here all the time to be alone, although not so much after your attack on Aunt Evie and Uncle Lucas. The gazebo lost a great deal of its charm after that night."

Maeven snorted, although the noise sounded suspiciously close to a laugh. "Well, it's good to know I wasn't a complete failure in everything I did."

"If there is one thing I have never considered you, it is a failure."

She harrumphed. "Do you know how bloody *frustrating* it is to work so long and hard and sacrifice so much? To have all these grand plans and schemes and almost—*almost*—see them succeed, only to be beaten, defeated, and crushed time and time again? And not by the enemies I was expecting or planning for, but by people and magic and forces I never even *considered*. That I had absolutely no *control* over. It's enough to drive me mad."

Anger, scorn, and bitterness dripped off her, hot enough to scorch through my own body. I knew she was talking about Everleigh Blair ruining so many of her plans over the years, but I also got the sense she was talking about me too.

"I could say I'm sorry that I killed Milo."

Maeven let out a harsh, caustic laugh. "Don't bother lying to me, Gemma. Not now."

Yes, that would most definitely be a lie, so I didn't utter the words.

"Did my mother tell you what would happen?" I asked, changing the subject. "How I would connect with the gargoyles and use them to protect Glanzen? Is that why you kept calling me the gargoyle queen?"

"Partially," Maeven replied. "During one of our little chats in the Caldwell Castle library, Merilde told me that you would have powerful magic, that you would do great things as queen. She was quite insufferable about it. I was ready to wring her bloody neck just to get her to shut up."

"But?" I challenged.

"But I don't think she saw your future as clearly as she did that of other people. Merilde called you the gargoyle queen, but I don't think she knew what it truly meant."

Suspicion filled me. "But *you* knew what it meant."

Maeven shrugged. "All I saw was a quiet, shy little girl who always had her nose buried in some storybook. Hardly a queen."

"But?"

"But there is a prophecy about three queens," she grumbled. "It's quite famous, or rather infamous, at least in the Morricone family."

According to that prophecy you mentioned, the Ripley princess is far more powerful than anyone suspects, Bridget DiLucri's voice whispered through my mind, along with Milo's reply.

Just because Dahlia Sullivan and my mother believe some moldy old prophecy doesn't mean that it's true.

The two of them had said that in Milo's tent. I hadn't paid much attention to their words at the time, but it seemed as though Maeven had given the idea quite a lot of consideration over the years.

I eyed the Mortan queen. "I never thought you would be one to believe in prophecies, especially since they're as common as sunshine. You wouldn't believe how many of them I've heard over the years. Mostly from one lord or another, claiming how our love is supposedly written in the stars."

Maeven let out a derisive snort. "You're right. Most of them are inane nonsense. I never really believed in prophecies—until about sixteen years ago."

I started to ask what had happened back then to change her mind, but then I realized exactly what—or rather *whom*—she was talking about. "You mean Everleigh Blair. She's one of the queens in this so-called prophecy."

Maeven nodded. "Yes."

She fell silent, staring out over the pond. When she spoke again, her voice was much lower and softer than before. "The prophecy predicts the rise of three queens. The first is a gladiator queen."

I frowned. "But gladiators are a Bellonan tradition, not a Mortan one. So why would there be a Morricone prophecy about a gladiator queen?"

Maeven shrugged again. "I have no idea why this prophecy is so prominent in my family, but it's been handed down for generations, and every single Morricone is told it from childhood. Although growing up in Maximus's shadow, it seemed impossible to me that it would ever come true. I thought no one could ever defeat him, not even a gladiator queen. But, of course, Everleigh tricked me into killing him, so I suppose she won that honor after all."

"Who are the other two queens in the prophecy?" I asked, suspicion filling me.

Maeven looked at me. "A gargoyle queen, of course. As if you hadn't already guessed."

This time, it was my turn to stare out over the pond and try to make sense of her words. I still didn't think some prophecy had foretold everything I would do over the past few months, and I wasn't going to put much belief in it now. But I wanted to know what else the prophecy said, so I turned back to Maeven.

"And the third queen?"

Her lips pressed together, and she didn't answer me—but she didn't have to. Out of the corner of my eye, I spotted that stand of liladorn by the gazebo steps, and I thought about everything the sentient plant had said to me over the past several weeks in all the places I had encountered it.

"Not-Our-Princess," I murmured, repeating the liladorn's nickname for me.

Maeven frowned. "What? What nonsense are you spouting?"

I gestured at the vines. "That's what the liladorn calls me—Not-Our-Princess." I paused. "Which means it *does* have a princess—someone who will eventually become a queen in her own right."

Maeven's lips puckered with displeasure again, indicating that I was right—and what this had all really been about from the very beginning. At least, to her.

Suddenly, I saw everything the Morricone queen had done over the past few months in a new light. Why she had stopped Milo from killing me at Myrkvior, why she had let me escape his workshop, why she had tried to throw Leonidas and me together at the Summit, even why she had saved me with Merilde's potion in this very spot just yesterday. Shock zipped through me, along with more than a little admiration.

Maeven Morricone had been playing a long game with me this whole time—and she had bloody *won*.

"You really did need me, didn't you?" I accused. "That's what you said to Delmira when I was eavesdropping on the two of you at the Summit. You needed me to play my part, to become this supposed gargoyle queen in order to further the prophecy. To help *Delmira*. So *she* can be queen. So *she* can rule Morta and the rest of the Morricones someday."

"Yes," Maeven muttered through clenched teeth, as though that one simple word, that one soft admission pained her more than she ever wanted anyone to know, especially me. "I bloody *needed* you, Gemma."

A laugh bubbled out of my lips. "Well, you have a funny way of showing it, considering that you tried to murder me at Seven Spire all those years ago."

"As I said before, I didn't believe in the prophecy back then."

"And now you do?"

"I've learned not to discount or dismiss such things out of hand." Her face hardened. "Besides, I haven't worked this long and hard and suffered this much for Delmira *not* to become queen."

"But Leonidas is next in line for the throne," I pointed out.

I'd killed Milo, which meant Leonidas could return home to Morta without fear of his brother trying to murder him again—and start positioning himself to be king. Leonidas hadn't said anything to me about it, hadn't talked at all about his future plans, but my heart still wrenched with pain, just as it did every time I'd had a similar thought over the past few weeks.

Maeven laughed, the sound tumbling out of her lips and splattering all over me like the coldest rain. "Just when I think you might actually have a small glimmer of intelligence, you go and say something stupid like that. How disappointing, Gemma."

I waited for her to explain her cryptic, mocking words, but instead, she rose to her feet, and I did the same.

"Why did you give me the cure to Milo's poison?" I asked. "You could have let me die. I'd already defeated Milo and become this supposed gargoyle queen. You didn't need me to fulfill your prophecy anymore."

"Oh, I quite enjoyed watching you gasp for breath," Maeven purred. "I'll always treasure that memory."

My hands balled into fists, but I forced myself to keep my voice level. "Why did you save me?"

"Because for some reason I will never truly fathom, Leonidas adores you, and he would have been devastated by your death." She paused. "I know what it's like to live with that sort of pain, and I did not want that for my son—not even if it meant letting you live."

Questions filled my mind about whom she had loved, and when, and why—Leonidas and Delmira's father, perhaps? But I knew she wouldn't answer.

"Maeven Morricone, always so generous," I drawled. "Perhaps we should nickname you *the queen of kindness*."

She ignored my insults and looked around the gazebo. Her gaze settled on an empty spot on the floor, and an image flickered off her and filled my mind—Dahlia Sullivan drinking the vial of amethyst-eye poison that had been meant for Everleigh Blair the night Maeven and some other members of the Bastard Brigade had failed to assassinate the Bellonan queen.

"I've always wondered what Dahlia was thinking when she willingly drank that poison," Maeven said, giving voice to her own memory. "What prompted her to do that, rather than trying to escape. Lucas Sullivan might have been disgusted by her actions, but Dahlia was still his mother. He would have helped her."

"Perhaps she didn't want him to have to choose between her and Heinrich, and her and Everleigh," I suggested. "Perhaps Dahlia was afraid Lucas would choose his father and his lover over her. Perhaps she didn't want to risk knowing the answer to those questions. Or perhaps she just didn't want to spend the rest of her life rotting in a cell before being executed."

Maeven jerked her head, although I couldn't tell if she was agreeing with me or not. "All reasonable theories."

"What's yours?"

Her lips puckered in thought again, and her amethyst eyes grew dark and distant. "I don't think Dahlia cared about being imprisoned or even executed. I think she took the poison to spare her son from further harm. In the end, I think Dahlia loved Lucas just a tiny bit more than she did Morta. That she cared more about her son than she did about doing her duty and furthering the Morricone legacy. I know the feeling."

Sorrow wisped off Maeven like a cold fog, and the ghostly tendrils of it sank deep into my own heart. Was she talking about her own love for her children versus her duty to Morta? Or something else entirely? Before I could ask, she straightened up to her full height and looked down her nose at me again.

"I will be leaving soon to take Milo home to Morta," she said. "This particular threat is at an end."

I frowned. "*This* threat? Is there *another* threat? A *different* threat?"

"That remains to be seen." She stepped even closer to me, her face hardening. "But know this, Gemma. Tonight, we are friends, but tomorrow, we are rivals again. Milo's death changes *nothing* between us. Do you understand?"

Interesting that she'd said *rivals* and not *enemies*, but I didn't point that out. Instead, I arched an eyebrow. "In other words, you'll keep trying to undermine me and my family, and we'll keep thwarting your plots. Does that sound about right to you?"

Maeven's lips pinched together in anger, even as a bit of weary resignation flickered off her. That tiny flare of emotion prompted me to speak again and to reveal something I had thought about for a long, long time but had never shared with anyone, not even Uncle Lucas.

"I think Dahlia was just tired."

Maeven's eyebrows drew together in confusion. "What do you mean?"

"I think Dahlia took the poison because she was so bloody *tired*. Of lying and scheming and pretending to be someone she wasn't. I think she just wanted it to end, in a way."

Maeven stared at me, considering my words.

"Sometimes, I think that you're tired too," I continued. "Just as tired as I am, as all the kings and queens and other royals eventually are."

"And what do you suggest I do about that?"

"You could stop. Just . . . *stop*," I replied. "Stop scheming and plotting and trying to kill all the other royals. Why don't you just stop and bloody *rest* for a while? Would that truly be so terrible?"

Maeven huffed. "And do what, exactly? Take up beekeeping like your grandfather has done and let someone else run my kingdom? Please. You know me better than that."

She was right. I *did* know her better than that, but I could also hear the faintest trace of wistfulness in her voice. Perhaps I knew the queen even better than she knew herself.

"Besides, Everleigh told me once that Morricones don't get to finish out their lives in quaint little cottages in the countryside, and she was absolutely right about that," Maeven continued. "Morricones rule—or we die. Simple as that. As do gargoyle queens. Something you would do well to remember, Gemma."

"I remember every single lesson you have taught me. They are some of the reasons why I am still alive today."

Maeven blinked, and she seemed truly surprised by my

compliment, such as it was. She studied me a moment longer, then dipped down into a deep curtsy, a gesture of equalness and respect from one queen to another.

I mirrored her motion, although both of us never took our eyes off each other. Then, together, we both rose.

Maeven glanced around, more memories flickering off her. Then she whirled around, stalked away from the gazebo, and disappeared into the shadows.

Gone for now, but not forgotten, and never, ever truly defeated.

CHAPTER THIRTY-ONE

The Sword and Shield Tournament resumed three days later. Given everything that had happened during Milo's attack, the arena had been closed so that workers could remove the rubble from the gargoyle statue, along with the Mortans' bodies.

Since Bridget DiLucri had fled, Kai was now the clear favorite, and he easily advanced through his bouts. Then, in the championship round, he drew first blood in less than a minute to win the tournament, as well as give the Crimson Dragons the overall troupe championship for the year.

Adora, who was now serving as ringmaster for the entire tournament, rushed forward and lifted Kai's arm into the air, officially declaring him the winner. The arena erupted into raucous cheers, and Reiko clapped, yelled, and whistled louder than anyone else. I also cheered wildly, along with Leonidas and Delmira. Lord Eichen was also quite exuberant, as were Grandfather Heinrich, Father, Rhea, and Alvis. Even Maeven politely applauded, although she shot an annoyed glower at the Mortan who had lost to Kai. The female gladiator ducked her head and slunk out of the ring to escape the queen's ire.

After that, the usual ceremonies were held at the arena, while the celebrations spilled out into the fairgrounds and plaza

beyond. And of course yet another royal ball was held that night
to celebrate Kai's victory. Almost everyone in the throne room
was in a jovial mood, and a palpable sense of relief filled the air,
mixing with my own.

Still, despite our victories large and small, things weren't
perfect. Milo might be dead, but Wexel was still missing, and
Bridget had escaped and returned to Fortuna Island, along with
most of her geldjager mercenaries. I had no doubt she and the
rest of the DiLucris were already plotting their next move against
Andvari, as well as the other kingdoms. And of course I couldn't
stop thinking about that mysterious *other threat* that Maeven had
alluded to. But those were all worries for tomorrow. Right now, I
was going to enjoy tonight.

I was standing in a corner of the throne room, sipping cider
with Reiko, when Kai swaggered over to us. As the tournament
champion, he'd been the most popular person at the ball tonight,
and everyone had wanted to speak to him, including Eichen, who
had practically talked his ear off for the last half hour.

Reiko smiled at Kai, although a wave of sadness gusted off
her. Earlier, when we had been getting ready for the ball, she had
said that the other dragon morph didn't have a reason to stay in
Glanzen now that the tournament was over. But given the emotions surging off Kai, she was very wrong about that.

Kai leaned down and kissed Reiko's cheek. She accepted his
affection, then drew back, not so subtly putting some distance
between them.

"So . . . when do you leave?" Reiko's voice remained neutral,
although the dragon on her hand scrunched up its face, as though
it didn't want to hear his reply.

"Leave?" Kai frowned. "What are you talking about?"

Reiko gestured over at the other members of the gladiator
troupe. "I heard some of the other Crimson Dragons talking.
They're eager to return to Ryusama so they can celebrate the

championship and spend the yuletide season with their families."

Kai's frown deepened. "Why would you think I'm going with them?"

Reiko shrugged. "Because you're the leader of the Crimson Dragons, and you just won the biggest tournament and championship of the season. You should go home to Ryusama and spend the next few months touring, doing exhibition bouts, and enjoying your reign as the best gladiator in all of Buchovia. Just like you did last year after winning the Tournament of Champions during the Regalia Games."

Kai shrugged back at her. "I'm tired of touring and winning tournaments. It's not nearly as fun and challenging as it was when you were part of the troupe." He grinned, his face crinkling with both warmth and arrogance. "But you're right about one thing. I *am* the best gladiator in all of Buchovia, just as you are the best spy."

Reiko rolled her eyes at his teasing, even as an answering grin crept over her face. I took another sip of my cider, hiding my own smile.

Kai stepped even closer to Reiko and stared down at her, his golden eyes bright and hopeful. "I thought I would stay in Andvari for a while. I've just received an offer from a wealthy benefactor to train with a different troupe, in hopes of helping them win the championship next year."

Reiko frowned. "What benefactor?"

Kai tilted his head toward Eichen, who was talking to Alvis, along with Maeven. Eichen must have noticed our stares because he stopped talking long enough to toast us with his own goblet.

I bit back a laugh. Of course Eichen would steal Kai away from the Crimson Dragons to help Adora and the Gray Falcons, along with his other grandchildren and their respective troupes. I toasted the lord with my own glass, silently applauding his ruthlessness, at least when it came to all things gladiatorial. Eichen grinned back at me, then turned to Alvis and Maeven, who actually deigned to join the two men in conversation.

"That is, if you want me to stay," Kai said, a hesitant note creeping into his voice. "If you would rather I leave—"

Reiko stepped forward and toyed with one of the gold buttons on his crimson jacket. "I didn't say that," she replied, then looked up and grinned at him. "You know, having a gladiator around could be a good thing. Gemma gets into so much trouble. I need someone to help me keep her in line."

I snorted. "Lest we all forget, *you* were the one who decided it was a good idea to sneak into a mercenary camp all by yourself."

"That's what spies do," Reiko murmured, never taking her eyes off Kai. "And I *am* the best."

He grinned back at her. "Yes, you are."

Reiko stood up on her tiptoes and whispered something into Kai's ear that made his eyes flash bright and hot. He slipped an arm around her waist and started whispering back to her, even as their two inner dragons eyed each other with hungry, passionate interest. They were all so wrapped up in each other, they didn't notice when I slipped away.

I went to the gardens, of course. They had been my escape from royal balls for my entire life, and I saw no reason to change that now. But instead of going to the gazebo, I headed to the gargoyle's right eye. As always, no one else was in this section of the gardens, so I sat down on my mother's memorial bench and traced my fingers over the silver plaque that bore her name.

"I wonder if you saw this moment too," I murmured.

I glanced around, hoping my magic would rise up and show me another vision of Merilde, but it didn't. Even now, after everything that had happened, I still couldn't completely control my power. But that was okay. Because I knew something now that had eluded me for so many years—that my magic was a part of me and that the storm of power, *my* power, would always be there when I truly needed it.

As would the liladorn.

The vines were curled around my mother's plaque again, and one of them reached out and patted my hand in a comforting gesture. I ran my finger along the vine, scratching it just like I would Grimley's head, and for once, it quivered and leaned into my touch.

Thank you, Not-Our-Princess. That familiar voice sounded in my mind. *That spot was itching.*

The vines slithered down and retreated back into the shadows. Strangely enough, the liladorn was growing on me, along with its dry sense of humor.

Another familiar presence filled my mind, as footsteps whispered through the grass and a shadow appeared at the edge of the hedge maze—Leonidas.

He hesitated a moment, then strode forward. I got to my feet, and he stopped in front of me, uncertainty creasing his face.

"Mother has informed me that she is leaving in the morning," Leonidas said. "She is taking Milo's body back to Morta to be buried at Myrkvior."

I nodded, since Maeven had told me as much during our talk in the gazebo a few nights ago. "Will you go with her?"

"Do you want me to go with her?" Leonidas countered in a soft voice.

I knew what I was *supposed* to say, what *duty* dictated I should say. That yes, Leonidas should go and support his family and see his brother laid to rest, no matter how murderous Milo had been. But for once, I didn't do the right thing, the proper thing, the dutiful thing.

"Of course I don't want you to go. I don't want you to go anywhere. But Milo is dead. The crown prince of Morta is dead—

which means you are now the heir." I shook my head. "I can't ask you to give up being king."

"Why not?" Leonidas asked.

I threw my hands out wide. "Because you could do so much bloody *good* as king. You could be such a wonderful leader for your people. You could do all the things you always wanted to, all the things you always *dreamed* about but never thought you would have the chance to implement. I can't ask you to give that up, not for me, not for anything. I would *never* ask you to do that."

Leonidas nodded, his face serious. "I know, and that's one of the many things I love about you. That you would let me go, and do my duty, and be king, even though we could never be together." A fierce light sparked in his eyes. "But I care less and less about duty these days, and more and more about you, Gemma."

He hesitated again, then reached into his pocket, drew out a box, and cracked open the top. I gasped.

A stunning silver ring lay inside. The centerpiece was Grimley's snarling gargoyle face—the Ripley royal crest—done in pieces of black jet, with midnight-blue shards of tearstone making up his horns, eyes, nose, and teeth. All around Grimley's face, strix feathers had been engraved into the silver, and tiny amethysts glittered here and there, turning the design into something that was both Andvarian and Mortan at the same time.

"I hope you like the ring," Leonidas said. "I've been working on the design with Alvis for weeks now."

"So *this* is what you were always sketching in that black journal." I couldn't stop staring at the ring. "It's beautiful."

"Not nearly as beautiful as you are, Gemma."

Leonidas drew the ring out of the box, then went down on one knee in front of me the way he had so many times before. He held the ring up and out to me, his gaze on mine.

"I never wanted to be king of Morta, and I have no desire to be king now. I'm not giving that up for you, because you are so much more than all of that. You are the queen of my heart, Gemma Ripley," he declared in a loud, strong voice. "You always have been, and you always will be. So I would like to make it official, and be the king of yours as well." His lips stretched into a wry grin. "Or at least the king consort."

My heart soared at his words, but I forced myself to do my duty, one last time. "Maeven tried to make us get engaged at the Summit. Are you certain this is what you truly want?"

Leonidas nodded, his gaze never leaving mine. "I've never been more certain of anything. So, Gemma Ripley, will you do me the honor of letting me be your king consort? Please?"

There he went with that bloody *please* again, the one word that always made me want to say yes to whatever he was asking. Oh, who was I kidding? I would have said yes to Leo no matter what he said.

Tears pricked my eyes and streaked down my face. Words abandoned me, so I nodded and held out my shaking hand. Leonidas grinned and slipped the ring onto my finger. He pressed a courtly kiss to my hand, the way he had so many times before, then surged to his feet. I reached for him, and he for me, and our lips crashed together—

"Yes!" a voice called out. "Finally!"

Startled, we broke apart.

Delmira was here now, along with Reiko, Kai, Grandfather Heinrich, Father, Rhea, Alvis, Eichen, Adora, and Maeven. They were all smiling and clapping, except for Maeven, of course. Her expression was more resigned than anything else, but she tipped her head to me, and I did the same to her.

Then Leonidas wrapped me up in his arms again and swung me around, and I was far too happy to think about anything but how much I loved him, and how much he loved me, and how we were going to spend the rest of our lives building one tradition after another.

After a round of hearty congratulations from our friends and family, everyone returned to the ball. Leonidas started to head in that direction, but I grabbed his hand.

"I have a surprise for you too."

"What?"

I gave him a mysterious smile. "You'll see."

I led him to a completely different section of the palace, albeit one that still overlooked the Edelstein Gardens.

Some of the walls here had been hit by Milo's lightning the night of the treasury attack, and purple scorch marks still streaked across the gray stones. I moved past the walls and waved my hand, and two stone doors on a nearby tower swung open.

Milo's lightning had blasted the roof clean off this tower, which was a bit taller and wider than its neighbors. The rubble and debris had been cleared away, and the night sky shone above in all its dark and glorious wonder. This tower had stood empty and abandoned for as long as I could remember, but a few days ago, I'd asked Alvis and the palace metalstone masters to spruce it up. Now a large fountain bubbled in the center of the open-air tower, and hollow spaces had been carved into the walls, starting at the ground level and going all the way up to the top.

As Leonidas and I moved deeper into the tower, two amethyst eyes appeared in a space along the floor. Then two more eyes in a space halfway up the wall. And more sets of eyes in other spaces throughout the entire tower.

The eyes crept forward out of the shadows, and the strixes appeared.

Leonidas stopped and turned around in a slow circle. "A rookery," he whispered in an awed voice.

After Lyra had asked the strixes to stop fighting, Rhea and her men had removed the saddles from the creatures. Some of the strixes had immediately flown away, but many had been too injured to leave, so Rhea had ordered them to be brought to the palace so that they could be healed. Her kindness had sparked my own idea to turn this tower into a rookery. Not just for the injured creatures, but for any strix who might wish to stay here.

Of course, the palace gargoyles hadn't particularly liked having a bunch of strixes in their midst, but I had asked them to give the other creatures a chance, and the gargoyles had grudgingly agreed. Truth be told, I thought some of the gargoyles, especially Fern and Otto, were fascinated by the strixes, which were so similar to the gargoyles and yet so different at the same time. Either way, Grimley, Fern, Otto, and Lyra had vowed to make sure that no fights broke out between the various creatures, and so far, everyone seemed to be getting along well enough.

I supposed that was the best I could hope for, as was so often the case when it came to most things between Andvari and Morta.

A whisper of wings sounded, and Grimley and Lyra spiraled down into the tower and landed on the flagstones in front of us. Violet was riding on Grimley's back, and she cheeped at us in greeting.

Lyra bent down and studied the ring on my hand. "Shiny!" she chirped in her high singsong voice. "I like it!"

Grimley huffed. "Alvis could have made my face bigger."

"Well, I think it's absolutely perfect." I tilted my head up and kissed Leonidas.

Grimley huffed again. "Is this what it's going to be like from now on? Will we find the two of you kissing every time we show up and want to go flying?"

Lyra squawked out her agreement. "No more kissing, only flying."

Laughing, Leonidas and I broke apart.

"We're not the only ones who want to go flying." Grimley paused. "Isn't that right, Violet?"

The baby strix cheeped and waggled her wings again. At first, I thought she was just agreeing with the gargoyle, but Violet kept beating her wings hard and fast, and she slowly lifted herself up. And then . . .

She started flying.

The baby strix zipped up off Grimley's back and sailed through the air above our heads, cheeping with glee the entire time. A few seconds later, she coasted to a stop and landed on the gargoyle's back again.

"I'm so proud of you!" I smoothed my hand down Violet's feathers, and she let out another happy cheep.

Grimley rolled his eyes. "She finally got the hang of it earlier tonight, and she just couldn't wait to come show you."

"She wants to go flying too," Lyra chimed in.

I petted Violet again, then turned to Leonidas. "What do you say? Feel like a moonlit ride?"

"With you, Gemma Ripley? Always." Leonidas stepped toward me, heat sparking in his eyes. "But first, I'd like to request a little more kissing, if my queen is so inclined."

I tilted my head at him. "This queen is very much inclined. Kiss away, my king. Kiss away."

Leonidas's grin widened, and he drew me into his arms. His lips came down on mine, and the rest of the world fell away.

Even without the surprise of the engagement or the rookery, tonight would have still been so very special. So many things had finally come to an end, especially when it came to Merilde and Maeven, and how they'd been all twisted and tangled up together with their visions and prophecies and schemes for the future.

But their past had led to this new beginning for Leonidas and me. And not just for us, but for all the strixes and gargoyles, and Morta and Andvari too. As strange as it seemed, I would always be grateful to Merilde for keeping her secrets from me, and to Maeven for believing my mother and in the prophecy that supposedly bound us all together.

But for right now, Grimley, Lyra, and Violet were here, and Leo was in my arms, and I couldn't think of a better ending to the night—and the beginning of our life together.

I had always loved being a princess, and then a spy, and then the gargoyle queen. But sometimes just being Gemma was the most wonderful thing of all.

ACKNOWLEDGMENTS

My heartfelt thanks go out to all the folks who help turn my words into a book.

Thanks go to my agent, Annelise Robey, and my editor, Erika Tsang, for all their helpful advice, support, and encouragement. Thanks to David Pomerico and everyone else at Harper Voyager and HarperCollins. Thanks also to Lauren Fortgang and Tony Mauro.

Thanks to Amanda Bouchet, Jeffe Kennedy, Gayle Trent, and Rachel Vance for all their help, support, advice, encouragement, and friendship through my ever-evolving writing career.

And finally, a big thanks to all the readers. Knowing that folks read and enjoy my books is truly humbling, and I hope that you all enjoyed reading about Gemma, Grimley, Leo, Lyra, Violet, and their adventures.

I appreciate you all more than you will ever know.

Happy reading! ☺

ABOUT THE AUTHOR

Neikirk Image Photography

Jennifer Estep is a *New York Times*, *USA Today*, and internationally bestselling author who prowls the streets of her imagination in search of her next fantasy idea.

She is the author of the **Gargoyle Queen**, **Crown of Shards**, **Elemental Assassin**, **Section 47**, and other fantasy series. She has written more than forty books, along with numerous novellas and stories.

In her spare time, Jennifer enjoys hanging out with friends and family, doing yoga, and reading fantasy and romance books. She also watches way too much TV and loves all things related to superheroes.

For more information on Jennifer and her books, visit her website at www.jenniferestep.com or follow her online on Facebook, Instagram, Goodreads, BookBub, and Twitter: @Jennifer _Estep. You can also sign up for her newsletter at www.jennifer estep.com/contact-jennifer/newsletter.

THE CROWN OF SHARDS WORLD

CAPTURE THE CROWN
A Gargoyle Queen Novel, Book 1

Jennifer Estep returns to her Crown of Shards world with an all-new trilogy and a bold new heroine, who protects her kingdom from magic, murder, and mayhem by moonlighting as a spy.

TEAR DOWN THE THRONE
A Gargoyle Queen Novel, Book 2

Crown princess. Clever spy. Powerful mind magier. Gemma Ripley of Andvari is all those things—and determined to stop an enemy from using magical tearstone weapons to conquer her kingdom . . .

KILL THE QUEEN
A Crown of Shards Novel, Book 1

Gladiator meets *Game of Thrones*: a royal woman becomes a skilled warrior to destroy her murderous cousin, avenge her family, and save her kingdom.

PROTECT THE PRINCE
A Crown of Shards Novel, Book 2

From a court full of arrogant nobles to an assassination attempt in her own throne room, Everleigh Blair knows dark forces are at work, making her wonder if she is truly strong enough to be a Winter Queen . . .

CRUSH THE KING
A Crown of Shards Novel, Book 3

After surviving yet another assassination attempt orchestrated by the conniving king of Morta, Queen Everleigh Blair of Bellona has had enough. It's time to turn the tables and take the fight to her enemies.